I0635511

IMPERIAL RECRUIT

BOOK TWO OF THE IMPERIAL MARINES SAGA

TERRY MIXON

YOWLING
CAT PRESS

Imperial Recruit

Copyright © 2021 by Terry Mixon

All rights reserved. No part of this book may be reproduced or transmitted in any form or by any means, electronic or mechanical, including information storage and/or retrieval systems, or dissemination of any electronic version, without the prior written consent of the publisher, except by a reviewer, who may quote brief passages in a review, and except where permitted by law.

This is a work of fiction. All names, characters, places, and incidents are the products of the author's imagination, or are used fictitiously. Any resemblance to actual persons, living or dead, events, or locales is entirely coincidental.

Published by Yowling Cat Press ®

Digital edition date: 6/21/2023

Print ISBN: 978-1947376656

Large Print ISBN: 978-1947376663

Cover art - image copyrights as follows:

algolonline (Caroline Rosa Nicolette Atkinson)

Donna Mixon

Cover design and composition by Donna Mixon

Print edition design and layout by Terry Mixon

ALSO BY TERRY MIXON

You can always find the most up to date listing of Terry's titles on his Amazon Author Page.

Note: the links below (ebook only, obviously) redirect you to my website where you can click a button to go to Amazon. This allows me to participate in Amazon's associates program and earn a little more. Sorry for any inconvenience.

The Last Hunter

The Last Hunter

Bonds of Blood

Alpha Strike

The Enemy Revealed

Command Authority

The Grand Conspiracy

Shield of Humanity

Fog of War

Ships of the Line

Operation Liberty

The Empire of Bones Saga

Empire of Bones

Veil of Shadows

Command Decisions

Ghosts of Empire

Paying the Price

Recon in Force

Box Sets

The Empire of Bones Saga Volume 1

The Empire of Bones Saga Volume 2

The Empire of Bones Saga Volume 3

The Empire of Bones Saga Volume 4

Humanity Unlimited Publisher's Pack 1

Humanity Unlimited Publisher's Pack 2

Want to get updates from Terry about new books and other general nonsense going on in his life? He promises there will be cats. Go to TerryMixon.com/Mailing-List and sign up.

DEDICATION

This book would not be possible without the love and support of my beautiful wife. Donna, I love you more than life itself.

ACKNOWLEDGMENTS

I want to thank the folks that support me on Patreon. You got to read this book as I was writing it and that kept me working. You have my deepest thanks.

In particular, I want to thank those patrons that supported me at the $10 level:

Bryan Barnes
Tony Craven
Dave Dolan
David Goldstein
Eugene Humbert
Christian A. Michelsen
John Page
Keith Ramsey
Carl Rumbolo
Dale Thompson
Raymond Wang
Clark Williams

Finally, I want to thank my readers for putting up with me. You guys are great.

1

——————

"Andrea! Hurry up, or you're going to miss breakfast! And don't slide down the banister!"

Andrea had just reached the top of the stairs when her guardian, Grace Tolliver, called out from the kitchen, so she hopped up onto the polished wooden banister and slid adroitly down it. Her guardian had scolded her about that far more times than she could count, warning that she'd fall off and break her neck, but she knew her balance was more than good enough to make it. Besides, she loved the rush.

And she needed all the positive energy she could get today.

She landed on her feet with almost no skid and slowed to a more sedate pace as she walked into the kitchen. The large house had several dining rooms, including one capable of seating more than a hundred people, but the kitchen was where they ate as a family when there were no guests.

Grace stood at the stove with Saanvi Modi, their matronly cook. Based on the heavenly scents floating through the air, they were frying bacon, one of her favorite foods.

Her guardian had been an indifferent cook—at best—six years

ago, but now even the veteran culinary warrior that ran their kitchen had to grudgingly admit that Grace had mastered breakfast.

Her other meals could use some work, but they weren't terrible on the few occasions Saanvi allowed Grace to take the lead with them. Fei, on the other hand, wasn't allowed to boil water unmonitored.

She was sure that her guardian's focus on that one meal came from Andrea's reverence for it. Pancakes, eggs, bacon, and orange juice had made up the first meal she'd eaten after they'd rescued her from the Singularity, and it still held a power over her that defied words.

Na Fei and Kayden Harmon already sat at the nook table, sipping coffee and chatting quietly about something. Together with Grace, they formed both a triad of marriage and her own personal guardian council.

She took her usual seat beside Fei and poured herself some orange juice.

"Are you ready?" the dark-haired woman asked with a smile that lit up her face, highlighting her Asian genetics even after generations away from her homeworld and its influences.

"I'm nervous," Andrea admitted quietly. "While I hope everything works out the way I want, it could all come crashing down. What do I do if they rule against me?"

The former marine noncommissioned officer shrugged slightly. "You keep living the way you're living now. Sadly, things don't always go the way we'd like. As a backup plan, living in Iron Mountain with us is a fair consolation prize, wouldn't you say?"

That was undoubtedly true. Back when she'd been in the crèche, she'd lived under a virtual death sentence. She wondered if the survivors of Keeper's discipline were free of the relocated crèche and being taught how to rule the Singularity yet.

That life had once been her destiny—if she'd survived to adulthood—but she was much happier having left it behind. Keeper hadn't spared any of them the knowledge that two-thirds of the two hundred girls—all genetically identical to the adults of the Andrea Line—would be dead at her hand before they matured.

Andrea had traded that life for a much freer one in the Terran

Empire. The downside was that as a genetically engineered being, she was legally a thing rather than a person. That meant that she had no rights, and if not for Grace's protection—and that of Duke DeSantis—she'd have spent the last six years in the hands of Imperial Intelligence.

If, of course, they hadn't dissected her.

Now that she'd grown to know the people of the Empire better, she honestly doubted that that had ever been on the table. The insidious idea had been Singularity propaganda. Even so, that didn't mean that Imperial Intelligence wouldn't have been happy to lock her up in some secret facility to study her at their leisure.

If things went well today, she'd finally be recognized as a human being and wouldn't need to fear that fate any longer. If things went differently, well, she'd have to accept whatever the Empire decreed.

She dreaded rejection because she wanted to become an Imperial Marine more than anything. She'd seen the platoon that Grace and Fei had led fight to save her and knew that was a goal that she could devote her life to.

Grace carefully set a tray holding platters of pancakes, eggs, and bacon on the table and took her seat next to Andrea as Saanvi began tidying up the cooking area.

"Don't be so nervous," her guardian said with a smile. "It won't be bad news."

"I think you're being too optimistic," Andrea said with a sigh as she began loading down her plate with her favorite foods. She slathered the pancakes with butter and poured a generous helping of syrup across them.

"I hate you," Fei said, eyeing the pancakes. "I just gained half a kilo from looking at those things."

"Now, now, my dear," Kayden said, patting the Asian woman's arm. "Having met you when you were in active service, I can assure you that any padding you've added has been integrated into your increasingly gorgeous form in ways that only enhance your exotic beauty."

Fei narrowed her eyes at her husband. "Allow me to assure you that there's no complimentary way to tell a woman that she's gained weight. I recommend you stop talking before banishing you to the couch starts sounding like a good idea."

Kayden grinned unrepentantly. "We have plenty of guest bedrooms, so I think I can avoid the couch. In any case, I made sure that we purchased the very best, and they have no lumps.

"Still, that was perhaps ill phrased. You're a beautiful woman, and you've always been so. Only now, you have *curves*."

Grace laughed. "You're not helping yourself, Kayden, but you're not wrong either. Fei, you're still as tough as you ever were, but I have to agree with our husband that curves suit you."

"Could we go back to talking about me before this conversation gets filled with all kinds of gross lovey-dovey noises?" Andrea mock complained. "I have to be able to keep breakfast down if I'm going to survive the day. You wouldn't want me to pass out, would you?"

"Everything will be fine," Grace said in the tongue, the language of the Singularity. She was completely and flawlessly fluent now, a far cry from the truly execrable accent she'd had six years ago. Andrea and Kayden had seen to that.

It wasn't necessary, since Andrea had been quick to pick up Imperial Standard, but it was a caring gesture that was just like her guardian.

"Thank you," Andrea said, reaching over to squeeze the woman's hand.

As they dug into their food, Andrea hoped that the extra calories she was taking in might one day lead to some of those curves that her mentor was developing, but she knew *exactly* what she'd look like as an adult.

The Andrea Line—of which she was a genetic member, though they thought her dead—didn't have any genetic randomization. She'd been raised by a woman that had epitomized what she'd look like as an adult.

At the age of eighteen, she was almost as tall as Keeper had been and had filled out just about as much. A few more years and she'd see Keeper in her mirror every morning, right down to the stylized bird-of-prey tattoos on her forehead and cheeks.

Frankly, she was almost to that point already, and that was the stuff of nightmares. Still, it wasn't like she had a choice in the matter. Some things in life simply had to be accepted.

Once they'd made it to the Empire, they'd tried to have her tattoos removed, but that had proven unexpectedly challenging. They were somehow imprinted into her skin at a genetic level. Once burned away—which had been almost as painful as getting them in the first place—they'd returned over the next several months.

No, for good or ill, she'd never be rid of her connections to the Andrea Line or the Singularity.

The four of them ate with cheerful jabs and commentary about what was going on around the manor house, and that relaxed her. Maybe she was wrong to worry. Perhaps her concerns would turn out to have been misplaced.

She might as well hope so, since she couldn't affect the outcome of today's events. Today was the day she'd become human in the eyes of the Empire, or she'd be consigned to remain a thing.

* * *

FEI'S UNEASE grew stronger the closer they got to the capital city. She'd been a combat marine for almost two decades before her retirement and knew what it felt like when she was walking into an ambush.

Grace—frighteningly enough—was the optimist of their triad. Kayden had a more realistic view of the universe and considered everything with a jaundiced eye.

She was the pessimist. If something could go wrong, Fei knew that it would, and thus it needed to be planned for.

Unfortunately, there was very little they could do to mitigate anything about this situation, and she was worried. Civilians frowned on people fighting their way out of social ambushes with flechettes and plasma grenades.

Unlike some of the vehicles that she'd traveled in over the years, their air car was spacious and comfortable. Decadent, even. Kayden was flying them in with Andrea up front as the unofficial copilot.

Well, in actuality, he was letting the girl—the young woman—fly the air car, and her attention was locked on the instruments and their surroundings. There wasn't any mechanism for Andrea to earn a license, though she was good enough to do so. Still, she could always use more seasoning.

That left Fei and Grace sitting in the spacious rear, where they could talk. Thus far, the conversation had been about trivial things, but Grace seemed to have sensed Fei's darkening mood.

"What's the matter?" her wife asked softly.

She'd pitched her voice low enough that Andrea *probably* wouldn't be able to hear her, though the girl's hearing was just as enhanced as the rest of her. If she truly focused her attention on what was going on behind her, she'd hear enough of their conversation to understand what they were talking about.

That wouldn't do.

Fei activated the privacy screen over where she and Grace sat. The sonic dampening field was very subtle, and Andrea would hopefully miss it since she was so focused on flying. Truthfully, she could've initiated an implant call and avoided any chance of her girl overhearing them, but Grace needed to hear her actual voice this time.

"It feels like we're walking into an ambush," Fei said. "All my instincts tell me that an enemy is waiting for us at the Ducal Palace."

Grace raised an eyebrow. "I trust your instincts far too much to pooh-pooh the idea, but I don't think anybody's going to be shooting at us. That said, you're right that there are other kinds of... unpleasantness that could be sprung upon us. What are you thinking?"

Her wife's voice had changed. It might've been six years since they'd served as active-duty marines, but the woman beside her once again sounded like the officer in command of a marine combat platoon, and she'd just requested a briefing from her senior NCO.

Fei approved. While things certainly might not be that grim, it never hurt to be prepared for surprises.

"I don't know," she admitted. "Since this is supposed to be about Andrea, it's likely that either her request to be recognized as a human being is about to be denied, or there's going to be some kind of gotcha.

"We've been coming into this with the assumption that the worst that could happen is that they say no. What if that's not the case? What if someone says that she's still property, but in contravention of Imperial tradition they're seizing her now that she's no longer a child and that Imperial Intelligence will take possession of her?"

Grace's expression darkened, and her eyes flashed. "Duke DeSantis would shred what was left of them once I'd finished demolishing them. He's my liege lord, and he won't allow that to happen."

Fei raised an eyebrow in a manner designed to show skepticism. "He has a liege too. What if the emperor has decided to change the rules? If that happens, Duke DeSantis will have no choice.

"Something about what's going to happen today is going to be a very unpleasant pill to swallow," she prophesized grimly. "I don't know how, but I can feel it coming. Mark my words."

"I hope you're wrong," Grace said quietly. "If you're not, there's going to be hell to pay."

Fei nodded. If push really came to shove, she'd implement Operation Gamma. It was an escape plan that she and Kayden had put together without telling their wife. Given an opportunity, she could get them into orbit and onto a ship that was waiting to take them away under assumed names that Kayden swore were absolutely legitimate, though illegally obtained.

The last six years had been wonderful, but if giving that up allowed them to save Andrea, she'd walk away from this life without looking back. Her husband had once been a smuggler, so he'd know how to establish them someplace safe where they could create a new life.

No matter the cost, Andrea was leaving with them today. On that, she swore her very life.

* * *

SENIOR SERGEANT JOHN PAGE stood at the back of the raised platform with his fellow drill instructors as Lieutenant Evans spoke to the platoon. It had been grueling, but the twelve-week training cycle was finally over.

He was looking forward to a little quiet time now that the soon-to-be marines were moving on. The platoon had shrunk by a third, but the civilians they'd started with had become larval marines. They'd mature with time and experience, but the foundation was there now.

Once the lieutenant had finished speaking, Page formed the platoon up and marched them to the battalion area, where Major Craig Martelle gave another address before sending the newly minted marines off.

All that done, Page turned to Sergeant Sophia Gomez as they walked toward the training barracks and the small party they'd set up for the recruits—marines—that didn't have family here today.

She'd put in as many hours as he had, and it showed. She looked exhausted.

"What are you going to do with your time off?" he asked.

His companion shrugged, her face haggard under her straight-brimmed, round drill instructor's hat. "I think I'll head out to one of the wilderness areas and spend some time alone. Get up whenever I want, do whatever I want, and not have any kind of schedule for a couple of weeks."

Now that the training cycle was over, they had four weeks off before the next one arrived. A few weeks of that was for staff to unwind once they'd cleaned the area up. One week was free, but the rest required them to have leave accrued.

He knew Sophia had the time banked because she rarely took leave at all. He was in the same boat. His work gave him purpose, and he didn't take time off unless he had to use the leave or lose it.

Thankfully, he wasn't going to be forced away from the base this time. He'd taken a cruise at the end of the last cycle and spent the time in his cabin, going over the training schedule in detail. It had improved things for this cycle, he thought, so it had been time well spent.

He led her to the cramped conference room the drill instructors used on the third floor and chatted over little things while half the team made their way in. The other half was getting the party kicked off downstairs, and they'd join them soon enough. In any case, they were linked in via their implants.

"I'll keep this short and sweet," he said with a grin. "You've all done a terrific job, as usual, and you've made me proud. Together, we've shaped up another fine batch of marines for the Empire.

"It'll take us a week or so to undo the damage this cycle did to the training area. We'll grab some bodies from battalion, fill in all the bunkers they built, and sweep for unexploded ordinance starting tomorrow. Without recruits on hand, we'll decadently kick off at 0800.

"Once that's done, you're free to sign out. Have a good time, and don't get arrested because I'm not posting bail this time."

That was the same spiel he always gave, and they laughed like they always did. That done, he dismissed them, but Sophia held back.

"You should take some time off too. Why not take a week or two and do something crazy?"

He shook his head. "I prefer the sedate life. Going out into the wilderness might be interesting, but I've got things to do. Maybe next training cycle. Go relax, Sophia."

She reached out, gripped his arm for a moment, and walked out.

He really should take some time to actually relax. Maybe next cycle. For now, though, he needed to work up a plan of attack to get the training area cleaned up. He was allowing a week for the work, but he'd prefer to be done in five days. That would let him spend more time focused on prep for the next cycle.

Before he got started, though, he really should tag up with the LT. As far as officers went, the man was pretty laid back, but it was best to clear the slate now. The man was probably already champing at the bit to be done so he could head out on his next adventure. That was good, since it meant Page would have the place to himself.

He rose and headed for his commanding officer's office.

2

_____

Andrea handed control of the air car back to Kayden as they approached the Ducal Palace. The flight patterns here were much tighter than over the city itself, and under the coverage of the Ducal Guard and their weapons systems, so she didn't want to chance making a mistake. She was a pretty decent pilot, but this wasn't the time to make a mistake and drift out of the cleared lane.

Kayden took over smoothly, brought them adroitly through the flight pattern, and set them down on the landing pad they'd been assigned. Like the one at their home, this one was large enough to accommodate even military craft, so there was plenty of room.

There was also space beside it for the dozen people waiting for the passengers to disembark. Front and center among them was Reginald Fowler, Duke DeSantis.

He was Grace's liege lord and the man they'd rescued after the Singularity had captured his heavy cruiser. She knew that he thought very highly of Grace and that he personally liked her, but he was the emperor's sworn man. That meant that whatever happened today, he was bound by his liege's will, no matter what he might personally prefer.

She knew maybe a third of the others were ducal functionaries, but at least two new figures seemed to be people of importance. Those would be the officials that had come from Terra bearing word of her fate.

Andrea studied the two as her family climbed out of the air car and arrayed themselves in an almost protective wedge around her. According to Fei, first impressions could often be wrong, but evaluating a potential enemy was a skill that everyone needed to nurture. These two held her future in their hands, so she examined them closely.

Duke DeSantis was obviously senior, as the new people stood slightly behind him and off to one side. Yet, they were not part of his entourage, and they had their own, smaller entourages behind them. She suspected that they were from a somewhat lower social stratum but powerful in their own right, based upon their bearings.

The more prominent of the two was a thin, hawkish woman with a haughty expression. She seemed the type that was used to obedience and who saw herself as better than those around her. That boded ill.

The man was shorter and plump. It only took a cursory examination to determine that he didn't exercise enough, not even close. Or perhaps he was too in love with rich foods.

Andrea had a hard time understanding people like that. Why would anyone intentionally disregard their body? She couldn't imagine the man even jogging around the landing pad without running out of breath.

Sometimes Imperials really confused her.

Duke DeSantis stepped forward and smiled. "Grace, it's always good to see you and your family. I trust everyone is well."

Andrea's guardian stepped forward with a smile of her own and took her liege's hand. "We're doing very well, thank you. We had a nice party for Andrea's birthday last week and were sorry that you couldn't make it, but we understand your busy schedule. I'm sure she'll tell you herself how much she appreciated your gift."

The man turned to the two unknowns, his smile dimming somewhat. "Allow me to introduce the Imperial representatives. This is Marla Treadshaw, Countess Dayton."

The woman inclined her head slightly but only after Grace had bowed hers. Some kind of power game, obviously. The woman's Imperial title was higher than Grace's, so she was above her in Imperial standing and was emphasizing the disparity.

"And this is J. Russel Macumber, Earl Still Water."

The overweight man smiled at Grace and bowed. He then took her hand into his.

"Allow me to compliment you on your amazing work inside the Singularity, Baroness Iron Mountain. Quite daring and an incredible blow against the Singularity. Well done."

Andrea considered his response for a moment and decided that there was actual admiration in his tone. That, of course, didn't mean that he'd react well to her if he had some animus against the Singularity itself. She'd quite literally be the face of his enemy. Still, it might be a hopeful sign.

Grace returned his smile. "The pleasure is mine, Your Excellency. Allow me to introduce my spouses, Lady Na Fei and Kayden Harmon, as well as my ward, Andrea."

Andrea bowed moments after her guardians did. There was some type of mandated bowing height that she hadn't quite mastered yet, so she always paid attention to those around her for guidance.

"Let's retire to my private chambers so that we can discuss this matter in solitude and comfort," the duke said, gesturing toward the palace.

The group made their way inside and to the duke's private chambers. They lost all the functionaries along the way, so there was only Andrea, her three guardians, the duke, and the two visitors at the end of the journey.

A series of small tables and chairs had been set up so that they could take refreshments in a cozy environment. Not a formal setting, so perhaps that was good.

Once they were all situated around the tables, a servitor took orders for drinks. Andrea noted that the two visitors ordered alcoholic drinks even though it wasn't even noon.

The duke ordered tea, and she did the same because the tea at the Ducal Palace was delicious. Her guardians took either water or tea themselves. Once everyone was served, the servitor bowed his way out and closed the doors behind him.

"I feel like the elephant in the room," Andrea said into the momentary silence. "You'll forgive me if I'm a little nervous about that."

Grace shot her a look, obviously not agreeing with her direct approach.

Nevertheless, that was how Andrea worked. If there was a problem, she faced it and dealt with it. Tiptoeing around trouble often made things worse, in her estimation.

The noblewoman's eyes narrowed as she considered Andrea. "I suppose that we can get right down to business. As I told His Grace earlier, His Majesty and the Imperial Senate have negotiated at length over the last several years about your status, One Twenty-Four."

"My name is Andrea Tolliver," Andrea insisted. "One Twenty-Four was the name given to me by the Singularity and the Andrea Line, and I'm no longer a member of either of those groups."

"In any case," the woman continued as if Andrea hadn't spoken, "dealing with how to recognize genetically engineered beings inside the Empire, where they're legally considered to be property, is complicated when there's a living example among us.

"Many of the senators didn't favor changing the law because they see the Singularity and its rulers—correctly, in my estimation—as one of the greatest threats to the Terran Empire. His Majesty was less convinced but unwilling to overrule the senate. Frankly, I believe that the 'solution' they decided upon only makes the problem worse.

"Yet they did agree on a course of action that will satisfy literally no one, which is often the case with the Imperial Senate. Your legal name is of some importance in this matter, so I will make note that you identify yourself as Andrea Tolliver and update the Imperial records to reflect that. You will still have One Twenty-Four listed as an alias because that's just how the law works."

"And what *is* the decision?" Grace asked, her voice holding more than a hint of impatience. "What's to become of Andrea, Countess Dayton?"

The woman smiled slightly, showing no actual amusement. "Not that they asked for my opinion in the matter, but they've decided to perform something of an experiment with her."

Andrea felt herself tense. Was this it? Were they really going to send her somewhere to be dissected?

She saw that Fei and Grace had also tensed and noted that Fei's hand was sliding toward her waistband. That was alarming as it raised the stakes in this confrontation significantly.

They'd been scanned for weapons, of course, but she wouldn't put it past the former marine sergeant to have acquired something that was undetectable. This situation had to be short-circuited immediately.

The duke raised his hands in a conciliatory gesture. "Let's take a step backward from that statement. There will be *no* experimenting on Andrea. That was *exceptionally* poorly phrased."

Something in his posture told her that he was aware of the implied threat in Fei's motion. He commanded the sector militia, so that probably shouldn't surprise her.

Her mentor's protectiveness made her feel good, but she didn't want Fei to get into trouble. Whatever fate was coming, it was hers to bear. Her guardians had given her six wonderful years, and she wasn't going to see them throw the rest of their lives away.

"Whatever the emperor and the Imperial Senate have decreed, I will accept," Andrea said in a level tone. "There need be no conflict today."

Fei's hand didn't retreat one millimeter, and her expression remained grim. "Then I think *Her Excellency* had best trot out the rest of her so-called statement. What exactly do the emperor and Imperial Senate want of Andrea?"

The two noble visitors seemed utterly unaware of the danger they were in. No, on second thought, while the man seemed somewhat amused, something in his eyes told Andrea that he was quite aware of what was happening.

That implied that he knew Fei was armed and was in some manner prepared to react to any hostile action. That was very interesting and led her to immediately reevaluate him. There was more to him than met the eye.

The countess was obviously unaware of the growing danger. Her reaction to the tension was to slightly raise her nose and sniff, her expression colored with disdain.

"His Imperial Majesty and the Imperial Senate have issued a dispensation that will, if certain milestones are met, grant recognition of humanity and Imperial citizenship upon Andrea Tolliver," she said, disapproval clear in her voice. "He has ordered that she be inducted into the Imperial Marines for training.

"However, you should understand that her status is linked to her success. If she graduates from basic training, then her status becomes permanent. If she fails, her temporary status will be revoked, and she once again becomes property.

"As an adult, she's no longer something to be watched over and would be taken into the custody of Imperial Intelligence for detailed study."

Grace surged to her feet. "Are you telling me that His Majesty is taking back something that he gave me?" Her voice was low and dangerous.

The woman jerked back slightly, likely unused to such a direct confrontation. "Remember your place, Baroness! I will tolerate only so much from those beneath my station. Am I clear?"

Grace didn't back down. In fact, she took a step forward, her expression hardening even more. "I hear you just fine, but if anything happens to Andrea, I'm holding you *personally* responsible. I've killed to protect her, and I won't let someone's social status exempt them from the consequences of putting her in danger. Am *I* clear?"

Of the two, Grace sounded *much* more intimidating, Andrea decided, and far, far too fierce for safety under these circumstances. Fei and Kayden rose to back Grace up, and the situation was on the verge of spinning wildly out of control.

Duke DeSantis and Earl Still Water had also risen, leaving only Andrea and the countess sitting. The tension in the air was so thick that it felt like syrup. Or a room with a hydrogen leak that needed only a single spark to set it ablaze.

The rotund man stepped between Grace and the countess, his hands held up imploringly. "I beseech you to allow me to explain the circumstances in more detail before you resort to the level of intimidation that only an Imperial Marine can bring to bear so well, Major."

Andrea wasn't certain that bringing Grace's retirement rank into this situation was the *wisest* decision—and how did he know what it was, anyway?—but it made her guardian take a deep breath and focus her attention on him.

"My tolerance for bullshit has just run out," she said coldly. "Talk fast."

"Andrea will enter marine training tentatively recognized as an Imperial citizen. That terminates your guardianship, as she is of age. If she fails to graduate successfully, she becomes Imperial property for five years—the same amount of time as an initial marine enlistment—before she is returned to you. That was the senate's price for their agreement.

"Compromise is occasionally a bitter pill to swallow, but there are guardrails to ensure that Andrea comes to no harm. In fact, once the five years are done—if she cooperates—her Imperial citizenship could be restored on the recommendation of the Imperial Intelligence director and made permanent."

"Then why didn't you lead with that?" Grace demanded.

"Allow me to apologize for my associate's lack of empathy and common sense." That was accompanied by a glance at the countess that wasn't in the least complimentary.

Countess Dayton's face twisted in anger. "You forget yourself, Still Water. I'm not someone you wish as an enemy."

"They say a man is defined more by his enemies than his friends, so I'll take my chances."

None of his words did anything to erase the fury on Grace's and Fei's faces. Kayden's expression was more urbane, but Andrea could see the fire in his eyes too. She needed to defuse the situation before they did something that they couldn't walk back.

"It doesn't matter what the price of failure is because I'm going to succeed," she said firmly, resisting the urge to stand. "I *will* become an Imperial Marine. Never doubt it."

Duke DeSantis nodded, looking a little relieved as the tension in the room came down a notch. "That would be the simplest solution. I suggest that you give this your absolute best effort because you're potentially blazing a trail for others who might one day come behind you."

He spared the countess a glance. "There will, unfortunately, be those opposed to your success. They'll try to trip you up, place obstacles in your path, and hate you for who and what you are. Be better than them because—rightly or wrongly—the Empire will judge those that come after you by your actions."

Fei nodded slowly and moved her hand away from her waist. The three of them relaxed a bit further and sat again.

The only one in the room who seemed unaware that a potentially deadly fight had just been averted was Countess Dayton. She sat there with her lips curled in disdain.

"Don't overestimate yourself, One Twenty-Four," she said with a sneer. "The Imperial Marines are a discerning lot—evidence in this room to the contrary—and I think it unlikely that you'll make the grade.

"And Imperial Intelligence has an... unsavory reputation. I wouldn't count on surviving five years under their so-called care. Things like you will always be things."

"Enough!" Duke DeSantis barked. "You've delivered your news, Your Excellency. Retire to your rooms at once, and I'll come by to speak with you—in detail—shortly."

The woman rose to her feet and exited the room without a word.

"This is utter bullshit," Grace growled into the silence. "The Empire is supposed to be better than this. Are we just as bad as the Singularity?"

"Sadly, there are competing interests at play," Duke DeSantis said. "And nobility doesn't miraculously grant honor or humanity. Trust me when I say that you're already a far better human being than that woman, Andrea.

"Grace, you have my word that I'll make certain that Andrea is well treated if she washes out of Imperial training. The facility that Imperial Intelligence would use if it comes to that will be located on DeSantis, and I will make absolutely certain that there are liberal visitation rights and that one of my representatives would be present at all times to make certain that no harm comes to her. I'm sorry, Grace, but that's the best I can do."

He turned his attention to Andrea. "The best solution to this problem, as I said, is absolute vindication. Prove to them just how good you really are, young woman. As of this moment, you're an Imperial citizen with all of the rights and privileges that entails. You're going to have one shot at keeping them, so I suggest you impress your trainers."

Well, that certainly put the load firmly on her shoulders, didn't it? Not that she intended to fail. She'd do this for herself and for her family, and God save the bastards who got in her way.

3

Even though things had calmed down significantly once Countess Dayton had been ejected from the meeting, Fei wasn't feeling any better about what she'd heard. She had to keep Andrea away from Imperial Intelligence, no matter what restrictions they might supposedly be subject to.

Their unofficial motto was "It's easier to beg forgiveness than to ask for permission," and that attitude infused their organization. She had to protect Andrea from them at all costs.

Fei believed Duke DeSantis would do everything in his power to make certain that Andrea was taken care of, but Imperial Intelligence couldn't be trusted. They'd find a way to game the system.

She could tell from the way Grace was scowling that she understood that just as well as Fei did. Kayden had worked for Imperial Intelligence as a source for years, and he didn't trust them either. In this matter, the three were of one mind.

Her family had been concerned that Imperial Intelligence would try something ever since they'd returned to the Empire with Andrea. Honestly, it had only been a matter of time, and it now seemed that that moment was at hand.

According to the scenario that Duke DeSantis and the Imperial representatives had laid out, Andrea was supposed to get a real shot at the Imperial Marines, but Fei found herself doubting that that was how things were going to play out. Imperial Intelligence would benefit significantly more from her failure.

There would also undoubtedly be other forces in the Empire that would dearly want to see someone from the Singularity fail. If any of the genetically altered beings that ruled the Singularity were recognized as a human inside the Empire, that would set a precedent that would have far-reaching consequences for centuries to come.

Sadly, there was nothing she could do to protect her girl from any of that. Andrea was going to be on her own in a hostile universe with only her wits to protect her.

Duke DeSantis had done everything that he could to calm their fears, and she could see his efforts were having an effect on Grace and Kayden. Then again, since she was the group's pessimist, she'd worry enough for all three of them.

After a few more minutes of de-escalation, the duke rose to his feet with a smile. "I realize that this has been unsettling, but I'd like you all to join me for lunch to celebrate. My chef has prepared something that I think that you'll like, Andrea."

The family rose and started toward the exit.

Earl Still Water softly cleared his throat and waved a hand at Fei. She turned toward him and raised an eyebrow.

"Yes, Your Excellency?"

"If you've got a few minutes, Lady Na, I'd like to speak with you about a private matter."

She made her excuses to Grace and the rest before turning back to face the portly nobleman. He gestured toward the table at which he'd been sitting and beckoned for her to join him. She retrieved her tea and sat across from him, both interested and concerned about what he might want.

"I've had an opportunity to review your full service record and noted that you were quite an accomplished marine," he said. "I'm about to make an offer that would allow you to provide some level of protection for Andrea, and I ask that you consider it fully before indulging in any impulses to reject it out of hand."

That unexpected statement made both of her eyebrows rise slightly, which for her was an expression of pure astonishment. While it was always possible that someone had the pull to see portions of military service records, he was acting as if he'd seen much, much more than just sanitized summaries.

"That's *quite* a statement, Your Excellency," she said slowly. "As I'm sure you're aware, my military service record is classified, even for Imperial nobility. I can't imagine under what circumstances you might have acquired it, as it shouldn't have been part of the consideration of Andrea's case. I think that you'd best explain yourself."

"Not an unexpected reaction," he agreed with a nod. "First, I have a revelation. There's more to me than meets the eye."

He looked down at his large belly. "And by that, I mean more than simply the physical. May I ask what kind of weapon you have concealed at the small of your back?"

"What makes you think that I'm armed?" she asked warily.

"I'm no fool, Lady Na," he said, his lips curling up into a genuine smile. "When you thought you'd have to defend Andrea, your hand moved toward a weapon. I'm familiar enough with the gesture of someone preparing to wage violence against another.

"Everything I've told you and your family today is true but incomplete. Now, as they say, I'll show you mine if you'll show me yours."

That last made her smile slightly. "It's been quite some time since I've heard that pitch. It's a good thing my spouses aren't here, as they might object."

Before he could respond, she reached under her short jacket and pulled out a miniaturized stunner. She'd paid a lot of money to make sure that no scanner in the Empire could pick it up. Even its power supply was heavily shielded. All of those features made it highly illegal, not even counting the act of bringing it into the duke's presence.

She slid the weapon across the table and watched the nobleman pick it up. He examined it competently and even removed the power pack to look inside the grip. "A true work of art. The creation of

Anton Casey, unless I miss my guess. You acquired this weapon in the last year or so. Certainly no further back than two."

It took every ounce of willpower to keep herself from reacting. How could a nobleman recognize the work of a highly skilled underworld weaponsmith?

"Who are you?" she demanded, her voice hard.

The earl put her weapon back together and slid it toward her with much less energy than she'd used to get it to him. Then he reached behind his back and pulled out a stunner that was virtually identical to hers.

"He built this one for me five years ago. As you can see, some of the details in workmanship have improved with your model, and the materials are slightly different, but these weapons were made by the same artisan.

"He does first-rate work. I've known of him through cutouts for many years. I suppose that if I really wanted to find out who he was, I could, but that would damage an otherwise exceptional relationship."

He put his weapon away and smiled urbanely. "I'm exactly who I've claimed to be, but as I told you, there's more to me than meets the eye. Besides being a representative of His Imperial Majesty in this matter, I'm also a roving director with Imperial Intelligence."

His claim stunned her to her very core. She'd met Imperial Intelligence field operatives in the course of various missions. They were the faces that Imperial Intelligence allowed others to see.

For someone to claim to be a roving director was quite a jump. That meant that he was not only management but *senior* management. He might very well be the most senior Imperial Intelligence representative on DeSantis if his claim was true.

Rather than say anything, she chose to sit there and sip her tea. He watched her, seemingly unperturbed. He was obviously ready to allow her whatever time she needed to consider his statement.

"I'm somewhat at a loss for words," she finally admitted. "There's no way to prove anything you've said, so I'm not sure how *to* react."

"Duke DeSantis knows who I am. He's also aware of this conversation and will verify everything I've said and will say. You've trusted him—with good cause—over the last six years. I urge you to do so now.

"Now, allow me to explain my mission and my offer. The emperor ordered me to make sure that you understand that if Andrea does not make the cut for the Imperial Marines, she will be well cared for. I'm to handle the matter personally in the unfortunate event that it's required.

"I know that you have no reason to trust me. In fact, as a representative of Imperial Intelligence, you have many sound reasons *not* to trust me, yet here we are."

"Why tell me any of this? Now I'm far more concerned for Andrea than I was before."

He nodded. "That's understandable. Let me put all my cards on the table, which is a refreshing change of pace, believe me. I think that the Empire would benefit far more from Andrea succeeding than failing.

"Yes, having her on hand for five years would be illuminating, but you've already provided quite a bit of information. Detaining her for study gains the Empire very little.

"This business of regarding genetically engineered humans as property is odious and offends me more than I can reasonably express. It smacks of slavery or worse. I want to see that law changed just as much as the emperor does.

"Yet the Imperial Senate is an overly dogmatic organization and a selfish one. Trying to get them to do anything is very much like herding cats. Each and every one of them has their own agenda, and they think far too highly of themselves."

That almost made Fei laugh. The comment perfectly matched what she'd heard about the Imperial Senate. As a body, they rarely got anything worthwhile done because they were too busy hissing and swatting at one another, *just* like offended cats.

That wasn't how government was supposed to work, but when you had powerful people acting in their own self-interest, it was almost inevitable.

"So, now that you've shocked me again, what do you *really* want?"

Fei asked. "Why tell me any of this? Andrea's going to the Imperial Marines, and nothing I can do is going to help."

"What if you could help?" he asked, leaning forward with a serious expression. "What if you had an opportunity to protect her from people that might wish her harm? A way that didn't involve that oh-so-deniable freighter you have in orbit if things don't work out?"

Her mouth dropped open. No one could connect *Gamma* to them. That just wasn't possible. They'd been far too careful.

He smiled indulgently. "If one has to spy on someone, one should at least be good at it. I'm sure that no one else is aware of your contingency plans, but they aren't needed in this case. It would sadden me if I had to track you down, but rest assured that even if I'd been unaware of the ship, I'd have found you.

"Thankfully, our interests align in this matter, and we won't have to put one another to the test. Allow me to repeat my question. What if you had an opportunity to protect Andrea from people that might wish her harm? What would you do?"

"I'd do it," Fei said without hesitation. "If I could trust you."

"You'll have to make your own assessment of just how much you can trust me, but I'm here to offer you that chance. Andrea cannot know any of this, though. Her success or failure *must* be on her own. The Empire cannot be seen as meddling, and if she knew you were there, it would taint the accomplishment in her eyes.

"I want you to infiltrate the training battalion that she's going to be assigned to. I'm making an unscheduled, last-minute change to where she'll undergo training, so theoretically, none of the staff will be aware that she's coming until she's on their very doorstep."

He smiled grimly. "Even though the original unit was supposedly secret, I know for a fact that several members of its staff were replaced by agents of the opposition. Those people and their backers won't realize that anything has gone awry until Andrea fails to appear. By then, it'll be too late to locate her *actual* unit and place anyone on staff.

"Still, it's possible that they could bribe someone already there or that some individuals will act on their own to stymie her. To offset that, I'm offering you the opportunity to be embedded as an officer at the battalion level to counter them. Are you interested?"

"They're going to know who I am," Fei said. "It's all in my record."

"It won't be by the time you arrive. All references to the raid and your association with Andrea or Baroness Iron Mountain will be temporarily scrubbed.

"Andrea's records will also be modified. Her background will be marked as classified at the very highest levels, and few details given. Your identities have been a closely guarded secret since you settled here, for your protection and that of the Empire as a whole. I've made certain that remains true.

"Even Countess Dayton didn't know which system we'd be going to until we arrived. Now that she's aware of who you are, it will take some time for that information to get to her co-conspirators."

He smiled brightly. "Did I mention that she's part of the cabal determined to see Andrea fail? I'm sure that revelation shocks you, so I'll allow you time to gasp with dismay before we continue."

Fei grunted and shook her head. "Shouldn't conspirators be more… subtle?"

"You'd be surprised how stupid many in the nobility truly are. In any case, she won't be passing that information along to anyone else for quite a while. I've taken the precaution of monitoring her communications. If she tries to send word back to Terra—which I don't see, since none of the information she's acquired will advance their cause at the moment—it will simply fail to arrive.

"As will she, though only for a period of time. Her ship—on which I will *not* be traveling—will suffer an engineering casualty that will strand her in an out-of-the-way system for between four and six weeks.

"Added to the time it will take the cabal to learn that Andrea isn't where they expected, that should be enough time for her to complete her training without their interference. That will effectively neutralize the countess."

Fei ground her teeth. "Why don't you just arrest her?"

"At this point, she's done nothing illegal," he said with a shrug. "Even if I were to allow her to act, her wealth and power would easily shield her from serious consequences. It's better to foil her and those that think like her. That's far more punishing in the long run.

"So, are you willing to help Andrea seize her dreams with both hands?"

"If I'm going to be looking at the officers, who will be keeping an eye on her? What about the training staff and drill instructors?"

"I'm not going to meddle with them, but I've taken a step to assure you of my personal commitment by sending someone into training with her that has the potential to be an excellent ally for her.

"My daughter had already decided to join the marines—for some reason, my current line of work has inspired a rebellious nature in an otherwise well-mannered child—so I pulled some strings to delay her enlistment and redirect her to the training cycle that Andrea will be in. In fact, she will be in the same platoon.

"She has no idea that I've done this or that Andrea will be there. Knowing her as I do, she'll like Andrea and want to be her friend. I can make no guarantees, but I'm putting my blood into the potential fire with your girl, so that should show that I'm committed to this."

Fei wasn't sure about that but would have time to figure things out on site. If he was lying, what could she do about it? Nothing except be ready to act if things went sideways.

"Why me rather than Grace? Hell, why not both of us?"

"You are much more the 'hands on' sort. If action is needed, I think you're the better choice. Besides, your wife has a barony to run, and her disappearance might raise awkward questions. Your lack of public appearances would be much easier to conceal."

Fei considered his words and conceded the point. "I'm in, but if you betray me, I'll hunt you down."

He gave her a wry smile. "A threat not to be taken lightly. Let's hope that this is an unexceptional training session for everyone. That benefits both Andrea and the Empire."

Things were never that easy. Well, Fei supposed there was only one way to find out.

"When do I leave?"

4

Page rapped his knuckles against Lieutenant Evans's office door and went in when the young officer gestured for him to do so. The small space was cramped, and all the sports memorabilia on the walls only made it feel even more constricted.

The man was one of those guys that loved every kind of sport that he could try. Not only that, he wanted to excel at them all. He cut the very figure of the dashing marine officer. He'd have fit right in on a recruiting poster.

"Park it and tell me what's going on, Senior Sergeant," the sandy-haired officer said as he leaned back in his battered chair, lacing his fingers behind his head.

Page sat in one of the hardbacked chairs in front of the desk. "We're ready to start cleaning up, and we'll be set up for the next cycle, no problem, Lieutenant. What are you doing during the break? Sailing again? Doing a triathlon? Skydiving? Space races?"

The officer grinned. "You know me so well. No, this time I've decided to go old school. I'll be skiing."

Page frowned. "Skiing? I'm not familiar with that one."

"It's where you put flattened pieces of wood under your feet and slide down the side of a snow-covered mountain, letting gravity drive."

"That sounds… incredibly dangerous," Page said, unable to stop a note of alarm from creeping into his voice. "Are you at least going to be wearing armor or have a grav chute?"

Evans laughed and sat up. "Hell, no. There are varying levels of difficulty for the slopes, so some aren't all *that* dangerous. I'll hit the easy ones for about a week to get myself up to speed, and then I'll open things up. By the end of the trip, I'll have mastered the most difficult slopes. Mark my words."

Page had a mental vision of his lieutenant in the infirmary with every bone in his body broken. The man had injured himself doing various stunts in the past, but this time it sounded like he was considering something genuinely insane.

"Sir, don't you think that's pushing things just a bit?" he asked in his most reasonable tone. "Maybe you should stick to the safer slopes for this trip and build more experience before you take things to the next level. I don't think you're supposed to go all the way to expert in one vacation. What happens if something goes wrong? You could be killed."

"I'm a marine officer, Senior Sergeant," Evans said with a wide grin. "Danger is my middle name. I've got this covered, Mom. How hard can it really be?"

Famous last words for sure.

"You should come with me," Evans continued, a kind of light shining in his eyes. "We could dominate the slopes together, and when we're not skiing, we could be in the lodge, drinking something warm while socializing with the ladies. Come on. You need to get a life, Senior Sergeant."

"To have a life, you actually need to keep living it," Page said dryly. "I appreciate the offer, sir, but I've already got plans. Try not to maim yourself. This isn't a competition."

Evans gestured toward the wall covered with sports trophies that he'd earned. "*Everything* is a competition, Senior Sergeant. If you're not trying to win, you're losing, but I'll take your caution to heart and be a bit more careful than I might otherwise be. At least in the beginning.

"What about you? What exactly are your plans? And you'd better not say working. That's all you ever do."

Since Page didn't have any plans other than working, he'd have to spin a believable lie. "Now who's nagging? Gomez is going camping, and I might do something similar. Having a little intentionally disorganized time in my life might be relaxing."

Not a chance. He couldn't imagine anything *less* relaxing than wandering around a forest with nothing to do. Still, this was only to put the lieutenant off so that he didn't keep trying to drag him along on his vacation.

"Well, your loss," Evans said airily. "I'm leaving this afternoon, and I don't expect to be back until just before the recruits arrive. You know what to do when they get here, so I expect that you'll take care of business if I'm delayed, though I don't expect that."

"Sounds good," Page said as he rose to his feet. "Have a good trip, LT, and try not to break every bone in your body."

The officer rose with him and laughed. "Not a chance, Senior Sergeant. See you in a month."

Page headed back toward his office, his mind already focused on the cleanup tasks they'd start tomorrow. One cycle of marines was gone, but the next would be here in a month, and he had to be ready.

* * *

THE NEXT THREE days were a whirlwind of activity as Andrea prepared herself for the journey to come. She hadn't left DeSantis since she'd arrived. Now she was going to have to leave literally *everything* she'd known behind.

Not only that, she was going to be bereft of her support network. The people who'd helped her grow out of the introspective and somewhat strange girl they'd rescued from the crèche wouldn't be there for her now.

She felt adrift, and she didn't like it. Once she'd finished packing, she sought Grace out.

Her guardian—her mother in every way other than genetics—was in the library, reading an old-fashioned book. Grace said that she preferred words on printed paper. She said that, weirdly enough, she'd gotten the idea from her old battalion commander and his paperwork fetish. She liked the smell of the paper and ink and found the solidity of real books relaxing.

Whatever she was reading today, it was thick. The cover looked old and worn.

As soon as Andrea came into the room, Grace put a bookmark between the pages, closed the book, and gently set it on the small table beside her.

"All packed?" Grace asked with a sad smile. "How are you feeling?"

Andrea took a seat next to her. "I'm nervous but not scared. I've been working toward this moment for so long that I can't believe that it's really happening."

Grace took her hand. "That's not surprising. You're embarking on the most incredible adventure of your life. How could you not be nervous?

"It's going to be okay. Whatever challenges you face, you're strong enough to handle them. Anyone that assumes you're a pushover is in for a very, *very* unpleasant surprise."

Andrea nodded, but she wasn't certain that she agreed. "I've had a long time to think about how this could play out. I've seen how some people see these tattoos on my face and think they know me without even *talking* to me. They hate me because I came from the Singularity and for what these tattoos represent to *them*. That's going to happen at training, isn't it?"

"I'm sure it will," Grace said, squeezing her hand a little tighter. "The path you've chosen isn't going to be an easy one. In fact, it's probably going to be the most challenging career you could've chosen.

"Everyone has to fight for their place in the universe when they leave home. I realize that I haven't talked very much about my family, but my mother didn't approve of me joining the marines. She'd already planned my life, and I caused her no end of grief by choosing to live my life my way.

"I sent her a letter letting her know that I'd retired from the service and that I had you. Her response made it clear that I didn't need to bother coming home to visit. I wasn't welcome anymore."

A cold wave of shock washed over Andrea. "Because of me?"

Her guardian shook her head. "Because of her. She took an already broken relationship and sundered it completely because she couldn't accept my choices. Sometimes, that's the way it is.

"When people come into conflict with you because of how you've chosen to live your life, nod your head and let them go on about their business. If they try to interfere, that's when you take notice and stomp them.

"We've discussed the kinds of challenges that ordinary people face in marine training. You'll have an added layer because some of your fellow recruits—and even some instructors—will have a problem with you because you're from the Singularity. They're going to see it as a challenge to break you.

"Here's the thing to remember. They can't do that to you unless you let them. Simple dislike isn't enough to stop you from becoming a marine. They have to categorically *prove* that you're unfit, and the only way they can do that is if you fail to live up to expectations, do something that breaks the rules in a major way, or quit.

"When you get there, all of the recruits are going to be under tremendous pressure, yourself included. That's going to foster an environment where it's easy to lash out both verbally and physically. Be wary, but don't be the instigator. More than enough trouble will come looking for you as it is.

"If somebody tears a strip off of you, handle it verbally. If they physically strike you, put them on the ground in a bloody heap. That's the line. Don't cross it without real provocation.

"Use the minimum amount of verbal or physical force necessary. If you can avoid fighting at all, that's the best course, but the drill instructors are going to expect fights, and to a certain extent, they're going to encourage them."

That part had never made sense to Andrea. "Why would they want the recruits to fight?"

Grace smiled slightly. "Because you aren't joining a knitting club.

The marines want people who'll fight, so they have to recruit people willing to take a swing at someone else. They'll weed out the ones that are too aggressive. They want warriors, not sadistic bullies. And those that are too meek will get moved to the support branches.

"If you intend to make it in the Corps, you're going to have to show that you're willing to fight to be there. The goal is to be strategic, not brutal. You know a lot more about fighting than many of your fellow recruits and, potentially, some of your instructors. Gauge your response to the situation."

Fei had ruthlessly drilled her on hand-to-hand combat, among other things. She wasn't Fei's match in skill, but her added strength gave her a different kind of edge against those who didn't expect it.

Grace was still her mistress on the field, too, but the margin with her was smaller. Another year of intense training, and Andrea might be able to take her guardian. Maybe. Fei? Probably never.

Physically, Andrea was superior to run-of-the-mill humans. She was stronger and faster and had reaction times that occasionally seemed like dark sorcery to her family. The Singularity had designed the Andrea Line well.

Except for the facial tattoos, she looked unassuming but was more than a match for a full-grown man, and that had been true when she was twelve. At eighteen and with some training, she wasn't worried that anyone would be her match in a one-on-one fight, even if they played dirty.

"I won't strike first, but I will strike last," she agreed. "Fei was *very* firm about that."

"She's not wrong, but keep your implant recorders going at all times. You have plenty of storage, and you'll want to be able to prove that there was a provocation. The barracks will be monitored, but you can't count on that record. Cameras can be covered, and recordings corrupted.

"People will lie, too, right in the face of evidence to the contrary. It's human nature to protect what they've achieved, by fair means or foul. Some people will see you as the bogeyman, and they're going to make you out as the bad guy no matter what you do.

"After the first couple of fights, I suspect that the confrontations will become more subtle. Your enemies will look to sabotage you in ways that damage your results rather than your person at that point.

"You're trained in a lot of the equipment and procedures that you're going to be learning about in training. Fei has prepared you better than some active-duty marines, but that's not going to be enough.

"Once the drill instructors realize that you have that level of skill, they're going to work you harder. Their goal in training isn't to make sure that you meet minimum standards. Their goal is to find your limits and push you as far beyond them as they possibly can. They'll call in help if need be. You can't beat them. You can only survive them.

"That's going to make your bunkmates really angry because they're not going to be ready to go where you can. You'll be the smart girl in class that blows the curve for everyone else. That's something else that you're going to have to get used to and find ways to soften for them."

Andrea sighed. "It's going to be hard, but I'll conceal my physical differences and skills for as long as I can. I want to make friends, and this feels like how I make enemies."

"Being a marine is about being part of a team," Grace said gently. "You watched my platoon fight. They weren't a bunch of cowboys doing their own thing. They were a team working together, using one person's strengths to cover another's weaknesses. The enemy isn't your fellow marines. It's the people you're fighting. They'll eventually learn that and treasure what you bring to the table."

Grace rose and pulled Andrea into a tight hug. "You've *got* this. You have a spirit inside of you that just won't give up. Whenever things seem impossible, just remember that we're there in spirit.

"Now, it's late. We're really proud of you, and I know that you're going to make a terrific marine. Go get some sleep. We'll have a big breakfast in the morning, and then we'll all go to the spaceport to see you off."

Physical closeness had always been hard for Andrea, but she treasured this kind of contact with her family. She squeezed her guardian tight, though she was careful not to exert too much strength.

Her genetically enhanced muscles were roughly forty percent more powerful than an average human's, and she'd been diligently working out to improve them for years. Her trim form concealed tremendous power.

"I love you," she said, letting the tears come. "I'm going to miss you so much."

Grace kissed her on the forehead. "I love you too. We'll be there for your graduation. Count on it. Now git."

Andrea went upstairs but wasn't able to fall asleep. She lay in her bed, worrying about what was going to happen. She wanted to make her family proud.

She'd do everything that she could to succeed, but she couldn't escape the feeling that there was going to be more trouble than any of them had anticipated.

Well, whatever came her way, she'd deal with it. She'd survived the crèche, and she could survive Imperial Marine training. It wasn't like they were going to try to kill her, right?

* * *

BREAKFAST WAS TOUGH. Fei put on a cheerful face for her family, but she was already in mission mode. She'd been working hard for the last three days with her spouses to plan out what she could, but so many things were up in the air until she saw what kind of situation was waiting for them.

She'd last served six years ago as a noncommissioned officer. Now she'd be going in as an officer and working in battalion headquarters. Imperial Intelligence was supposed to handle her insertion, but things could always go wrong.

In fact, they almost certainly would.

Now, rather than translating Grace's orders into tactics, she'd be doing the strategic work herself. If she wanted to blend in, she'd have to perform the task well too.

Watching her daughter—because that was how she saw Andrea— suffering while trying to hide how she felt hurt. She wanted to tell her girl that she'd be right there, but that wouldn't do her any favors. Andrea had to learn that she could carry the load herself.

When they'd drawn the meal out as long as they could, Kayden flew them to the sprawling starport. Andrea was putting on a brave face, but Fei could tell the worry was still gnawing at her. She'd felt the same when she'd enlisted.

Andrea's ticket had her as a general passenger on a midsized liner. Since she was traveling to basic training, the Empire was paying for the trip, but the family had upgraded her to a private cabin.

Fei was traveling first class and would be in a separate section of the ship. There was very little chance that the two would run into one another under those circumstances, but Fei already planned to spend the flight in her cabin, even eating there.

When they arrived at their destination, first-class passengers departed first, so she'd be able to slip away before Andrea had a chance to debark.

Her girl was going out on her own. Fei was both proud and fearful for her. Lots of hugs, kisses, and tearful words were said as Andrea took her luggage and trooped off to the cutter with her head held high.

They waited until another cutter was ready to depart before Fei started saying her own goodbyes. Those hugs were heartfelt and tearful too. She'd never expected to find a family like Grace and Kayden, and it tore at her to be leaving them, even if only for a few months.

"You'll take care of her for us, won't you?" Kayden asked, enfolding her in his arms.

"Of course I will. This is going to be straightforward. There shouldn't be any serious complications."

Grace laughed with an edge of derision as she pulled Fei into a tight hug. "We all know that things are *never* that simple. Either Imperial Intelligence will try something, or this strange cabal will stick their oar in. Hell, some random asses will certainly get in on the game. We're not going to know until it's all over, but thank God that you'll be on-site to mitigate it."

Fei nodded and hugged her wife before kissing her deeply. Then she did the same with her husband.

She hadn't brought any luggage. Whatever she needed, she'd buy on the ship. It was pricey, but that had preserved the impression that she was going home with the rest of the family.

Now, with her own head held high, she boarded the cutter. Whatever came for Andrea now, Fei would stand ready to defend her from the shadows.

She pitied *anyone* that crossed her girl, and that included any of the officers that thought they'd manipulate things behind the scenes. It was her job to make sure that didn't happen, and she'd make absolutely certain that everything ran smoothly.

Now, if only the universe would cooperate with her plans.

5

Page spent the next four weeks getting set up for the arrival of the next cycle of recruits. With the other drill instructors away, he commandeered warm bodies from battalion to get everything configured just the way he wanted it.

This was pretty much how it worked every training cycle, and the familiar process relaxed him. This was the one part of the cycle where he could shape things to be just the way he wanted them without any interference.

The drill instructors started trickling back in over the week before the training cycle kicked off and helped him verify that he hadn't missed anything. To his annoyance, there was usually something that needed to be tweaked or that had somehow been overlooked.

Page spent the final day reviewing everything and found himself satisfied. Now he only needed to wait for the recruits.

They'd be flown from the spaceport in the evening and wouldn't get the ever-so-warm welcome until they were safely in his clutches.

Honestly, this was one of the most enjoyable times for him as a drill instructor. He'd meet the civilians that thought they could be marines and give them a few bad weeks. Those that survived the first month would almost certainly make it all the way through.

He was just finishing up the last of his electronic paperwork when he got a call from battalion. It was Major Martelle. The man frowned at Page through the vid.

"Senior Sergeant, I've got some bad news. Lieutenant Evans had an accident while on leave, and he won't be here for the recruits' arrival.

"It seems he got overly ambitious and tried a slope well above his skill level. An inconveniently placed tree and a moderate cliff put him in the local hospital. He's expected to make a full recovery, but his injuries take him out of play for this training cycle."

So, Page's vision of his lieutenant falling off a mountain had turned out to be basically correct. Perfect.

"What will we do for an officer, sir?" he asked.

"For now, you're in charge. I have every confidence in you, Senior Sergeant. If there is a problem that you can't handle, call me no matter the hour, and I'll make the magic happen."

"Will do, sir. Thank you."

He wouldn't call, of course. Page knew every aspect of training marine recruits backward and forward. He could handle any curves they threw at him. Unless something very unusual happened, he didn't anticipate anything that would require an officer to make a decision today. Or even this week.

He called Gomez and asked her to come to his office ASAP. She arrived a couple of minutes later, and he told her the news.

She shook her head in bemusement. "I can't say that I'm shocked. With the LT's idea of fun, it was only a matter of time before he maimed himself. I'm glad to hear that he's going to be okay."

"Me too. Did you enjoy your trip into the woods?"

She nodded, heading for the coffee maker to get them each a cup. "I really needed it. Being able to set up a tent in the middle of nowhere, sleep as long as I like, and do whatever I want really relaxes me. I assume you stayed here."

That had been a statement, not a question.

"I find what we do relaxing. Honestly, who wouldn't?"

She laughed. "This is some of the most stressful work in the Corps, and you find it relaxing. What's wrong with you, John?"

He grinned. "I thrive on stress. Seriously, I don't know what I'd do with unstructured time. I like having my days all laid out. That kind of order *is* relaxing for me. I don't like chaos, and I don't like surprises."

She shook her head, sat down, and sipped her coffee. "Then I sure hope there are no surprises for you this training cycle. We wouldn't want to ruin a relaxing twelve weeks of basic training."

He laughed and hoped that she had the right of it.

* * *

MOST PEOPLE WOULD'VE FOUND a four-week trip on a liner relaxing, but it hadn't turned out that way for Andrea. She'd forced herself to leave her cabin and meet new people, but she still felt isolated.

It wasn't that the majority of her fellow passengers were overtly hostile to her—though some of them were—but enough recognized what her tattoos meant for her to get a series of dirty looks even on an otherwise enjoyable outing or meal. That was honestly about average when she ventured out in public and why she didn't do it all that often.

Andrea missed her family. Every night she questioned whether she'd made the right decision. This was what she'd wanted, but that didn't make the process any easier.

She'd ended up spending a lot of time in her cabin rather than taking meals with the other passengers. She'd slept, read, and exercised using martial arts katas, since the gym was a bad place for a confrontation because it showed exactly how different she was from normal humans.

Not only had Fei drilled her in hand-to-hand combat as used by the marines, Andrea had taken instruction in a number of other styles to augment her capabilities.

She wasn't a master of any of them—not by any means—but the additional moves that she'd added to her repertoire might one day allow her to surprise someone who wasn't expecting them. With her speed and strength, an unexpected move could be devastating if applied correctly.

When the liner arrived at New Dallas, she felt as if she'd been cooped up for half her life. The liner ferried its passengers to the main spaceport via cutters, and once she was on the ground, it was only a short walk to where a marine pinnace was taking on what she assumed was a group of soon-to-be recruits.

Since Fei had claimed a pinnace as part of her booty from the raid, Andrea had experience with them. Kayden had trained her in piloting one, though she wasn't nearly skilled enough to fly unsupervised. As Fei had said, Andrea knew enough to spectacularly crash one in a pinch.

Her mentor was probably right.

The pinnace's interior was crowded with young people, so she found an open seat and strapped herself in. There were a couple of marines in flight suits going through the compartment, showing everyone how to strap themselves in, and she realized that she probably should've waited to be instructed on how to do that just to maintain her cover.

Nobody around her seemed inclined to talk, so she settled herself in and observed the people watching her. Her tattoos had once again garnered the attention of those that were close enough to see them.

The girl seated beside her, a redhead, seemed like she was about to speak, but one of the marines chose that moment to come over to her. "Where did you get those tattoos, and why the hell would you do that yourself? Do you know what they mean?"

This moment had been inevitable, and Andrea had been dreading it for years. There was nothing she could do to put it off, so she faced it squarely.

"The tattoos represent one of the castes of the Singularity, Corporal," she said calmly. "As for why I have them, I didn't have a choice. I was a child when they put them on me, and they're not removable."

Concealing them would've made her life *so* much simpler, but her very genes rebelled against going that route. That meant that she had to prove that she was worthy of being human despite her origin.

"Well, I'll be damned," he said, shaking his head.

Without saying another word, he turned and headed over to his comrade. They had an energetic discussion that revolved around her based on their gestures. The corporal went into the control area while the other man watched her with narrowed eyes.

A minute later, an officer stepped into the compartment and headed straight for her with the corporal at his heels. He stopped in front of her and studied her closely.

"Are those genuine?" he asked, his voice toneless.

"Yes, sir. I was rescued from the Singularity as a child."

"Who rescued you, and how old were you?"

"Imperial Marines rescued me during a raid when I was twelve years old, sir. I've been raised in the Empire since then. They gave so much for me that I'm here to dedicate myself to doing the same for others."

"Let me see your orders."

She handed him the old-fashioned folder that contained her orders and her redacted records. Even though she had electronic copies in her implants, not all recruits had that capability, so she'd been carting paper around and would continue to do so until she was at the base.

He flipped them open and scanned several pages before stopping to read something in more detail. He looked up at Andrea and examined her face more closely.

"Both your orders and records back up what you've said, Recruit, but I've never heard of anything like this. What's your story?"

"I'm sorry, but I've been told that I can't divulge anything further because it's classified, sir. Everything that I can say is in those records."

The man grunted noncommittally, closed the folder, and handed it back to her. "I can only imagine the tsunami of crap that you're about to walk into, Recruit. The people around us don't know what you represent, but there are plenty of marines at the base who do. Why would you subject yourself to something like this?"

"Marines just like yourself gave their lives for me. The only way I can repay that debt is to become an Imperial Marine myself."

"I don't envy you or your training staff," the man said. "Good luck, Recruit Tolliver. You'll need it."

He returned her folder and made his way back into the front of the pinnace.

The corporal and his companion continued to stand at the front of the compartment, glaring at her as the pinnace prepared for takeoff. Yes, these were going to be fun times.

A large boy—or young man—of perhaps a hundred and ten kilos with long brown hair and a nose that was rather too large for his face leaned across the aisle and stared at her.

"What kind of freak are you?"

Well, that hadn't taken long.

6

Fei made it down to the port without any trouble and immediately got herself on a flight to the base with other marine personnel by presenting her orders. She took care to be sure it wasn't the same vehicle that would be carrying any recruits before she boarded.

The trip took about an hour, and once she'd disembarked, she quickly found a base map and located the 225th Training Battalion.

She snagged a ride from some of the others that had been on the cutter, and they dropped her off in front of a wide, imposing building made of formed plascrete that brought back mixed memories of her own past.

It was evening, yet the place was bustling. They had an incoming crop of recruits, so everyone was getting prepared for the influx.

She marched to the person acting as the charge of quarters—basically the enlisted person responsible for dealing with any general issues like visitors or com calls after regular hours—and presented her orders again.

The female corporal examined everything and then pointed down the hall toward a set of stairs. "The major's office is on the third level, ma'am. Turn right, fourth door on the left."

Fei thanked the woman and headed in the indicated direction. She was still in civilian clothes, but her orders were to report to the battalion commander upon arrival. It wasn't like she'd drawn uniforms yet or even had a place to change.

She made her way up the stairs, down the hall, and stopped at the indicated door. The outer office was manned by a sergeant whose nametag read Jackson. He smiled pleasantly as she entered, focusing his attention on her.

"May I help you?"

She presented her orders a third time. "I'm reporting to the battalion commander."

The sergeant took and scanned them. Satisfied, he returned them.

"If you'll have a seat, Lieutenant, I'll see if Major Martelle is free to see you."

Fei took a seat, and three minutes later, the sergeant indicated that she could go in. She rapped twice on the door with Major Craig Martelle's name and entered as soon as the voice inside commanded her to do so.

The man's office was neat to the point of obsessiveness. Everything was regimented and ordered, even though there was quite a bit of material on shelves and hung on the walls. The major was obviously a meticulous man.

He was of average height with closely cropped brown hair and piercing eyes. He sat behind a desk that was absolutely clear of paper or any other distractions. Unlike her last battalion commander, the major apparently was not someone who fetishized paper.

She stepped in front of the desk and braced to attention. "Lieutenant Na Fei reporting as ordered, sir."

"At ease, Lieutenant."

She relaxed slightly with her arms behind her back as the major examined her. She expected him to ask for her orders, but he seemed content to simply observe her.

"You're former enlisted, aren't you?" he finally asked. "I'd guess either a sergeant or senior sergeant. Am I right?"

"Yes, sir."

He smiled slightly. "It's the posture. Officers tend to be a little laxer in how they stand. If you want to blend in as an officer, you're going to have to learn to relax a little, Lieutenant Na.

"I received an electronic copy of your orders just two hours ago. I assume that's when your ship arrived in orbit. Curious. I usually know that an officer is being assigned to my unit well in advance. I can't recall how long it's been since I've had anyone just show up, particularly an officer.

"That last part makes this an *interesting* curiosity. Why are you here, Lieutenant, and why didn't I know that you were coming?"

She shrugged slightly. "It's in my orders, sir. As to why you weren't notified ahead of time, I can't speak to that."

He grunted. "I see. We'll get someone to assign you quarters once we sort things out, but I still have a few questions. Your service record says that you left the service six years ago, and yet here you are back in uniform, metaphorically speaking.

"I find that gap curious. Actually, I've used the word 'curious' too many times. Once this many curious things happen, I tend to get suspicious. I'll ask you again, Lieutenant, why are you here?"

"I'm here to serve the Empire, sir, in whatever capacity you see fit."

He took that in silence before finally nodding. "I see. We're going to have an interesting time getting to know one another, Lieutenant Na. Well, it just so happens that I have a spot in need of filling.

"One of my adjutants went on emergency leave a few months back, so that leaves me with an opening. I'm going to assume that that's what you were sent to fill. I've never known the personnel branch to be this prompt, but I suppose I can't rule it out."

Then he smiled. "But I have a better idea. One of my platoon leaders was in an accident while on leave, and I just got word that he won't be returning to duty anytime soon. That means you get the nod.

"You can head to Bravo Company, First Platoon's barracks and get yourself settled in. We're expecting the recruits to arrive in the next hour, and your drill instructors are already deployed to receive them. That means you're going to have to catch up with them on the fly.

"There's just enough time for you to draw uniforms and gear and get yourself settled in before all hell breaks loose. Welcome to the 225th Training Battalion, Lieutenant Na. Don't screw this up."

Na blinked in surprise, confident that this *wasn't* what Earl Still Water had had in mind. She hadn't planned on being anywhere near the recruits, but she was a lieutenant in charge of a training platoon, so they were going to see her.

Still, the odds of Andrea being assigned to the same platoon as she were low. The problem was that without being in battalion headquarters, she wouldn't be able to keep an eye on her charge. That was going to make her job significantly more difficult.

"Might I get a listing of assigned personnel and trainees, sir?"

The major nodded and forwarded a file to her through her implants. She started going over it quickly and stopped, her mouth almost falling open in shock.

Andrea was assigned to her platoon.

"Don't let the unexpected situation overwhelm you, Na," Martelle said. "Your NCOs are experienced. They'll keep you from messing up as long as you listen to them. Hell, you already know that. Now get moving. Orientation waits for no one."

She was so screwed.

* * *

PAGE HAD JUST FINISHED PUTTING away his coffee mug and was headed toward the parade ground with Gomez when he got a call from the inbound pinnace.

That was unusual. He hoped it didn't foreshadow some kind of problem.

"This is Senior Sergeant Page," he said into his wrist unit.

"Senior Sergeant, this is Lieutenant Gregson, the copilot on your pinnace. We have something of a situation with one of your recruits. It's odd enough that I felt you needed a heads up.

"There's a girl in your group that looks like she's from the Singularity. I'm not sure what her story is, but she's got what looks like a valid set of orders."

Page frowned. There were certainly people from the Singularity who migrated to the Empire, but very few of them ever joined the Imperial Marines. Even if they had, he wasn't sure how that mattered.

"Forgive my asking, sir, but how did her origin come into play?"

"She's got a full set of facial tattoos. I'm no expert, but I know that means some kind of social standing there."

That deepened the mystery. "Can you describe the tattoos? Maybe have a picture forwarded to me?"

"I'm sending it now."

An instant later, an image popped up in his implant feed. It showed a perfectly normal-looking girl with dark hair and tattoos in the form of a hawk on her face. The bird's head was on her forehead, and it was turned slightly to the side to give it depth. The cheekbone tattoos seemed to have the bird's wings in a diving configuration.

It was a striking, aggressive tattoo and one that he was unfamiliar with.

He double-checked the Corps databases for that particular tattoo and came up empty. Whatever it was, they'd either never encountered it, or it was classified at a higher level than he was able to access.

"Thanks for the heads up, Lieutenant," he said. "Was the girl confrontational, or was someone aggressive toward her?"

"It started out with one of the corporals questioning her presence. Once that was done, I went back and checked her orders for myself. After I left, one of the other recruits started giving her crap, so I'd imagine this will be a problem for you going forward."

Perfect.

"If you don't mind my asking, how do you plan on dealing with someone from the Singularity inside your training platoon?" the officer asked, his tone curious.

That was a great question. One, unfortunately, that he didn't know the answer to.

"I'm going to have to play that by ear, sir. Once you land, we'll get the recruits off the pinnace like usual, and I'll make certain that she gets all the attention that she deserves. Thanks for the heads up."

"No problem, Senior Sergeant. Good luck."

Once the com link terminated, Page turned to Gomez. It only took a minute to fill her in.

She scowled thunderously. "That is complete bullshit. I don't know who or what she is, but the fact that she has tattoos means that she's a genie. The Empire doesn't even recognize them as people. How could she possibly be here?"

Page's feelings were mixed. The girl might be a clone—or rather a being created from a human-designed template—but that didn't mean that she wasn't a person.

Still, he had to keep in mind that not everybody felt the same as he did, and Imperial law was clear. Clones and created beings *were* property, though the manufacture of such was an extremely grave crime.

Yet, somehow, this girl was here with seemingly valid orders for training. He couldn't imagine how that was possible, but he'd have plenty of time to find out.

"I don't know," he finally said. "Once the pinnace lands, I'll take lead while you tear someone up to get the recruits' attention. We'll get them out of the pinnace and onto the parade ground for the shark attack like usual.

"Once we've got them all sorted out, you and I will pull her aside and get some answers. Let's not make a big deal about this until we have those answers. Clear?"

Gomez nodded, obviously unwilling to fully agree. "I don't like this. The Singularity is our enemy, and we don't need to be training their clones about how we fight."

"Let's be sure of the situation before we act," he cautioned. "It's our responsibility to be evenhanded, and I'm not going to do this girl wrong unless she deserves it.

"Pass the word to everyone else so that no one is caught off guard. We need to be on the same page by the time that pinnace lands."

She nodded and jogged ahead to inform the others.

He stood on the side of the parade ground and shook his head. This wasn't shaping up to be the best training cycle he'd ever run. Chaos was starting to seep in, he'd lost his lieutenant, and now he had a real mystery on his hands.

What else was going to go wrong?

7
_____

Andrea considered ignoring the boy's rude question but decided to turn the confrontation back on him.

"What kind of freak are you?" she asked, mimicking his tone.

Her flip answer made the boy scowl even more fiercely. If he hadn't been strapped in, he probably would've tried to lean forward and be more intimidating. If he unstrapped himself, though, he risked drawing the ire of the noncommissioned officers who were watching the events unfold without bothering to hide their interest.

They gave no visible clues about what they'd do, but she was pretty sure that they'd intervene if an actual fight broke out. Words were probably acceptable, but she needed to avoid *too* much provocation.

The boy didn't seem to feel the same limitations.

"I've heard about you Singularity freaks," he sneered. "You aren't even human. You don't belong in the marines, freak. Hell, you don't belong in the Empire at all."

"You're an ass, Claudio."

The scornful exclamation came from the curvy redheaded girl seated next to Andrea. "I don't even know her, but I already like her better than you. You've been nothing but a jerk this entire trip. If someone doesn't belong in the marines, it's you."

The boy glared at the girl. "All you do is sit around mooning about how exciting it's going to be in the marines, Diana. You don't have what it takes to fight. You'll be washed out inside a week."

"I suppose we'll find out," the girl said with a sniff. "I'll still put my money on us."

She turned to face Andrea, making a point of ignoring the boy. "Hi. I'm Diana Randall, and I'd like to be your friend."

Andrea smiled. This sounded like some kind of ploy against the boy, but even fake friendship might be nice.

"I'm Andrea Tolliver, and contrary to what you might hear, I'm not really that bad of a person. This tattoo doesn't define me."

The redhead laughed. "I promise I won't judge you. Ignore Claudio. He's just a jerk from some backwater that figures the Imperial Marines are all about beating people up. He wouldn't understand strategy and teamwork if it bit him in the ass."

"We'll see about that once we get to the base," the boy said grimly. "You two better hope you're nowhere near me because I'll make it my mission to run you both out."

"I see what you mean," Andrea told the girl thoughtfully. "He *is* a jerk. So, what do you think the odds of us actually being assigned to the same training platoon are?"

The redhead shrugged. "No clue. The marines make it relatively difficult to find out what happens during basic training. I suppose they want to keep up their mystique.

"All I know for sure is that they'll run us ragged as soon as we arrive. Once that's done, they'll use whatever magic they have to assign us to training platoons, and then the fun really starts."

Andrea knew far more about the kinds of tactics the drill instructors would use, though that wouldn't make surviving them any easier.

She really hoped that she got assigned to the same platoon as the redhead. It would be nice having a friendly face to deal with instead of people like Claudio. Jerks were a dime a dozen, but friends were worth their weight in gold.

They chatted, each relaying a little bit about their background as the pinnace flew on. They'd only just begun the inevitable questions about Andrea's life inside the Singularity when the pinnace came in for a landing.

It settled down almost gently, and the ramp at the rear lowered. Two women and a man in marine uniforms wearing strange hats with circular, straight brims made their way into the pinnace. The two women spread down the aisles, while the man stopped at the head of the ramp.

"Welcome to Bravo Company, First Platoon of the 225th Training Battalion, recruits," he said in a tone that easily carried to everyone inside the pinnace. "My name is Senior Sergeant John Page, but you will call me Drill Instructor. As of this moment, you're mine. Trust me when I say that isn't something I'm going to be bragging about anytime soon."

Someone up one of the aisles chuckled, which drew the attention of one of the women in the strange hats. She stalked over to the amused girl and glared at her with her hands on her hips.

"Do you think Drill Instructor Page is funny, Recruit?" the woman demanded.

The girl got a deer-in-the-headlights look, obviously having no idea how she was supposed to respond. Unfortunately for her, there was *no* right answer, and she was about to become a negative example.

The female drill instructor leaned forward until the brim of her hat almost touched the girl's forehead. "Come to think of it, Drill Instructor Page *is* a funny guy. Would you like to laugh at Drill Instructor Page, Recruit?"

The woman stared into the girl's eyes and said nothing for a few seconds while the pinnace sat in dead silence.

Getting no answer, the woman grinned. "Since you seem to be mute, I think push-ups might help you find your tongue. On your feet!"

The woman turned and shouted at all of them. "Everyone on your feet! I want you worms off my pinnace in thirty seconds. Twenty-nine... Twenty-eight... Twenty-five... Ten... Three..."

Andrea had heard about this particular trick and knew that it wouldn't end well for any of them. Sometimes you just had to play the game, even when the rules were stacked against you.

She released her restraints and rose, grabbing her pack. When she saw that Diana was having difficulty with her restraints, she reached down and undid hers too.

"Come on," she said. "It'll be better to be toward the front of this mess."

Since the two of them were out of their restraints before the other recruits, they were able to hurry down the ramp and onto the ground.

And it was ground. They hadn't landed at a port. The pinnace sat in the middle of a well-groomed field surrounded by long, squat buildings. Those would be barracks, she realized. This was their training area.

She hadn't expected things to kick off quite so rapidly, but one of the goals of basic training was to knock you out of your comfort zone and make you lose your emotional and physical equilibrium.

The three drill instructors waiting in the field—two male and the other female—wasted no time getting into Andrea's and Diana's faces.

"On the deck, recruits!" the man shouted. "Keep pushing until I get tired."

Andrea dropped her bag, lowered herself into the front leaning rest position, and started doing push-ups. She made sure there were flaws in her technique and went much slower than she could under normal conditions. She'd do what she judged was enough and then slow down as if she were tired.

The goal was to avoid standing out too much. She wanted to be in the upper third of this initial assessment but not at the top. That would help offset her origin while not making it look like she was smug about what she could really do.

The truth of her capabilities would come out, though. As soon as the medical personnel began going over her records, they'd realize that she'd been holding back, and then there'd be fireworks.

Andrea wasn't precisely sure what kind, but it would undoubtedly be exciting. Yet, for now, her goal was to fit in. First impressions mattered.

As the rest of the recruits finally exited the pinnace and began doing their own push-ups, she was able to see the lead drill instructor out of the corner of her eye. Senior Sergeant Page stood at the top of the pinnace's ramp with his hands on his hips, his head swiveling as he observed them.

One of the female drill instructors—the same one that had berated the girl—stepped up next to him and said something, pointing at Andrea. With all the drill instructors shouting at the recruits, hearing what they were saying was impossible, but they were obviously talking about her.

The recruits around her were already having trouble maintaining their form, so she started allowing her butt to rise. That was how the body tried to cheat the exercise. Soon enough, they'd all be doing it.

Except maybe Claudio. The jerk was still pumping out the push-ups, glaring at Andrea and Diana. Of course he was breezing through the physical part of this.

And based on the fact that there was only one pinnace of recruits, that made her suspect that they'd be in the same platoon. Andrea wasn't going to be able to escape him so easily.

Well, whatever came, she'd face it. She was going to become an Imperial Marine, and none of these people—recruit or drill instructor —was going to stop her.

* * *

It took a surprisingly short time for Fei to draw her uniforms and essential gear. One of the battalion runners escorted her to each location where she got equipment, and the man checked items off a list. All the stations were open because they were about to receive recruits.

Once they had her fully outfitted, the runner showed her to the barracks. It was similar to the one that Grace's platoon had occupied, and she almost found herself walking toward the senior noncommissioned officer's room before she stopped herself. Those days were over.

The runner led her upstairs to what would've been Grace's office six years ago. The small office fronted a set of quarters. They were small but complete, including a private head and a minuscule kitchen. The same was true of the noncommissioned officers' quarters. After all, it wouldn't do for the recruits to see their leaders using the can or showering.

The rooms were full of the previous occupant's belongings, though several enlisted men and women were hurriedly packing everything. It wasn't like she had anything to fill the empty space.

They'd leave the food and consumables, so she was basically set.

The office was filled with sports memorabilia: trophies and pictures, mostly. The earnest young man who usually ran the platoon looked like a happy-go-lucky daredevil in some of the images. She was sorry that he'd hurt himself but glad that he'd recover.

Once she was settled in and the man's belongings were gone, she stepped into the office and looked out over the parade ground through the window. A few barracks had lights on, and Fei realized that the training groups were probably at different points in their individual training arcs.

Some of them would be getting close to graduation, while others had probably only just arrived themselves. That was somewhat different than it had been during her day. The training battalion she'd attended had had all the recruits dropped on them at the same time.

Talk about utter chaos.

Still, that put a load on both the ranges and the equipment being utilized. Having everything staggered made more sense. It seemed even the Corps could learn new tricks.

Down on the parade ground, she could see a pinnace, and spread around its base were people doing push-ups. The bright lights kept the encroaching darkness at bay, but the view was still distant enough to make identifying Andrea impossible.

What she could see were a pair of drill instructors standing at the head of the pinnace's ramp, clearly illuminated by its interior lights. They were watching the recruits, and she knew they were making judgment calls about which ones needed a little more attention.

Her download indicated that the lead noncommissioned officer was Senior Sergeant John Page, and she had a brief summary of his service record. He'd been doing this kind of training for quite some time and had an excellent record for turning recruits into marines. She hoped he wouldn't have a problem with Andrea's background, but there was nothing she could do about it if he did.

A senior sergeant was a fairly high-ranking NCO for a platoon, but in this case, there were five other NCOs performing drill instruction duties. They'd be rotating their time so that none of them were on duty for more than about ten hours. That allowed them to run the recruits ragged without exhausting themselves.

She scrutinized each of the people doing push-ups and eventually decided which one was probably Andrea. The girl's tattoos were going to make her life difficult.

Fei's too. The very first person Senior Sergeant Page would come to talk to about Andrea was her. How was she going to handle that?

She wasn't supposed to know Andrea, and there was nothing in their records to connect them. Fei had to avoid showing the girl favoritism because she wanted her to succeed on her own, but she also wanted her to succeed. It was going to be a delicate balancing act.

Well, as Grace often said, if it was easy, anyone could do it.

Shouting from outside brought Fei's attention back to the scene in front of her as the drill instructors got the recruits on their feet and began herding them off. Whatever belongings they'd brought with them would be confiscated, they'd have their heads shaved, and then they'd start the process of being issued uniforms and equipment.

Once that was complete, they'd be shown where they'd be sleeping, educated about how the barracks were set up, and get the basic ground rules. By the time that was all done, it would be after local midnight. Unless she missed her guess, the drill instructors would be waking them up around four hours later.

They'd get just enough sleep to be completely and utterly exhausted. That pace wouldn't slow over the next dozen weeks either. They'd toughen up or wash out.

Andrea had an advantage in that she had genetic enhancements and marine-grade medical nanites and implants. Fleet used the same implants, but their nanites were less capable. Those little machines would help Andrea recover faster, which was already enhanced by her efficient metabolic processes. The end result was that she'd be able to keep up better than any of the other recruits, which would make her *very* unpopular.

Well, that was a problem her girl would just have to deal with.

She needed to get herself in uniform and be ready to meet with Senior Sergeant Page. Somehow, she'd have to lead this platoon without Andrea laying eyes on her or hearing her name.

She wasn't sure how she was going to manage that, but she'd figure something out. She had to.

8

Page stood at the top of the pinnace's ramp, considering the strange girl, as the drill instructors moved through the recruits on the parade ground, making them do push-ups. This kind of welcome was called the shark attack and was a staple of basic training.

They had to keep the recruits off guard to lower their defenses against what was coming. They didn't want to generate resistance, so they focused on keeping the situation as locked down as possible so that the drill instructors' authority was never questioned.

There was no doubt in his mind that the girl had come from the Singularity. Even though he hadn't been able to find any information on that particular tattoo, he could tell from the way it was drawn that it was authentic. This wasn't something that someone had cooked up out of thin air just to distinguish themselves.

Still, he needed to get as much information about the girl as he possibly could before he confronted her.

And there *was* going to be a confrontation. One couldn't allow a genetically engineered being into the Imperial Marines without asking pointed questions. They didn't have to be aggressively asked, but she still needed to be pressed.

He tapped into the database that contained the incoming recruits' data and quickly located her. Rather than reviewing her background first, he scanned her orders. One could often determine interesting facts from who initiated them and where they came from.

Directions to report to Imperial Marine basic training came from the Corps' office of personnel. Each specific set of orders tended to originate on the planet the recruit came from. It was also interesting to note how far away the world of origin was from the training center they were placed at.

In this case, it looked like the girl—Andrea Tolliver—came from a planet named DeSantis that was about four weeks away under normal travel conditions.

Interesting. She'd been ordered here right about the same time that the last training cycle was wrapping up. That was fast for this sort of thing.

To make sure that there weren't too many recruits going to any one location, the office of personnel filled each training platoon over the course of half a year, and the orders were cut at least three or four months in advance of the recruit's arrival date.

Yet, in this case, it looked like there was no history before they came down four weeks ago. There wasn't even a request for training from the girl or her family. It was almost as if the Empire itself had declared, "You're going to Imperial Marine recruit training," and she'd said, "Okay."

He doubted very seriously that that was the case, but her orders *were* unusual.

Page switched his attention to her personnel jacket. As anyone experienced knew, the record for a new recruit was painfully thin. It would list the basic facts about her: her planet of origin, information about close family in case there was an injury or death during training, and that kind of thing. As someone who had never served before, she would have no previous service record.

Even so, the amount of information listed for Tolliver was thinner than he'd expected. It listed her name, planet of origin, and her guardian: Grace Tolliver. There was a link in the woman's name that led to an Imperial Marine service record.

He clicked on that to find out the woman's history and discovered that she was a retired major. Considering the age on the public record, that was surprising. He'd have expected someone of that age to be a senior lieutenant, at best.

The accrued service time didn't match up with what was required for retirement either. Significant portions of the woman's record were under seal, including her last assignment. She must've done something to warrant being promoted, and that had allowed her to retire six years ago.

Six years.

He flipped back to the younger Tolliver's record and discovered that she had been resident on DeSantis for six years. In fact, the date of her arrival and the elder Tolliver's retirement were identical.

And, if he put his mind to the task, it wasn't tough to come up with a likely explanation. The Imperial Marines occasionally conducted raids across the border with the Singularity. If the elder Tolliver had led one of those assaults and somehow laid hands on the girl, that might explain something of the situation that he was dealing with.

It wasn't going to make unraveling the mystery any easier, but knowing where someone came from often made dealing with them less complicated.

The girl's record indicated that she was a genetically engineered being and had originated in the Singularity. There was an Imperial dispensation attached to her file that allowed for training in the Imperial Marines. It stipulated that by Imperial decree, she was recognized as human on a probationary basis and that only successful completion of basic training would make that condition permanent.

Since the girl's future was on the line, she'd be what marines liked to call "extremely motivated." It also meant that others would be willing to do just about anything to see that she failed. That was a complication that he didn't need.

Well, nobody had bothered asking him what he wanted, so he'd just have to muddle through.

He finished going over the records for all the recruits while the rest of the drill instructors got them in motion toward the warehouse building where they'd start the intake process.

As soon as that was underway, he and Gomez would corner the girl and ask those pointed questions. They might as well also get a complete medical scan while they were at it.

He sent a message to the battalion medical officer, and the man agreed to meet them at the intake clinic.

Personally, he couldn't wait to hear the girl's story. She was going to be a wrench thrown into his smoothly working machine, but his curiosity was piqued. Who was she really, and how had she shown up on his doorstep?

Page closed the files and marched along behind the ragged lines of recruits. He'd find out very shortly. He hoped Tolliver was ready for a rough twelve weeks because there wasn't going to be smooth sailing for any of them now.

* * *

BASED on what Andrea had learned from Grace and Fei, she expected to have her head shaved and then be issued equipment. Instead, Senior Sergeant Page gestured for her to accompany him.

A little uneasy, she did so.

He led her outside and joined the female drill instructor that had yelled at the girl in the pinnace. Together, without saying a word, they led her to a different building. Waiting inside was a medical center, complete with an officer that looked like a doctor.

Unlike the medical centers she was familiar with, this one seemed designed to quickly process a lot of people. No doubt the rest of the recruits would be run through here at some point to make sure that they were healthy.

Senior Sergeant Page turned to face her once they were inside. "Recruit Tolliver, before we begin, I've examined your records, and I'm astonished. I've met people from the Singularity before, but it's always been over the sights of my rifle.

"I've also seen some with tattoos before—specifically, officers and troops of the warrior caste—though I've never seen that particular pattern. Are those real? How did you get them?"

She braced to attention. "I was rescued during a raid into the Singularity when I was twelve, Drill Instructor. These tattoos are authentic, but I wasn't raised in the Singularity past when I was a child. They don't define me."

"That's where you're wrong, Recruit. They certainly do define you. If you've rejected your heritage, why keep them?"

"My guardian had them removed—with my approval—Drill Instructor. Something about the tattooing process changed the cells in my skin, and the damned things came back. I can't get rid of them and keep my own face."

"That's... inconvenient," he allowed. "Your records lack detail, so tell me what role you were designed for in the Singularity."

She didn't want to irritate the man who had total control over her life, but she had to set the ground rules.

"There are some things that I'm not allowed to talk about, Drill Instructor. Things that were declared classified. I'm sorry, but that's going to limit some of my responses."

He considered her for a moment and then nodded slowly. "I'm provisionally willing to accept that. If I'm not satisfied with what I hear, we'll go find an officer and see what they can pry out of you. Now, give me the details you can."

"I was raised to be part of the Andrea Line. I suspect that my former line sibs would be insulted at my appropriation of their name. The woman in charge of the marines who liberated me was named Grace Tolliver. She was my guardian until I reached adulthood and received an Imperial dispensation to attend training here."

Page looked thoughtful. "I'm not familiar with the Andrea Line, so explain what it is."

"The Singularity has a caste system, Drill Instructor," Andrea said, trying not to sound like she was lecturing. "Basically, starting at a middle-grade managerial level, the Singularity begins tattooing the various lines designed for those tasks. Stacked one on top of another, there are various levels—or castes—of authority. The Andrea Line is one of the twelve lines that are part of Singularity's ruling caste."

He blinked, apparently surprised. "You're saying that you were designed to be part of the leadership of the Singularity?"

"Yes, Drill Instructor."

"Then this is even stranger than I'd expected. I'm going to step out of the room while Doctor Grey gives you a complete exam. Because you're female, Drill Instructor Gomez will remain in the room with you. You'll cooperate with the doctor and follow Drill Instructor Gomez's instructions. Is that understood?"

Andrea nodded. "Clear, Drill Instructor."

He stepped out of the room, and the doctor gestured toward the table. "If you'll sit on the table, Recruit, we'll begin the examination. I'll do everything I can via scanner while Drill Instructor Gomez holds up that wall over there and make certain that nothing untoward occurs."

Andrea had quite a bit of experience with medical examinations, and this one was no different. She was scanned in various ways, blood and tissue samples were taken, and then it was over. If anything, it was less extensive than some she'd endured. She even got to keep her clothes on.

The doctor had to have noted the fact that she had implants and a nanogenerator, but he didn't mention them. When he finished the exam, he excused himself and went outside.

Drill Instructor Gomez said nothing, merely leaning against the wall and staring at Andrea with an unfriendly expression.

Five minutes later, the door opened, and Senior Sergeant Page walked in alone. He stared at her for a few seconds without saying anything, and then he sighed.

"Doctor Grey will get back to me with the detailed results from your labs, but you've already shocked me. How did you end up with military-grade implants and a marine nanogenerator?"

His words struck Drill Instructor Gomez like a lightning bolt. She came off the wall and stared at him.

"Seriously?"

Page nodded. "He said you've had them for a while. How exactly did you get them, Recruit?"

"Parts of that story are classified, Drill Instructor."

"Explain it to me as well as you can, and I'll decide if that's sufficient."

"During the raid, there was a need to access a secure Singularity computer system. I did that for them. Later, there was going to be fighting, and the Fleet officer in command of the ship ordered the doctor to install the implants and nanogenerator if I agreed."

"He knew I wanted to become a marine, even then. I needed to fight, and he knew that they'd help me survive and protect the marines around me."

Page's eyebrows shot up. "You've fought Singularity troops? How?"

"I can't give you any details other than the fact that I did, but yes. I've risked my life and killed for the Empire."

Page's expression became a mixture of disbelief and astonishment. "I think that we need to have a *much* longer conversation about this, Recruit. One with an officer present."

Well, hell.

9

Fei expected to meet with Senior Sergeant Page once things had settled down, so she was more than a little concerned when she received a summons back to battalion, courtesy of Major Martelle.

By that point, she'd already gotten into uniform and had her quarters—such as they were—squared away, so all she had to do was head directly over, already worried about what might've gone wrong.

When she arrived, the major was seated behind his desk and looked annoyed. Worse, he wasn't alone. Standing in front of the desk, turned half toward her, was a man wearing a senior sergeant's tabs and holding a drill instructor's hat.

She stepped in front of the desk and braced to attention. "You sent for me, sir?"

"At ease, Lieutenant," the major said. "This is Senior Sergeant John Page, your lead drill instructor. He's just come to me with a problem that I suspect you're already aware of."

"Sir?"

Martelle leaned forward and fixed her with a stern look. "Don't feed me that line, Lieutenant. I think I now understand the general shape of the game you're playing, but I don't know *why* you chose to play it.

"You came out of retirement to accept a position here after being out of service for six years. Coincidentally we've got a recruit that was rescued from the Singularity six years ago. That strains credulity. Would you like to try your explanation one more time before I decide exactly how I'm going to respond?"

Fei sighed and gave in to the inevitable. "You're absolutely correct, sir. Imperial Intelligence sent me to keep an eye on her because forces are working to make certain she doesn't graduate. I wasn't meant to influence her attendance in any way. Only to make certain that no outside groups interfered."

Senior Sergeant Page gave her an assessing look. "You were on the raid that retrieved her, weren't you, ma'am?"

"I was," she confirmed. "I've been keeping an eye on Andrea since we rescued her, so you could say that I have a vested interest. As I said, I wasn't here to interfere, just to keep an eye on the situation."

The major didn't look impressed. "Do you think that I'd allow external influence inside my battalion?"

That was a loaded question if ever there was one. "When you're talking about Imperial nobles and their plots, none of us can control what they do, sir. Before Imperial Intelligence changed her training location, they became aware that a clique of nobles had inserted personnel into her original training unit to sabotage her chances.

"This wasn't a hypothetical situation, sir. This was cold, hard fact."

Major Martelle didn't say anything for a full minute. He just stared at her, his expression flat. When he finally did speak, his tone matched his expression.

"I can't say that I'm happy to hear any of this, Lieutenant Na, yet there's nothing overtly wrong in what you were instructed to do. If I'd done what Imperial Intelligence likely intended, you'd have had no direct influence over what occurred with your ward.

"Only now, you're in command of her training platoon. I suppose the correct thing for me to do would be to pull you back to battalion because of the conflict of interest. Still, I have a few questions, and I know that Senior Sergeant Page does as well.

"I'm told that she has military-grade implants and a marine nanogenerator. How did she get those?"

"The Fleet officer in charge of our ship during the raid made her the offer of receiving them as a reward for using her genetics and a passcode that she'd overheard from her Singularity instructor to help us recapture a Militia vessel—a heavy cruiser—taken by the Singularity and free what was left of her crew. A lot of lives were saved because she helped us of her own free will.

"I was only a sergeant at the time and didn't have any say in the matter, but I don't disagree with the decision. She's wanted to be a marine ever since I began training her. I was the one tasked to make sure that she stayed alive during the fighting."

"How could you put a twelve-year-old girl in a position to fight someone?" Page asked coldly. "I can't begin to say how irresponsible that is. Ma'am."

Fei laughed a bit bitterly. "It's not like I *encouraged* her, Senior Sergeant. I ordered her to remain on the raiding ship, but she smuggled herself aboard a boarding pod and was on the captured ship before we knew that she'd stowed away.

"Once she was there, I put her in the safest place I could and armed her to defend herself. She used a sniper rifle from cover and killed several attacking Singularity troops while defending engineering with me.

"Look, we started the raid with the full platoon of combat marines. We ended with just a handful left alive. That fighting was some of the worst I've ever seen, and we were damned close to being overrun. Her assistance helped turn the tide."

Page looked interested. "You said you trained her? How?"

"Before the fighting? I showed her how the weapons worked, put her in unpowered mercenary armor, and taught her enough to make a last-ditch stand if the Singularity tried to take the raiding ship.

"On the captured ship, I showed her how to link her implants to her weapons and use them to fire from concealment. She acted as a sniper and made a real difference. She proved her loyalty and courage that day.

"When I got out of the service, some thoughtful souls had taken one of the marine pinnaces aboard the ship we freed and stocked it with all kinds of interesting equipment. Equipment that would be extremely useful in training someone to become an Imperial Marine. I claimed it as my booty, and over the last six years, I've done what I can to impart some knowledge to her about how to use most of it."

Martelle and Page exchanged a look.

"Your record indicates that you have quite a bit of combat experience, so I'm going to assume that she's coming into this with a larger range of knowledge than most recruits would have," Page said. "That's going to make an interesting challenge since she's mixed in with people that don't know their ass from a hole in the ground."

"I'd say that I'm sorry, Senior Sergeant, but I'm not," Fei said. "I already knew that the deck would be stacked against her, so I did what I could. She has experience with as many weapons as I could get my hands on, she can use powered armor well enough to get by, and she can fly—for certain values of the word—a marine pinnace. I'd give her better than 50/50 odds that she could take off and make a survivable crash landing.

"Her genetics are also going to cause you some headaches. I told her to obscure her capabilities, but she was designed from the ground up to be an enhanced human. She's around half again stronger than she looks, her reaction times are off the charts, and she's *incredibly* bright.

"She's also dedicated and caring. She's a truly good person. Someone who doesn't deserve to be discriminated against, though it's going to happen. Hell, I'm sure that it's *already* happened.

"How *you* treat her isn't up to me. I'm a marine, and I trust the Corps to do right. What happens next is up to you."

Martelle considered them both and shook his head. "Senior Sergeant Page brought her here to answer some questions, but I think you've assuaged my curiosity. It would probably be best if she doesn't realize that you're here, so I suggest we keep that fiction in place.

"I'm not going to pull you out of the platoon because I think your experience and insight would be beneficial. Page, see that the recruits get a version of the chain of command that still has Lieutenant Evans running the platoon.

"As for the rest, we'll play it by ear and hope that we don't get any outside interference. If the girl has what it takes to become a marine, I'm not going to deny her that opportunity.

"That said, she's going to have to be more thoroughly vetted than any of the other recruits. This isn't going to be a pleasant experience for her. She's going to run into trouble with other trainees and, potentially, even some drill instructors, though I expect the senior sergeant to mitigate that to some degree.

"You're not going to be able to interfere with that. I think you'll have the most challenging job of all, Lieutenant Na. You'll have to oversee training remotely and sit on your hands while she struggles.

"Senior Sergeant Page, you'll make sure that the girl is pushed *hard*. We have to be sure of her character. She has to be put through the wringer."

Fei finally felt the knot of tension inside her start to relax. She was going to be able to keep an eye on her girl.

She'd trained her well enough to take what was coming, but it was up to Page to referee the scrum. That would have to be good enough.

"Oh, there's one other thing," Martelle added with a slight smile. "Since you know her training better than anyone, I'll rely on you to work with Senior Sergeant Page to devise some challenging 'extra credit' exercises for her. Our training is meant to push the recruits to the edge and beyond. I'll rely on you to make sure that happens."

So, in effect, Fei had just made Andrea's training significantly more difficult. Perfect.

* * *

PAGE LEFT the impromptu meeting in the major's office and escorted Tolliver back to the warehouse to get her gear. He left the actual work of that to Gomez while he returned to his office to think.

He sat at his desk, allowing himself a few minutes to think. The situation had grown complicated in a hurry. He needed to plan for what was coming and start visualizing potential obstacles.

The first likely obstacle was Lieutenant Na. Not that he thought she would actively obstruct him and his people, though he couldn't rule that out, but she was an unknown with an agenda of her own. That was undoubtedly going to introduce complications he'd rather avoid.

There was also the matter of exactly how much information he could pass along to the other drill instructors. They had to be made aware of some of the challenges they were going to face, but he had to be circumspect, since they didn't need the full story.

He'd tell them as much as possible. If they didn't know to plan for complications, something would come up to bite them in the ass. That wasn't a position a drill instructor wanted to be in. He and his people always tried to envision as many potential issues as possible to mitigate adverse outcomes.

And he was quite sure that Tolliver was going to generate some adverse outcomes.

A follow-up conversation with the marines in the pinnace had revealed that Tolliver seemed to have made a friend and a rival on the flight out. A friend would be helpful to the girl because getting through basic training was a team exercise. It would be useful to foster that friendship from behind the scenes and keep an eye on the obvious antagonist.

Not because Page wanted to stop the boy but because he wanted to manage the confrontations. Seeing how the girl responded to someone acting directly against her would be a handy tool in judging her character.

What he wanted to avoid was any possibility that the confrontation could spill over into something that would be career-ending for either of them or make the platoon as a whole take sides.

He didn't know anything about the boy at this point, not even his name. He had to get that information as quickly as possible and start assessing the likely outcomes of their budding competition.

With proper management, he could balance the two to the point that they'd become foils. That kind of rivalry inside a training platoon usually goaded everyone to try harder.

Unless it was allowed to poison the whole unit, which he and his people wouldn't allow.

Well, this particular Gordian knot would have to wait until tomorrow. He needed to get some sleep, but first, he needed to talk with the new officer and see just how much trouble he was in.

10

The medical exam and her trip to battalion headquarters—though no one had actually spoken to her there—delayed Andrea long enough that she drew her gear long after the rest of the recruits had finished and departed.

The waiting marines took their frustrations out on her, and she couldn't blame them. Even so, the process went smoothly enough. They stripped her down and put her into a scanner that noted her measurements precisely and printed uniforms for her that fit perfectly.

The rest of the gear she drew was familiar enough, Fei having educated her in its use over the last six years. She hadn't lived the life of a marine, so it hadn't been constant training, but she'd learned what marines did with the gear and how they did it.

Once she had everything she needed, including personal items for brushing her teeth and showering, Drill Instructor Gomez put her in a chair and cut her hair off. She'd known it was coming, but the event was still traumatic.

The drill instructor made her sweep up her own hair and dump it into a bin. Then she escorted her to the barracks that would be her home for the next three months.

The long room on the ground floor was bustling with activity when they arrived. The other recruits had claimed their bunks and seemed to be working at setting everything up.

Andrea turned to Drill Instructor Gomez to find out where she needed to go, but the drill instructor withdrew without a single word. It looked like she was on her own.

"Over here!" a voice called out.

Andrea spotted Diana about halfway down the side of the barracks, waving at her. She hefted her duffle bag and hurried over.

The curvy girl looked completely different with her long red hair gone. It made Andrea wonder how she looked now.

The area her new friend was waiting in was set up very much like what she'd grown up with inside the crèche. There were two small bunk beds, one on top of the other, and two wall lockers side by side. Diana had claimed the lower bunk and the leftmost wall locker. Andrea could tell because the doors were open, and all of Diana's gear was laid out inside it.

"They gave us instruction on how everything was to be done, so I went ahead and left my wall locker open so that you could see how you need to put yours. The beds aren't going to be made a specific way tonight, but they're going to teach us how to do them tomorrow. Also, don't walk into the center of the room. That's off-limits to us. Where did you get off to?"

The other girl's eyes were bright with curiosity, but there was no obvious malice. Maybe she really was that friendly.

"They gave me a medical scan and asked me some questions," Andrea said with a shrug as she started unpacking her gear and putting it away. "That's not surprising, really. They're curious about where I came from, and I think they're worried that I'm a spy or something."

Diana's left eyebrow rose. "Are you a spy? That might be something my father would think was interesting."

"Your father? Is he one of those people that likes spy thrillers?"

"That's probably about the safest way to explain him, yes," the girl said with a laugh. "In fact, he loves spy thrillers to an unhealthy degree. In any case, let me help you get set up so that we can get some sleep. I'd wager that we're going to get a *very* early wake-up call."

"Earlier than you'd think if my guess is right," Andrea said as she eyed the layout in Diana's locker. "They'll let us get a little sleep, and then they'll make a huge ruckus to totally disrupt us way too early in the morning.

"It's supposed to keep us off balance and start deconstructing us before they put us back together in ways that are useful to the Corps."

As they put Andrea's gear into the wall locker, Diana smiled at her. "You seem to know quite a bit about what's going to happen. Considering your background, that's kind of weird, isn't it?"

"Not as weird as you think. I was rescued by marines, and two of my guardians are ex-marines. I've had six years to pester them for details of what basic training might be like. They didn't tell me any of the really secret stuff, but I got a feel for how things worked."

Diana chuckled. "I picked a good partner, then. You have the inside straight on this game."

They'd almost finished putting Andrea's gear away when something struck the back of her wall locker, knocking its contents over. The two girls startled and leaped backward.

Moments later, Claudio stuck his head around the side of the locker and grinned evilly at them. "Sorry about that, girls. Space over here is kind of tight, and I accidentally hit your lockers with my shoulder. Hope I didn't mess them up too much."

Andrea had never heard a more insincere excuse in her life. She felt her eyes narrow to slits. This guy was going to be an *epic* pain in her ass.

"That's too petty," she growled. "Why don't we make ourselves a wager, big man. We'll start doing real training tomorrow. Let's do this man to woman and keep it out of the barracks. Best one wins."

He considered her for a moment and then shrugged with a grin. "You might as well accept that I'm going to kick your ass. Think about that while I get some sleep. Night night, girls."

The man's head vanished, and she could hear him laughing with somebody on the other side of the lockers. He was her neighbor. Great.

Diana was fuming as they started putting the wall lockers back into shape. "You can't let him get away with this."

"He's bitten off more than he can chew," Andrea said in a low voice. "I don't trust him to stay in his lane, so I'll be pondering my revenge for when he pulls more of this crap."

It only took them a couple of minutes to get the wall lockers back into order. Unlike those in the crèche, these used thumbprints for the locks, so hers should be safe enough from casual intrusion.

Andrea stripped out of her outer clothes, put them in her locker for tomorrow, climbed onto the top bunk, and wiggled under the covers. Her internal chronometer said that it was almost one in the morning. She figured they had a couple of hours before all the fun started.

Everyone—including her—was going to be exhausted. Her enhanced metabolism would help, as would her medical nanites, but it still wasn't going to be enough.

Senior Sergeant Page knew what she had under the hood and would make sure that she was worked harder than anyone else. The goal was to push her, and they would.

Fun times ahead.

With that cheerful thought, she closed her eyes and forced herself to relax. Lying awake until they came would only make tomorrow worse.

* * *

THERE WAS a knock at her office door half an hour after she'd left the major's office. She opened the door after confirming that it was Page and gestured for him to have a seat.

She ignored the desk and took the uncomfortable chair beside him. "I'm sorry that all this is coming as such a surprise to you, Senior Sergeant. As I told the major, if I'd had my way, no one would've ever known why I was here.

"I'm not trying to influence how you treat Andrea; I just want to be sure that she gets a chance to succeed on her own merits. Only now, I've got to make sure that these recruits do the best they can and learn everything we can teach them, which I'm sure is exactly what you were already doing."

Page considered her for a few seconds and then nodded. "I haven't formed an opinion about the girl yet, but I can already tell that her presence is going to be divisive. Basic training, as you already know, is stressful by design.

"The problem I see is that she's going to be a magnet for trouble, so not only are we going to have to see that she gets stress tested and trained, we're going to have to make sure that no one does anything they shouldn't.

"There are going to be fights. We just need to keep them from becoming general brawls and make certain that nobody gets seriously injured."

"Then I think we're in agreement," Fei said. "How do we do that?"

He leaned forward. "Could you share more about your background so I can figure out what you're bringing to the table?"

Fei began going over places that she'd served, tasks that she was trained in, and what her work had been like six years ago. She hadn't made senior sergeant or officer, but she'd been a working sergeant in charge of a combat platoon.

Sadly, that left her ill prepared to be in charge of the training platoon as an officer. Her experience revolved around taking the strategic decisions and turning them into tactical directions.

Page quickly seconded her concerns. "Did you actually attend officers' school? If not, you'll be walking into some blind spots."

"I know," she admitted with a sigh. "And I'm going to have to work hard to try to figure out what they are and correct them as we move forward. Thankfully, you're doing tasks that you're familiar with, so you'll know if I'm missing something.

"I'm going to try to stay out of your way as much as possible, but this is going to be a delicate situation. We're going to have to work hard to foresee the problems Andrea's presence will cause for the rest of the platoon and the issues they might cause her."

"I'll have my instructors keep an eye out for trouble," he said.

"Once we have the lay of the land, we can generate some separation between her and any really hardcore haters.

"We can't protect her entirely—and I wouldn't want to—but we have to make sure that the fire happens under controlled circumstances so that we don't get an explosion."

"What about the staff?" she asked. "Are we going to have trouble with any of the drill instructors?"

"Possibly," Page said in a grudging tone. "They're going to wonder why we're keeping your presence a secret from the platoon too. How should we handle that?"

"Tell them the basic truth. That I'm somebody that has experience with Andrea and her capabilities, and my presence here is to make sure that not only does she get the training that she needs but that it's done in an evenhanded manner.

"I'm giving directions, but you and your people are going to be carrying them out. If we all know what page we're playing from, we might be able to manage an understandable tune. If we're working at cross purposes, somebody is going to get hurt, and I don't want that."

He nodded, his expression approving. "I think that's a good start, ma'am. We'll tweak whatever plans we make as we move forward. We'll only have the recruits for twelve weeks, so I don't have to train you to be an officer. I just have to shield everyone from your inexperience in this role, including you.

"I'm assuming that once she makes it into the marines, or washes out, that you're going to return home to your family. Let's make the best we can of the situation and hope we don't run into any insurmountable problems."

"I love your optimism. When do you intend to wake the recruits?"

"0430. As you might expect, their day is going to start with a bang. I'll be running the show but handing things off to Sergeant Sophia Gomez at 0700 to get some sleep. You don't need to be awake for that, and I suggest you get what sleep you can. As soon as we run into problems, we'll be coming to see you.

"You'll need to meet all the DIs before lunch, so I'll set that up. As far as food goes, I suggest you have a runner grab you something. The recruits will be around and about, so you'll need to stay inside until you know their schedule."

Fei rose and extended her hand. "That works for me, Senior Sergeant. We'll make this work."

"I wouldn't get ahead of myself if I were you, ma'am," he cautioned as he shook her hand. "There's still plenty of time for things to drop into the crapper."

That was so damned true.

11

Page's internal chronometer woke him at 0400. He was tired, but the schedule didn't allow him any extra time to sleep. He'd have to wait until he was off to catch a few more hours of shuteye.

He dressed quickly because the other drill instructors would be done eating breakfast and already preparing to receive the recruits. Today was going to be a continuation of the shark attack, so they'd all be in attendance.

Basically, intake was a feeding frenzy that devoured anyone that didn't move fast enough or failed to do what the drill instructors ordered. The slow or noncompliant would get all of the negative attention they could handle to ensure that there were no repeat performances.

It was a somewhat brutal tactic, but it was also quite effective.

He grabbed a ration bar from his desk for breakfast as he made his way down the stairs. As he walked, he briefly conferred with the other DIs via his implant coms. Half of them were going to the pit to wait for the recruits while the rest were lined up outside the barracks.

The pit was a sizable sawdust-filled exercise area surrounded by sandbags. There was a raised platform at one end where exercises could be demonstrated, and there was plenty of space to spread the recruits out so that they could get far more individualized attention than they wanted.

The drill instructors in front of the barracks would receive the recruits as Page sent them running out. The bum's rush would get them off balance, and the DIs would keep them that way.

This process would continue on and off over the next couple of weeks to see who broke. Better to find out early. If they couldn't take the shark attack, then they probably weren't cut out to be marines in the first place. Combat was an unforgiving environment.

Satisfied that everything was ready, he exited onto the ground floor and found a handy trashcan. It was a pressed metal affair with a lid made of the same material. It was relatively light and made an *incredible* amount of noise when thrown.

Which was kind of the point.

He walked down the center aisle of the barracks, looking at the sleeping recruits. At this point, they'd been through a busy day and had no idea of the trauma that was awaiting them. The thought made him smile.

He paid particular attention to Tolliver. She was the only recruit with military-grade implants, so identifying her took only a moment. Six other recruits had civilian implants, but they'd only be of marginal usefulness in this environment.

They'd probably want to keep the fact that the girl had military-grade implants and a marine nanogenerator to themselves. The information that she had something the rest of the recruits didn't might cause additional friction.

Then he reconsidered.

Maybe demonstrating that she already *had* military-grade implants would drive the others to work harder if done right. Seeing what someone with implants could do might encourage them to increase their efforts.

Of course, that would make Tolliver even more unpopular, but that could also play into his plans.

Page made a mental note of the girl's bunkmate. He needed to find out whether she was a friend, an enemy, or merely someone who was horrified to be anywhere close to Tolliver.

He'd be able to sort that out in short order as the barracks' public areas were monitored via concealed vid cams. It wouldn't take long to get a grip on the recruits' interpersonal relations.

When his internal chronometer indicated that it was 0430, he grinned. It was time to get this party started.

* * *

As Andrea had expected, the morning wake-up call came long before dawn. It was, however, significantly louder than she'd foreseen.

The first hint that something was going on was a loud metallic crash. Andrea sat bolt upright and almost fell off her bunk. Even though she'd been expecting something, the shock value was far greater than she'd anticipated.

Striding down the center of the room after the metallic trashcan that he'd thrown, Senior Sergeant Page bellowed at them. "On your feet, recruits! It's a glorious day!"

As everyone started scrambling, he continued. "Welcome to your first day of training. I want everybody standing next to their bunk, in uniform minus your jacket and cover—that's your hat—in sixty seconds. Anybody not ready by then will regret it."

Andrea vaulted off the top bunk, narrowing missing Diana as the girl hurled herself toward her locker. Since Andrea had slept in her undergarments, it was a simple matter to pull on the uniform she'd stripped off yesterday. She sat on the lower bunk and hurriedly put her boots on, tying the old-fashioned laces as quickly as she could.

Dressed in what her internal chronometer said was just over fifty seconds, she picked one side of the bunks and stood at attention behind the yellow line painted on the floor. She could see across the open space as everyone on that side of the barracks was still scrambling to get ready.

Diana was a few seconds behind her, but she reached the line on her side of the bunks and stood at attention before Senior Sergeant

Page stalked back down the center of the room, his eyes taking everything in.

"Everyone freeze!" he said in a loud voice. "Your time is up. Because you couldn't be ready on time, I'm adding thirty minutes to this exercise period. I'm certain that your platoon mates will thank you for that later."

Andrea understood that kind of peer pressure quite well. In the crèche, the girls had disciplined one another quite firmly. She was certain that some of the methods they'd used wouldn't be tolerated here, but the tactic would still be effective.

Frankly, she was grateful that she'd gotten ready on time. She was coming into training with enough baggage and didn't need to be the one causing trouble for everyone else.

"If you're ready, line up outside," Page shouted. "Move out!"

Andrea and Diana raced out of the barracks and found three drill instructors waiting for them. The sky was still dark, but bright lights on tall poles lit the area quite well. Drill Instructor Gomez seemed to be in charge and directed everyone to three lines painted on the pavement.

"Toes behind the lines and spread out an arm's length away from the person to your left. I don't care where you are in the formation, but make certain that there are a similar number of people in each line. Move it!"

The process was far from straightforward, since no one knew what they were doing, but they managed it even as the late arrivals began filtering out of the barracks. She was pleased to see Claudio scowling as he ran out.

Day one, and he was already falling behind. She'd make sure to mention that to him when the time came.

Senior Sergeant Page stepped out of the barracks when the last of the recruits made it out. He stood in front of them, surveying them like they were spoiled food in the pantry.

"That was an utterly pathetic performance, recruits. Going forward, everyone will be standing in formation in under two minutes. I expect each of you to *encourage* your fellow recruits to move faster, or the platoon as a whole *will* suffer the consequences.

"Now, for your first lesson. When I say 'right face,' you will turn ninety degrees to your right. When I say 'forward march,' you will begin marching in step to my cadence, starting with your left foot. Your *left* foot."

He gave them all a stern look. "Right face."

Andrea turned to the right, pivoting on the ball of her left foot and the heel of her right. Then she brought her left foot forward to stand next to her right. That was the way that Fei had shown her to do it.

Very few of the other recruits moved with anything like that kind of precision. It was more like shuffling their feet to get into position.

"Forward march."

The platoon staggered into motion. At least a third of them stepped out with their right foot.

"Your other left, recruits," Page said. "Your left, your left, your left, right, left."

He followed actions to words by stepping with the indicated feet. His voice was easily loud enough to carry to each of them. That helped to sort out some of the chaos but not all. Not by any means.

Around them, Andrea could see other platoons that were already up and in motion. Unlike their platoon, these recruits were orderly, and their steps all happened in unison. Their drill instructors were singing strange songs that the recruits sang back as they jogged. It was all… very odd.

She was sure that Senior Sergeant Page would've liked to have gotten them to where they were going faster, but idiots that they were, they couldn't move in unison, so they walked until they arrived at an area about fifty meters square that was surrounded by sandbags. The interior was filled with a thick layer of sawdust. The scent of it tickled her nose.

At one end, there was a raised wooden platform, and Senior Sergeant Page jogged over to it as the drill instructors—including two more that had been waiting there—moved them into what was obviously an exercise area.

"Welcome to the pit, recruits," Page said, his hands on his hips. "This is where we'll do a fair bit of your morning calisthenics for the next few weeks, *particularly* when you screw up. You're going to grow to hate this place. Spread out as the drill instructors indicate and prepare for the worst morning of your lives."

No matter what happened today, it wouldn't come close to being the worst morning of Andrea's life. No one was trying to kill her. Yet.

The drill instructors got everyone separated so that they wouldn't inadvertently come into contact with those around them. Of course, this process involved lots of shouting and some pushing. She imagined that that was going to be a staple of basic training.

Once the recruits were spaced out the way the drill instructors wanted, they began patrolling the pit's interior. Their eyes seemed to be everywhere, looking at everyone. No lapse was too small to be corrected.

Senior Sergeant Page spent a few seconds looking over the crowd and nodded in apparent satisfaction. "The first exercise you will learn is the push-up. Trust me when I say that you will become *extremely* familiar with it over the next twelve weeks. Observe as I demonstrate."

He dropped down on the platform to rest on his toes and palms with his back straight, facing at a ninety-degree angle from the recruits. "This is the front leaning rest position. You'll note that my back has no bend or sag. As you do your push-ups, you will keep your back perfectly straight and your head up so that your face is forward. You will tuck your elbows in as you descend and keep going until your elbows break the plane of your back like this."

He lowered himself until his elbows were on the same plane as his body. He then pushed himself back up.

"That seems easy, doesn't it? Trust me when I say that maintaining such a clean posture will become most difficult once you get tired. Which you assuredly will."

He rose to his feet and smiled grimly. "Everyone drop."

Andrea quickly planted her hands on the sawdust and kicked her feet out behind her, raising her head so that she was looking forward. The rest of the recruits were slower and less agile, but it only took a few seconds to get all of them into the front leaning rest position.

"Now, push until I tell you to stop."

Andrea began doing push-ups. She kept her posture straight and didn't try to rush. That probably wasn't going to help her, but she had to try.

The drill instructors moved among the recruits, correcting their posture and demanding they move faster. Andrea complied, her body able to handle the load.

As the platoon did more push-ups, butts started to rise, and someone eventually declared that they couldn't do any more. That was immediately demonstrated to be a *bad* idea.

The drill instructors swarmed that person. They came in from every part of the pit, all shouting at the same time. The general thrust of their orders was to keep pushing and not to stop. All demanded more from the unfortunate recruit.

Andrea continued doing her push-ups, focusing just on herself. With her greater strength and endurance, she could keep going longer than a regular human. She was feeling pretty pleased with herself right up until Senior Sergeant Page arrived with a couple of sandbags in hand.

He grinned at her and put them on her back. The added weight made doing push-ups correctly far more difficult, and that situation wasn't improved when Drill Instructor Gomez added two more bags. The things had to weigh at least ten kilos each.

Page squatted down beside her as she continued pushing. "Don't think we've forgotten about you, Tolliver. Since you're in better physical condition than your fellow recruits, we're having a special weight vest put together. Once we add in arm and leg weights, you'll have just as much fun as everyone else."

As the additional weight on her back sapped her strength, her arms began trembling, and her posture suffered. That didn't stop her from giving it everything she had. She wasn't going to fail. Even with the weights, she was going to keep going until she had nothing left to give.

"Get that butt down, Recruit," Drill Instructor Gomez barked. "Tuck those elbows back in and keep pushing. I'm not tired yet."

Gomez stood directly over Andrea until she couldn't do another push-up. Her face planted in the sawdust when her arms failed, and it clung to her sweat-covered face and got into her mouth. Yuck.

The drill instructor grunted, though Andrea couldn't tell whether it was in satisfaction or displeasure. She then moved on to yell at someone else.

Andrea sucked air in and tried to get herself back into the front leaning rest position, spitting out the wood-flavored grit as best she could.

Training was going to be just as much of a pain in the ass as she'd expected. Worse, really. She'd have to work harder, but she wasn't going to give up—no way in hell.

Senior Sergeant Page shook his head as he jumped back onto the low platform. "Pathetic. Well, I'm not going to lower the standards of my beloved Corps for the likes of you. If you want to be Imperial Marines, you're going to have to perform at a higher level.

"That's only the first of the exercises we're doing today. If you think you're tired now, you have absolutely no idea what you're going to feel like in an hour.

"Some of you are doing so poorly at this point that it might be necessary to move you to a remedial platoon where you can be worked until you perform at the level this training demands. You *definitely* won't like that, so I suggest you dedicate yourselves to the process of impressing me *right now*."

With that, he began instructing them on how to do jumping jacks. Drill Instructor Gomez and another man arrived with a short length of rope to tie two sandbags together. That done, they produced a second rope and repeated the process. They then hung the improvised weights on each of her shoulders.

That meant that she had to support four sandbags while doing jumping jacks. It wasn't impossible, but she was going to do far worse than she would've under normal circumstances.

The next hour was going to be hell.

12

_____

During her exploration of the platoon's command-and-control network, Fei discovered that they used vid cameras to keep an eye on the battalion's public spaces. That meant that she was able to monitor what was happening at the pit without actually being there.

She watched wryly as the drill instructors piled sandbags on Andrea to make her work harder. She felt some sympathy for the girl but not much. She'd known what becoming an Imperial Marine would take, and this was only a down payment.

Andrea had come into this with advantages that the rest of the recruits didn't have, so it was only fair that she had to work harder to achieve her goals. Nothing about this process was going to be easy, and it wasn't meant to be.

Once the recruits had no energy left, the drill instructors shouted them to their feet and walked them around the pit a few times in formation to let them cool down before marching them to the medical center for their intake exam.

Fei knew that the recruits would be released to clean up once that was done and then taken to eat breakfast. This was only a foretaste of what they had coming to them over the next twelve weeks, and she wondered how many of them really had the grit to tough it out.

That was the real secret. If someone could do what was required and buckle down to learn what was offered, they'd almost certainly pass basic training. It was the ones who refused to comply or gave up that didn't make it.

She knew that Andrea didn't fit into those categories. Barring any outside influence, her girl would make it.

Page and one of the female drill instructors left the recruits and headed back toward the barracks. It was game time.

That forewarning gave her enough time to find a small briefing room that would be sufficient to hold them, and she let Page know where she'd be. The two entered the briefing room a few minutes later.

Page gestured to his companion. "Lieutenant Na Fei, this is Sergeant Sophia Gomez, my second. Lieutenant Na is going to be our commanding officer while Lieutenant Evans is recuperating. She's only here for this rotation."

The smaller woman's eyes narrowed as she took her seat. "Forgive me if I say so, ma'am, but I can't help feeling that there's more to the story. Are you here because of Tolliver?"

Fei nodded, not even trying to hide the truth. "Yes. I have experience with her, and I'm cleared to know all the details of how she came to be in the Empire.

"That said, while I'm guiding this platoon, I'm not influencing how the training goes for her. That falls to Senior Sergeant Page and your team.

"She's been given an Imperial dispensation to be here, and I expect her to get a fair shot at completing the training. That doesn't mean that she's going to get a pass.

"You're going to work her just as hard as anyone else and push her past the breaking point. The only thing I demand is that if you have a bias, you set it aside."

The woman considered her and then shook her head. "That's not the whole story. What's your *real* connection to her?"

Fei smiled coolly. "The details of that are classified. All you need to know is that I'm playing referee. If there's going to be trouble with bias, I'm going to see it, and I'm going to act. Be evenhanded with all of the recruits—including her—and we're not going to have a problem.

"Because of my connection to her, we won't be letting the recruits know about me. She knows me, so we'll leave Lieutenant Evans listed as the platoon leader. Is that clear?"

Both of the noncoms nodded.

"Excellent. Now, how is day one going?"

Page smiled. "The first day is always fun. You get to take people that think they want to be marines and run them into the ground. Honestly, while the later portions of the training are more rewarding, these first couple of weeks are more enjoyable. A little browbeating isn't going to hurt them."

"I think this group is going to be lively," Gomez allowed. "That'll make things a bit more chaotic than usual, but I think this is a good set of people. We're going to run some of them out because I can already see a few that aren't going to put in the effort it takes to make it."

"We'll have our share of bullies and sadists, just like every single group I've ever trained," Page added. "They'll want to lord it over the others and think that being a marine is all about fighting and killing. We'll identify the worst of them and kick them out.

"That isn't to say we won't have jackasses. I already know of one that's going to be a pain in Recruit Tolliver's ass. He's decided to run her out of the Corps. We'll keep an eye on their interactions, but I'm not going to intervene unless things get out of hand."

He watched her closely, obviously wanting to see how she reacted.

Fei shrugged. "We all have asses to deal with in life, so that's good training. Hopefully, she'll find allies to help her. In any case, I'm not worried if you're not."

That answer seemed to satisfy him, though Gomez seemed less convinced. Well, it would take time to show them that she was sincere.

"Okay, run me through the plans for today, and then let's go over the next few days," Fei said. "I've got a lot to take in, and I need to do my part to make this the most rewarding and painful training cycle for the recruits that I can."

There were interesting times ahead for both Andrea and her. She'd be ready. She only hoped her girl was.

* * *

ONCE PAGE and Gomez had finished their meeting with Lieutenant Na, he waited until the officer had returned to her office before he called the available drill instructors to a meeting in the same room.

Two of the DIs would keep an eye on the recruits as they had their first group meal after they'd cleaned up. Then they'd shepherd them back to the barracks so that instruction could begin.

Page had initially intended to take that time off, but then he'd reconsidered. He needed to be the face the platoon saw going forward. That meant he'd be exhausted by noon, but that couldn't be helped. He'd deal with it.

The two absent drill instructors would be listening in on the meeting via their implants. If they had anything to add, they'd be able to do so remotely.

Before he could even start talking, Gomez shared her opinion of the situation. "This is bullshit. Lieutenant Na is here to interfere on behalf of that thing, and we need to talk to the major about it."

Page gave his friend and subordinate a stern look. "Before we start discussing options, we need to brief everyone on the situation, don't you think?"

He turned his attention to the other two drill instructors without waiting for a response. Sergeants Rafael Engel and Lucy Carmichael had been with him almost as long as Gomez, and he trusted their insight and wanted to hear from them before things got heated.

Engel was built like a bear and dominated the other end of the table. Having seen the man in the shower, Page knew that he had as much hair as a bear as well. Even though that type of condition could be treated these days, Engel seemed to enjoy having a pelt and encouraged the jokes about how primitive he was.

Carmichael was the exact opposite, being of slight build with exquisitely delicate features. Beneath that harmless-looking exterior was a bulldog. She was one of the most aggressive drill instructors he'd ever met, and she didn't know the word "quit."

She could run any recruit into the ground, and he wasn't willing to bet that she couldn't do the same to Tolliver, even with the girl's advantages.

The two drill instructors that weren't present were sergeants Stephan Bluefield and Gail Wright. They were both very competent, but he had no idea how they'd respond to the situation. The same was true of Engel and Carmichael. Only Gomez had tipped her hand.

Once he had their undivided attention, he laid out the basic facts about Tolliver and her situation. He then passed on some of the information about their new platoon leader. He didn't mention that there was more to the relationship between Na and Tolliver than he was telling.

When he'd finished, he let the conversation flow based on what his associates were thinking. As he'd expected, there was a fair bit of consternation. No one liked the Singularity, and the idea of training someone from one of their senior lines generated some strong feelings.

Also, as expected, Carmichael was the voice of reason. The slight twang to the woman's voice betrayed her rural upbringing and always made him smile. It was as if she'd come from the old state of Texas on Terra. He could see her riding a horse and wearing a big hat without any trouble whatsoever.

"If the girl was rescued when she was twelve years old, then it's not exactly like she's a hardened enemy," Carmichael said in her easy drawl. "Even though she was indoctrinated until she was twelve, she's had a marine officer undoing all of that over the last six years. I feel pretty confident that whatever she learned as a child has been successfully counteracted, at least mostly.

"But that doesn't mean we won't have trouble with or about her. Just like Gomez, there are plenty of marines with perfectly valid reasons to hate anyone from the Singularity."

She turned to face Gomez directly. "I'm not saying that you're wrong, Sophia. What I *am* saying is that it isn't right to blame children for the actions of adults. We need to judge her on her merits, not her past."

"Technically, she's not even a person," Engel said, his voice a low rumble. "Imperial law is clear. She's property."

"That's sheer and utter crap," Carmichael shot back, glaring up at the big man. "People are people. Anything else smacks of slavery and all kinds of other unwholesome things that I won't accept.

"And you need to keep the dispensation she was given in mind. If she finishes training, her recognition becomes permanent, and that's a wedge that somebody means to drive into the Empire to change the law itself.

"If you don't think that's the emperor's hand at work, then you're an idiot. Ask yourself this, are you really going to be the one that stands up to the emperor?"

That silenced the conversation for a few seconds, but Gomez was more than ready to jump back in. "What about the lieutenant? She's here because she has knowledge of Tolliver. She's got a bias and wants to see the girl succeed."

"And you don't?" Page asked, inserting himself back into the discussion. "I thought we all wanted to see every single recruit succeed. Sometimes they're not suited, and we run them out, but we don't know enough about Tolliver to make that call yet.

"Sophia, you need to get a grip. You're prejudging Tolliver without even trying to understand her. You need to focus on figuring out how she's different than the Singularity troopers that killed your friends. She *is* going to be different, and you need to do some hard thinking to make sure you understand that."

Gomez shook her head. "Why should I? I can do my job and still dislike the girl. I don't think she has what it takes to be a marine, and I don't think she should be allowed in. Are you going to hold that against me?"

"No, but don't let it cloud your judgment. The goal is to see what she's made of. If she's got what it takes to become a marine, then we're going to help her. If she doesn't, then we're going to end her career before it starts. I don't want to see anyone's biases getting in the way of doing what's right for the Corps. Is that understood?"

There was a lot of grumbling, and Page could tell that no one was pleased with him laying down the law, but that didn't stop him from doing it.

"I can't say that I'm happy about it, but I'll do it," Carmichael said without hesitation. "Sophia, if she's got Singularity sympathies in her, we'll find them and run her right out the door."

Gomez grunted. "I just don't like this situation. It stinks."

And that set the tone for the remainder of the meeting. There were some questions that he couldn't answer, and some he simply avoided or pretended ignorance. Eventually, things wrapped up, and he dismissed them to get about their duties.

The next twelve weeks would be interesting. He couldn't wait to see how Tolliver did, but he also knew that her presence would affect everyone around her. The only unmitigated truth he could see was that things weren't going to be boring.

13

Andrea and the rest of the platoon were marched to the clinic she'd been at last night and given a rigorous examination. Even though she'd already been looked over, the same doctor was there and ran her through even more detailed scans with equipment that had obviously been brought in just for her.

The exams ate up a couple of hours, but the drill instructors eventually herded them back to the barracks and promptly abandoned them with calls to be ready for chow in half an hour.

She grabbed her shower kit from her locker and headed for the showers with the rest. She stank and was sore in places that she hadn't realized had muscles.

Andrea walked through the area with the toilets and discovered that the shower itself was coed. That only surprised her for a moment before she understood. There was no such thing as body modesty in the marines.

When she'd been on the raiding ship, she'd seen and experienced that, even if only a little. This had to be the drill instructors' way of training the recruits about it. It would've been less shocking if they'd explained it, but this was also another test.

Even as the rest of the recruits—male and female—were blinking in shock and murmuring to themselves, Andrea stripped off her uniform and undergarments, dumped them into a bin by the door, and walked boldly in.

She selected a shower and started soaking down as if this were the most natural thing in the world, though she was *acutely* aware that everyone was staring at her.

The boys started in next, and the girls followed more hesitantly. Andrea could hear them muttering among themselves even as the boys were making jokes. And staring.

A few moments later, Diana took the showerhead next to Andrea, her eyes darting around at the people near them. The redhead—was that still true when she had almost no hair on her head?—seemed to want to cover herself at every turn.

"Did you know that we were going to be showering with the guys? Is this even legal?"

Andrea smiled wryly. "I didn't know, but I can't say that I'm surprised. Marines have to armor up without body modesty, and this is one of the best ways I can think of to get rid of it.

"Of course, the marines are all professionals. These guys are just losers."

As she said the last, she jerked her chin toward where Claudio was lathering up while eyeing both of them. His expression said that he liked what he saw.

Yuck.

Though honesty compelled her to admit that even for being an ass, he wasn't hard on the eyes. He had muscles in all the right places and was fit. If he hadn't been such a jerk, he might've made pleasant eye candy.

"I can't stand the fact that he's staring at me," Diana muttered. "It's degrading."

Andrea used the body wash to cover her entire body. It wasn't as if she needed shampoo.

"Put that out of your head. You can't control what he does, only how you react to it. This is as much a test as everything else we're going through. If you can't adjust to the fact that we're naked in the same room as the guys, that will be a strike against you.

"Just ignore him ogling you. If he can't get past this, it'll trip him up, and he'll wash out. Be smarter than him."

Her friend stared at her for a moment, unmoving. "Holy crap, that's really deep. You've thought about this, haven't you?"

Andrea nodded. "When I got into armor for the first time, I was surrounded by guys, and I'd never even *met* a male before. It was hard, but necessary.

"You need to accept that none of this is going to be easy. That'll give you a leg up when it comes to the mental game that the drill instructors are playing with us."

"You've been in armor? Really? How?"

"We don't have time for that story now," Andrea said. "I'll have to tell you what I can later. Hurry up."

Her friend resolutely turned her back on the rest of the showers and cleaned herself off as quickly and efficiently as she could.

Andrea exited the showers as soon as they were done, grabbed a towel, and dried herself off—no need to worry about her nonexistent hair.

That done, she marched back to her bunk, completely naked with her chin held high. Wrapping a towel around herself would've only undone the mental headspace she'd built.

She opened her locker and started dressing in a deliberate, unhurried manner. Diana moved more quickly but tried to emulate what she was doing.

Claudio sauntered up, naked. He boldly put his hand on his hips and assessed her.

"I was wondering if those weird tattoos went everywhere. The good news is that you'd look great if you put a bag over your head."

She pulled her panties up and put her hands on her own hips, letting her bra dangle from one fist as she stared at him just as boldly. "Are you going to talk to the medics about that thing?"

He gave her a quizzical look, his grin fading slightly. "What?"

"That," she said with a gesture toward his lower half. "I understand they can use modern medical techniques to make up for genetic deficiencies like that. Surely they can enlarge it enough to bring it up to something, well, average. Maybe."

Claudio's mouth opened as if he were going to say something, but no words came out as he started turning red.

His bunkmate chose that moment to walk by and laughed. That made Claudio's face darken even more.

"You bitch."

"Sure," she agreed, "but marines can be bitchy. You can't be a marine with that little thing. That's like bringing a penknife to a knife fight. You've got to have something that you can do battle with, you know?

"Talk to the medics. I bet they can fix you right up. Well, at least enough not to humiliate yourself. Come on, man. Marines have standards."

That was too much for Diana. Her friend burst into laughter, bending over at the waist with howls of amusement.

The girl's reaction wasn't isolated, since Andrea hadn't spoken all that softly. Far from it. The entire platoon seemed to be laughing now.

This incident wasn't going to improve her relationship with Claudio, but she didn't care. He'd been looking for a fight, so she might as well get this party started.

She noted with amusement that the boy's hands had moved down to shield himself. She made sure that her implants captured that particular image because it would provide her with needed entertainment when things got tough.

"You're going to regret this," he promised darkly.

"Not as much as your last girlfriend, I'd wager." She made a shooing motion with her hand. "Get going, Tiny. I'm hungry, and looking at your micro junk is making me lose my appetite."

He stormed around the wall locker and was immediately accosted by his bunkmate. "How's it hanging, Tiny?"

That caused even more raucous laughter.

Diana grabbed her shoulder. "Oh, my God! I can't believe you did that! You've turned this whole thing around and made it about him. I *love* it!"

Andrea smiled with satisfaction. "It was pretty funny, but he'll try to make me pay for it. Come on, let's get dressed and get something to eat. I'm starving."

* * *

FEI HAD SUMMONED a runner from battalion to grab something for her from the mess hall. Her last meal had been a long time ago, and she hadn't been able to sleep at all.

The food was of excellent quality, but that wasn't a surprise. The Imperial Marines prided themselves on providing good food.

People on the outside always told stories about how terrible military food was—particularly coffee—but that just wasn't the case. The meal wasn't gourmet—not by any means—but that didn't mean it wasn't wholesome and well prepared.

When she'd finished eating, she piled everything back onto the tray and set it on the edge of her desk to wait for the runner to come back for it.

Her new office was eerily bare now that all of Lieutenant Evans's personal effects had been removed. The spartan nature hardly mattered because her attention was going to be laser-focused on her girl and the rest of the recruits under her care for the next three months.

To do that right, she needed to understand what they'd be going through. True, she had her own memories of basic training, but she couldn't trust them as a roadmap.

Senior Sergeant Page had created a detailed timeline of the training program that the recruits would be going through, and she began perusing it in detail. She needed to understand the most significant tasks and where she fit into the scheme of things.

The first three weeks revolved around the customs, courtesies, and traditions of the Corps. They'd also learn basic first aid, leadership and core values, and proper uniform wear.

And then there was marching. So much marching. They'd hate close-order drill by the time they were done, but they'd learn to do it in their sleep, almost literally. It would teach them discipline that might one day save their lives.

It wasn't to say that the next few weeks would be all bad, though. They'd learn hand-to-hand combat skills and make several runs at the confidence and obstacle courses too. Those were very fun, in her opinion.

It would be interesting to see how Page and the rest of the DIs compensated for Andrea's implants and genetic advantages during this phase. Balance would be critical. They had to make her work hard, but they couldn't make her tasks impossible in the process.

None of the other recruits had military-grade implants. A few had civilian rigs, but they wouldn't be nearly as useful in this kind of environment.

The process of taking these bright kids and molding them into marines was more of an art than a science, and she had to trust that Senior Sergeant Page and the rest of the DIs knew what they were doing.

Really, she didn't need to trust in that. Their records spoke for themselves.

Still, Sergeant Gomez definitely didn't seem like she'd welcome Andrea's presence. Fei imagined that there would be other drill instructors who were displeased about the idea of someone from the Singularity being present too.

And that didn't even count the recruits themselves. There were going to be confrontations and fights inside the training platoon. The only way she could do her job while making sure that Andrea could take care of herself was to work from behind the scenes and leave Andrea to focus on the training and her fellow recruits.

As hard as that was going to be, it was the right course of action.

She'd just finished going through the training schedule and had begun going back to the beginning to learn it in more detail when there was a knock at her door. That would be the runner on his way back to pick up her tray.

"Come in," she said, after verifying her assumption through the door's vid feed.

The door opened, and the runner came in. Rather than grabbing her tray, though, he braced to attention and extended a data chip to her.

"This just came in for you, ma'am."

She took the chip and frowned. "Where did this come from?"

The young man shrugged. "I'm not certain, ma'am. Battalion commo caught me in the hall and asked me to deliver this when I picked up your tray."

Without waiting for more instructions, the young man picked up her tray and exited the office.

Battalion sending her a message this way was kind of peculiar. If they wanted her, they could've just sent a message directly.

With a mental shrug, she plugged the data chip into the computer built into her desk. It immediately demanded a password. Sadly, she had no idea what the password was supposed to be.

There was a password hint bubble, so she moved the cursor over it, and a question appeared.

"Who makes the best damn stunners in the known universe?"

Her blood went cold. This came from Earl Still Water.

She typed in "Anton Casey," and the screen cleared to show Still Water sitting at a desk, his brow creased with a frown.

"Lady Na, I'm sorry to be the bearer of bad news, but it seems that my plan to sideline Countess Dayton has failed. She disappeared around the same time you left, but I wasn't aware of her absence until almost a full day later.

"I believe that she took passage on the same liner that you did, though I still have to find some evidence of that. That means you need to increase your vigilance.

"I've included a contact number and code phrase in an attachment to this message that will allow you to contact someone in Imperial Intelligence that will be able to assist you. I realize that you're disinclined to trust them or me, but don't hesitate to use them if you need anything. Good luck, and please try not to kill the odious woman if she's really there."

His image vanished as soon as she accepted the file, and the recording deleted itself. She supposed she was lucky the chip hadn't burst into flames.

She needed to talk to the major right now because that woman had enough money to corrupt *anyone*. It was only a matter of time— and probably not very much of that—before something ugly happened.

14

Page stood at the front of the classroom, staring out over the recruits. They were a fairly average-looking bunch, except for Tolliver. Her tattoos virtually leaped off her face without her hair to soften their impact. Whoever had designed the damned things had done an excellent job because they definitely made for a fearful visage.

"Good morning, recruits," he said, tearing his eyes away from her to look over the rest of the class. "I hope you've enjoyed your first taste of training. The next twelve weeks are going to be difficult. Three months sounds like such a short time until you get here.

"Today, we'll start teaching you the academic basics about what Imperial Marines are and what we do. You may think that you have an idea already, but let me assure you that your visualization is incomplete."

He stopped for a moment with his hands on his hips and allowed his eyes to survey the crowd. "Most people believe that Imperial Marines live simply to fight. While we do fight, that's only a small portion of our duties. We're also responsible for general security and performing damage control and rescue operations on board a ship.

"In fact, I'd say rescue operations are actually a larger part of a marine's duties throughout their career than fighting. Not only would you be responsible for lifesaving actions aboard your own ship during battle, but you're going to come across ships in distress. Believe me, that happens far more often than one might imagine.

"In those kinds of situations, you'll be the ones responsible for ascertaining what's going on and saving as many civilian lives as possible. That means you need to have a broad education about how to save lives as well as end them. Quite the contradiction, isn't it?

"In addition to that, we're going to be covering other topics like the history and customs of the Imperial Marines and other requisite academic matters. Trust me when I say that we're going to pack your heads full of knowledge over the next few weeks and that there will be tests."

One of the recruits raised his hand. It was the boy that had been giving Tolliver so much grief.

"Yes?"

"Why didn't they make us learn this stuff before we came to training, Drill Instructor? Shouldn't we be spending our time here on more important things?"

"Do you think that ending lives is more important than saving them, Baker?"

The boy's mouth hung open slightly as he realized he might've made a mistake. "I'm sorry, Drill Instructor. I was talking about things like the history of the Corps and the other noncombat book learning. All of that won't matter if a recruit can't fight or be trusted, right?"

Ah, things became clearer. This was part of his battle with Tolliver. Well, maybe he should let this play out a little bit and see where it led.

"Are you concerned that some of your fellows might not have what it takes when it comes to fighting, Recruit?"

The young man nodded and even smiled a little. "Two people, Drill Instructor. One of them is an enemy of the Empire, and the other just doesn't have what it takes to fight."

"Those are serious allegations," Page said gravely. "This might come as a surprise to you, Recruit, but often the ones that think they're the best suited for fighting are the worst fits for the Corps.

"If you think that there are people here that don't have what it takes, then I'll allow you to prove it. Tomorrow, we'll make our first run at the confidence and obstacle courses.

"Would you say, Recruit, that you're as good as the two you've mentioned? If so, perhaps we should have a little competition to see if they can keep up with you."

Baker's eyes widened as he realized where this was going. Then they narrowed, and he nodded.

"I can do that, Drill Instructor. I can prove to you that they don't have what it takes to be marines."

"What if they prove the exact opposite?" Page asked with a cool smile. "Does that make you unfit? An interesting question and one that I'll have to explore in more depth tomorrow. I assume that you're talking about Tolliver and Randall?"

The boy nodded. "Yes, Drill Instructor."

"Very well, then. I'll allow you to prove that you've got what it takes, but for today, you're just going to have to learn all that boring academic material anyway.

"Now, we'll start with the history of the Imperial Marine Corps and what it means for us to be marines. On top of that, we'll start layering in other subjects so that you'll have a solid foundation to understand what it means to be an Imperial Marine by the end of the first three weeks of training. Open your books, and we'll get started."

* * *

ANDREA FOUND the morning classes interesting in ways that she hadn't expected. Fei and Grace had passed along a lot of Imperial Marines Corps history, but having it laid out like an academic course, with concrete examples of what people had done over the past ten thousand years, had really put things into perspective for her.

Each of the book's examples had built upon others and set up a theme that had been missing when each of the stories was told individually. She could now see how the Corps' customs and traditions had built up over the millennia to become what they were today.

That wasn't all her doing that, of course. She was smart, and she knew it, but the implants she'd had since she was twelve were unbelievably good at parsing data to develop options and insights that weren't necessarily obvious.

She'd flipped ahead in the book—an actual *book* that they'd issued to each of the recruits—and quickly scanned several chapters in advance. The page flips had been far too rapid to retain anything, but her implants had recorded what she'd seen and had boiled it down, looking for insights and patterns.

Once she'd arrived in the Empire, she'd done some research on her implants and discovered that there were some interesting variations to what seemed at first glance to be ubiquitous hardware.

To begin with, the general populace could also get implants if they wanted, and many of them did. Civilian implants were far less capable than the military versions, which were optimized for tasks that civilians wouldn't encounter.

For academic tasks like she was using hers for now, the civilian models were excellent at picking up data and finding correlations and presenting reports and insights to any given data.

The military-grade implants that she had could do the same but were different in many ways. First, they were hardened against interference and monitoring while the civilian models were less so.

The versions used by Fleet and the Imperial Marine Corps were physically identical but subtly different. There was software built into the marine versions that involved controlling armor, weapons, and performing other tactical tasks, whereas the Fleet versions were angled toward ship operations and space combat.

That wasn't to say that hers didn't have that kind of information built into it as well, but those tasks weren't given the same priority that things of a tactical nature were.

For example, a threat assessment scan of the recruits in the classroom would've rated them as potential threats and give her possible avenues to disable or kill them. She bet that that wasn't something Fleet personnel used regularly, if at all.

She was making the assumption that Fleet implants even had these capabilities. They might not. The marine versions might be the more capable set. Unless she had a chance to talk with a Fleet person and compare notes, she might not ever find out either.

It was a safe bet that they'd scrub her implants and remove her nanogenerator if she failed basic training, so she needed to use every advantage she had now to succeed. This was her one chance, and she didn't want to waste it.

She considered all that while standing in line to get lunch at the battalion mess hall. A couple of the drill instructors had marched them from the classroom and made them do push-ups while they waited to get inside.

They'd placed them in line without the option of switching locations, so she wasn't next to Diana, and that was fine. It gave her time to ponder everything that she'd learned today.

The available foods were set up cafeteria-style, except for cheeseburgers and fries. Those were cooked on a grill as she watched and were the most popular choice by far.

She'd had cheeseburgers before and liked them. After all, her metabolism required more calories than the average human, so she was always happy to add something to her plate. She'd found very few foods that she didn't care for, which was lucky. Being a picky eater while needing so many calories would've been a huge pain in the ass.

Andrea decided to go with cheeseburgers on toasted buns, a heaping pile of fries, and a soda. Soft drinks were still popular in the Empire, and the extra sugar would certainly be useful.

When she'd piled her tray high, and added lettuce, tomatoes, and condiments to her cheeseburgers, she found a long table at the edge of the room with a gap between her and the other recruits and sat down.

"Are they any good?" Diana asked as she sat across from her a few minutes later.

Andrea nodded, chewing on a bite of the first cheeseburger. "They're just a bit greasy and have a really savory flavor. I approve. The french fries are crisp on the outside and soft on the inside. Who could ask for more?"

"So, what do you think of what Claudio did?" her friend asked, changing the subject as she took a bite of her cheeseburger and nodded approvingly.

"It's just the kind of crap that I'd expected him to pull. Honestly, I think this confrontation was inevitable, so it makes sense for me to grab the bull by its horns and deal with him once and for all."

Her friend raised an eyebrow. "And you think this will settle things? If you kick his ass, that'll just piss him off even more."

Andrea didn't disagree. Claudio seemed like the type that didn't give up easily. She'd have to thrash him severely and then keep doing it until he decided the pain was more trouble than the dominance he wanted to achieve.

"There's not much that I can do about it," Andrea said as she dipped a fry in catsup and popped it into her mouth. "He decided to be my enemy the moment he laid eyes on me, and that means I'm going to have to take him down as many times as he comes charging in. I'm sorry that you got caught up in it."

Diana shrugged and grinned. "I'm not afraid of a challenge. While the drill instructors might be pitching this as something that's going to get somebody thrown out of training, I don't believe that for a second. They just want to use the competition between the two of you to encourage the rest of us to greater efforts. Or maybe use Claudio's behavior as a negative example. It doesn't take a genius to figure that out."

Andrea pursed her lips and stopped just as she was about to take a bite from the second cheeseburger. "Really? What's your reasoning?"

"Working in the Imperial Marines is a team effort. To succeed, we're going to have to add our skills to the group and improve everybody's odds. Everything we're learning now will increase our fundamental skills, yes, but only in ways that will help integrate everything together by the end.

"The training is meant to build up individuals now, but it won't be long before things move to training teamwork and finally to working as a platoon. They want us to succeed as a group, not as one person being better than the rest.

"Just like every successful team, whether it be sports or some type of work effort, you want to have one person's strengths help cover another's weaknesses. The person with the weaknesses will have their own strengths that will support other people on the team.

"Would it be great to have somebody great at everything? Or maybe have a team full of them? Sure, but how likely is that?"

That was a pretty deep consideration of the challenge they were facing. Andrea hadn't thought about it from that angle.

"They'll use Claudio to force us to do better," her friend continued, "and when we thrash him, he's going to have to try harder. My guess is that the drill instructors will use that to build competing squads based on him and us. Then the teamwork starts.

"At some point, they're going to have to settle the conflict, and I have no doubt that they've got a plan to do just that. They've been training recruits for ten thousand years. They've got plenty of data on what needs to be done.

"We just need to focus on succeeding within the bounds of what they find acceptable and let Claudio make mistakes that are going to get him in trouble if he doesn't learn what the boundaries are."

Andrea considered her friend for a moment and then nodded slowly. "Wow. You really *have* this thought out. I had no idea that you were so analytical."

Her friend blushed lightly and shrugged. "I've always been good at gauging what people will do. And, weirdly, my implants seem to be angled more towards figuring out those kinds of things.

"I think my father paid somebody to tweak my software to figure out these kinds of interpersonal entanglements and conflicts more effectively. It's kind of spooky, really."

Andrea finished the last of her cheeseburgers and fries and polished off the pudding she'd picked for dessert. It wasn't as much as she needed, but it was as much as she was going to get.

They only had a limited time to eat, and people weren't allowed to go back for seconds. That was probably going to prove challenging in a few more days because they'd be piling her up with gear and she was burning calories like they were going out of style. She'd have to have a talk with them before too long about increasing her caloric ration.

Almost as if she'd been reading her mind, Drill Instructor Gomez appeared at Andrea's elbow. "On your feet, Tolliver. It's time for you to make another pass through the chow line. Doc says you need more calories than everybody else, since we're stacking you up with weights.

"We wouldn't want you to fall out just because we're working you a little harder. I want to see you sweat all the way through this because of hard work, not starvation."

That last was said with a little bit of a smirk and more than a hint of a glare. Drill Instructor Gomez didn't like her. Not one bit.

Well, there wasn't a whole lot that Andrea could do about that. She'd just have to manage. At least she wouldn't have to do it on an empty stomach.

15

Fei wasn't able to meet with Major Martelle until early that afternoon, as he was off inspecting a platoon in the field. She was sitting in his outer office when he got back, though.

He strode in dressed in field gear, gestured for her to follow him into his office, and closed the door behind them.

"I always enjoy inspecting the recruits," he said as he started divesting himself of the gear, putting it neatly on a side table. "Though I will admit that going on a field march isn't my idea of a good time. What about you, Lieutenant? What do you think about marching?"

She shrugged from where she stood in front of his desk. "As a noncommissioned officer, that wasn't exactly something that I could avoid. When it came time to march, I just wanted to get to where we were going in the best condition we could, as quickly as we could."

He sat behind his desk and raised an eyebrow at her. "Pragmatic. I like that. What's going on that has you haunting my office?"

"I've gotten word of potential trouble. I'm not exactly sure what can be done about it, but you need to know what's happening."

Martelle frowned, leaned forward to put his elbows on the desk, and steepled his fingers. "That doesn't sound promising. Tell me."

Fei did, leaving nothing out.

Martelle sat unmoving at his desk as he considered her for a few seconds, then he grunted and leaned back in his seat. "I suppose this kind of interference was only to be expected. Sadly, there's not much we can do without more information. This woman has only been on the planet for a day, and if she came alone, she's going to have to drum up people to assist her.

"Those people are going to need to contact other people that have connections to this base and then try to find people willing to work with them to sabotage Recruit Tolliver. All of that will take time.

"Believe it or not, this is actually a point in our favor. They don't know that we know they're coming, and that will give us an opportunity to catch the infiltration."

"And how do we go about doing that, Major?"

"Start with the drill instructors. You're going to have to brief them about the threat so that they can be on the lookout for strangers and for odd behavior by their comrades.

"I really hate starting a witch hunt, but the most likely place to find someone that can sabotage Tolliver's efforts is with the drill instructors. That's going to be bad for morale because nobody likes being considered a potential traitor.

"Sadly, you can bet that one of them will be approached. If the person making the pitch is skilled enough, and if they offer enough compensation, one of the instructors might be tempted, particularly if they already have some kind of grudge against Tolliver because of her origin or nature."

Fei fought the urge to rub her face. "I'm sure that's all true, sir, but how does that help us? We're highlighting the weaknesses, but I don't see any way to reinforce them."

He grinned at her. "You appeal to the drill instructors as marines, and you make sure that they understand that there will be a reward if they resist temptation.

"The person that approaches them is going to want to prevent them from reporting the contact, even if they decline the offer. They're going to offer them a great deal of money to listen to their offer and then keep quiet about it. That gives the enemy leverage over them later, too, so it's a worthwhile investment.

"You should tell them that they can keep that money, so long as they inform us of what's going on. We can then use them to lure their contact into a place where we can capture them. If the enemy is wily enough, that's not going to be easy, but it's not going to be impossible either.

"I suggest that you speak with Senior Sergeant Page and let him deal with the other noncommissioned officers. He's got a long working relationship with each of them, and he knows them far better than you do.

"If he can get them to buy into the plan, then they'll be on the lookout and can play this in a way that benefits them financially and won't embarrass the Corps. They're marines, so I choose to believe that they'll do the right thing, particularly if they know that we're watching."

Fei snorted a little. "That's a bit cynical, sir. I like it. What do we do if they're approached and don't come to us with this information? Or what do we do if we find out one of the drill instructors is secretly working with someone on the outside and their drive to stop Andrea is stronger than their loyalty to the Corps?

"I don't want to overreact to the situation, but I'm afraid that my toolbox is a little short on strategic tools. My training is as a combat noncommissioned officer. If someone is a threat, I'm inclined to deal with them directly. That's probably not the most prudent response to something covert like this."

Martelle chuckled. "It's really going to depend on what they try and who they try it with. Until we start seeing the shape of what they're doing, we won't know how to react.

"It's an almost certainty that their initial actions won't involve trying to harm Tolliver. Their goal is to make her fail. That doesn't require anything convoluted if they could get someone on the inside to stack the deck against her.

"For that plan, one of the drill instructors would be perfect. They would be in a position to make her success far more problematic. If you weren't the one in command of the platoon, you'd be an excellent target to turn as well. Honestly, you might still be approached if they don't know that Lieutenant Evans was replaced.

"If that happens, rather than putting someone in the hospital, it might better suit your goals to at least listen to their sales pitch. See what kind of information you can pull out of them.

"Unless Countess Dayton is aware of your presence here, she's not going to be able to warn them to be on the lookout for you. That's a potential ace up our sleeves, but it's one with an expiration date.

"Since you've met the woman, it won't take her very long to realize that they've made a tactical error in approaching you if that's what they choose to do. It's always possible that they'll discover that Lieutenant Evans isn't here before they make an attempt, but if they're expecting him and find you, that will make them start asking questions. You're going to have to make some decisions when that happens."

She thought about that for a few seconds and then nodded. "While it might make things somewhat easier if we had one of them in custody, we can't count on being that lucky. The best we can probably hope for is to catch them when they attempt to make their intrusion. I'll talk to Senior Sergeant Page and make him aware of the possibility. Then I'll let him brief the other drill instructors."

Martelle nodded. "If you learn anything, inform me at once. I'll talk to a few of my specialists and make certain that our data net is as secure as possible. If someone tries to penetrate it, I'll want to know. If I find anything out, I'll let you know immediately and expect you to do the same."

"Yes, sir."

She double-checked where Andrea was and then headed back toward the barracks. Her girl was eating lunch, and so it was safe.

The situation had become far more complicated than she'd hoped, and the potential for things to go wrong was growing with every passing minute. She needed to talk to Page as soon as possible and let him know what was going on.

Somehow, they were going to have to get in front of this thing. They needed to figure out the enemy's plan of attack and slap them down hard.

She smiled coldly. This might be more entertaining than she'd anticipated.

* * *

PETER BRYANT ARRIVED at the meeting place early. It disturbed him that anyone had known how to contact him without going through his usual cutouts. Not only didn't he know who the potential client was, he didn't even know what they wanted to hire him for.

If, of course, this wasn't just some kind of trap.

He'd considered refusing to meet at all, but that entailed a danger of a different kind. Someone that knew his identity and how to get to him was a threat, and he needed to know who they were.

Since they knew his identity, they could've already tried to kill him if that had been their goal. If that was accurate, this first meeting should be relatively safe because they had something that they wanted from him.

That left him the challenge of finding an acceptable meeting place. The would-be client had wanted privacy, but each of the locations that they'd suggested could've easily been a trap. He'd rejected them immediately and sought a neutral location. That was a daunting task, since he knew absolutely nothing about the person or persons on the other side.

In the end, they'd been able to settle on a location that provided a high degree of privacy yet still allowed him to feel secure. The location was a trade-off for the potential client, but this meeting wouldn't have taken place if they hadn't agreed.

Big Tony's was a relatively plain-sounding name for an Italian restaurant, but in this case, the name was misleading. Big Tony's was a high-class establishment that catered to both the city's elite and those discerning members of the underworld who needed to meet with them without anyone being the wiser.

Tony Giovanni was also a close friend. They'd grown up together, and the two had long ago worked out the boundaries through which they could be both friends and colleagues in the shadowy world that lurked just beneath the surface of everyday civilization.

The big man wouldn't allow anything untoward to happen. Not only would that be bad for his friend, but it would also reflect poorly on him as the host of this meeting, so he wouldn't tolerate it.

When Peter walked through the door, Tony was already waiting and gestured for him to step into one of the side rooms. He nodded to his bodyguards and joined his friend.

"She's already here," the big man said without waiting for him to speak. "I've got her set up in one of the private rooms with full com shielding. She came alone."

"Are you sure? Some of the other patrons might be hers."

Tony shook his head. "I know everybody that's in the building right now, one way or another. I don't believe any of them are working for her. She's not anybody I know either. Based on how she carries herself, she's used to giving orders. Be careful."

The mystery was getting even deeper. How could someone brand-new to the area know who he was yet still be cocky enough to walk into Big Tony's like they owned the place?

Well, he supposed there was only one way to find out.

"I guess I'd better go see her. Could you get me a coffee? I could use one of your specials right about now."

His friend smiled. "I'll see you two settled, and then I'll get you both coffees."

Peter settled his guards close by, but he'd go into the meeting alone. He was armed and could defend himself against a single opponent unless she was far more skilled than he expected.

When Tony escorted him into one of the small dining rooms at the restaurant's rear, Peter found himself looking at a thin, hawk-faced woman. As his friend had said, her expression was more than a bit superior.

Peter had nothing to base his feeling on, but he didn't believe that she was part of the criminal underworld. If anything, she was either a politician or a noble. He'd rather deal with straightforward criminals than either of those kinds of people.

The woman rose slowly to her feet, looking as if she didn't want to give him the basic courtesy. Definitely a noble.

"So how are we supposed to do this?" she asked. "I confess that

I'm not that well-read on the intricacies of negotiation with organized crime lords."

He gave her a small smile and an even smaller bow. "I'm not so organized as all that. Why don't we just have a seat and talk about how you found me. In fact, it might be a good thing to start with who you are."

She laughed. The sound contained no amusement, only disdain. "I'm not going to give you my name. What I will do is give you a hefty retainer for the mission that I want you to carry out for me."

"I don't do business with people that I don't know," he said with a shake of the head. "I also don't do business with people that don't come through my regular conduits. You've already got two strikes against you, madam. Unless you want me to walk out right now, I think you'd best meet me partway."

She considered him briefly and then shook her head. "No. I represent a group of Imperial nobles, and I'll pay extra because of the unusual method we're doing business, but don't think that means you have the option of declining."

He felt the hair on the back of his neck start to rise along with his temper. "An outright threat is strike three. It might be inconvenient for me to kill an Imperial noble—which I have no doubt you are—but it wouldn't be the first time. You need to consider your next words *very* carefully, or this meeting is over, and so are you."

For the first time, she smiled in a way that looked perfectly natural. "Now *that's* more like what I'd imagined dealing with a criminal mastermind would be like. See? Perhaps we should agree that there's no need for threats from either of us.

"Considering the amount of money that I'm willing to pay upfront for your consideration in this matter, don't you think you'd prefer to know what we're talking about before you threaten to kill me?"

Before he could answer, the door behind him opened, and Tony brought in a coffee service on a small cart. It was very old-fashioned, but his brew had a reputation that wasn't to be ignored.

The big man set the service up on the table, poured them each a cup, and then stepped out of the room, closing the door softly behind him.

Certain that he was probably making a mistake, Peter finally took a seat and gestured for the woman to do the same. "For the amount of trouble that you're already causing me, you'd best make this worth my time."

She smiled like a shark and mentioned a number that was significantly higher than he'd been ready to hold out for. "And that's just the retainer. Once we've discussed the mission that I want you to carry out for me, then we can negotiate the actual fee for services."

Well, it looked like this negotiation was going to be significantly more interesting than he'd anticipated. He wondered exactly who she wanted dead because that kind of money meant there'd be one or more bodies for him to dispose of in the very near future.

16

———————

Page received notice that the lieutenant wanted to meet with him while the recruits were having dinner. He'd just woken up from a quick nap.

He stopped by his office and grabbed a ration bar and a bottle of water. He probably wasn't going to get a real dinner today, so he might as well prepare for that.

Being the smart man he was, he made a note to replenish his stock. This training cycle would probably be rougher than most, and it always paid to be prepared.

He grimaced as he finished the bar and threw the wrapper away. Why couldn't they make survival rations that tasted halfway decent? Maybe it was to keep hungry marines from eating everything in sight.

Actually, that kind of made sense.

Once he'd finished, he went to the lieutenant's office door and knocked. She called for him to enter a moment later, and he did.

Lieutenant Evans's belongings had been removed, but it didn't look as if Lieutenant Na had replaced them. The walls and shelves were bare. Since she was only going to be here for twelve weeks, he suspected she probably wouldn't do any decorating.

That had to be kind of strange for her. He made another mental note to contact supply and verify that all the necessary basic items for a functioning office would be delivered tomorrow. He needed his officer operating at peak efficiency even when her attention was focused elsewhere.

He came to attention in front of the desk. "You asked to see me, Ma'am?"

She nodded and gestured toward one of the chairs. "I've got some bad news, and then I got some worse news."

Great. He took a seat and listened as she filled him in on the information she'd gotten from Imperial Intelligence. He felt his stomach sink at the news because he immediately knew what the worst part was.

The noble that had come chasing Tolliver was going to try to find someone on his staff that they could turn for money. That meant that he'd have to be on the lookout for a friend sticking a knife in his back.

Sadly, he could already feel his mind turning toward the most likely candidate: Gomez. Her dislike of Tolliver made her a juicy target for someone like the noble and her henchmen, whoever they ended up being.

Well, there was nothing he could do about it, at least not directly. That was one of the lessons he'd learned early in life: you could only be responsible for your own actions. Other people had to take responsibility for the things they chose to do.

Right or wrong, everyone had a vision of what was in their best interest. No amount of arguing was really going to change their minds, not if they had what they thought were compelling reasons.

"So, what are we going to do?" he asked slowly. "If the person that's followed Tolliver here has as much influence as you say, they're going to be able to throw a lot of money and other enticements at my people. How do we prevent them from being tempted into doing the wrong thing?

"Or is that how we're going to handle this at all? Do we just accept the shocking yet inevitable betrayal and wait for one of the drill instructors to try something? I have to say that that's not my favorite option."

Na shook her head. "I'd rather be proactive. We need to find a way to bring your people onto our side. I understand that some of them don't like that Andrea is here, and they'd prefer that she didn't graduate.

"Balanced against that, we have their careers as Imperial Marines. That has to count for something. No marine really wants to betray their fellows.

"Your people are probably some of the best at what they do, and they're your family. Given the options I see, I don't think they'd be inclined to betray you personally. If they know that you're looking for trouble, that's got to discourage betrayal.

"And that fits in very well with something that Major Martelle suggested. If the bad guys intend to turn one of the drill instructors, they're going to have to approach them with a lot of money to even consider the offer and not tell someone about it, even if they decline.

"What if we authorized them to keep the hush money, so long as they informed us that they'd been contacted and then they worked with us to try to stop whoever was perverting the process? That way, they'd get the benefit of keeping the money and upholding the honor of the marines. A win-win situation."

Page considered the idea. "Is that legal?"

"So long as they pay the taxes and report it to their superiors, I think it might be. In any case, I can send a message back to my Imperial Intelligence contact, and I'll wager that he can make certain that no one gets into trouble. He wants this to succeed as much as I do, even though I'm not sure his motives are as pure."

"Let's say that's the way we go," Page said. "Are we really sure it's going to work? Tolliver has a lot of baggage simply because of where she came from, and some of those folks that are approached might not see stopping her as being at odds with being a marine.

"The Singularity *is* our enemy, and they're going to think that perhaps Tolliver shouldn't be allowed to graduate even if the means of stopping her are dirty."

Na sighed. "It's a risk. We're still going to have to keep our eyes open, but we can at least give them the opportunity to do the right thing. If they know that we're watching, they're not going to be able to be too overt in their actions.

"Their best opportunity to succeed at this was with our ignorance. Somebody working behind the scenes might have been able to engineer a situation or series of situations that guaranteed her failure to graduate. That option is off the table now.

"I think with the balance of our foreknowledge and your people's consciences, we'll be able to stop anything like that. Obviously, you're going to have to watch Tolliver very closely going forward, and if things start happening that don't make any sense, you're going to have to act."

He had to agree with her logic, but that opened a new set of pretty ugly possibilities.

"If they can't stop her with subversive tactics, then they're going to have to do something significantly more overt to ensure that she doesn't graduate. To me, that means an attack of some kind. They'll have to try to kill or maim her so severely that she's washed out of the service.

"I suppose they could also try to rig up some set of circumstances that made her look as if she'd done something so heinous that she'd be thrown out, but that's a lot less straightforward than simply killing her. How do we keep an eye out for that without sending up all kinds of red flags?"

The lieutenant crossed her arms over her chest. "Before Andrea left to come here, I told her to keep her implant recorders running at all times. She's got plenty of storage space to save that kind of data for twelve weeks. If she does—and I have no reason to expect that she won't—she'll have a record of *everything* that happens around her.

"I did that so that when the inevitable fights break out, she'll have proof that she didn't start them. I get that a certain amount of conflict is not only necessary but desirable. Still, with all the strikes she has against her, I wanted there to be no doubt about what had actually happened.

"If she's doing that, that'll provide some evidence in her favor if someone tries to frame her somehow. While I'm certain that implant recordings can be manipulated, she wouldn't be able to do so without it being detected."

"That will be useful if it comes down to that," he agreed. "Let's hope it doesn't. Our best bet is to catch them when they approach my people if they do. I can't see my people betraying their oaths as drill instructors like that."

The creed of an Imperial Marine drill instructor had its roots in the Marine Corps of the United States of America back on prespaceflight Terra, back before all the individual nations were absorbed into the Terran Republic and then later into the Terran Empire. It was almost word-for-word identical to that sacred promise even after so many millennia.

It said, "These recruits are entrusted to my care. I will train them to the best of my ability. I will develop them into smartly disciplined, physically fit, basically trained marines, thoroughly indoctrinated in the love of the Corps and the Empire. I will demand of them and demonstrate by my own example the highest standards of personal conduct, morality, and professional skill."

If one of his people betrayed that creed, it would kill him.

"Well, I think I understand the problem that we're facing, Lieutenant. I think I'd best go speak with my people and make sure that the worst-case scenario never comes around."

He rose to his feet and smiled at her. "Yesterday, I was kind of annoyed at the level of complication that Tolliver's presence was creating. Now, I think I'm going to take this as a challenge.

"Now I'm looking forward to figuring out exactly what's going to happen next. Playing chess with opponents that I don't even know is going to be an interesting test, and I look forward to defeating them on the field of battle, no matter what kind of battle this actually turns into."

Then he gave her a cold, sharklike grin. "If things do go bad and someone tries to harm one of my recruits, I'm going to come down on them like a platoon of Marine Raiders dropping from orbit."

She matched his grin with one of her own as she stood and extended her hand. "And I'll be right there with you, Senior Sergeant. You can count on it."

* * *

Once dinner was over, and they'd finished cleaning up the barracks to the drill instructors' satisfaction, Andrea climbed onto her bunk and collapsed, completely wrung out.

The amount of work they'd put her through while wearing weights made her ache all over, and this was only the first day. She knew that the next twelve weeks would feel like an eternity and that by the time she'd finished training, she'd feel as if she'd been run over repeatedly by a cargo truck.

Her bunkmate didn't look much better, but at least Diana wasn't completely exhausted. She could tell that when her friend's head popped up to look at her.

"So, what do you think about day one? Did you have as much fun as I did?"

Andrea groaned and covered her face with her arm. "You think this was *fun*? You're sick."

Diana laughed. "Oh, I wouldn't say that I had an incredible amount of fun in the ha-ha sense, but sure, this was fun. We got to do things that I hadn't even dreamed about doing before, and this is only the *beginning*. I can't wait to start learning how to do things with powered armor, flechette rifles, and all that other stuff. This is going to be *terrific*."

Andrea couldn't argue with the general concept. Working with those kinds of things *was* a lot of fun. Still, learning the equipment wasn't just an isolated task. They did it so that they'd know how to fight. That meant killing and death. Not exactly what she'd call fun under any circumstances.

"Powered armor is a blast to operate," she allowed, moving her arms so that she could look at her friend, "but we're learning how to use it because it protects us from getting shot. Flechette rifles are also awesome, but we're going to use them to kill people that are trying to kill us. So, while training can be fun, I wouldn't say that the use of it is always going to be a pleasure."

Her friend hoisted herself up to sit beside her on the top bunk. "I remember you saying that you've used armor and flechette rifles before, among other things. You had to use them to fight, didn't you?"

Andrea nodded. "I didn't get to use powered armor in the

fighting, but I've trained in it since then. I was wearing modified mercenary unpowered armor back then.

"I did get to use a flechette rifle to defend some marines against attackers on the raid where I was rescued. I can't talk about the specific details of that operation, but I had to kill people, and that was the furthest thing from fun that I can imagine.

"I was terrified and angry and a whole lot of other emotions that were hard to process."

"That had to be difficult for a little girl," Diana said, her voice filled with sympathy. She put her hand on Andrea's leg and squeezed it gently.

"Actually, it wasn't as difficult as you think," Andrea said with a shake of her head. "I was raised in a school where those that didn't fit in or didn't succeed at the level expected of them were killed.

"The crèche started out with two hundred girls. By the time they graduate, only a third of them will still be alive.

"Worse, the ones who have survived will have been molded into ice-cold monsters that only care for their line and the ruling caste of the Singularity. Trust me when I say that it's not the kind of place that makes one feel love and joy toward their fellow human beings.

"It didn't make me happy to do what I did, but I didn't feel the slightest bit of remorse for killing those men and women at the time. They would've done worse to me if they could have. Now? I don't know how I'd feel.

"In any case, while it's definitely fun to do the training, I recommend that you never lose sight of what our ultimate goal is. Basic training is meant to weed out those that can't fight or that the Marine Corps doesn't want for other reasons."

Diana took a deep breath and nodded. "When you're right, you're right. Still, today was fun. I think that you can look for joy even in ugly places, Andrea. Not everything we do is work or business, but even when we're working, we can still find something pleasurable about it.

"Like, for example, what we're going to do to Claudio tomorrow."

The idea of that actually did make Andrea smile. "We really should work out a plan in advance. If we're going to be making a run through the confidence course and potentially the obstacle course, that will put him at a disadvantage, and we need to make sure to capitalize on that as much as possible.

"This is our chance to make sure that everyone else knows what taking us on means. If they want to try to bring us down, we want them to know just how much of a risk that will be for them personally. We're not people that they want to mess with, and they need to understand that at a visceral level."

Diana looked impressed. "Well, okay then. What do you have in mind?"

Andrea held her hand up and then raised herself to her feet to look over the wall lockers beside them to make sure that Claudio and his bunkmate weren't listening.

They weren't there, so that was good. Considering that they were restricted to the barracks at this point, they had to be in the bathroom or taking a shower. Either option was good enough for her.

She dropped back down to sit beside Diana. "The confidence course is designed to help build teamwork. It will be hard for him to get through it without failing if he's operating alone. That may mean he's going to have a partner that we don't know about yet.

"The key to getting through is assessing each obstacle and figuring out how we can work together to help *both* of us get past it. Anyone trying to get through the confidence course solo will end up doing something that makes their failure inevitable. If we can work together like a well-oiled machine, assisting one another over the hard parts, then we're going to beat Claudio."

"Do you know anything about the obstacles we'll be facing?"

Andrea shook her head. "My guardians were intentionally vague about that. I'm already coming into this with advantages that the rest of you don't have, even though the drill instructors are packing me down with weights. My implants are going to help me with the problem solving, though, and that's something that they can't stop me from using."

Diana cocked her head. "Really? Tell me more."

"I have marine-grade implants, and they have software built into them that helps me with tactical problem solving. They're going to suggest potential solutions that we can utilize on the confidence course.

"It might not be as helpful in the obstacle course. Those obstacles are meant to be done solo, so finding ways to work together on them will be more difficult.

"Still, there may be parts of the obstacle course where we can help one another, but we won't know until we get a look. We'll be able to make plans for our second run through, though, and I'll help you assess things that didn't work as well as we'd like. Sometimes, all you can do is try to do better the second time.

"I expect that you're going to have some insights that can help me with this. Teamwork isn't exactly my strong suit, and I'm going to be counting on you to help me beef up my interpersonal skills.

"I just don't see the human angle as clearly as the rest of you. If you see something that will help me bond with the other recruits, please help me, even if it's something that makes me uncomfortable."

Diana extended her hand and grinned. "You can count on me, partner! We're going to figure this out, and we're going to have fun doing it."

Andrea couldn't help but smile at the girl's broad grin. She really liked Diana, even though she was so different from her. Maybe it was *because* she was so different.

She was really looking forward to thrashing Claudio. That really would be a lot of fun.

17

F ei tried to get some sleep, but rest proved elusive. After a couple of hours, she just gave up. She needed to do something. She needed to feel like she wasn't just waiting for an inevitable disaster to strike.

She rose from her uncomfortable bed, dressed in her uniform, and went to her utilitarian desk. The built-in computer system was able to monitor the vid pickups placed around the battalion area.

There were pickups scattered across the entirety of the base, she was sure, but she didn't have the authorization to tap into those feeds. With the problems looming over them, perhaps she needed to see about rectifying that.

If someone wanted to sneak into the barracks, they wouldn't have an easy time of it. They'd be crossing several monitored areas just to get into the general vicinity around the barracks itself.

That wasn't so critical if the enemy was going to use an insider as their weapon of choice. However, if that didn't work out for them, they'd have to get up close and personal, which meant a much greater likelihood that they'd be spotted.

How would they go about mitigating that outcome? Hell, how were they going to get onto the base at all? It was heavily guarded.

To her mind, that meant they'd have to subvert the security systems. That was, after all, the easiest way to slip into a location without being detected. Her old platoon had had an expert at that kind of thing, and she really wished she had Corporal Riggio Gomez helping her now.

Interesting. While the name was ubiquitous in the Empire, she wondered if her old tech specialist was related in some way to Sergeant Sophia Gomez, the hostile drill instructor.

She paused her original line of thought and brought up Sophia Gomez's record. She no longer had access to Riggio's, but she had an archived copy from six years ago in her implant records.

A quick check confirmed her wild speculation. The two *were* related. Extremely closely, in fact. Brother and sister. The odds against that were quite literally astronomical.

Unless Earl Still Water was playing even more games.

Why would he do something like that? What purpose could it possibly serve?

Fei sighed. There was no way she'd be able to guess the answer. She'd just have to accept the data and see if she could use it at some point. For now, though, she needed to focus on the problem at hand: the barrack's vulnerability to penetration.

When human beings relied on electronic monitoring devices for their safety and security, they tended to forget that those same devices could be subverted. If that happened, most people were caught flat-footed.

She didn't want to be caught like that, and she refused to rely on others for Andrea's safety. That meant she needed to cobble together a backup system that she could use without fear that the enemy could subvert it.

That really made her wish that she had the specialized gear to use for that kind of thing and an expert to set it up. The types of combat remotes that she was used to using were easily visible because of their size.

The same was true of most of the monitoring around the barracks. No one bothered to hide the fact that the recruits were being watched. Why should they? After all, that was only to be expected.

She sighed. She was just going to have to accept aid from a source that she didn't want to even speak to. She had no doubt that their help would come with a price, but sadly for her, it was a price she was going to have to pay.

Fei brought up the file that had been attached to the message from Still Water. It galled her to have to approach Imperial Intelligence for any kind of assistance whatsoever, but if anyone would have the type of equipment that she needed, it was them. They were, after all, spies.

She input the code into her desk before she could change her mind. Even at this late hour, somebody picked up on the other end on the first ring. They only answered with voice.

"Go."

"I need some equipment," Fei said without identifying herself. "Authorization code Zeta Charlie Bravo Epsilon Mouse."

"Hold one… Authorization confirmed. Stand by while I forward your call."

She frowned. Forwarded her call to who? She'd just called Imperial Intelligence. Who were *they* calling?

The channel was clear for almost three minutes before the vid screen came to life with an image so surprising that she jerked back in shock. Grinning at her while wearing a shirt of eye-searing yellow flowers was Riggio Gomez.

"Sergeant… No, Lieutenant Na. This is an unexpected pleasure. What can I do for you?"

"Riggio? What the hell are you doing on New Dallas?"

"I live here. I retired here to be near my parents after… everything. I gotta say that I'm a hell of a lot more surprised to see you here and back in uniform.

"Still, this probably isn't the most secure way of catching up. What do you need that I can help you with?"

"High-end surveillance equipment that isn't patched into the main grid. Stuff that won't be found unless someone is looking really closely. Not the kind of thing that a civilian can get their hands on."

He scratched his chin, still smiling. "You called Imperial Intelligence to get connected to me. Who does that suggest I'm working for?"

"Really? You went to work for *them*?"

"Only as a tech guy. I leave the spy crap to those with the right kind of personality. On the plus side, I can get what you need, and my supervisor told me that you have carte blanche. If you need it, I can provide it.

"And, for your peace of mind, I'll report solely to you for the next twelve weeks. Imperial Intelligence will only hear from me if I need something, and they don't get to dictate my actions. It's like old times. You get to call the shots, and I'll make the magic happen."

Fei wasn't sure how much of that she should believe, but this was *Riggio*. They'd bled together and almost died together. Better yet, he liked Andrea.

"I can't imagine your presence here—and mine—is coincidental," she said after a few seconds. "Strangely enough, your sister is a drill instructor in my unit, which screams intent. Someone is playing a game of some kind. Are you *really* on my side?"

His expression was deadly serious. "I figure I owe you and Lieutenant Tolliver my life. That doesn't even count my share of the haul, which set me up for life and lets me do great things for my family.

"For the next twelve weeks, I'm your Huckleberry. I hadn't heard that my sister was involved in anything, though I knew she was on the base. Since she's a drill instructor, I can guess why you're here. Is Andrea really that old now? I guess so.

"I owe her some too. She betrayed her people to save us, and I'll damned well give her my all. I'm your man. One hundred percent. Tell me what you need, and I'll make the magic happen."

She briefly wondered if she could believe him but decided that was being idiotic. She'd known and worked with Riggio for years. If he said that he was on her side, he was.

Besides, she was out of options.

"I need surveillance gear to keep watch over a barracks and all of the approaches to it so that I can have continuous coverage of both the inside and the outside without anyone knowing that they're under surveillance. This has to be with the assumption that somebody is going to be looking for the vid cameras and bypassing the official feeds."

"I can get you that equipment tonight if you need it."

Fei considered that. The late hour meant that very few people were awake, and she could spend the hours of darkness planting the vid cameras around the barracks. That would give her a backup monitoring system in place before the enemy was likely to strike.

"I'm on the marine base. Am I going to need to meet you somewhere else?"

Riggio laughed. "No. Tell me where, and I'll be there in an hour."

"225ᵗʰ Training Battalion, Bravo Company, First Platoon. For God's sake, wear something that blends in."

He laughed again. "I can be subtle. See you shortly, Sarge. It's good to be working with you again. I've missed that."

"Me too. See you on the parade ground in an hour."

Fei killed the channel and turned her attention to creating a more detailed map of the area around the barracks, noting which areas of approach would be best monitored and which ones would be covered from multiple angles. Riggio could double-check her work when he got here.

Depth of coverage was going to be critical. If an approach was only visible to one camera, it might be vulnerable to being spoofed. If all the approaches were covered by multiple cameras, even if some of them were discovered and neutralized, there was a good chance that word would still get to her if anyone tried to breach the perimeter.

She spent about forty-five minutes working before she rose to her feet and started out toward the parade ground. It was time to meet an old friend.

* * *

PAGE MANAGED a few hours of sleep and felt refreshed when he woke the next morning. That might have had something to do with the fact that he'd slept in till 0700. Luxury.

He dressed, went to the mess hall, and had an actual meal before returning to the barracks to meet with the recruits. They'd already been to the pit, so they'd just finished cleaning up when he arrived.

Under normal circumstances, they wouldn't be going to the confidence course until the second week, but it was within his purview to shake up the schedule.

And he wanted to. He needed to see exactly what Tolliver was bringing to the table and determine how clever she was. To a lesser extent, he wanted to know what her bunkmate was like.

The same was true of Claudio Baker and his bunkmate, Justin "JR" Handley. He'd already decided to tap Handley to be Baker's partner on the confidence course. Sending anyone to do the obstacles alone was just asking for trouble.

He wanted to set up a rivalry between Tolliver and Baker. Once that was going, he'd control its intensity to keep them poking at one another and get the platoon operating at a higher level than they might otherwise be inclined to. He'd have to keep a very close eye on everything to make sure that things didn't escalate too far, though.

The recruits were busy getting their bunks made when he walked into the barracks. "Morning, recruits! I hope you're ready for a march. You've got three minutes to be finished making your bunks and lined up outside. Move!"

That set off a flurry of activity behind him as he walked back out to where the lines were painted on the ground. A few people were right behind him, but most came out minutes later. The last recruit hit the line thirty seconds after the deadline.

"Pathetic! Everyone drop and give me thirty."

They'd eventually learn to move faster, but that would take them a few days if history was any indicator.

Once they'd completed the push-ups, some of them needing to be yelled at by one of the other drill instructors for flawed form, he got them back on their feet.

"You recruits continue to disappoint me," he said, his hands on his hips. "You have got to pick up what we're doing faster and be more on the bounce. It may not seem like it right now, but we're giving you extra time. By next week, you'd better be finished getting your bunks and lockers set up before one of the drill instructors arrives, or there's going to be trouble. Pick up the pace, recruits!

"Now, I hope all of you are ready for a nice road march. The confidence course isn't too far away, but it'll give you some practice moving in formation and keeping time. Marching is one of those fundamentals that every marine needs to understand at a cellular level, so pay attention.

"You may not know this, but marines love to run, and marching is the foundation for running as a unit. By the time you're done with basic training, you're going to have learned that you can run a lot farther than you'd have ever thought possible.

"Now, let's get a move on. Right face!"

Once everyone was turned, he got them marching down the road. He then began educating them about cadences. Cadences were ditties that helped them focus on their timing and improved their breathing because they had to sing along.

Many were also crude and generally unacceptable in polite company. Yet the tradition was so ingrained into the Corps that no one would dream of changing them. It was merely the way things were done.

Another benefit of singing together was that it built a sense that the platoon was a single entity in their minds. Each little bit of that the drill instructors could do to drive that point home was helpful.

It took them roughly half an hour to march to their destination. The course was positioned near the barracks because every training platoon would be using it at one time or another.

There were places on the base that they'd be marching to that were many kilometers distant, usually up and down steep hills and through brush that would be challenging to get through even for a trained marine, but that was for later.

He'd made sure that no one was scheduled to use the confidence course this morning. A combat team was scheduled to use the obstacle course in the afternoon, but the platoon would be long gone by then.

He stopped the recruits and turned them to face him with the first of the confidence course obstacles behind him. It looked like a ladder built on a gigantic scale and then propped up so that it was on a gentle slope.

Only looks could be deceiving. The ladder-like surface was three meters wide to allow more than one recruit on it at a time and was stout enough to support the weight of many recruits.

The obstacle's apex was about four meters off the ground, which was covered in sawdust and had a few safety pads to prevent injuries when someone fell. The logs that made up the "steps" on the six-meter length of the ladder angling up to the apex were slightly more than half a meter apart. The same was true on the descending side.

Honestly, it had always looked like a squat tent to him. It was a significant first step in building a recruit's confidence in their physical abilities, but there were many more that followed it. Together, they could intimidate the uninitiated.

"Listen up, recruits," he said, half turning to face the obstacle. "This is the Weaver. We call it that because you have to climb up one side and down the other by weaving your bodies between the logs, over one and under the next.

"The gaps average just over half a meter, but there are a few places where the gap is significantly wider. Those spots might require someone to help you. Or not, if you're that good.

"See how the side logs are painted red? Touching red will disqualify you, and you'll have to start the obstacle over. The posts holding up the apex are also red, you'll note. Stick to the center of the span, and you'll be fine.

"The confidence course is meant to drive home how essential teamwork is and also reveal personal limitations that you might not be aware of. Trust me when I say that we all have them and that being a marine means covering for your fellow marines.

"Today, I'm going to send Recruits Tolliver and Randall against Recruits Baker and Handley. We'll use three obstacles as a test. Whoever wins two out of three will get a reward. Those who fail will be punished.

"You see, when you make a point of going after your fellow recruits, you'd better have what it takes to back it up. If you don't, there will always be a price to be paid. Do you understand me?"

The platoon sounded off in unison. "Yes, Drill Instructor!"

"Excellent. Then let's be about it."

18

Andrea eyed the Weaver and started calculating the best way to handle it. They hadn't made her put on any of the damned weights this morning, so she'd be allowed to run the obstacles without them. That was going to give her a *significant* advantage.

Part of her wondered if that was intentional. Was Drill Instructor Page trying to make a point about her? If so, what was the message? That she was a badass?

That was probably true compared to the other recruits, but what good would that kind of messaging do them?

Then again, she supposed his reasoning really didn't matter. She needed to win this competition, and the key thing to remember wasn't her strengths. Instead, she needed to compensate for her partner.

While Diana was physically fit, she didn't have the same muscle density as the boys or Andrea. She'd have to work harder than the rest to achieve the same results.

Of their opponents, Claudio was the most buff. Handley wasn't out of shape; he just wasn't in as good a condition as the jerk.

Still, he'd have an advantage over Diana. JR and Claudio were going to be a challenge for the girls to overcome, and she'd just have to make it work.

To do that, she needed to improve Diana's chances. The only way she could see to do that was to work her way through the obstacle in front of Diana and use her greater strength to help her.

That wasn't meant to be an insult to her bunkmate. None of them had any experience running these obstacles, so being hesitant was natural. She expected her own performance would improve with time and experience.

Only this first time, they had to be better than the boys.

Drill Instructor Page stepped over to the front of the obstacle. "As you can see, it's wide enough for all four of you to go up at the same time. Here are the rules. You go over one log and then under the next until you reach the top. If you go over the top of the first log in the sequence, that means that when you reach the top, you'll need to go over the apex.

"Don't get yourself out of order, or you're going to have to try to go underneath the apex log, and that means that you're going to fall. There's padding underneath the apex to help mitigate some of that and sawdust in the other areas. The sawdust won't be that big a help, so my advice to you is to hang on.

"You're allowed to help your partner and hinder your opponents, but you cannot touch any of the logs that are marked in red. If you do, I'll call you out, and you'll have to drop off the obstacle and start again.

"The winner of this obstacle will be the first team that gets both of its members down the other side successfully. Now, get into position and wait for my signal to begin."

Andrea stepped over to the left side of the obstacle's front and spoke softly to Diana. "Follow me up and be ready to take my hand if you run into trouble. Our best option is to get as much of a lead as we can on these two. If they get in front of us, they're going to win.

"We can use my greater strength to offset that some, but you're going to have to move as quickly as possible."

Her friend nodded, and they set themselves up to begin.

Claudio and JR took up positions on the right side of the entrance. The big boy grinned at them.

"I hope you girls are ready to get stomped because this isn't going to be pleasant. At least not for you."

"Whatever you say, Tiny," Diana said smugly. "Let's hope you're big enough to reach between those logs. We wouldn't want to see you fall short. Again."

The boy's grin turned into an angry snarl just as Drill Instructor Page yelled at them to begin.

Andrea lost no time heaving herself over the first log and under the one just past it, flipping over in the process so that she could move more quickly while still getting her arms on the next log beyond.

The process wasn't too tricky, as the logs were close together, but she knew that there was a gap farther along that would make getting between them more difficult. She'd have to keep that firmly in mind so that it didn't surprise her when she reached it.

Just as she wormed her way around the second log, she could see that Diana was struggling slightly to get past the first one, so she reached back and lent her friend her strength. She was able to use her leverage to pull the other girl up and around even as she swung her legs free.

The maneuver almost made Diana fall. If she had, there was an excellent chance that she'd have yanked Andrea with her. They'd gotten lucky this time. She'd have to pay better attention going forward.

Claudio and JR were making decent time, but the obstacle was just as unfamiliar to them as it was to the girls. To her relief, it was causing them some grief too. JR seemed to be having difficulty understanding how to correctly weave between the logs and fell as he tried to maneuver past the second one.

Not only did he come loose, but he also grabbed the red log on the side, thus doubly disqualifying himself even before Drill Instructor Page yelled at him to start over.

The boy snarled and turned around to head back to the beginning of the obstacle. While it no doubt annoyed him, at least he didn't have to make up very much. Falling at the top or on the second half would've meant having to make up a lot more time.

Something for her to keep in mind.

With Andrea helping Diana move, they were doing almost as well as Claudio. He was starting to worm his way slightly ahead of them, but that wasn't going to matter so long as they could beat JR. This was a team exercise, after all.

When they reached the broader gap between the logs, Andrea reached over and locked her arm around the far log before using her greater body strength to lock her legs under the log behind them. That turned her into a human bridge that Diana could use to get across the gap.

"We're going to make it," Diana said triumphantly as she cleared the gap and helped Andrea pull herself over.

"Yes, we are," Andrea said with a matching grin.

Claudio had reached the apex of the obstacle and was maneuvering himself across the top. JR was halfway back on the first half of the obstacle and trying to make up time. Andrea could see that he was pissed that his partner hadn't waited for him. Apparently, Claudio wanted to get to the end first, whether or not his partner made it.

With a little bit of work, Andrea reached the apex right behind Claudio. She'd have really loved to finish before him, but she doubted that was going to happen. So long as the two girls came in behind him, but in front of JR, it didn't matter.

Andrea climbed over the apex and locked her legs underneath the log on the other side. She reached back for Diana and pulled her friend up on top of the peak.

That done, she was about to unwind herself when there was a sharp impact against the side of her boots, and they came loose from the log that was providing her with leverage.

She pinwheeled in the air and made a grab for one of the logs, missed, and slammed face-first into the padding. The impact drove the air out of her lungs.

"Whoops," Claudio yelled down with a grin as she sat up, gasping.

"Sorry about that. Looks like my tiny feet got in your way. Better luck next time."

Andrea snarled in rage as she staggered to her feet, raced back to the beginning of the obstacle, and began climbing up as fast as she could.

She half expected Claudio to knock Diana off the obstacle as well, but he didn't. Instead, he settled for speeding down the other side.

JR had reached the Weaver's apex and was on his way down the other side in pursuit of Diana, but he wasn't going to catch up with her. Her friend had too big of a lead now. Barring the girl falling off, she was going to make it.

It now fell to Andrea to show the boys what she could *really* do.

She stopped pretending that she was a normal human being and took the obstacle on with all of her strength and dexterity. She basically flew up the first side of the obstacle, weaving between the logs like an eel. When she reached the apex, she kicked off with her feet and actually arced over the top log without touching it before snagging the log on the other side and flipping herself underneath it, using her legs to hook onto the log beyond it.

That put her almost face-to-face with JR, and she wondered if he was going to try to knock her off like Claudio had. If he did, he was going to deeply regret it.

Something in her expression must've conveyed her feelings because he held out a hand as if to ward her off. "Take it easy! I'm not going to screw with you!"

Rather than respond, Andrea took his words at face value and raced down the far side of the obstacle, almost catching up with Diana before the girl climbed over the final log and landed on her feet.

Two seconds later, she was standing beside her friend, glaring at Claudio. "If you *ever* touch me again, I'll punch you square in your ugly face."

"Bring it," he said, his voice low and hungry. "Let's do this."

"Recruits!" Drill Instructor Page roared.

Andrea braced to attention as Page walked up beside them. He glared at her momentarily before turning to face Claudio.

"I suppose I should've been more explicit, so I'm going to rectify that lapse right now, recruit. Striking another recruit with your hands or feet while working one of the obstacles is not permitted. Doing so again will result in you having to start the obstacle over. Is that clear?"

"Clear, Drill Instructor!" Claudio said, all traces of his smirk gone.

Page stared at him for a few seconds and then turned toward Andrea. "You'll note that I didn't say that striking another recruit was *always* disallowed. You are marine recruits, and it's expected that there will be some level of conflict.

"What I do expect is for you to keep that down to a level where it's not going to come to the attention of the drill instructor cadre or to harm another recruit to the point that they require medical treatment beyond cuts and bruises. Is that clear, Recruit Tolliver?"

"Clear, Drill Instructor!" she said.

He turned toward the rest of the platoon. "Am I clear, recruits?"

"Clear, Drill Instructor!" they all said in unison.

"The first obstacle goes to Recruits Tolliver and Randall. Now, I want you all to pay close attention to what I'm telling you.

"You saw how fast Tolliver was able to navigate this obstacle by herself. Let it sink in. That's why we make her wear weights during physical training because she's not being stressed at the same level of physical exertion that you are.

"Never doubt for one second that she's stronger than you, has more than enough endurance to run you into the ground, and—even with every bit of impediment we put in her way—she's almost certainly still going to outperform you in tasks like these."

His words were like a blow to Andrea's stomach. She'd wanted to fit in, but he'd just made that impossible. She was always going to be different from them. Something to be feared. This was what she'd dreaded.

"Recruit Randall handled this obstacle well enough," Page allowed, "but she did a lot better in the first half than in the second. That's because she had help. In fact, she had the most support that a single person could give.

"Being a marine means being part of a team, and you'd do well to remember that. Don't be like Recruit Baker and leave your teammate behind. It doesn't matter how fast *you* are when someone on your team *doesn't* make it.

"And never forget that the caliber of your team depends on how much effort you put into it. Any team that has Recruit Tolliver as a member will have an advantage over the rest when the drill instructors allow it.

"Listen very closely to me now, recruits. Tolliver is an example of what the warriors from the Singularity can do, but she *is not your enemy*. She's your *teammate*.

"Judge a person on their merits, not their past. That doesn't mean that everyone in the Corps needs to be your friend. I can't stand some marines, but that doesn't change how I behave towards them.

"If you're good enough to graduate from this course, each and every marine becomes your brother and sister. Families fight among themselves, but they turn a united front to outsiders. Together, we *will* defend the Empire from our enemies. Never forget that."

Andrea watched the platoon out of the corner of her eye and could see at least a few people seemed to be considering his words. That didn't stop some of them from glaring at her, but the only genuinely outraged expression belonged to Claudio.

She knew that she was going to have more problems with him. All of that talk about brothers and sisters didn't matter to him. He'd had a chip on his shoulder since the very moment they'd met. He wasn't her friend and never would be.

So be it.

Now, they had two more obstacles to run, and she was going to do everything within her power to crush Claudio's dreams of victory before lunch.

19

Peter spent more time thinking about the woman's offer than he really should have. That involved staying up late in his darkened library, sitting in a comfortable chair while pondering his options.

His first inclination was to refuse outright. His second inclination was to have the woman killed. Honestly, that was what he needed to do, and he knew it. The way she'd treated him demanded it.

Unfortunately, the amount of money she'd offered for the job was significant. Just the consideration fee was more than he usually charged for killing anyone other than a political or public figure. The kill fee itself was staggering.

Every time he thought that he had the issue settled in his mind, he found himself thinking about what the organization could do with the extra money. His organization brought in quite a bit of income, but a chunk like that would allow him to expand.

The woman really wanted this girl dead.

The whole situation was a conundrum that he wasn't sure how to resolve, so he spent more time than he'd have customarily allowed considering the various options.

Once he'd finally gone to sleep, he'd dreamed about the target.

That was more than a bit disturbing, since he didn't have much of a conscience to begin with. When he'd started working for the organization, he'd been an enforcer. That meant that there had been plenty of people he'd had to make examples of over the years.

Sometimes that involved an injury to make a point, and other times someone had had to die. If he'd had any moral qualms about that sort of thing, not only wouldn't he have advanced in the organization, but he'd have paid a price himself.

Even so, this unknown girl from the Singularity had haunted his dreams. It wasn't that he was inclined to show her mercy or anything so dramatic, but the fact that she preyed upon his thoughts at all was both unusual and unsettling.

Once he'd risen the next morning and taken his breakfast alone on the small balcony of his suite, he stared out over the city as it began coming awake and considered Andrea Tolliver.

He knew next to nothing about the Singularity itself, other than what everyone thought they knew. Working in the underworld, he knew better than to take any information at face value. There were always nuances, half-truths, and outright lies told by those in power to direct the anger of those they ruled toward anyone other than themselves.

The truth was always messier than anyone would have you believe. There weren't just two sides to any issue; there were dozens, hundreds, or thousands.

He buttered his toast and enjoyed the warm crunch of it as he watched the birds fly overhead. Did any of this really matter? Was it her background that was causing him to pause?

Peter couldn't imagine why that would be. He'd dealt with people from many different cultural backgrounds, so why should the Singularity be any different?

Or was it merely her appearance? The woman had given him a picture of Andrea Tolliver. She'd had no choice, since one usually wanted to make certain that a hired assassin killed the right person.

He brought up the image in his implants and again examined the girl. The picture had been taken at some type of meeting because the girl was seated reasonably close to the person taking the image, and she seemed to be looking directly at them.

He wondered whether or not the image had been captured by the woman who'd hired him. Had she sat in front of the girl at some point?

If so, why? Why would an Imperial noble be meeting with someone from the Singularity? It all seemed very strange.

He'd, of course, recorded the meeting with the woman. It was safe enough because even if he were ever arrested—unlikely at best with the pull he had here—everything in his implants was encrypted to the point that no one could access its contents. He'd paid top money to make certain of that, not only for himself but for his senior lieutenants as well.

Using a still image of the woman, he'd been unable to locate anything about her in the public databases, so he tasked one of his associates with contacting other worlds farther toward the core of the Empire to make surreptitious inquiries about her identity.

He wouldn't use the information as blackmail material because the consequences to his reputation for betraying a client would be too significant, but he wanted to know who he was doing business with.

That drew his attention back to the girl's image. She was young and looked relatively normal for a girl her age except for those tattoos. Someone had inked the image of a bird of prey on her face.

A bold statement, indeed.

The hawk's head on the girl's forehead was partially turned to present its screaming beak in profile. The wings and claws were portrayed on her cheeks as if the bird were diving toward the viewer.

It was an intimidating image and one that he didn't really understand the purpose of. Why had the girl kept it?

No matter.

The woman had offered an awful lot of money to stop this girl from graduating. Her preferred method was an assassination, but Peter wasn't convinced that that was the right way to lead this off. Such an outcome would undoubtedly guarantee a robust response from the authorities.

If the goal was simply to make sure that the girl didn't graduate,

there were subtler means at his disposal. A severe enough injury
would mean that the girl would never be able to become an Imperial
Marine.

Or some type of manufactured scandal might disqualify her just
as effectively. In fact, there were several options available to him, and
he wasn't going to dismiss any of them out of hand simply because his
client was bloodthirsty.

In fact, his irritation with the woman edged him toward resisting
the ultimate solution. After all, the woman had deeply annoyed him,
and he wasn't going to just give in to what she wanted so quickly.

Still, the main question just didn't want to go away. Why did an
Imperial noble want this girl from the Singularity dead?

He'd probably never know the answer to that question, so he'd be
better off accepting that he was going to take the job but do it in his
own fashion. He'd begin with the more subtle attack methods and see
if he could wash the girl out quietly.

If he couldn't manage that, there was always the option of
assassinating her directly. He had twelve weeks to carry out the
contract, contrary to the woman's desire to have it done as quickly as
possible, and he wasn't going to rush the process.

In fact, delaying the project would annoy the woman even more,
so that was what he'd do.

His mind made up, Peter finished his breakfast and consulted a list
of contacts in his implants. He knew more than a few people who
worked on that base.

He usually didn't have any reason to get onto a military facility,
but several contacts there in the supply system were useful in
procuring restricted things that he could either sell or co-opt for his
own use.

It was time to see if he could turn those contacts into a method of
locating Andrea Tolliver and then setting up a means to observe what
was happening around her.

Once he'd done that, he could formulate a plan to begin the
process of eliminating all opportunities for the girl to graduate.

Peter smiled at the thought of how much grief he was going to
cause the Imperial noble before this was all done. This would both

be a pleasure and a profitable undertaking. Who could ask for more?

* * *

FEI AND RIGGIO had spent the early morning planting vid cameras all around the battalion area and around the pit. They'd also hit the mess hall and finished out at the confidence and obstacle courses. Those were the primary locations where Andrea would be during the first few weeks of training, so that was where they'd needed to focus their efforts.

By the time they'd finished, dawn was already upon them, and it was too late for her to head back to her quarters because the risk of being spotted by the recruits was too high. They'd still have to go into the barracks after the recruits left for the day to plant vid cameras there too.

To pass the time, she and Riggio decided to hit a distant mess hall to eat and catch up.

The two of them went through the line, collected their food, and retired to a table at the corner of the room where no one could listen in on them. Once they were seated, she focused her attention on her companion and started eating.

"So, let's talk about your new employers," she said between bites. "I can't imagine how you ended up working for them. Or imagine why you'd want to. You did pretty well for yourself when everything was settled out from the raid. What the hell happened, Riggio?"

He grinned at her as he dug into his own omelet. "You're right about that, Sarge. Or rather, LT, I should say."

"You can call me whatever you like. It's not like you're on active duty."

"Why don't I stick with Sarge for old times' sake? They approached almost two years ago. I've been on New Dallas for over a year. That can't possibly have anything to do with Andrea."

Fei shook her head and chuckled. "You haven't met the guy in charge of this operation. He's the kind of person that thinks further ahead than the rest of us. He's known that Andrea would probably be attending basic training for years. He's had plenty of time to move elements into place to support that, including you.

"I think he knew exactly what he was doing when he recruited you. It might seem disconnected, but if I'm right, they've been preparing for this moment for years.

"You were a good choice for him because you have the right skillset and you're well disposed toward her. You weren't going to be instantly offended at the idea of helping somebody from the Singularity. That can't be a coincidence, Riggio. I'm just not buying that."

Her companion ate a couple bites of his omelet, his brows furrowed, and then he sighed. "I suppose it's possible. In the end, it doesn't really change anything for me. I chose to get into this work because I was bored. Sure, I made more than enough money off the raid to live a life of luxury if that was what I wanted, but it isn't.

"I like doing things like this. I needed this kind of excitement in my life. I seriously considered rejoining the marines before I got this offer.

"If you're right and they picked me because Andrea was going to be here, then they picked the right guy for the job. I'll do whatever it takes to help her get through this. The kid's got a spine. The marines could really use somebody like her.

"Better yet, the Empire needs to understand that not everybody from the Singularity is bad."

He raised an eyebrow and smirked slightly at her. "Now, what's this I hear about you getting married to Kayden Harmon and Lieutenant Tolliver? Is that true? If so, then I think you might understand somebody from the Singularity a lot better than I do."

She laughed. "You're incorrigible! Yes, we did get married, and no, I'm not going to give you any details.

"Still, I have gotten to know Kayden and Andrea very well over the last six years. There's a lot to like about the regular people from the Singularity. There's also a lot to like about what those designed for the ruling caste can become if they're freed from their indoctrination.

"I refuse to believe that people like Andrea are bad simply because they come from the Singularity. I think my contact with Imperial

Intelligence wants to see her succeed because that will open the door for people here in the Empire to see the people from the Singularity as human.

"If we're going to avoid fighting wars with the Singularity for the rest of eternity, we can't be so hyper-partisan that extermination seems like the only way to end the fighting. That's true on their side as well as ours."

The two of them ate quietly for a minute before Riggio finally nodded. "Well, that's way above our pay grades, Sarge. Right now, we need to focus on the task at hand. If someone's going to come for Andrea, we need to be ready for them.

"That means that we need to have some kind of response team. I'm afraid that the two of us can't keep a constant eye on everything and still be ready to respond with force if need be. If they send someone to kill Andrea, we're going to need people ready to respond at a moment's notice. How exactly are we going to handle that?"

Fei had been thinking about that very thing ever since she'd found out that Dayton had arrived on New Dallas. She thought she had a workable plan, but it was really going to depend on how well she could sell it.

"I'm going to talk with the major in command of the training battalion. He may be able to help us solve this problem. If he can't, I'll have to talk with somebody else from Imperial Intelligence and try to convince them to support us even more.

"Until then, we'll just have to hope that they don't come looking to kill her as their first option. If their goal is to keep her from graduating, they have room to be subtle. All it would take is a serious training accident, and she's done.

"She's a really tough girl, but there are so many potential ways to be maimed that you can't really plan for all the possibilities. Yet, somehow, we're going to have to make sure that we try to anticipate anything they might try to do.

"We're going to have to look for places where a saboteur could break something in such a way that it looks like it's an accident or mischance and still hurts my girl badly enough that she could never serve as an Imperial Marine."

Fei shook her head and sighed. "And not only do we have to protect her, we have to make sure that she doesn't know that we're doing it. If we want this moment of hers to have the effect that it should, she needs to succeed on her own merits. We can't be revealed as having pulled strings to help her. Not only would that damage her confidence, but it would taint everything that she accomplishes."

Riggio drank down his milk in one long gulp and set the empty glass back on his tray. "That's a real challenge, but I think that we can do it. According to the vid feed, the recruits are at the confidence course now. That allows us to get into the barracks and wire it up.

"We don't know how long they're going to be gone, and I don't know exactly how difficult it's going to be. You're going to have to keep watch while I do the work to make sure that none of the drill instructors interrupt us. That means we need to get moving."

Fei drank the last of her coffee, loaded all her utensils and plates onto her tray, and followed Riggio to drop them off for cleaning. The clock was ticking, and they needed to get this job done before the recruits got back.

Andrea was counting on them, even if she didn't know it.

Their mutual enemies wouldn't wait forever to strike, so they needed to be ready to react when the time came. If they played their cards right, they might be able to capture someone and unwind the conspiracy behind the scenes without tipping off Andrea.

If Fei locked Dayton up, that would be the end of this nonsense, and that was just what she intended to do.

20

_____

The second obstacle looked somewhat anticlimactic to Andrea. It was only a tall wall of shaped wooden planks that the two of them had to get over. That was it. The only no-touch zones were the side logs and the braces that kept the obstacle upright.

Well, and it being twice her height.

"I don't think I can get over that," Diana told her quietly.

Andrea grinned at her. "This is where teamwork comes in. To get us both over, we need to get one of us to the top so that they can lean down and grab the other one's arm and pull them up.

"Basically, the way I see this working is that I'll help you get to the top, and you'll brace yourself along the upper edge. Once you're secure, I'll jump up, grab your arm, and use you as a lever to pull myself over. Then we both drop down on the other side. Easy peasy."

Her friend looked uncertain. "That sounds simple, but I'm not sure I can get up there, even with your help."

"I'll get you there. When Drill Instructor Page gives us the signal, I'll get there first, and you put your foot in my hands. I'll boost you up to the top.

"Once you're there, swing one leg over and brace yourself across the top so that you're not going to fall. Be extra careful that you don't go too far, or you might lose your balance.

"Once you're stable, I'll jump up as high as I can. I should be able to come within arm's reach of you. Honestly, I might even be able to jump up and reach the top by myself, but I'm not sure. In any case, this is a team exercise, and I want to show them that we're working as a team. This is how marines do it."

Diana smirked. "I can totally see that on a T-shirt."

Andrea laughed.

Drill Instructor Page walked to stand in front of the obstacle to reiterate the rules. It was just like he'd said before. They could obstruct one another, but they couldn't use their fists or feet for a deliberate strike.

The goal was to get both people over the top of the obstacle and down safely on the other side. It seemed simple enough, though she knew it was going to be complex in execution.

Particularly for their opponents. The boys didn't seem to understand how to work together. If she and Diana played their cards right, they'd get across this obstacle and have won this competition in less than thirty seconds.

When Drill Instructor Page gave the signal, Andrea raced to the wall, turned, and cupped her hands into a stirrup for Diana. As soon as her friend had a foot in place, she straightened and lifted the girl with all her strength.

Diana shot up the side of the wall and almost entirely over it before she grabbed on for dear life. The girl's squeak of dismay was absolutely adorable but not very marine-like.

The end result was Diana hanging onto the top of the wall with her body on the far side, struggling to get one leg back over the top. It looked like the situation was touch and go for a moment, but then Diana hooked an ankle over the top of the wall and began pulling herself back up.

Claudio and JR had tried to get up the obstacle separately and failed. Yet, they proved they could learn because Claudio quickly had the other boy shoving him up the wall.

His ascent was far less dramatic but much more effective than

Andrea had expected. She didn't see what he was doing until moments before his head struck Diana's arm and caused her to lose her grip on the obstacle and fall off the other side, landing with a loud thud and a stream of curses.

"Look, Ma, no hands!" Claudio said with a grin as he levered himself over the top of the obstacle and reached down to help JR up. "Good luck climbing that all by yourself, genie."

Furious, Andrea backed up and then raced toward the obstacle. When she was just a few steps away, she hurled herself up the wall and used her legs to add just a bit more kick off the wood to get herself up the obstacle. It was *just* enough that her fingers barely reached the top of the wall, but they *did* reach it.

Her grip was tenuous, to say the least, but Claudio was already pulling JR over the wall. If she meant to get on the other side of the obstacle and beat them down, she had to act now.

She drew upon the well of strength inside her and pulled with all her might, levered herself over the top of the wall, and plummeted down the other side.

Unfortunately for her, the boys landed just moments before she did. They'd won.

The two boys high-fived one another, and she considered punching Claudio's lights out. Once again, he'd interfered with her team, and this time it had cost them their victory. Almost worse, he'd insulted her.

Senior Sergeant Page stepped over and examined the red-faced Diana. "Are you hurt, Recruit?"

The girl shook her head. "No, Drill Instructor. I've only bruised my pride."

"It happens. You've got nothing to be ashamed of. Unlike Recruit Baker."

He stepped into Claudio's space and almost touched his nose to the boy's. "I will not tolerate that kind of language in my platoon, Recruit. If I *ever* hear that word come out of your mouth again, you will rue the day you were born. Is that clear?"

Claudio looked utterly taken aback. "But it's true, Drill Instructor."

"It's a derogatory term that you will eliminate from your vocabulary. Put it in the same category as any racist or sexist words you might have heard and never utter it again. Am…I…clear?"

Claudio stiffened. "Yes, Drill Instructor."

Page held his position for a few seconds and then pulled back to look at Andrea and Diana. "The interference was within the rules. Sometimes things don't go your way. Sometimes you can nudge an enemy and ruin their plans. You've got to be ready for those unexpected little things.

"This obstacle goes to Recruits Baker and Handley. That ties the sides. It looks like we're going to need a tiebreaker to settle this once and for all."

Page led them to the third obstacle while the platoon followed closely behind. It looked interesting and more than a bit intimidating. Two ropes led up to a series of bars set like ladders laid flat across a pool of water to another pair of ropes on the far side.

It was obviously designed so that a person could climb the rope and then use the rungs to get across before sliding down the rope on the far side.

While it was a straightforward obstacle, Andrea suspected that it was going to be a challenge for Diana. This would require a lot of upper body strength, which would put her friend at a disadvantage.

Page stepped in front of the obstacle and put his hands on his hips as he smiled coolly at them. "This is a relatively simple obstacle, recruits. You're going to climb up the rope and then go hand over hand across the water before climbing down the far side. Once the first person has reached the rope on the far side, the second person can begin traversing the obstacle. Any questions?"

Andrea shook her head. This obstacle wouldn't make it easy for Claudio to interfere with them. While it was certainly possible to reach across to where the other team was, there'd be no way to "accidentally" bump into someone and send them tumbling down.

To interfere on this obstacle would require a deliberate punch or kick, and that wasn't allowed. The real threat to finishing this obstacle would be getting Diana across faster than Claudio. And since she couldn't help the girl, this was all going to be on her shoulders.

It was irritating that they had to do this obstacle because Claudio had cheated, but she was proud of their performance thus far. They'd proven themselves as a team.

"How are we going to handle this?" Diana asked.

Andrea shrugged slightly. "There's no way we can work this obstacle together, so you're going to have to go first and just do the best you can. I hope you're a good climber."

The girl grinned at her. "I might be better at it than you think. I've been practicing."

"Do the best you can," she repeated, "and I'll try to make up any lost time. Be careful of Claudio. If the bastard tries something, I'm going to punch him in the face."

Once Page gave the signal, Diana started up the rope. Claudio went first for the other team, and he was faster than Andrea's friend but not by nearly as much as she'd feared. Diana really had been working out.

Claudio reached the rungs and started across with Diana only a couple of seconds behind him. This was going to be a tight race. That would give her a chance to put one final win in their column.

When Claudio reached the far side, JR began climbing. Three seconds later, Andrea started up after him.

She'd had years of practice climbing ropes just like this one before she'd left the Singularity, and she'd kept up that exercise. Her rope climbing skills were superb.

Andrea swarmed up the rope like a spider climbing a strand of its own webbing. She reached the top of her rope at the same time as JR, and she knew that they would win this competition.

So, of course, that was when things went horribly wrong.

JR botched his transition from the rope to the rungs and fell. If it'd been toward the water, she'd have let him fall and continued on her way, but his trajectory was going back toward the ground where they'd started, and that meant he was going to suffer an undoubtedly catastrophic injury.

It took every bit of her enhanced reflexes and strength to lunge back as far as she could while still gripping the rope with one hand. Even with all her advantages, she only barely caught the boy's pants leg as he fell, and his weight swung him back underneath her. She added what momentum she could to his swing to get him back up to the rungs.

To her shock, the maneuver actually worked. Her swing carried him just high enough that he could grab on to one of the rungs on her side, and he latched on for dear life.

Sadly for her, that was when her hand on the rope came loose, and she fell. Even with his precarious position, JR tried to grab her, but he missed.

Andrea pinwheeled through the air and slammed into the water face down. The impact drove the air from her lungs, but she seemed otherwise uninjured.

It took a moment for her to reorient herself and kick back up to the surface of the water. She sucked air in even as she started swimming back toward the rope.

JR had maintained his grip on the rungs and was continuing across. That put her *way* behind, and she doubted that she'd be able to catch up.

It turned out that she could still climb, but being soaked made it a lot harder. By the time she reached the rungs, JR had already gotten down the rope on the far side, and the competition was over.

She didn't let the loss stop her from giving everything she had going across the rungs and down the rope on the far side. She landed lightly on her feet and was immediately pulled into a hug by Diana.

"Are you okay? Oh, God! That looked horrible!"

Andrea was a little embarrassed at the public display of affection with the entire platoon looking on but realized that trying to extract herself from the girl's grip would only make things worse.

"I'm fine," she assured her friend. "No damage done, except to my ego."

Drill Instructor Page stepped up beside them and nodded. "The third obstacle goes to Baker and Handley. I declare them the winners of this competition."

Andrea felt as if she'd been punched in the gut.

This was a bitter pill to swallow. She'd allowed Claudio to beat her, and he'd won by cheating. She might've made up for it on this last obstacle, but she couldn't stand by and allow someone to be maimed or killed when she could've stopped it.

Circumstances had worked against her, and she'd lost.

"That said," Page continued, "I want to commend Recruit Tolliver for her quick thinking and even quicker action. She likely saved Recruit Handley from a severe injury.

"Learn a lesson from this, recruits. If your options are to save one of your fellows or perform better at something, choose your fellows *every single time*. Well done, Recruit Tolliver. Well done."

A glance toward the rest of the platoon showed that they approved. In fact, they cheered.

That wasn't something that she'd ever expected to see. It seemed that she'd lost the competition but earned a tenuous place inside the platoon.

A look at Claudio showed that he was furious that the drill instructor had stolen his thunder. He was going to continue to be a thorn in her side, and the events of this morning had only hardened his feelings.

Handley gave her a grateful nod. She might not have made a friend in him, but he was obviously disposed to give her a chance.

On balance, it'd been a good morning. A really good morning.

21

Page stepped to the center of the platform beside the fighting area and looked out over the recruits. The last three weeks had really allowed him to get to know them. Perhaps they didn't realize how closely they'd been observed, but he now had a good feel for who would make it and who wouldn't.

Of course, that didn't count the recruits that had already washed out for one reason or another. Some of them hadn't fit in, but others had refused to put in the effort required to be an Imperial Marine.

That was about par for the course at this point. The next several weeks would step up the pressure and wash out even more. At that point, they'd be getting down to the meat and potatoes of being a marine.

"Welcome to week four of marine training, recruits," he said, pitching his voice to carry over the entire area. "I want to take a moment to congratulate you for completing the academic section of your training. You've picked up the history and background material appropriate for this stage of your development. If you graduate, this is only the beginning, but it's a good foundation.

"Now we'll start teaching you the nuts and bolts of being an Imperial Marine. Today we'll start with the basics of hand-to-hand combat. You're going to learn how to use your hands and feet as weapons over the next two weeks.

"You'll also be issued training weapons and begin the process of learning how to use them. There's a lot to pick up, so you'll be worked even harder than before. Big surprise, right?"

That sent a dark chuckle through the ranks.

Once their amusement had passed, he continued. "The fighting field will be the one area where you're going to be encouraged to fight one another full out. I understand there have already been several scuffles inside the barracks, but those don't count.

"Here, your fighting style will be scrutinized, and any bad habits that you've developed will be corrected. We're going to train you how to maim and kill your opponents with or without weapons so that they don't do the same to you.

"I know what you're thinking. You're going to become Imperial Marines, fighting in powered armor with flechette rifles and plasma grenades. Why do you need to know how to fight with your bare hands?"

He grinned at them. "That's a great question. The problem with fighting in a technological society is that sometimes you find yourself out of ammunition, and you have to make do. Teaching you the basics of hand-to-hand combat will also form a foundation to teach you other useful battlefield skills later.

"I'm not going to explain exactly what that means at this point, but I suspect you'll be able to figure it out as the training progresses. Let me be very clear. The fighting here will be more dangerous than a fistfight in the barracks. This means that you're going to have to be more deliberate and careful in what you do. It also means we have medics standing by and a field medical facility right at hand."

He stopped for a moment to look at each recruit individually to make sure they knew that his gaze was upon them.

"Since the chance for injury is higher, there are going to be ground rules, and I expect them to be followed to the letter. This is not the place for you to work out your frustrations with your bunkmates. Is that clear?"

"Yes, Drill Instructor!" they shouted back in unison.

"Excellent. Some of you probably already know a few things about fighting. For almost all of you, that knowledge will prove a hindrance because we're going to have to train the bad habits out of you and teach you how to do things properly.

"Let's start off with finding out who thinks they know how to fight, just to see where we're starting from. If you've received any formalized hand-to-hand training, raise your hand."

About a third of the recruits raised their hands. That was about average. Almost all of those would be some form of martial arts. They likely had a few bad habits in their styles that would have to be corrected. That wouldn't be a challenge.

"If your training only lasted a couple of years or hasn't been something that you've pursued recently, lower your hands."

Most of the hands that had been raised now dropped. That left him with six recruits that thought they had some type of advanced training that they were continuing.

He noted that Recruit Tolliver still had her hand up. Honestly, knowing what he did about her mentor, he suspected that she was the only one who really knew anything compatible with what they were about to learn.

"When I point at you, I want you to briefly explain the type of training you've received and how long you've pursued it."

He pointed at the first recruit and listened as she explained about receiving training in one of the myriad martial arts prevalent throughout the Empire and that she had achieved a second-degree black belt.

Page nodded. "That's good. The dedication you've invested in learning it will carry over even if the specific techniques do not. Next."

He continued going through the recruits, saving Tolliver for last.

When he finally pointed toward her, she spoke. "I've received six years of basic marine hand-to-hand combat instruction, Drill Instructor."

Page pursed his lips. "I'll need a bit more information, Recruit. What exactly did that entail?"

"Six years of almost daily instruction, bare hands and with

weapons that are commonly used in the training regimen of an Imperial Marine, Drill Instructor. My teacher was a qualified marine hand-to-hand combat instructor."

That was actually something of an understatement. Lieutenant Na had both graduated from and received a teaching certificate in the advanced combat course. The real question was how much of that knowledge she had passed on to her student.

If Tolliver had been training with basic combat forms for six years, she'd be more than capable of wiping the fighting ground with any of the other recruits. If she'd been given any of the advanced classes, she might be even more dangerous than that, considering her other physical enhancements.

Page considered asking for even more details but decided that he'd rather judge her skill level for himself. That would serve the dual purposes of demonstrating to the recruits that they had a lot to learn and put Tolliver on notice that she wasn't the biggest dog in the pack.

"That sounds very impressive, Tolliver, yet I wonder how much you've actually picked up. If what you say is accurate, then the next few weeks of hand-to-hand training will only be covering the very basics of what you already know."

He took off his drill instructor's hat, set it down on the platform, and jumped down to the ground. He gestured for the recruits to back away until only he and Recruit Tolliver were left standing inside a circle of observers.

"Attack me," he said.

"Drill Instructor?" she asked hesitantly.

He made a gesture with his hands. "I'm not asking you to maim me, Recruit. I want you to try to put me on the ground. This is your chance to strike a drill instructor without reprisal. Let's see what you've got."

She'd respond one of two ways: either she'd be hesitant, or she'd come after him with everything she had. He suspected the latter, so he prepared himself.

Tolliver raced in and punched at his head. He was glad that he'd been prepared for her attack because she was faster than he'd counted on.

He moved his head clear and struck back. She blocked his blow and tried to grapple with him, but her technique was rushed. That allowed him to use a counter move and break free.

The two of them circled one another. She was obviously assessing his skill level and deciding what the best way forward would be.

Rather than giving her the time to make up her mind, he charged in and launched a kick at her midsection. She twisted, her hands grabbing his foot and heaving him past her. Damn, she was *strong*.

He hit the ground and rolled, coming to his feet just in time to meet the charge he'd expected. Only he thought she'd be farther away. Instead, she was already in his face.

This time, he wasn't able to dodge the fist she slammed into his midsection, and he discovered that knowing she was roughly half again stronger than a girl her size should be did absolutely nothing to minimize the stunning shot.

Page tried to use his skill and get out of striking range, but she kicked his legs out from under him and slammed him into the sawdust with all of the force that he'd have expected from a full-grown man.

She landed hard on top of him and jammed his arm behind his back, effectively ending the fight.

He tapped the ground with his free hand, and she immediately released him and backed away.

Page climbed to his feet and brushed sawdust from his face as the recruits gazed on in awe and horror. Others might have been humiliated at having a recruit beat them, but he was always willing to recognize an accomplishment.

Besides, this fight wasn't over yet.

"That's pretty good," he admitted with a grin. "You're faster than I expected, even knowing what I know about you. You're going to be able to use that to your advantage on the battlefield, but I think there are a few things that your instructor hadn't gotten around to teaching you yet. Have you heard about the advanced course?"

Tolliver nodded warily. "I've heard of it, Drill Instructor. I can't say that I've been trained in anything from it."

"Thought not."

Without saying another word, he launched himself at her and

pulled out some of the dirtiest, nastiest tricks he'd learned in the advanced course. It was going to stretch his skill to get her, but he wasn't going to allow himself to be beaten by a recruit.

This time when she tried to counter punch him, he not only pulled her off balance, he kicked her legs out from underneath her while grabbing her uniform and hurling her off to the side.

She landed hard and rolled, not quite making it back to her feet before he landed on top of her. She squirmed, but he was able to lock her arm behind her back.

Tolliver proved her experience by immediately tapping out. Many people would've kept resisting, but she'd recognized that the fight was over without the drama. His positive opinion of her and her mentor grew.

The two of them rose to their feet and circled one another again for the third and final bout. He liked the fact that she wasn't intimidated by him. She wasn't afraid to throw a punch or take one. That was going to count for a lot going forward.

He took two steps forward and struck at her head with his fist, but it was only a feint. His real attack was the knee that followed up to her gut. The surprise strike drove the air out of her lungs and sent her staggering back.

Page expected that to be the end of the fight, but she didn't go down. She was still struggling to breathe, but her fists were up.

Damn, she was *good*.

Hoping to end the fight quickly, he stepped into range with her, and they traded blows. She got one good strike to his chin before he popped her one on the side of the head. She staggered to the left, and he was on her.

Even with his larger size, she *almost* kept him from forcing her to the ground, but he managed to kick her legs out from under her again and pinned her.

When she tapped out, he climbed to his feet and stepped away until she rose.

"Are you okay, Recruit?" he asked, not bothering to hide the fact that he was a little winded.

She nodded, rubbing the side of her head. "Yes, Drill Instructor. That was… educational."

"It was meant to be. Allow me to commend your trainer. You've got a good grounding in basic marine hand-to-hand combat, though you've got a lot of dirty tricks from the advanced course to learn if you graduate.

"Unfortunately for me, that means I need to find something to do with you for the next few weeks, since you're not going to learn anything new from this segment of training. The solution is to put your skills to use and allow you the opportunity to help teach your fellow recruits to fight."

She blinked. "Drill Instructor?"

He grinned. "I think you understood me. For the next few weeks, it's going to be your responsibility to help instruct your fellow recruits on how to fight. I'd wager that will teach you a few things and try your patience more than you can possibly imagine."

It would also give him deeper insight into what made her tick. He was already inclined to think she would make a good marine, but seeing how she took a position of authority would be a window into her soul.

He only hoped she was up to the challenge.

22

Peter was pouring himself a cup of coffee in his office when Charlie knocked on the door and stuck his head in. "That woman is here."

He immediately knew that the man had to be talking about his troublesome and unwelcome client. Honestly, it had taken longer than he'd expected for her to come looking for answers.

"Tell her that I'm with a client and that I'll see her as soon as I'm free. Keep her held up at least twenty minutes."

"You got it, boss," Charlie said with a grin as he headed back out.

As Peter sat at his desk, he made a mental bet with himself. His suspicions were confirmed when there was shouting outside, and he smiled inside as the door burst open a few seconds later.

"Don't try to put me off," the woman snarled. "Why haven't you carried out the job that I hired you for?"

He stared at her coldly for ten long seconds without speaking. "It's a good thing that I told my client to go into the next room because I *expected* you to burst in.

"This isn't something that I'm willing to tolerate. My people won't even let you into the building next time. You'll need to call for your updates from here out."

She planted both of her palms on the top of his desk and leaned over it to glare at him. "I *have* called for updates, and all I've heard are excuses. You've had weeks to kill the girl, and you haven't.

"Why not? I believe that I made it abundantly clear that this needed to be carried out in a timely fashion."

He leaned back in his chair and smiled slightly. "Timely can mean many things. It can mean quickly, as I assume you think it means, or it can mean at the appropriate time, which is what I interpret it to mean. Doing the job to my satisfaction requires that I raise as little suspicion as possible. That takes time."

"I paid extra to make certain that this happens quickly, and your delaying tactics are pissing me off. Get with the program and take care of the girl now."

Peter shook his head. "Not going to happen. You don't have to live on this planet once the job is done. Could I send someone to the base to shoot her? Certainly, only that would draw law enforcement attention.

"I need to make sure that their suspicions are never aroused. As I recall, I told you several times before I agreed to do this that I was going to do it in my own fashion. You had every opportunity to approach someone else, yet you didn't. I wonder why that was?

"Oh. That would be because I'm the best at what I do. So rather than telling me how to do my job, why don't you leave me to take care of this in the manner that I think best?

"You don't even need to be here, you know. You can go back wherever it is that you came from. So long as the money is in escrow, your presence is not required or desired."

If anything, the woman turned even redder than she had been before. "I'm not going anywhere until this job is done. If you want any peace whatsoever, you'll get it done as quickly as possible.

"If that girl isn't dead within the next week, I'm going to be coming here every single day. If your thugs try to stop me, I'll bring my own to make certain that I get in.

"Understand this very clearly. I'm not someone that you can toy around with. Just like you threatened me on that first day, keep very clearly in mind that I can end you.

"And before you think that you can just threaten me with death again, you should know that I've already informed certain associates that if I disappear, you're the one responsible, and you'll end up regretting ever crossing swords with me."

He stared at her, his eyes hard and unblinking. "I'm taking steps to see that everything happens in the sequence that I want it to. If you show up with thugs, you'll survive the experience, but they won't. I put word to that effect out right now so that anyone stupid enough to work for you is marked for death. Good luck hiring anyone.

"We're done here. You can walk out that door, or Charlie can throw you out. I don't care which. No, scratch that. I'd *prefer* it if Charlie throws you out so that I can watch you bounce down the stairs. Now, get out."

With steam virtually rising from her hair, the woman turned and stalked out. Charlie followed and closed the door after her.

Peter waited for a full fifteen seconds before he began to chuckle. That chuckle turned into a full laugh, and moments later, he leaned back in his chair, roaring.

He hadn't had this much fun in years. Pissing that woman off was a reward in its own right. He hadn't expected that.

Once he'd gotten his mirth under control, he looked up a number on his computer. He'd already contacted several people that worked on the base and had laid the groundwork for the job, but it was time to get things started.

As he'd told the woman, this operation was meant to be subtle. If his people performed as he desired, no one would suspect foul play. The girl would survive, but circumstances would prevent her from completing her training and thus satisfy the terms of the contract.

The fact that the girl would live *would* piss the woman off, and that would make him laugh even harder. She *really* wanted Tolliver dead, so he was determined to complete the contract while *not* killing the girl if possible. It was pure pigheaded stubbornness on his part, but he wasn't going to be bullied.

Over the next few days, Andrea Tolliver's circumstances would change for the worse, but she'd survive. He had no idea what would happen to her after that, and he didn't care, but his business with the woman would be complete, and he could move on with his life.

* * *

FEI SAT at her desk going through the paperwork that a marine training platoon generated and once again thanked the gods that it wasn't her real job. She couldn't imagine how Grace had lived with this for so many years.

It wasn't difficult work, but it kept her at her desk far longer than she preferred, going through data to formulate the reports she needed to send up the battalion every single day. She'd known that Grace had spent a lot of time in her office but hadn't imagined that there'd been so much data manipulation. It was far better to be the senior NCO of a platoon than to be an officer.

Even so, the last three weeks had shown her what she needed to do, and she'd fallen into a routine. She saved the drudgery for the afternoon while reserving the morning for going through all the data she and Riggio were collecting, looking for anything that might stand out.

Not that she'd found anything. Things had been far too quiet, and she was getting worried.

She was just wrapping up a series of reports covering the last week when there was a knock at her door.

"Come in," she said briskly as she cleared the display above her desk.

When the door opened, it didn't reveal one of the drill instructors or someone from battalion. Instead, Earl Still Water stood in the hallway.

"I hope I'm not disturbing you," he said with an urbane smile.

"Not at all," she said as she stood. "Come in and close the door behind you."

He stepped into the office, closed the door behind him, and locked it. He then looked around at the utterly bare room.

"I love what you've done with the place. It absolutely *screams* minimalism. Don't you think you should at least have *something* on the walls and shelves?"

She ignored his attempt at humor and gestured toward the chair in front of her desk. "I'd offer you something to drink, but as you can see, I don't have anything in stock. When did you get to New Dallas?"

The noble sat and grimaced. The seats weren't designed to encourage people to linger, so she wasn't surprised. That suited her fine, as she rarely wanted to meet in her office anyway.

"I've been here a few days, but I didn't think it needful to contact you until I'd nailed down a few things. I can now confirm that Countess Dayton did arrive on the same ship that brought you and Andrea here.

"She didn't come down to the surface via the usual cutters but had a charter pick her up in orbit. It took her to a private spaceport that my people have now identified, and I have confirmation of her arrival via their surveillance feeds.

"I'd have come on an earlier flight, but until a short time ago, I wasn't confident that she'd taken the liner, and I needed to make sure before I committed. That woman is far more resourceful than I'd have given her credit for.

"Since she's here, I'm actually surprised that nothing has happened yet. She doesn't seem to be a patient sort."

Fei nodded, having resumed her seat. "I was thinking the exact same thing. It's kind of creepy how she's just waiting. I figure she's acting through local intermediaries. Perhaps that's what's holding her up.

"I've got a couple of people keeping an eye on Andrea during the day. People from battalion masquerading as support personnel. They're never far from where she is. I worked with Major Martelle to get them assigned.

"I've also used Riggio to get everything monitored on our own private network so that we can be certain that no one is slipping into the barracks or creeping around the battalion area."

She sighed and scrubbed at her face. "Honestly, that was all I could think of to do. Until they show their faces, we're not going to be able to strike at them.

"What about you? Are you able to use any of your super-secret spy stuff to find out where she's hiding? I assume she's not too far away. If you can find her, perhaps you can take her into custody before she makes her play."

He shook his head. "As suspicious as her activities are, they don't violate the law. I've got nothing with which to charge her. I have people searching for her, and once they locate where she's hiding, we'll begin monitoring those that come into contact with her. Perhaps she'll incriminate herself.

"As for why she hasn't acted, that's an interesting question. I don't see that staying true for much longer, though. Andrea is a quarter of the way through the training regimen, and from everything I've heard, she's doing quite well.

"When she makes it past the halfway point, her chances of washing out will be relatively low. If there's not an attempt made in the next week or two, I'll have to reassess whether or not Countess Dayton is actually still here.

"Perhaps she wasn't aware that Andrea was on the liner and was only taking it to get out from under my thumb. If so, it's possible that she took another transport and isn't here at all."

"No," Fei said with a shake of her head. "She's around here somewhere. I can feel the hairs on the back of my neck standing up. It's not going to be much longer before she strikes. I'm doing everything that I can to be ready for it, but it's nerve-wracking."

He nodded. "I've informed the Imperial Intelligence personnel on the base to more actively monitor people coming in and out to determine if we have any unexpected visitors. They have your contact information and will let you know at once if they detect anything unusual.

"I trust Riggio will be able to monitor everything in the battalion area for you and provide every assistance you need. He's a very resourceful man, as you well know."

She raised an eyebrow. "He thinks it's a coincidence that you hired him and then stationed him here two years ago, but that isn't true. You knew back then that you were going to send Andrea here, didn't you?"

The man smiled slightly. "I believe in planning as far in advance as I can when an operation is in the offing. Yes, I approached your former subordinate specifically with this operation in mind, but I'm glad that I did so because his services have been extremely helpful in a number of other matters. He's a credit to your training."

She considered the noble for a few seconds and then shook her head. "I still don't know what to think about you. Imperial Intelligence has been a blight on so many operations that I hesitate to trust anything you say, yet you really do seem to care about this.

"Why can't the run-of-the-mill Imperial Intelligence operatives be this straightforward?"

"Just like every other organization, we have our share of bad apples," the earl said with a sigh. "We try to weed them out but, unfortunately, the way they reveal themselves is usually in a manner that costs lives.

"I wish we didn't have the reputation that we do, and I'm trying to see that things change. Hopefully, over the next ten years or so, I'll have cleaned this particular sector of its worst offenders.

"The people you dealt with on a day-to-day basis as an Imperial Marine weren't usually the problem. It was the people that they reported to. Getting rid of those bad apples is significantly more challenging.

"Some of them are so stupid and self-centered that you wonder how they could possibly have managed to rise to the level of incompetence that they've reached. I really wish that someone had come along to take care of this problem years ago, but it's fallen into my lap, so I'll see it through.

"The emperor is making certain that the other sectors are getting similar treatment, so I anticipate that Imperial Intelligence's reputation will improve over the next few decades."

He rose to his feet and brushed his pants off. "Well, I'd best be going. I've got transport to take back to the city, and I have that woman to find.

"Keep an eye on your girl. I expect trouble will come knocking before very much longer, and you'll need to act with dispatch and discretion.

"In addition to the people that you have working for you from battalion, don't forget that Riggio can call on others. If someone makes an unexpected appearance, I'd rather not see them dealt with through normal channels. Those kinds of people demand lawyers, and then we'll never get anything out of them.

"Since this is an Imperial Intelligence matter, I'm claiming priority for our organization. All of the Imperial statutes support this, but I'd rather not make a big deal about it. So, when they make their move, I want to be able to make mine as quietly and quickly as we can."

Fei rose to her feet and smiled coldly. "I'll be happy to turn whatever's left over to you. It really depends on how much resistance they're prepared to give me when the time comes."

Personally, she hoped they fought like hell because she wanted to hurt the bastards. Particularly Dayton.

Who knew? Maybe the gods would smile on her just this one time.

23

During the process of helping guide her fellow recruits through hand-to-hand training, Andrea quickly discovered that they weren't a very appreciative bunch. They barely trusted her to begin with, though they'd been neutral over the last several weeks.

Drill Instructor Gomez would delegate groups of the recruits for Andrea to keep an eye on as they practiced what they'd been taught, issuing any minor corrections that she could to their form or technique.

It hadn't taken her very long to learn that a friendly tone and being apologetic about any corrections earned a much better response than telling them what they'd done wrong.

She wasn't quite sure why. Even after living inside the Empire for six years, she still really didn't understand how to interact with people. Her background made it difficult to really understand how to be friendly. The crèche never developed anything like that in her that she could build upon now.

That had occasionally led to some unexpected situations. Growing up, she'd sometimes done something wrong and couldn't figure out what, even when it had been explained to her. At other times, she'd found people's behavior incomprehensible.

Why did everyone have to be so different? Growing up, her line sibs had been almost identical to herself in how they'd behaved and thought. Even though she'd been an outlier in the crèche, she'd still been much more like them than she'd been to anyone since.

Yet if she graduated, she'd have to be a sister in arms to these people. She'd be assigned to a platoon, and her squad mates would have to become even closer to her than she'd ever imagined possible.

She wasn't certain how that would take place, particularly when so many people still viewed her with suspicion and distrust.

Well, that was a problem for later. For now, she needed to focus on the details of her current assignment. Fortunately, correcting most of the issues that she saw and adding words of encouragement wasn't all that difficult a process.

She really enjoyed helping Diana. The girl was nice, but she didn't know how to fight. Her personality wasn't very confrontational, which was odd in a marine recruit.

On the other end of the spectrum, there was Claudio. Andrea had expected the boy to confront her physically at some point over the last three weeks, but he'd shown surprising restraint.

After the obstacle course, he'd seemed willing to hold his peace, even though he hadn't taken his victory very well. The way that Drill Instructor Page had flipped things around had pissed him off, and it was evident that he was still looking for a way to even things up.

Honestly, she was surprised that he hadn't tried to push her around. Maybe he was more worried about her than he wanted to let on.

The lesson that Page had given them all about being marines had been instructive and illuminating. It was possible to win at something and still feel as if one had failed. Conversely, one could technically lose and think that they got the better end of the deal.

Sometimes the process was more important than the outcome. If one came into something with the right mindset and tried their very best, they might not win, but they wouldn't embarrass themselves.

Four days had passed since Page had tapped her for this extra duty. The recruits didn't study hand-to-hand combat all day long, but they did devote several hours a day to the process. The rest of their time was spent learning other tasks that a larval marine needed to know, and she was grateful that she didn't have to play instructor for them as well.

She'd been thinking about that while running Diana and some others through throwing drills. She probably shouldn't have allowed the situation to distract her, but she couldn't help herself.

The downside of that became apparent when Gomez spoke from right behind her. She hadn't even heard the woman approach.

"Stop chatting with your friends and go help the others," the surly drill instructor ordered. "I'll take these recruits, and you can work with the half that you don't seem to be inclined to associate with."

Andrea opened her mouth to argue but snapped it closed when she saw the drill instructor's expression.

"Yes, Drill Instructor," she said as she moved to the other side of the fighting field, shooting Diana an apologetic glance.

On the other side of the field was her least favorite person in the entire platoon: Claudio. He looked even less pleased to see her headed his way than she was to be going toward him. This promised to be less than pleasant.

"I know that you don't want me over here any more than I want to be here," she said before he could open his mouth, "but we'll just have to make the best of it. Why don't you show me what you're doing, and if I can suggest any improvements, I will. Let's keep this professional, shall we?"

The boy glowered at her and then gestured for his bunkmate to come at him. His technique wasn't terrible, but there were several things that could be improved on.

She tried explaining it to him a couple of times and even had JR throw her to make a point, yet the boy seemed unable to grasp what she was saying.

"I can't understand why you don't seem to get this," she grumbled. "This is a basic throw. Come on, Claudio. I thought you were a fighter."

Her comment only deepened his scowl, and he dropped into the stance that they'd been practicing. "Why don't you see what I'm doing wrong for yourself?"

She dropped into her own stance with a shake of the head and made a slow-motion pass with her fist at his head. The speed at which she'd struck was insulting, but she wasn't exactly in a great mood.

That was where things went sideways.

With more speed than she'd expected and far better technique than he'd demonstrated thus far, Claudio grabbed her arm, twisted his body, and hurled her just like he'd been supposed to all along.

She squawked in surprise as she flipped through the air and tried to land in a way that wasn't going to hurt. His skillful attack was so unexpected that she failed and ended up slamming into the ground on her back. The sawdust puffed up around her as though there'd been a miniature explosion, and she felt every eye on the fighting field swivel toward her.

Blinking in shock, she narrowed her eyes at Claudio as she sat up. "You suckered me! You son of a bitch."

He grinned down at her. "I don't know what you're talking about. Maybe you're just a better instructor than you thought. Nah. That can't be right. I must just be that good."

"Stop playing around and up the ante," Gomez called from the other side of the fighting field. "Since Baker seems to understand the basic throw, show him how it's countered."

Andrea rose, brushing sawdust off and shooting a dark look toward the drill instructor. All that did was make the other woman grin wolfishly.

"You were playing dumb this entire time, weren't you?" she asked as she walked in a slow circle around him. "You've received some kind of training that you didn't tell Drill Instructor Page about. What was it?"

"Nothing official," he said smugly. "Just some stuff that I picked up here and there. If you really want to know how good I am, there's only one way to find out, isn't there? If you can avoid cheating, that is."

She stopped dead in her tracks. "Cheating? You mean that thing you do when you influence events in a competition that fall outside the rules? Like, say, using your head to knock someone off an obstacle? Or kicking somebody's feet out from under them? That kind of thing?"

"Don't be such a baby. If you don't like playing rough, you shouldn't be a marine. If you're not cheating, you're not trying.

"But speaking of cheating, what about using those perversions inside your body? That's sure as hell cheating. Nobody else here has that kind of tinkering, so you shouldn't be able to use all that extra speed and strength. If you want to fight me, you've got to tone it down to what a *real* human can do. Otherwise, it doesn't mean anything."

"I *am* a real human, moron," she said as she glared at him. "Just because the Singularity refined the human genome to the point where it could do things better and faster than you personally can doesn't mean that I'm not human. I still have the same DNA that you do."

"Tolliver!" Gomez said as she stomped up. "Stop flirting and start fighting."

"Here's how we're going to do it," Andrea said flatly. "I'll tone my strength and speed back until I think it's fair. I'm not going to be as weak as the average female, and you're just going to have to accept that."

"If I think you're cheating, I'll call you out," he declared. "I can hit you as hard as I want?"

"Bring it." She looked over at JR. "You get to play referee. If you say stop, we stop. I expect you to keep this fight clean."

The boy glanced at Claudio uncertainly but nodded. He gestured for them to separate.

Andrea backed up a couple of steps and dropped into a fighting crouch. She knew that Claudio would probably try to fool her again, and she wasn't going to leave him the opportunity to win by default. If he wanted to take her down, he was going to have to work for it.

When JR told them to begin, she started circling to the left, but Claudio drove in like a bull. She waited for him, feinting a punch toward his face and then kicking at his knee.

To her shock, he hopped over her kick and lashed out with a side kick of his own, connecting solidly with her midsection.

Andrea staggered back, her breath partly knocked out of her as he charged in. He wasn't playing around, and she needed to get her act together.

He pressed his advantage and discovered that she had a few tricks of her own. She'd used a retreat to make him think that she wasn't ready to fight. Instead, he'd overextended himself, and she used his lapse to strike back.

She grabbed his arm even as she fell backward, planting her feet on his midsection and drawing her knees in. When he was directly over her and moving as fast as she could get him, she extended her legs explosively and hurled him through the air behind her.

It turned out that she *might* have used just a little bit more strength than she probably should have because he went a good distance before he came crashing down. Unlike her, he landed well, rolled, and popped up on his feet, facing her.

"Son of bitch," she grumbled as she jumped up and turned to face him.

"I've been called worse," he said as he charged back in, his fist swinging at her head.

The situation was rapidly devolving into a brawl. She was supposed to be teaching him something about throws, but this was obviously a play for dominance. One that Drill Instructor Gomez seemed disinclined to stop.

In fact, Andrea could see the woman watching the fight, and it seemed as if she was enjoying the spectacle.

What was her game? Did she just want to see Andrea get beaten up, or did she want to catch her doing something that she shouldn't? The woman was devilishly hard to read.

The only thing Andrea knew for sure was that Gomez didn't like her. What she intended to do about that was still a mystery.

They traded blows for a couple of seconds before he got a strike past her guard and his fist smashed into her chin. The blow half-stunned her, and he was on her before she could shake off the effects.

He definitely wasn't playing around, and she needed to end this before he found a way to take her down.

Even half stunned, she blocked his next few strikes and then planted a fist in his sternum.

To her annoyance, that didn't slow him down at all. He'd obviously taken shots like that before and knew how to handle himself.

The problem was that she'd allowed herself to stand still too long, and now he had her just where he wanted her. In the midst of the exchange, he kicked her leg and spun her partly around before grabbing her arm and levering her over his hip and into the ground.

Pinned face down, she tapped out, expecting him to release her. Instead, he jammed her arm a little further up, making it hurt.

"That's one," he whispered in her ear. "I hope you enjoyed it because I'm about to serve you up another one just like it."

Then he released her, hopping back out of any possible retaliation range.

Andrea levered herself up to a sitting position and shook her head to get the cobwebs out. She'd been acting like this was some kind of game, and she needed to stop.

Now that she'd seen Claudio fight, she thought she had a good idea of how he'd react to various attacks, and it was time to put her training to use. It would also be an excellent time to let her marine implants do some modeling and show him how a marine really fought.

Once she'd risen to her feet, she made a "come and get me" gesture and just stood there waiting for him to attack. He didn't disappoint.

Claudio charged forward, stopping just outside of her striking range for just a beat and then dodging to the side, lashing out with another sidekick toward her body.

Her nerves and thought processes worked a little bit faster than an average human, and in conjunction with the programs in her implants, she had time to assess that slight hitch in his stride and guess at what was coming.

She grabbed his foot when it came into range and then dropped down low, sweeping his other leg out from under him. Even as he slammed onto his side, she was on top of him.

He still struck at her with his elbow, but she deflected his attack, using her other arm to snake around his neck and slide behind him, latching down into a chokehold even as her legs wrapped around his torso to keep him from tossing her off.

Claudio struck at her repeatedly with his elbow, but he couldn't get a good angle and eventually had to tap out or lose consciousness. When he did so, she sprang away, not trusting that he wouldn't try to hit her again.

"You know, you're pretty good," she said with a grin. "I don't really understand why you felt you needed to hide those skills. Was that just so that you could get me into a fight? You didn't need to do that. All you had to do was ask."

"I wanted to wait until the time was right," he said as he jumped back to his feet and tilted his neck to the side, making the bones pop. "And I didn't want you using any of those enhancements on me. It wouldn't be fair."

"You mean like you used my lack of knowledge about your training against me? Sounds like bull to me. So, we've got one more fall to settle this. Are you ready to dance again?"

"Stand easy," Drill Instructor Gomez said.

Surprised, Andrea took a step back and turned to face the drill instructor.

"You two seem to think this is all about you. What a bunch of towering egos. In the marines, we're all about teamwork. I think we should settle this third fall with your bunkmates."

The woman gestured for JR and Diana to come closer. "Basic fighting rules, recruits. We'll do one fall. Get into positions and then begin."

Andrea sighed. She had a deep suspicion that her team was about to lose another competition. Based on Diana's resigned expression, she felt something similar.

Her friend dropped into what might loosely be called a fighting stance even as JR grinned and charged in.

And that was when her friend executed the throw they'd been practicing flawlessly, sending the surprised boy spiraling through the air as she flipped him over her hip. When he slammed into the ground, she was right there and pounced on him.

There was a lot of flying sawdust and a couple of squawks, but her friend came out on top, hooting her victory as JR tapped out.

"Well, well, well," Gomez drawled. "Nicely done, Randall. The victory goes to your team."

JR climbed to his feet with a half smile on his face. "That was actually pretty cool. Good job, Randall."

When her friend came close, Andrea held up a hand, and Diana smacked her palm into it, a grin on her face. "Claudio isn't the only one who can hold a couple of things back. Thanks for the instruction."

Even as Andrea congratulated her bunkmate, she could see Claudio shooting daggers at them and knew that this had only elevated his rage toward her. Not only was the fight between them not over, she suspected that it was going to get even hotter moving forward.

She spared a glance at the rest of the platoon and saw that their opinions seemed neutral once again. They weren't going to hold this victory against her, but they also weren't going to give her any real credit for it either.

If she was ever going to find a way to get them to accept her, she would have to do something different. She just wished she knew what that was.

24

Fei leaned back from her desk and rubbed her tired eyes. She was exhausted. Not only had she had to do the mountain of paperwork required for a training platoon, she'd had to keep an eye out for trouble that could come from any direction.

Had Still Water been wrong? Had Dayton actually come to New Dallas? If she had, surely she'd have acted by now.

Over the last few weeks, Fei had spent uncounted hours watching video of the recruits in the barracks and around the training area. She'd slept with one eye open, waiting for someone to sneak into one of the areas under observation and do something nefarious, yet there'd been nothing.

Well, if nobody came for Andrea, she'd be able to finish her training in another couple of months. Then it wouldn't make sense to go after her at all because the precedent would've been set. Basic training was Dayton's only chance to stop this from happening. If she failed to act, so much the better.

Fei was about to go get lunch when her computer signaled an alert through her implants. Something had triggered one of the vid feeds that they'd installed almost a month ago.

It would have to have been more than motion because there was a rudimentary algorithm running in the network that she and Riggio had planted so that it didn't go off anytime someone happened by. No, this had to be something unusual.

She quickly brought up the feed in question and saw that it was inside the barracks itself. It showed a drill instructor walking down one side of the bottom floor, his stride purposeful. Nothing unusual there, so what had triggered the alert?

Then the man glanced over his shoulder as he reached Andrea's locker, and she realized that it wasn't one of the drill instructors assigned to her platoon.

Fei ran a quick facial recognition scan against the marine database and got a hit. Only, the person in question wasn't a drill instructor at all. He was assigned to the supply section.

That instantly raised more red flags than she could count. This was it.

She sent a quick message to Riggio, alerting him that they had trouble as she scanned the other feeds to determine if the intruder had backup. She found none. The only person in the barracks beside the intruder was her.

He'd probably planned it that way, figuring the officer was unlikely to come down to the recruits' level. He'd likely had the barracks under observation, but she hadn't known to flag him.

Riggio responded that he was on the way and had summoned backup. That would be armed Imperial Intelligence personnel. She hoped not to need them, but it was always good to have reinforcements.

With only a single intruder, she made the snap decision to proceed before Riggio got there. She was a trained combat marine, and if it came to a physical confrontation, she could handle a supply guy.

She opened the drawer of her desk and pulled out her illegal stunner. She should probably get permission from the major to have an official weapon, but if push came to shove, she'd deal with the repercussions.

With her weapon in hand, she headed quietly down the stairs while maintaining watch on the vid feed through her implants. The intruder was still working on bypassing Andrea's lock. He was definitely up to something.

Fei took a moment to access the official vid feed and discovered that it had been bypassed. It didn't show the intruder at all. That wasn't a shock, yet it was another sign that this was the action she'd been expecting from Dayton.

Since her rebooting the official feed might notify him that he was under observation, she left the situation with it to be resolved later. She was recording everything in her computer and through her implants, so if she needed evidence at a later time, she'd have it.

When she reached the ground floor, she moved slowly and deliberately as she exited the stairwell. She didn't want to give the man any indication that he was about to be caught in the act.

In fact, she wanted to *literally* catch him doing whatever it was that he intended to do. That was going to tell her exactly how far Dayton was willing to go in these initial stages.

That being the case, she paused a couple of bunks away from where the man was working and waited to see what he did through the covert vid feed.

It took him another fifteen seconds to finish bypassing the lock. He again looked around to make certain that he wasn't under direct observation, which did him no good because she had the unofficial vid feed to keep an eye on him.

He reached into his pocket and pulled out a bottle of body wash as he opened the locker. It was the exact same kind that the recruits were issued. The man opened Andrea's shower kit and quickly swapped her tube of body wash with the one he'd brought.

That was good enough for Fei. Now she had the evidence that she needed.

In two quick steps, she stepped around the wall lockers on the center aisle side and confronted him before he could close the locker door.

"What are you doing?" she demanded. "Who are you?"

She expected him to come up with some excuse, but he surprised her by lunging forward and striking straight at her head with his fist.

The move was a textbook marine hand-to-hand combat strike,

and she blocked it automatically. Her counterstrike to his gut should've disabled him, but she discovered that he was wearing some kind of unpowered body armor underneath his uniform. The strike hurt her hand more than it hurt him.

The intruder followed up faster than she'd expected, as well, lashing out with a kick that forced her to dodge back to minimize the hit but still sent her staggering into the center aisle.

She quickly reassessed the situation and decided that he was more of a threat than she'd anticipated. She needed to end this right now.

Fei brought her stunner up to shoot him, but he struck her hand with his fist, sending the weapon spinning away. He then kicked her in the side, sending her slamming into a bunk across the aisle.

Her mass and momentum were enough to shove the bunk half a meter back and to the side, scarring the bright wax on the floor. He was on her in a moment, trying to end the fight.

With a grunt, she used an elbow strike at his head to force him back a step, and that allowed her to get clear of the entanglement. It wasn't enough breathing room to completely reset the fight, but she knew that her training and experience were better than his.

All she needed was a couple of seconds to get her feet back under. She'd been overconfident and needed to break the cycle before he used that against her in a way that she wasn't going to be able to block.

Her opportunity came when he tried to take her down. He struck at her head again, and she had just enough warning to twist to the side, grabbing his wrist as she threw him into the wall locker next to her.

He struck hard but had turned his body to take the impact on his upper back. The throw's kinetic energy was transferred into the wall locker, tipping it into the bunk behind it with a metallic screech and a crash. That, in turn, went over and took out the lockers behind it.

Like a row of dominoes, everything from the impact point and past began falling over.

She was peripherally aware of the mess but was too busy trying to follow up on her strike to pay it much mind. That was a problem she'd deal with later.

The intruder recovered much more quickly than she'd hoped, lashing out at her with a kick as she tried to close in. One that didn't connect because she'd been expecting something very much like it.

He might be wearing torso armor, but his legs weren't nearly as protected. She grabbed his ankle and fell on his leg with her entire weight, hearing a satisfying crack as she hit the floor with all of her mass.

The man screamed but didn't let the injury stop him from pulling a knife from the small of his back and slashing at her. She raised an arm to block the strike, and he opened her forearm from wrist to elbow.

It hurt like bloody hell and gushed blood.

The wound would cause her problems if she didn't take care of this guy right now.

With his mobility impaired, she was able to jump back and grip her injured arm tightly to try to mitigate some of the blood loss. She kept her eyes on him as she backed toward where her stunner had ended up. He wasn't going to be able to pursue, and she'd stop him here and now.

Only it seemed he'd prepared for that eventuality too. He dropped his knife and pulled a marine-issue flechette pistol from concealment, raising it with far more competence than she'd hoped to see as she threw herself behind Andrea's wall locker.

Flechettes tore gaping holes in the locker itself but missed her as she kept moving, putting distance between the man and herself.

That wasn't going to be enough to save her. Nothing in the barracks was heavy enough to use as cover rather than concealment.

That was when Riggio raced into the barracks, firing a flechette pistol of his own as he advanced. The intruder jerked and spasmed as flechettes slammed into his body. Blood went everywhere, and he collapsed against the wall locker.

The unpowered body armor would've given the man some protection, but at least one of the flechettes had struck his head. There was no way that was survivable.

Still, Riggio was a professional, and she'd trained him herself. He advanced in a sliding combat step until he was able to reach out with the tip of one of his boots and kick the man's weapons away from his body.

Only then did he verify the intruder was no longer a threat and holstered his pistol, though he didn't turn his back on the corpse.

He yanked off his shirt and backed to her side, wrapping her bleeding arm in the makeshift bandage. "You let that yahoo get the drop on you, Sarge? I'm disappointed. I figured that even after six years, you were still too badass to let that happen."

She sighed. "I underestimated him. The database said he was a supply guy. Who expects a supply guy to fight like a line marine?"

"I get you, but don't think I'm ever going to let you live this down."

Two women in unpowered combat armor, with flechette rifles at the ready, raced into the center aisle and began assessing the situation.

Riggio jerked his chin toward the door. "Secure the building, but don't shoot any of the first responders. We don't want a friendly fire incident."

The women nodded and began sweeping the ground floor to make sure that it was clear.

Riggio turned his attention back to Fei. "I can already see that some people from battalion are headed this way through the main feed. We've got maybe two minutes before you're going to have a lot of questions to answer."

Before she could respond, he walked over, grabbed her stunner, and stuffed it into his pocket. "I'll just hold onto this so that you don't have to explain where it came from. Since I'm working with Imperial Intelligence, that's going to give me some cover."

Fei stared at the wreckage of the first floor. Not only was it going to be impossible to clean up in time to hide the fact that something had happened, it was now a crime scene. There were going to be military police *everywhere* inside of fifteen minutes.

She had no idea how she could keep Andrea from finding out that something was going on.

The first thing she needed to do was let Page and Major Martelle know what happened. Then she was going to have to answer all those questions.

"Maybe they'll let me get my arm fixed up before they start interrogating me?" she ventured.

Riggio laughed. "Keep dreaming."

Sadly, he was probably right.

25

P age was about to send the recruits to the mess hall for dinner when he received a priority call from Lieutenant Na. He accepted it at once and found that she'd sent a voice-only, prerecorded message.

"There's been an incident at the barracks. We had an intruder. You need to get the recruits to a safe place in case this wasn't an isolated incident. I'll let you know more when I can. Na out."

He accessed the vid network and tapped into the feed coming from the barracks. Everything looked normal. That couldn't be right, considering the message he'd just received. Had it been tampered with?

He accessed the battalion network, found the feed in question, and ordered it to reboot itself. The image vanished and then reappeared a moment later with a completely different scene.

The bottom floor looked as if a battle had been fought there. Lockers and bunks had been knocked over—some of them seemed to have been shot up—and there were marines scattered throughout the area.

Lieutenant Na was receiving medical attention while an obviously dead man in uniform was being examined by others. Major Martelle was there, and so were the MPs.

Dealing with recruits meant an unending parade of complications, but he'd never faced an outright attack.

The lieutenant was right, though. If the woman after Recruit Tolliver was willing to directly attack the barracks, then the risk of her attacking the recruits out in the open was far too high. He needed to get them out of here right now.

He motioned to the two marines that were providing security, and they jogged over. He filled them in on the situation and watched their level of paranoia shoot through the ceiling. They were disguised as support personnel but had flechette pistols and stunners under their uniform jackets.

That now seemed like far too little protection, and he felt just as exposed as they did. Well, they'd just have to do the best they could.

That task done, he stepped over to Gomez and stood beside her as she watched the recruits sparring. She raised an eyebrow when he gestured for her to follow him a little farther away. He wanted to be distant enough that Tolliver couldn't overhear them with her enhanced hearing.

Once they were safely away, he turned his back to the recruits so that there wasn't even a chance that someone could read his lips. "There's been an incident at the barracks. It seems that Lieutenant Na surprised an intruder, and there was a fight.

"The barracks is trashed, and the intruder is dead. We can't take the recruits back there, and worse, we don't know that there isn't another prong to this attack. We need to get the recruits to a safer location without tipping them off that that's what we're doing. Ideas?"

Gomez's jaw dropped a little as he spoke, but then her expression clouded with fury. Moments later, her eyes became slightly unfocused with the look of someone that was accessing their implants.

"Holy shit! It looks like the LT is down. I can't get a good look at the dead guy's face, and when I scroll the feed back, it just goes blank. Somebody's been screwing with it."

She started to say something more but then froze. "Son of a *bitch*! That's my brother standing there!"

Page examined the feed and tried to figure out who she was talking about but couldn't. "Which one is he?"

"He's the guy in the center of the third group standing next to Major Martelle. The one whose hair is out of regulation."

That helped him spot the man. He was dressed in marine duty fatigues, but she was right. His hair was a little bit longer than regulations allowed for.

"What's your brother doing here?" he asked, knowing that she probably didn't know the answer.

Gomez turned her back on the recruits, grimacing. "He lives on New Dallas, but he works for Imperial Intelligence. Oh, that's not the story he tells other people, but I know that's what he does. He's a tech guy, but he retired from the marines a while back. He shouldn't be there."

Page absorbed the information, and it all came together in his head. "So, you're saying that he was a marine who left the service a while back. Would that be six years ago, around the same time Recruit Tolliver was rescued from the Singularity?"

It was as if a light bulb had gone off behind her eyes, and Gomez clenched her fists. "Holy crap, how could I have missed that? The timing is too close, and he has all that extra money to throw around. He was on the raid that rescued her.

"That means that he was a member of Na's platoon. He knows *everything*. He's been here this entire time because of Tolliver. He's been lying to me for two freaking years!"

Page put a hand on her shoulder. "Tear a strip off of him later. We need to get the recruits moving. Do you have any ideas about how we can get them to safety without spilling the beans?"

Gomez frowned furiously and began pacing. "We're going to have to jump to another part of the training. We're not supposed to go into space for another couple of weeks, but I think we need to kick off zero-G and vacuum orientation right now.

"Next week is supposed to be field exercises, but that's a little too accessible for my taste. If we get them straight to the landing field, we can have them on board a pinnace and into orbit before anyone knows what we're doing."

He considered the idea and decided that he liked it. It would put the training out of order, but that wasn't necessarily a bad thing. They could recover from any hiccups this caused.

He could pitch this as a surprise exercise. With some care, it didn't have to be dangerous. Well, any more dangerous than the rest of basic training.

Another bonus would be that the small orbital the marines used was also used by Fleet for the training of their own people. There'd be a number of Fleet recruits and officer trainees present in the area doing patrols with small craft. They'd challenge anyone who wasn't supposed to be there and provide a layer of protection that the recruits wouldn't get on the ground.

All in all, it was an excellent plan.

"Pass the word to the other instructors while I get things in motion. I'm calling in a pinnace, so we'll depart from here. We can't afford to delay any more than we have to.

"I'll also make sure that the orbital knows that we're coming. That should give us a couple of weeks of relative safety while Lieutenant Na and Major Martelle get things sorted out down here. Go."

Gomez ran to inform the other instructors while Page turned to face the fighting field. He stared at the recruits with his hands on his hips for a few seconds while he initiated the implant call to the field to scramble a pinnace.

Page smiled grimly. Tolliver's enemies had tipped their hand. Now, if they tried anything else, he'd be ready for them.

He hoped they did because they'd deeply regret crossing blades with him and his people. No one threatened his recruits or attacked his officers. He'd make them bleed if they tried again.

* * *

PETER GOT word of the problem right after lunch. A contact inside the military police called and gave him the lowdown on the fiasco.

Base security was in an uproar, and his contact said that someone had confronted the man he'd sent. There'd been a fight in the barracks, and at least one person was dead. The contact didn't know whether it was his man or someone else.

He instructed her to find out and call him back. Then he summoned his lieutenants.

Jomos Carfio and Lucinda Drake took the news stoically once they'd sat down at the table to the side of his office, drinking their coffee. They silently considered their options once he'd finished laying out the facts as he understood them.

"This has the potential to go really bad, boss," Jomos said, scratching his dark beard. "What did the guy you sent know about us?"

"I recruited him very carefully," Peter said. "He had a sizable gambling debt with the Mackie family. I had our people pretend to be with them and offered to forgive his debt in exchange for this job.

"I made sure that we paid off the debt through a cutout, and our people told the man he was no longer welcome at any of the Mackie gambling halls. So far as he knows, he's working for the Mackie family. So far as the Mackie family knows, this guy paid off his debts on his own. Nothing he says or does can lead back to us."

The burly man nodded. "That's good, so far as it goes, but if base security finds out about the debt and manages to dig too deeply, they'll find out that he didn't pay it back. That's gonna raise some questions if anybody from the Mackie organization talks. Still, there's nothing we can do about it."

Lucinda leaned back in her chair and grimaced. "The best outcome for us is if our guy is dead. If they start asking him pointed questions, the vanishing debt will raise their level of suspicion even higher. Far better if all they have is a body and no motive.

"How long will it be before we hear back from your contact in the military police? I'd really like to know if our guy is dead or sitting in a box."

"It'll take as long as it takes," Peter said, his tone calm. "She's not going to ask any questions that would draw attention to herself, and I support that attitude. She's our eyes and ears on that base right now, and she'll get us all the information she can as soon as it's safe to do so.

"All our man was supposed to do was replace the girl's body wash with a bottle that had drugs mixed in. She'd use it without ever realizing that it was tampered with.

"Once she started behaving strangely, they'd have her tested and find that she'd taken a prohibited substance. She'd have denied it, and they wouldn't have found any evidence of it in her locker because no one would feel the need to test her body wash. It would've been good enough to get her kicked out of the marines."

Jomos rose to refill his coffee mug and turned back toward the table as he stirred sweetener in. "Our guy wasn't supposed to start a fight, I assume. How did it happen, and how did someone end up dead?"

Peter shrugged. "We might never know his motivation. Whatever the case, it's done, and we have to deal with the fallout."

"What's our next step, boss?" Lucinda asked.

"It looks like we'll have to kill the girl, so I want to hear your ideas before I make any final plans. What would you do?"

"I think we should have one of our other people on the base get their hands on the sniper rifle and kill her as soon as possible," Lucinda said.

Jomos shook his head. "That's going to cause them to ask even more questions. I think we should have someone sabotage one of the small craft that they use in space. If we can make it crash, lose atmosphere, or something else that will destroy the evidence of tampering and kill the girl, it might be written off as an accident."

Peter considered the options they'd proposed. Each of them had its pluses and minuses.

"Let's do both," he decided. "We can set up a direct attack, and if that doesn't work out, we'll have the backup plan that you've proposed, Jomos."

"You'll need to arrange an accident for that damned woman too," Lucinda said, a hint of venom in her tone. "She brought this trouble down on us, and we can't let her just walk away once the contract is fulfilled. The way she smirks makes me want to shoot her between the eyes."

Peter agreed wholeheartedly. His contacts had finally gotten back to him with her identity. Sadly, openly killing a countess would bring far more attention than he was willing to tolerate.

Still, she had to travel home again at some point, and she was likely to do so in a commercial ship. If he sent someone along to make sure that she never completed her journey, that would satisfy him while keeping suspicion off his organization when her death came to light.

Lucinda was right. When this was all wrapped up, he and his organization had to be the only ones left standing. One way or the other, Countess Dayton was going to die too.

"We'll talk about what can be done to her once we finish handling the problems we've currently got. We'll wait for our military police contact to give us more information about what's going on and then finish formulating our plans.

"Each of you will be responsible for the plans you've proposed, so I want you to get working to make them happen. We've got several people on our payroll at the base, but most of them aren't going to be suitable. Find someone that you can work with and begin formulating your plans."

One way or the other, they'd finish this stupid job. It was too bad that Andrea Tolliver had to die, but at least she wouldn't have to live with the shame and anger his original plan would've left her with. He supposed it was cleaner this way.

26

Andrea's thoughts of dinner were disrupted almost as soon as they'd finished fighting practice for the day. They'd barely formed up to begin marching to the mess hall when a roar jerked her eyes upward as a dark shadow passed across the training field.

A marine pinnace raced over them, seemingly only a few meters up, its thrusters howling as it flared into an abrupt landing next to the fighting field, generating a massive cloud of dust.

An inexperienced observer might be forgiven for believing that the small craft had just crashed, but she knew that it hadn't. The pilot had just performed a high-speed combat drop and killed the pinnace's velocity at the last moment. She knew that because she'd seen it done before.

Not nearly so elegantly, but Kayden Harmon wasn't a trained marine pilot, only an ex-merchant who was very good for a civilian.

Before the dust had even started settling, the ramp at the rear of the pinnace began lowering, and Drill Instructor Page appeared at their sides as if by magic.

"Into the pinnace! Move! Move! Move!"

Even though she had no idea what was going on, Andrea didn't hesitate. She grabbed Diana's arm and dragged her into a run. The two of them were only slightly ahead of the rest of the platoon. Everyone had learned that when a drill instructor told you to do something, you did it right then.

They hadn't received any further training on the acceleration restraints since they'd been delivered to the base, so there was a lot of fumbling as everyone found seats and began strapping themselves in.

Page stalked in after them and shook his head in disgust. "Pay attention to detail, recruits! There are four lines of seats. I want this platoon separated by squad, and I want it done now. Move it! We lift in thirty seconds."

Sadly, it took over forty seconds to reorganize themselves into the appropriate seats. While they were doing so, the last of the instructors and support staff charged up the ramp and sealed the pinnace. They strapped themselves into the line of seats not being used by the recruits.

As soon as he was satisfied with how the platoon had arrayed itself, Page strapped himself in. He must've sent a signal to the pilot because the pinnace lifted with a burst of heavy acceleration, pressing them all sideways in their seats.

It probably would've made a lot more sense to have the seats facing forward, but a marine pinnace was designed for powered armor, and that required space for them to move.

That meant the seats were arrayed in lines along the outside bulkhead facing inward with matching lines of seats on the inside facing out. The wide space between them was where armored marines would move.

Even though the acceleration was pushing Andrea to the side, it wasn't too much to deal with. The pinnace had compensators to help deal with some of the acceleration, and the seat's padding was sloped in such a way that it provided some support, even at full acceleration.

It soon became apparent that the pilot wasn't going to slow down now that they'd lifted off. They continued to pile on the acceleration to the point that Andrea was glad that she was physically enhanced. She felt sorry for her fellow recruits.

The drill instructors seem to be handling everything without any trouble. Of course, even if they *were* feeling some discomfort, they weren't going to allow the recruits to see them sweat.

Since no one was telling her anything, she had plenty of time to wonder where they were going. Why had they left the fighting area in such a dramatic fashion?

From everything that the drill instructors had told them, there were still several days of hand-to-hand instruction left. What purpose did this little surprise serve in advancing that?

Unfortunately for her curiosity, no one seemed inclined to give them an explanation. Instead, the pinnace flew higher into the sky, its thrust seemingly unending.

Andrea attempted to interface her implants with the pinnace and was somewhat surprised when they connected successfully. They hadn't bothered to block read-only access to anyone with marine-grade implants, including her.

The pinnace was definitely on its way to orbit. It wasn't scanning ahead so much as it was scanning behind, and that confused her. Were they worried about being chased? Another inexplicable mystery.

Because the pinnace wasn't scanning the area where they were going, she couldn't determine their destination. Perhaps they were doing a suborbital flight where they briefly left the atmosphere and then came back down to another location on the planet itself.

Her curiosity frustrated, she turned to look at Diana, who was seated beside her. She pitched her voice low to keep the drill instructors and recruits around them from overhearing her.

"Can you access the pinnace's scanner feed?"

Her friend shook her head. "My implants don't have the necessary authorizations. We're not supposed to get the marine-grade implants until a few weeks before graduation. Why?"

"Because we're headed to orbit. I'm not sure what's going on, but this seems unusual. Weren't we supposed to continue our hand-to-hand training for another couple of days?"

Her friend nodded. "That was my understanding. Why would they break the training regimen?"

"To surprise us," Claudio said from his seat just on the other side of Diana, his tone condescending. "They're obviously trying to put us off our game. They want to see what we do under pressure."

Andrea thought about it and nodded. That would be in line with some of the things the drill instructors had done so far.

The recruits had been told that the next stage of training was going into the field. That should've lasted a couple of weeks, and they'd have learned to shoot flechette rifles and do all the other necessary field tasks. They'd then have moved to the orbital phase of training, where they'd start learning how to operate in space.

Everything was happening out of sequence, but maybe that was their plan. Nothing that Fei or Grace had told her indicated in what order the training would take place.

The acceleration lessened slightly, and she looked up as Drill Instructor Page unstrapped himself and walked to the front of the compartment.

"Listen up, recruits. We've decided that it would be in your best interests to swap the field training exercises with orbital operations. We'll arrive aboard the orbital used for small craft training and vacuum operations within the hour.

"This training segment will take approximately two weeks, and then we'll move back down to the planet to continue ground operations. I'm sure you all have questions, but you're just going to have to find out the answers as you go.

"Once we reach the orbital, you'll be given quarters, and we'll see that everything you need is provided. There's going to be a little bit of a delay because some of the supplies you'll need will have to be requisitioned from a nearby Fleet operations center.

"For safety purposes, you'll receive a series of safety orientations. I understand that you haven't eaten yet, so we'll start off with that, but expect to be up late getting the necessary training that will keep you safe in space.

"Some of you already have basic skills in that area, and we'll be leaning on those recruits to help make certain that none of you put yourselves or others in danger. If one of those recruits tells you to stop doing something, I expect you to obey immediately. Is that clear?"

"Clear, Drill Instructor!" they all shouted.

He gave them a stern look and then resumed his seat, leaving them to think about what he'd said.

Andrea didn't know why this change was happening, but it felt as if it wasn't normal. Something had caused it, and she was really curious what that could be.

Well, no matter. She needed to focus on the job at hand. If she was any judge of circumstances, this would reignite the competition between her and Claudio, and she needed to make sure that she stayed on her toes. Everything else would sort itself out.

* * *

THE MEDICS TOOK Fei to the battalion doctor once they had the bleeding under control. He grunted and poked at the wound as he was cleaning it out and prepping it for regeneration.

"I suppose it's not as bad as it could be, as far as knife wounds go. You didn't bleed out, and nothing was irreparably damaged. This wound is going to regenerate cleanly with a couple of sessions. What exactly happened?"

Fei looked pointedly at the MPs that were standing by the door. "I'll be answering that question and plenty of others very shortly, Doctor, so I think I'll just do it that one time."

From the smirks on the MPs' faces, she knew that she'd be answering that question and many more as many times as they wanted to ask them. Well, so be it.

The doctor shrugged and went about his business. Roughly half an hour later, the wound was regenerated, and she was almost as good as new, though she had a scar that would need further sessions to completely eliminate. She'd been down this road before.

The MPs escorted her to the military police building, where she was joined by Major Martelle and Riggio in a spartan interrogation room. It seemed that the two of them had bullied their way into the room rather than being relegated to the observation room behind the one-way glass.

Seeing her former subordinate made her frown slightly. Why was she getting the brunt of the questioning? He'd been the one that had shot the intruder. Shouldn't he be on this side of the table?

Or had he even told them that he'd shot the man? Now that he worked for Imperial Intelligence, he might be playing that close to his vest. If so, he probably should've told her so that she could keep their stories straight. As it was, she intended to tell them precisely what had happened minus the classified parts.

A marine lieutenant with a nametag identifying him as Vega came in and frowned at Martelle and Riggio. "I'm not certain why the two of you were allowed in here, but I expect you to follow my lead. You'll be allowed to ask questions when I choose, and you'll answer any questions that I have. Is that clear?"

Fei thought he was a little snippy for a lieutenant speaking to a major, but since this was a criminal investigation, he might have more leeway than was usual. She thought he'd turn his attention to her, but he continued to stare at Riggio.

"Your name is Riggio Gomez?"

Riggio nodded. "That's correct, Lieutenant. I'm a retired marine."

"And yet, here you are in uniform, Senior Sergeant. Or is that even the correct rank? Since you're playacting, you might be making that part up as well. And aren't you a little young for that rank?"

Her friend shrugged slightly. "When you're good, you're good. The rank is correct for my retirement, and the reason that I'm wearing this uniform will become apparent shortly."

The investigator grimaced and shook his head. "I'm sure it will. So, you and Lieutenant Na surprised an intruder, and she killed him in the fighting?"

"Not quite. She was defending herself against him so effectively that he pulled out a flechette pistol. When I came into the barracks and saw her life in danger, I shot him. Personally, I'd have preferred to capture him alive, but that wasn't meant to be."

Lieutenant Vega raised an eyebrow. "Maybe I should have *you* sitting on the other side of the table, and perhaps you'd also like to explain why you were armed. I hope that that's a past-tense sort of thing, since you shouldn't be armed in this building. Were you authorized to carry that weapon?"

Riggio grinned. "Of course. You think I'd run around a military base with unauthorized weapons? I'll transmit my authorizations to your implants right now."

After a moment, Vega grimaced even more deeply. "Imperial Intelligence. I should've known. And what connection do you have with Lieutenant Na?"

"That's classified. I saw Lieutenant Na in danger of being killed, and I ended the threat. That's really all that's important, isn't it?"

"I need to understand *why* this person attacked Lieutenant Na. Perhaps you'd provide a little background information?"

"My duty is to support Lieutenant Na in this matter. This would be the place you ask her the questions."

The man sighed and turned to face Fei. "Lieutenant Na, would you care to elaborate on why this individual attacked you?"

She opened her mouth to speak, but Major Martelle interrupted her. "That matter is classified. My purpose in this room is to oversee what is allowed to be discussed and what is not, as I've been briefed on this matter.

"What I *can* say for the record is that this intruder wasn't supposed to be in the barracks. He was dressed as a drill instructor but had never served in that capacity. He was attempting to do something illegal when Lieutenant Na confronted him.

"Before he entered the barracks, he or someone associated with him compromised the monitoring system, and that wasn't cleared up until one of my drill instructors rebooted the system after the fight was over.

"While I can't explain why the man was there, it's critical that we determine what specifically he was doing. We're going to rely on you and your people to get us that information in an exceptionally timely manner, if you know what I mean. Is that going to be a problem, Lieutenant Vega?"

The investigator looked as if he wanted to chew the table in frustration. He was angry, and Fei could certainly understand why. Imperial Intelligence had gotten her just as worked up in the past by keeping her in the dark about certain details. Yet here she was with secrets that she wasn't going to explain.

"Pending confirmation with Imperial Intelligence, we will, of course, work in as delicate a manner as is required for classified information," Vega said, his tone almost surly. "And how exactly am I to do that when I know virtually nothing of the events in question?"

Major Martelle inclined his head toward Fei. "Lieutenant Na will explain as well as she can."

Taking her cue, Fei addressed what she could of the situation. "The intruder opened a recruit's wall locker and swapped out the body wash inside the shower kit. I'll identify which wall locker, but we're going to need you to test the tube he planted to see how it was tampered with.

"I physically observed him placing it into the kit. I believe that the recruit is unaware of this action, so it shouldn't reflect upon that recruit. Is that clear?"

"That really depends on where the evidence takes us. Is there anything else?"

She nodded. "The second thing we need to know is who the intruder was and what drove him to do this. All we have at this point is his name and real duties in the supply section.

"Since he can't talk, perhaps there's some information in his quarters or on his communication devices that could explain exactly what he was doing and why. We're going to rely on you to find that for us."

The lieutenant made a harrumphing noise. "We're already gathering some of that information. I'll make sure that we get the body wash to the lab to determine if it was tampered with. When I get the results from that, I'll get you a copy of the report through Major Martelle.

"I have to say that I'm deeply unhappy with this situation. I'll cooperate, but I want to know what's going on, and I'm not going to stop asking questions until I get answers."

Martelle shrugged, not bothering to commit to satisfying the man's curiosity.

Thankfully, that wasn't Fei's problem. Her job was keeping Andrea safe.

She wasn't certain where her ward was at this moment or how Page was shielding her and the other recruits, but she needed to find out. Once she did, she'd leave keeping them safe to him.

It would be her job to dig into what was going on here and make sure that the responsible parties were dealt with. Ultimately, that was Dayton, but sadly, Fei would have to work her way through the intermediaries to get to the woman.

Well, as her wife often said, if it was easy, anyone could do it. She'd just have to get busy and make the magic happen.

27

When the pinnace reached the orbital, Page instructed the recruits to remain where they were because he knew that there would be trouble, and he'd rather handle that in private.

The orbital was relatively small but modern enough. Everything inside was clean and well maintained, just as it should be, since this was also a Fleet training facility. The marine recruits and Fleet trainees made sure that everything was in the best condition possible. That was, after all, part of their training.

The problem was going to be the number of people aboard. Fleet took up a fair chunk of the orbital because their training in space was ongoing. The marine recruits came broken down by platoon, everything scheduled and choreographed so that each group got their training done before the next training platoon arrived.

The problem he was about to trigger was because he was about to wreck all that careful planning.

He'd taken the opportunity on the flight up to call Major Martelle and get verbal authorization, which fell under the category of begging forgiveness rather than asking permission. Still, the deed was done, and the major had approved.

That fact wasn't going to carry any water at all with the lead drill instructor currently running her platoon through the orbital training. She'd be *righteously* pissed, and nothing he said was going to change that. The two of them had to find a way to make this work while stuffing two platoons into the space that one customarily occupied.

Before that could happen, he needed to get the other platoon sergeant to at least stop screaming at him. That was probably going to be a challenge because Senior Sergeant Ingrid Gunnarsdotter had something of a reputation for chewing up the scenery when she was angry.

The two of them had been professionally cordial with one another for several years, but the woman had a chip on her shoulder, and it didn't take much to set her off. It was just his bad luck that she was the one on station now.

In the end, she wasn't going to have any choice about accepting him and his people. Major Martelle would've made that perfectly clear, and her platoon leader would've backed that up.

That didn't mean that the process was going to be easy or smooth. If he wanted this to work, he'd have to grease the squeaky wheel and find a way to bring her on board with what he was doing.

Frankly, he wasn't sure that he was going to be able to do that. Still, he was a marine, and he had to try.

Page entered her outer office and was about to speak to the corporal sitting at the desk when the hatch behind the young man opened abruptly, and Gunnarsdotter stepped out, her face a mask of incandescent fury.

Well, this was going to be fun.

The other senior noncommissioned officer was tall, blonde, and statuesque. Her family was of pure Nordic descent, even though they hadn't been on Earth in centuries. She certainly looked like what he imagined a Valkyrie would look like.

When it was about to reap someone's soul.

Her size made her somewhat intimidating as she scowled down at him, completely blocking him from even trying to get into her office. Not that he'd been inclined to even try to go in uninvited.

Instead, he raised an eyebrow as he looked up into her face and smiled slightly. "Senior Sergeant Gunnarsdotter, I apologize for my unexpected intrusion. Might we speak privately?"

The woman's eyes narrowed and slid to the side to look at the corporal, who was studiously working on his computer and making a point of ignoring *everything* that was taking place around him.

That was probably a wise choice on his part.

Page thought he could almost hear the woman's teeth grinding as she stepped to the side and gestured for him to enter. He stepped through the open hatch and glanced at her office.

It was exactly as he remembered, a closet with the computer and a cramped desk. How the large woman fit in there comfortably, he had no idea.

Somehow, she'd found a way to put a single visitor's chair into the corner, but he had no intention of using it. He was already at a height disadvantage, and he didn't want to sacrifice any more ground.

She put her hands on her hips and glared at him as soon as the hatch had closed. "What the ever-loving hell do you think you're doing, Page? This damn station is already stuffed to the gills with Fleet trainees and my recruits. What would make you think I'd have any desire to squeeze your platoon into the same area my platoon is already using?

"I don't give a tinker's damn what the major said. Give me one good reason why I shouldn't kick your ass back to your pinnace."

"Straight to business it is," he said dryly. "Somebody tried to attack one of my recruits and cut my platoon leader up in the barracks less than an hour ago. The intruder is dead, but I don't think that's the last of the matter. I had to get my recruits to a place where they wouldn't be easily accessible, and this station fits the bill."

Her already narrowed eyes closed until they were barely slits. "That's crazy. Who would attack a recruit, much less an officer in the middle of the marine base? Are you yanking my chain?"

Page shook his head and sent her a still image from the scene he'd recorded through the feed from the barracks after the attack. It showed how the barracks had been shot up, Lieutenant Na receiving medical care, and the dead intruder.

Gunnarsdotter's eyes became slightly unfocused as she took in what he'd sent, and then the color drained from her already-pale face. She refocused on him, and there was a blazing fire in her ice-blue eyes.

"Why would anyone do that? That's insane."

"It's complex," he admitted. "The recruit in question is a refugee from the Singularity. I suppose there's nothing outrageously exceptional about that, other than the fact that she's genetically a member of one of their higher castes, tattoos and all. Someone wants to make absolutely sure that she doesn't graduate."

Gunnarsdotter blinked in shock. "Really? I don't know much about the higher castes inside the Singularity, but I know that Imperial law says they aren't even human. How could she possibly be a marine recruit?"

"Are we really going to have that particular argument?" he asked softly. "She's an eighteen-year-old girl. Were her genes meddled with? Absolutely. Does that make her a thing? No.

"Even if that weren't the case, she's received an Imperial dispensation to attend training. If she graduates, the emperor will make that permanent, and she'll be legally recognized as human. That's why someone wants to stop her."

Gunnarsdotter opened her mouth to say something but then closed it again. Her gaze became distant, and she began pacing, obviously thinking.

Page didn't blame her and actually admired that she'd taken the time to think about her response rather than just saying the first thing that came to mind.

She waved for him to take a seat, and he did so, his behind regretting it immediately. This might, in fact, be the most uncomfortable chair he'd ever sat in. Still, it was the barest hint of welcome, so he wasn't going to turn it down.

The woman paced for a full two minutes before she stopped abruptly and turned to face him. "Even if I accept that everything you've said is true, this comes back around to my original question. Who is behind this, and what do they have to gain?

"Even if they stop this recruit from graduating, it's not going to stop this kind of thing from happening in the future."

He shrugged. "The intruder was a marine. From what I understand, he worked in the supply section but was masquerading as a drill instructor. The little bit of information that I got from Lieutenant Na following the attack indicated that he was attempting to plant something in the recruit's wall locker.

"If I had to guess, drugs or other contraband. Something like that would get her kicked out. What I don't understand is why the guy went off on the LT when she confronted him. He was armed with a knife and a flechette pistol, and he wasn't shy about using either one.

"The LT was unarmed and took a pretty nasty gash in the confrontation. Unfortunately for him, she's a mustang and used to be the senior NCO in a combat platoon, and she was more than capable of handling herself.

"I'm not entirely certain how he ended up shot while she was unarmed, but I'm sure the details will become clear as Major Martelle gets to the bottom of things and sends a follow-up brief for us.

"And that, Senior Sergeant Gunnarsdotter, is why I needed to get my recruits out of the crosshairs, and this ended up being the easiest place I could find to make that happen.

"I apologize for my unexpected arrival, but I didn't know I was coming until I called for the pinnace. I didn't call ahead because I figured it would be easier to explain the circumstances in person."

The tall woman sighed and seemed to droop a little as the fight went out of her. "This isn't going to be easy. If we're going to have everyone working here simultaneously, we'll have to hot bunk. That's going to cause a lot of bad blood between your platoon and mine.

"Do your recruits know about the attack?"

"No, and I'm doing everything I can to keep them from finding out. All they know at this point is that I've decided that it would be good to shake them up by bringing them here. I'd appreciate it if you'd play along with that."

She nodded. "I'll come up with something similar to tell my people, but they're going to see your people as interlopers. We won't be able to keep there from being confrontations and tribalism."

Page scratched his chin thoughtfully. "Actually, it might be worthwhile to encourage that sort of thinking, at least a little bit. I understand that we don't want any serious fighting, but Recruit Tolliver is a controversial figure inside my platoon.

"She's found a single friend and a dedicated rival, but everyone else seems to be waiting to see how things shake out. This entire situation with your platoon might get them to pull together in the face of a hostile outside group."

The tall woman stared at him for a moment and then slowly smiled. "So you're saying that I should encourage a little competition between the platoons? That's going to involve some hazing, you know. And my people are good. They might just trounce yours."

"I think you might be surprised. I happen to have a few credits I'm willing to put on the line for them. Unofficially, of course."

"Done. Still, you might be right. The situation is going to force your people to pull together. It's also going to force my people to work harder, particularly if they think they have to compete with yours. The trick is going to be keeping things within manageable limits."

He started to say something, but she held her hand up. "Don't think this makes the situation acceptable to me. I'm still pissed at the disruption you've dumped in my lap, and I'm not certain that your assessment of this girl is accurate.

"Since you're shoehorning her into my training area, I need to make an assessment of her character. That means I'm going to test her in my own way, and you're going to let me do it."

He felt his eyes narrow. "What do you have in mind?"

She grinned like a shark. "Nothing that's going to hurt her. Much. I just want to judge her character and assess what kind of person she is. I might have to accept your people because the major said so, but this is my price. Are you going to pay it, or do we rumble?"

Frankly, he wasn't sure that she meant the fighting part metaphorically. Still, he had enough on his plate, and he wasn't going to make this more challenging.

"Deal," he said as he stood, extending his hand. "I look forward to seeing exactly what you have in mind. Honesty compels me to say that she's a *lot* faster and stronger than you'd expect. She's also smart and determined."

That was true enough, but he held back the information that

Tolliver had received training from Lieutenant Na, had knowledge of things that no other recruit would have a clue about, and had marine implants and a nanogenerator. Those were his aces, and he wanted to see how Gunnarsdotter responded to that kind of surprise.

And he wanted to win the bet.

"Excellent," she said, actually rubbing her hands together. "Let's get things in motion. I figure the best way to make this work is to split the bunk room in half and put your people on one side. That'll create a kind of no man's land between the two platoons, but it should also create some unit solidarity in both groups."

"I can live with that."

This was going to force his people to pull together. And, honestly, he was tired of some of the whining and sniping they were still engaging in. It was time they found an enemy to stiffen their spines.

The only casualty of this might be Tolliver. She'd either make new friends in the next few weeks, or this was going to be the end of her.

28

Peter rubbed his face tiredly as he leaned back in his office chair. What a stinking mess this had become.

"What do you mean they're not on the planet anymore?" he demanded.

Jomos gestured toward the ceiling. "One of my contacts in Fleet indicated that there's some kind of kerfuffle at the Fleet training orbital. It seems that an unexpected load of marine trainees has crashed their party.

"Since I can't find any information about where the target is, I believe they've moved the platoon to a location where they think that we can't reach them."

"Are they unreachable?"

"Not nearly as much as they might hope. We've got just as many contacts inside Fleet as we do the marines, so while it's not going to be simple to get someone on board that orbital, it's not impossible either. I do think this is going to make Lucinda's option a little bit less likely to succeed, though."

That was certainly true. An outright assassination directly inside a Fleet orbital with no obvious means of quick escape or evasion wasn't going to be the best solution to their problem. Luckily, that wasn't the only arrow that they had in their quiver.

"It looks like you're going to have to make a trip up there to at least start working with some of the individuals that can get access to the areas that the marine recruits will be utilizing.

"I'm not sure how simple it'll be to sabotage equipment that will affect her. I'd prefer to keep the death toll to a minimum, but if we can't narrow the attack down to the target, we're going to have to make this messier."

His lieutenant nodded. "I've been thinking about that, and it may not be as tricky as you fear. Each of the recruits is assigned specific equipment for their use. In this case, I'm thinking of vacuum suits.

"If she's working outside and something goes wrong with her suit, so long as we can engineer the event to happen when she's nowhere near rescue, she's going to die, and it won't affect anyone other than her.

"I'm not certain at this point that I need to be there, so I'd prefer to work through cutouts. If we're going to generate a larger incident —say, the crash of a pinnace—it would probably make more sense for me to be there because I can see some of our contacts wanting to back out of doing that kind of work."

Peter thought about the various options available to them through that kind of sabotage and slowly nodded. "If there's a change in plans, they might not be able to communicate with you down here without raising suspicions on their end. I want to keep the command-and-control loop as tight as possible for this operation.

"To do that, you'll need to go to the orbital. What's your plan for doing so?"

"The supply system would be easiest. While Fleet uses their own personnel to manage all sorts of things aboard that orbital, the delivery of supplies is still handled by civilians. Admittedly, they're trusted merchants but still civilians. A small fraction of them have existing relationships with the organization.

"If I need to get aboard the orbital, we have one of the merchants that deliver supplies there on our payroll, as well as somebody in the supply section. I'd have to be packed aboard a crate with life support and transferred aboard the station, where our inside contact would see that I'm extracted without raising any eyebrows.

"I'm certain an orbital of that size has places to put me that are out of the way. Once the contract has been executed, I can get out the same way."

Peter shook his head. "That's not going to work. They've already had one attack. If something happens in orbit, they'll lock everything down until they can figure out what happened.

"Once you get everything lined up to execute, you need to get out of there. We can't afford to have them capture you because it'll lead right back to the organization."

Jomos nodded. "When would you like me to leave, and how soon would you like the mission carried out?"

"As soon as possible. I'd imagine that the equipment will be scrutinized very closely, as these recruits are not used to working in a vacuum. Everything needs to look good for the first several excursions. Wait for them to grow a little lax before you initiate the sabotage.

"And be careful. We haven't got a choice about carrying out this contract, but I don't want to lose anyone. You're very important to the organization and to me. This job isn't worth seeing you apprehended or killed."

The burly man stood and grinned. "You can rest assured that I'll be gone before anyone has reason to be looking for me. I'll talk to my contacts tonight and see about getting ferried up to the orbital sometime tomorrow. With any luck, we can close out this contract in a week."

Peter didn't say anything as Jomos left his office, but he couldn't help but be concerned. There was more going on than met the eye with this entire thing. The fight in the barracks had unsettled him.

He still didn't know why their contact had resorted to violence in the first place, and once he'd done so, Peter didn't understand how the marine officer had been able to fend off an armed attacker when she was presumably unarmed.

At least a little bit of information had made its way back to him. The officer his contact had assaulted was female and had apparently confronted the contact in the act of planting the evidence.

It would've been awkward to have his man captured, but it wouldn't have led back to him or the organization. Not after all of the hard work that he'd done to make sure the man thought that he was working for an entirely different crime family.

Unfortunately, now that violence had been committed, everyone's nerves were going to be frayed. He wanted to get this work done sooner rather than later, but he wasn't going to take any unnecessary chances, particularly with one of his trusted lieutenants.

If anyone captured or killed Jomos, that would lead the authorities directly back to his organization and him personally. That needed to be avoided at all costs. Even if it meant that they had to wait until Tolliver was back on the planet.

He cradled his head in his hands and wished for the millionth time that he had never met that damned woman. Well, he had, and he still had to deal with her when this was all over.

He picked up his portable com unit and dialed a number from memory. When someone on the other end picked up, he allowed a wolfish smile to cross his lips.

"Adrian, it's Peter. I have something for you. Can we meet?"

* * *

It was late by the time Andrea and the rest of the recruits had eaten, and the drill instructors had escorted them to where they'd be sleeping. To her surprise, the room was relatively small and didn't seem to have enough bunks. Every one of the recruits already there was glowering at her and her platoon mates.

"Listen up, recruits," Page said. "As marines, we often have to do things that force us to improvise. This is one of those situations for you.

"At this time, we only have enough bunks for half the platoon to be asleep at the same time. That means hot bunking. The same will be true of the recruits already here for training."

The man half turned to the hatch, just in time for an Amazonian blonde female senior sergeant wearing a drill instructor's hat to step into the compartment. Based on how the other recruits snapped to attention, this was their senior drill instructor.

"This is Senior Sergeant Gunnarsdotter, and she's the senior drill instructor for the platoon you will be sharing space with. You will extend every courtesy to her that you would to any of your usual drill instructors. If she gives you an order, you will carry it out immediately. Is that clear?"

"Yes, Drill Instructor!" they all shouted.

The woman took a single step forward and glared at the recruits on her side of the bunk room. "And the same is true of you when Senior Sergeant Page gives you an order. Is that clear?"

The other recruits shouted their understanding. That didn't do a single thing to tamp down the hostile looks that they were still shooting toward Andrea and her platoon mates.

"There are going to be limited training resources as well as sleeping accommodations," Page continued. "We will work out a training schedule so that everyone can still accomplish everything they need to learn, but it's not going to be comfortable, and there's going to be friction. I expect everyone in this compartment to keep their irritation within acceptable limits.

"Now, since only half of the recruits can sleep at a time, we're going to split you up and move to around-the-clock training. When I call up your name, select a bunk, and get some sleep. If I don't call your name, step over to the side of the compartment and get ready to have a very long night of learning the basics of vacuum safety."

Even as he was reading names off from memory, Drill Instructor Gunnarsdotter was doing the same. That was going to make the other platoon even crankier. Why couldn't they just hot bunk everyone so that the platoons were kept working as a single unit? It seemed as if they'd picked the worst possible solution to the problem.

That made her wonder if the choice was intentional. If they were avoiding the easy answer, then there was something about it that wasn't optimal. Or splitting up the platoons would produce something else that they wanted.

Were they looking to generate conflict between the recruits? She supposed it was possible.

In the end, her name wasn't called, so she wasn't going to get any sleep tonight. Neither were Diana or Claudio. Perfect.

Andrea started to file out of the compartment as Page gestured for them to do, but he quirked a finger in her direction and pointed at the tall, blonde drill instructor.

"Tolliver, I want you to accompany Drill Instructor Gunnarsdotter. She has some questions for you, and I expect you to cooperate fully, except where you cannot do so due to the information being classified. I expect you to be as forthcoming and cooperative as you can possibly be."

Well, that was great. Now she had to go with the strange drill instructor and be grilled about her background again. This would happen when she graduated and was assigned to a unit too. Everyone would want to know about her and her background. Again and again for the rest of her life.

She braced to attention and waited for the strange drill instructor to send her people out into the corridor and followed as directed. The strange recruits were all looking at her with rising suspicion.

Her tattoos had been unusual, she supposed, but now they knew there was something different about her, and people always hated or feared anything different. That was one of the sad parts of being human.

It seemed that it would be her continual struggle to fight for acceptance. Well, if that was what it took to make it easier for the next person from the Singularity, then she'd fight. Hard.

Gunnarsdotter led her platoon to what was obviously a massive airlock with both doors open. It filled the entire corridor. They all marched through it and into a wide area that held some cutters and other small craft.

The recruits didn't go toward any of the small craft but instead went to lockers and began pulling out vacuum suits. Another pair of drill instructors were already there and began inspecting the recruits as they dressed. Obviously, they still didn't trust that the recruits had the necessary experience to do the task correctly.

While that was going on, Gunnarsdotter gestured toward one of the cutters. "If you'll accompany me, Recruit, I have a few questions for you. Ones that I'm very interested in hearing the answers to."

The woman's tone didn't sound at all inviting. In fact, she sounded angry and suspicious. Did she have a grudge against people from the Singularity? From everything that Andrea had heard, there were going to be a lot of marines that felt that way. Yet one more hard fact of life that she was just going to have to live with.

"Yes, Drill Instructor," she said morosely.

With that, Andrea walked up the ramp and prepared to be interrogated. Again.

29

Fei was exhausted by the time the military police finished questioning her, and she'd gone back to the medical center to get another session of regeneration done on her arm. It was now late in the evening, and she knew that her day wasn't anywhere close to being over.

She knew that because she'd just gotten a summons to Major Martelle's office. She'd only *just* gotten back to her own office.

Even though there was still a lot of work going on downstairs, she was able to leave the barracks by the back door without disturbing the crime scene. She still wasn't sure exactly what was going to happen there. The body of the intruder had been removed, but the wreckage remained.

How they planned to replace everything so that the recruits didn't notice that their belongings had been messed with, she didn't know. Everything was regimented inside the wall lockers, but each individual would remember the little details about their kits and the placement of their things.

Hell, even the way they made their beds would make it obvious to some that something had changed. It was a dilemma that she wasn't quite sure how to solve. Luckily, she had a couple of weeks to figure out how she'd manage it.

She passed a couple of armed marines stationed at the back door and returned their salute. Another pair was parked in front of the barracks to make sure that no one disturbed the crime scene. Not that she expected anyone to try now.

She made her way across the battalion area and into the headquarters building. The major's adjutant gestured for her to go right in, so she did so. That was when she got her first surprise.

Seated just off to the side of the desk was Earl Still Water. Based on the half-empty tumbler of brown alcohol sitting at his elbow, he'd been there for a while.

He gave her a grin as she came in and a small wave of his hand.

"Have a seat, Lieutenant," the major said with a tired-looking gesture of his hand. "Serve yourself a drink if you like."

As an enlisted person, she'd never have been so bold, but it had been one hell of a day.

She walked over to the small bar set in the corner of the major's office, selected something that looked good, and poured herself a double. She wasn't going to allow herself to get drunk, but she certainly felt the need to unwind just a hair.

Then she took a seat next to the earl. "I see you've met my sponsor, sir. At least, I suppose that's the right word. The man who recruited me for this mission."

The major nodded. "The earl and I have been talking about the situation while we waited for you to finish your treatment. He's given me the same information you have but provided a bit more detail in some areas. I now feel that I understand the situation a little bit better.

"That doesn't make it any easier to solve, mind you. Just because I know who is here and why they want to stop Recruit Tolliver from graduating doesn't mean that I can keep them from doing so. At least it gives me all of the data I need to disregard any feints like this planting of drugs if that happens again."

She took a sip of her drink and nodded in appreciation at the smooth burn of the alcohol. "And we know for sure that it was drugs?"

Martelle nodded. "I'm given to understand that it's a common drug for people who want to excel in physical matters. It also has the side effect of making the user euphoric. As drugs go, it's not terribly addictive, but it would've been more than enough to get a recruit kicked out the door without any question."

"As opening sallies go, it was fairly pedestrian," the earl said. "Frankly, I can't see this as what Countess Dayton had in mind. She seems much more the bloodthirsty sort, and I can't see her being that subtle. This had to be the work of an intermediary that she hired."

"Have you had any luck in locating her or determining who she hired?" Fei asked.

"Sadly, no. She's concealed herself in a surprisingly effective manner. I'm not even sure what city to look in. As flamboyant a personality as she is, I'd have expected her to be at one of the most luxurious hotels, sequestered in the penthouse suite. Yet she's nowhere to be found.

"That doesn't mean that we're not going to have any luck in finding who she's working with, though. I have Riggio looking at the intruder's communications devices and computer.

"He's very competent at that sort of thing, as you well know. If there's anything to be found, he'll find it. The only thing that I'm uncertain of is whether he'll do so in time to stop them from trying again."

"Senior Sergeant Page moved the recruits up to the orbital that we use for space operations training," Martelle said. "It's causing a bit of a crowding issue and some grumbling from the other senior noncommissioned officer there, but it's going to keep Tolliver out of easy reach.

"Still, we're being careful because they managed to get someone on the base to do their dirty work. There's no guarantee that they're not going to try again with something a little bit more serious. It wouldn't take much of an accident in space to end up with a lot of dead recruits. I want to avoid that outcome at all costs."

Fei nodded. "So do I. Are they going to be able to shield them?"

"I have complete confidence in Senior Sergeants Page and

Gunnarsdotter. They are aware of the danger, and they're watching everything like protective mother bears.

"That said, I want to know who's responsible for actually carrying out these attacks, and I want them stopped. That's beyond the purview of the Imperial Marines unless someone authorizes me to drop a platoon into their laps, but I'd imagine that's something that His Excellency here can handle without any problem."

Still Water smiled coolly. "I believe I can work with the local authorities once we determine who the responsible party is. That said, I'm not going to rule out the need for a platoon of marines. I'm an inclusive sort of fellow, and I'd like to give everybody a chance to get some back for the blood that was spilled.

"Unfortunately, I'm not certain how easy that's going to be. Riggio may get lucky, but these seem like the kind of people who cover their tracks. We'll probably be able to determine their identities, but I wouldn't count on it happening in time to do us any good."

"Then what do we do?" Fei asked, almost growling in frustration. "You knew up front that Dayton was going to try something, and yet you had to let her make an attempt. Well, this was her free swing."

The noble turned to face her and gave her an expression of sympathy. "I understand how frustrating this is. I've got agents all across this planet doing their absolute best to locate her. If they do, I'll pick her up and put her in a box to question her.

"Unfortunately, that does nothing to stop the events already in motion. We have to fight this war on two fronts. One of those deals with Countess Dayton and the other one with protecting Andrea.

"I'm counting on you to work with Riggio and be the face of the efforts here on the planet. When we locate any information that gives us an angle to investigate, I want you front and center. With the major's permission, of course."

Martelle nodded. "Of course. When might we know what your man has found?"

"As soon as he tells me anything, I'll pass that information directly to you."

As soon as he finished speaking, the earl's eyes became slightly unfocused. "And I believe this is him calling now."

Fei sat quietly, watching as the man took the call, and took another sip of her drink. She wasn't sure that it was relaxing her, but it wasn't hurting.

After about thirty seconds, the earl's focus on the room returned, and he smiled. "He was able to find specific records inside the man's computer and some deleted communications on his com that give us a motive for his actions and *may* point us toward the intermediary party.

"It seems that our wayward supply specialist had a hefty gambling debt to a local crime syndicate. Someone from that syndicate forgave the debt in exchange for planting the body wash. Perhaps that explains why he felt the need to attack you, Lieutenant Na. Failure would've meant that he still owed them."

"What do we do with this information?" she asked.

"If you're feeling up for a trip, I'd like you to change into civilian attire and accompany me. It seems that we're going to a gambling den."

* * *

PAGE WAS MORE than a little concerned about how Gunnarsdotter would treat Tolliver, but his worry seemed misplaced as the girl showed no signs of distress once the meeting between the two concluded.

He was already putting his people through the introductory safety briefing for vacuum operations. It quickly became apparent that the girl was basically competent in vacuum operations and had a fair bit of familiarity with the gear used in space.

That would be useful at this stage of training because having a few recruits who knew what they were doing would make things safer for everyone.

He could see that her knowledge of the gear had not gone unnoticed by the other platoon. The more they took in of his platoon, the more their ire seemed to focus on Tolliver. That was interesting but not completely unexpected.

No matter where the girl went, she was going to face discrimination and hatred. In a way, it was similar to the racism that had plagued prespaceflight Terra. That had mostly ceased once the human race had moved to the stars, but it had never entirely disappeared.

Even after spreading to thousands of worlds, humanity still had quite a lot of variation in how it looked, but there was enough of a mixture that various genetic traits could pop up almost anywhere these days.

Maybe one day, humanity would be truly one, but it wasn't today.

Once the recruits were thoroughly engaged in suiting up for their first vacuum test, he sidled over to Gunnarsdotter. She was watching her people just as closely as he was watching his.

"Since both of you came out minus bruises or cuts, I'm going to assume that the conversation didn't go too badly," he ventured.

The blonde sniffed and didn't even glance in his direction. "She's more complicated than I expected. She talks a good game, but I'm going to have to see how she behaves before I can make up my mind for sure.

"I can understand why someone who doesn't know her might be inclined to make sure that she never becomes a marine. Those tattoos give me chills. Do you have any idea why she didn't have them removed?"

"Apparently, once the tattoo is applied, it becomes part of the genetic code of the affected skin cells. She'd have to literally have her face removed and regrown without a template.

"Hell, I'm not even convinced *that* would work. It's possible it's not just ink. The tattooing process might've also altered the entirety of her DNA to make that part of who she is."

The tall marine nodded. "I half expected something like that. I wonder what the Singularity will do once they figure out she's on the loose. They'd be furious if anyone managed to collect a genetic sample from their higher orders, much less their ruling caste. I can't imagine what their reaction will be once they learn that we have what amounts to a defector among us."

"Not a defector," he disagreed. "A castoff. Someone that didn't meet their standards. That's got to be a double insult. Not only does the

Empire have their hands on someone that's partially trained in their ways and has their complete genetic profile, but this is someone that they see as having been fatally flawed. Someone who should've been culled."

The woman partially turned to face him, still keeping her eye on the recruits. "Do you think that's sufficient to spark a cross-border incident or maybe even something more? Would they go to war over her?"

Page shrugged. "I don't know. I suspect they'd rattle sabers at a minimum, and demand that she be turned over to them. If she was still considered property in a legal sense, I'd imagine some Imperials would even consider doing it.

"If she makes it through training and receives a permanent dispensation, though, that's going to be a real stick in their eye."

Gunnarsdotter chuckled. "It's not like they've lacked reasons to go to war. The Singularity and the Empire don't mix. If either one of us comes up with even a half-assed excuse, we'll fight. Do you think the girl will make a decent marine?"

"You mean if she passes?"

The woman snorted. "Barring some kind of accident, she's going to pass. That's not a judgment based on her genetic enhancement but on her willpower. She won't give up, and that's the key to success in basic training. At least as long as you're not stupid, and she's far from that.

"There's still two months to go, but if she's made it this far, she's going to make it all the way. Once she gets into ground operations and starts working on the equipment that she's already had some training on—and don't think I didn't notice that she's done vacuum work before—she's going to continue to excel.

"How much does she know, and how did she learn it?"

"She was rescued during a raid, as I expect she's told you. Two of her guardians are former marines. One was the senior NCO of a combat platoon. The other was the platoon's officer.

"Both of them have been training her on and off for the last six years in marine operations and equipment. She probably knows as much about our equipment as someone who's already graduated.

Perhaps even someone who's been through advanced individual training just before their first assignment."

Gunnarsdotter considered that and then slowly nodded. "Then she's *definitely* going to make it. We need to take that into consideration when we perform more training. Put her under more stress by making her teach the others and forge some kind of alliances inside your platoon."

"We?" he asked, raising an eyebrow.

She smiled slightly. "I might have found myself somewhat invested in this process. I understand that I'm only going to be part of what happens here on the orbital, but I like her. That's actually kind of surprising because I don't like very many people, particularly recruits. She knows what she wants, and she's willing to fight to get it. I can appreciate that.

"I remember you said that she had a friend and an enemy inside your platoon. Have you considered how to cause the platoon to gel a little bit more tightly around her?"

"Do you have something in mind?"

"Make her a squad leader. Put both her friend and her enemy inside the same squad. As my platoon puts pressure on yours, they're going to grow to rely on one another more closely, and she's either going to excel in the role or fail completely. Either one of those outcomes will tell us something about her."

He'd actually been thinking of doing something like that already, so it was an easy choice to make.

"I'll do it. I can't imagine that's going to make Recruit Baker happy, but that's a just punishment in its own way. The boy has an attitude that I'd like to see broken."

"Which one is he? I might be able to help you with that."

Page smiled as he pointed Baker out. "I'm intrigued. Tell me more."

She started outlining a plan for getting his platoon more fully integrated while having her people lean in on the browbeating. It was audacious and perhaps a bit more aggressive than he'd have preferred, but he liked it.

Which meant that the recruits would hate it.

30

ndrea was exhausted by the time she got to her bunk, but sleep was short-lived. She felt like she'd only been asleep for a few seconds when someone shook her awake. It was Diana.

"We've got trouble," the girl said grimly.

She swung her legs out over the edge of the bunk and hopped down to the deck. With her enhanced musculature, the landing was no problem. She was only dressed in her underwear, but almost a month's worth of showering in mixed company had helped them all deal with any lingering body modesty issues.

It only took a few seconds for her to blink the sleep from her eyes and walk around the wall lockers and see what the trouble was. There was an argument taking place in the no man's land between the two platoons. She didn't recognize any of the people from the other platoon but had no difficulty seeing who was causing the trouble on her side.

Of course it was Claudio.

With a sigh of resignation, she headed straight for the troublemaker. He was in someone's face, waving a finger around under their nose in a way that would've gotten it broken if it had been her, yet the other person—a boy somewhat shorter than him but wider by half—simply smirked at him.

That was probably the worst approach to take with Claudio. He liked being the smug guy in the room, and having someone else do that to him had to burn.

She stopped a couple of steps away from the argument and put her hands on her slender hips. "What's going on here? People are trying to sleep."

That wasn't true anymore. They were all up and gathering to see the confrontation. No matter how this turned out, this was the flashpoint that she'd been dreading. She had to defuse it.

The other boy turned to face her, and his expression darkened. His smirk was replaced with a look of disgust.

"Well, look what the cat dragged in. We were just talking about you, genie. I was explaining to your boyfriend here why you didn't have a place inside the Imperial Marines and that you'd best be careful because your inexperience with vacuum gear could lead to accidents, if you know what I mean."

As threats went, it wasn't the worst she'd ever heard, though it wasn't that imaginative. What put her off her stride was the fact that Claudio seemed to be disagreeing. That *couldn't* be right. She was missing something.

She turned to face him, holding up a hand to silence her foreign detractor.

"What? *You* disagree with him? Am I still asleep, and this is some kind of dream? Someone pinch me."

The look Claudio gave her implied that she was four years old and stupid to boot. "I agree with every single thing he says, but he doesn't have the right to say it. That's *my* job."

"So you two are fighting over who gets to insult and degrade me? Neither one of you feels any disagreement with what you're saying, but you're going to wake up everyone because the guy outside the platoon isn't allowed to say those things and steal your thunder?"

"You're damned right," Claudio agreed with a half snarl and a rude gesture toward the other guy. "You might be a bitch, but you're *our* bitch. He doesn't get to talk about anybody in this platoon like that, not even you."

Andrea started to tell him that that was the stupidest thing that she'd ever heard, but Diana put a hand on her shoulder, leaned in close, and whispered into her ear, "Let him do this."

With her mouth still open, Andrea turned to face her friend and saw her resolute expression. She had absolutely no idea why Diana would want to see this continue, but she already knew that she had a weakness with interpersonal relations. Maybe something was going on that she just didn't get.

Instead of arguing, she threw up her hands in a gesture of surrender and stepped back. "Okay. I'll let you two settle your business. Whoever wins can keep insulting me, and the loser has to go back to his bunk with his tail between his legs. Have fun, boys."

The two of them turned back and resumed their argument. Yep, this was definitely the stupidest thing that she'd ever seen in her entire life.

"This is a *huge* breakthrough," Diana whispered in her ear. "Claudio doesn't like you any better than he did before, but he's associating you with the platoon and defending the platoon. He might not like you, but he's not going to let anyone outside it trash talk you. That's an incredible step forward."

"Maybe," Andrea said, unconvinced. "Right up until the point they start throwing down on one another, then this turns into a brawl, and we're all in deep, deep trouble. Why doesn't Claudio just let the guy come at me? It seems like he'd *want* to see the other guy try to take me down."

"It's because he wants to do it himself," JR said, stepping up on her other side. "If he lets this loser cut onto his turf, he loses control of winning the thing he's got going with you. He's not going to do that. So, as weird as this seems, he's got to defend you so that he can be the one to beat you."

"That's… crazy."

"If you were expecting Claudio to make sense, you haven't been following along with the rest of the audience. He's one of the most bigoted, self-important, egotistical jackasses I've ever met. He literally does think that everything revolves around him.

"What I don't think he realizes is the awkward position this is going to put him in tomorrow. No matter how this fight comes out, he and you are going to be closer than you were before. He's allowed a crack in his armor, and it's something that you can exploit if you do it right."

"Why are you helping me?" Andrea asked. "You're his friend, and I'm pretty sure that you don't like me any better."

"Eh, I'm not that bad. My feelings are a little muddier, but you're growing on me. Like a fungus."

Andrea laughed in spite of herself. The joke was just so unexpected. Almost as surprising as the admission that she was wearing him down. The idea of having done so was thrilling because it was what she'd wanted so badly to happen.

She was still trying to figure out how to respond when the fight finally broke out. She caught the first movement out of the corner of her eye as the unknown boy tried to kick Claudio in his junk, but as she personally knew, the ass was much better at hand-to-hand combat than he let on.

He grabbed the boy's leg, heaved it high into the air, and planted a kick of his own in the boy's torso, sending him flying back into a group of his friends, who all went crashing into one of the bunks.

"Uh-oh," she said under her breath as they *all* climbed to their feet and started forward. Even those that hadn't been involved in the fight were now stepping up to join their comrades, and she could hear her platoon gathering with a low growl.

If she didn't act *right this very moment*, there was going to be a monstrous brawl, and every single last one of them was going to be in deep trouble.

"You heard Andrea," Diana roared. "Nobody attacks one of our people! Get them!"

Shocked at the unexpected betrayal, Andrea was swept forward as her platoon charged. She had no choice but to block the first swing that came her way and gave in to her frustration by kicking the woman square in *her* junk.

And with that, the riot was *on*.

* * *

FEI WASN'T sure what to wear when meeting a crime family, so she decided to go with something severe and black. It would suit her scowl that way.

She met Still Water downstairs, where an air car had landed to pick them up. He nodded approvingly and gestured for her to climb into the back of the vehicle. When she was securely strapped into the luxurious car, he climbed in beside her, and it quickly took to the air as he secured himself.

"So, what's our plan, and exactly who are we dealing with?"

"The Mackie family is one of the premier criminal organizations on New Dallas. Honestly, I'm not certain why they would've gotten involved with this because that's not their strong suit, to go with a gambling metaphor. I won't be at all surprised if we find out that this is some kind of misdirection."

"Then why are we going? Simply to rule them out?"

He grinned at her as he opened the small built-in bar between them and the driver's compartment. He selected a dark bottle and poured them both a small amount before putting it away and handing her a glass.

"We're going to confront them as if they're the ones responsible, and then I'm going to have them use their resources to figure out who we should *really* be talking to.

"They'll want nothing to do with anyone from the Imperial Department of Justice—which I'll be masquerading as. In fact, they'll do *everything* in their power to make sure that we don't take a *very* close look at everything they're doing.

"They might have the local police paid to look the other way, but if I send a team to tear them apart, they're going to be very, very sorry."

"And what part am I playing in this?"

She took a sip of the drink and found it was a smooth but sweet liquor. She wasn't sure if she'd like it, but she wasn't going to turn it down either.

"Oh, you can be yourself. Tell them that since this was an act against the Imperial Marines, you're here to get a good look at everyone responsible. Add that if you determine that they're behind this, you've been authorized to put all of their facilities on the Imperial blacklist so that no military personnel will ever use them again."

That was actually a pretty severe threat. Military personnel were a significant percentage of the patrons to many businesses designed to separate them from their pay, including gambling dens.

Marines loved to bet money. Sadly, they were also very good at losing it. Being blacklisted would have a measurable impact on the crime family's bottom line.

"How are you planning on getting in to see someone in charge? Are you proposing that we just waltz in the front door and demand to see the boss?"

He grinned toothily at her. "That's *exactly* what I'm going to do. I'd imagine that it's not going to happen immediately, but rest assured that the process is going to be enjoyable for both of us."

"Are you expecting us to be in any danger? This is, after all, a criminal enterprise."

He shook his head. "I can't imagine them going after anyone that publicly. The last thing they'll want is a scene, particularly one with an Imperial noble present.

"But I'm not actually going to be doing most of the talking. I'll kick the door open, but I want you to do the grilling. You're actually much more intimidating than I am, and I plan to use that to our advantage."

She was still considering how that would work when the air car landed in front of a bright casino filled with well-dressed people. A uniformed woman immediately raced to the side of the vehicle and opened the door for her.

Well, she'd just have to figure it out on the move.

"Shall we go inside and see what kind of damage we can do to the house?" she asked Still Water with a grin.

31

Page had been asleep when the riot broke out, so it took him a couple of minutes to get himself in order and get to the bunkroom. The drill instructors who'd been training the recruits in the small craft bay had responded to the fighting, but they'd made errors.

First, they hadn't kept their group of recruits separated, so as soon as they saw that there was fighting, they broke ranks and joined in to assist their comrades. That only made the situation worse.

He arrived on the scene at the same time as Senior Sergeant Gunnarsdotter, and they waded into the fighting, separating the two sides.

A quick scan of his people showed injuries ranging from cuts and bruises to sprained limbs and the occasional broken bone. Nothing life-threatening.

He'd known that there would be a fight, but he'd expected it to be something less all-encompassing. Now that they had the situation under control, he had to figure out what had sparked the raging bonfire. Then he'd have to deal with the causes.

Luckily, just like the barracks down on New Dallas, everything here was monitored. He was able to access those feeds and scroll back to when Recruit Baker and one of the recruits from the other platoon had gotten into an argument.

He should've known that boy was involved.

With the volume they were shouting, it wasn't difficult to discover that the argument was about Tolliver.

No surprise there. Baker had serious issues with Tolliver, and apparently so did the other recruit.

The ironic portion of this entire incident was that they were fighting over which one of the two should put Tolliver in her place.

Morons.

Sometimes, recruits just didn't make that much sense to him anymore. Any pair of ordinary people would've decided to work together, but no, these two had to fight it out to see which one had the *privilege* of crushing Tolliver under his heel.

As if she'd been all that crushable to begin with.

The real excitement came when Tolliver joined the conversation. She started off—to her credit—by trying to break up the fight. Unfortunately, she ended up throwing her hands up in disgust and allowed them to figure it out themselves.

He supposed that she really hadn't had that much of a choice. It wasn't like either of them had been disposed to listen to her.

When the first strike came, he was happy to see that it was the boy from the other platoon that swung first. Baker ably defended himself and kicked the boy back into his friends, which knocked over a whole pile of them. That got everybody on their feet and facing off in what was already bound to be a brawl.

There was still a moment where the situation could've been salvaged, and he saw Tolliver open her mouth to say something, but then Recruit Randall exhorted the platoon to attack in Tolliver's name because Baker had been attacked.

He stopped the feed and backed it up, listening to everything said as closely as possible. There was a lot of noise, but he clearly noted that Tolliver had said no such thing. In fact, the expression of horror on her face when her friend had started the riot in her name was priceless.

Page froze the feed there and considered. There was no telling what Tolliver had been about to say, and at this point, she might not even remember. Her actions had been hijacked by her friend, and she'd basically been shoved into the middle of the riot.

Randall had started the fight, but in the process, she'd bound Tolliver firmly to the platoon by forcing her to support Baker, at least so far as everyone else was concerned. If Tolliver was backing up her worst enemy inside the platoon, how could the platoon not support her?

It was *brilliant*.

It also broke so many regulations that he could barely count them. Sadly, he now had to be the bad guy and punish them for doing *exactly* what he'd wanted.

He left the rest of the drill instructors keeping the two groups separated and sought out Gunnarsdotter. He found her leaning against the wall in the corridor, rubbing her temples.

"So," he said in a drawl, "did the confrontation work out quite the way you'd expected?"

The look she shot him was filled with tired disgust. "No. I expected there to be a little bit of pushing and shoving, not an all-out war. Now I'm going to have to start punishing people that I don't want to see kicked out of training. This is a nightmare."

He leaned up against the wall beside her and scratched his chin. "Nobody on my side was seriously injured. A couple have some fractures but nothing the medical center can't handle.

"I've reviewed the recordings, and I have to say things didn't play out *quite* the way I expected either. As we'd planned, Tolliver was the ignition point, but she didn't actually get involved in the fighting or encourage it until she had no choice.

"Ironically, it was her friend that shoved her into the center of things in such a way that it pulled my entire platoon together. I'm both horrified and impressed."

Gunnarsdotter nodded. "I saw that. That was a really insightful thing she did. As long as Tolliver keeps her mouth shut, she's bound to the platoon, and they're bound to her. That part worked out really well.

"Unfortunately, we can't let this riot pass without punishing people. Exactly how do we do that without permanently impacting them?"

He smiled. "I've got a few ideas. We've had them living side by side, but in retrospect, maybe that's not the best idea. Perhaps it would be better to have one platoon off training while the other sleeps and then switch them out."

The other drill instructor nodded. "That'll prevent future fighting, but what do we do about what's already happened?"

"I don't think there's any need to drag officers into this. We can handle this all on our own. I suggest that we do this."

He leaned over closer to her and explained his plan in greater detail.

She listened and slowly began to smile. "You know, that might actually work. They won't like it, but I think you've found probably the best way to handle it. I look forward to seeing how it turns out.

"I'll have to come down like the wrath of God on my people, but they need to know that other marines are still marines. They have to find a way to stick together."

"Agreed. Time to go make everyone *very* unhappy."

* * *

BECAUSE OF HER skill at hand-to-hand combat, Andrea hadn't been in any real danger during the fight. That hadn't kept her from getting hurt because she couldn't keep her attention in every direction she needed to be looking and still protect her platoon mates.

She'd been kicked and punched and even thrown, though she hadn't been seriously injured. The worst she'd suffered had been a couple of minor cuts and a lot of bruising.

Even though they were all in tremendous trouble, she'd had a blast. She'd never fought in a mass combat situation before and had found it exhilarating. It had been totally different than any kind of sparring she'd ever done.

Even so, her enthusiasm vanished as soon as she and the rest of the platoon were lined up against the bulkhead, eyes forward as Senior Sergeant Page stopped in front of them.

"I cannot *believe* the gall of you recruits," he shouted. "What in the universe makes you think that it's acceptable to brawl in my bunk room? Worse, to fight another platoon?"

He turned on his heel and pointed at them, running his finger down the line until each and every one of them had seen him looking into their eyes with condemnation.

"It's a bloody *miracle* that no one was seriously injured. By all rights, I should throw every single last one of you out of my beloved Corps. Have you no dignity? Have you no common sense? Where is your esprit de corps?"

He threw his hands up into the air and resumed stalking back and forth. "Who am I kidding? You people have no idea what esprit de corps is, and you have no sense of identity.

"About the only positive thing I can find about this sorry affair is the fact that at least you were defending one of your own, even if him getting into an argument like this was a disgrace.

"Let that be a lesson for you. No one can control stupid. The best you can do is try not to get any on yourself. And in this case, you have each failed."

Page pulled his hat off his head and rubbed his hand across his short hair. "There are going to be consequences that none of you are going to like. I came into this with the expectation that you could work with others, but you've proven me wrong, and that means that I'm going to have to be harder on you than I'd planned.

"As of right now, you can't stay in the same bunk room as the other recruits. The other platoon will work and train together while you sleep, and then you'll do the same. That means that at no time will you be sharing training space or bunkroom with the other platoon. That's going to make life more difficult for me, and I'm going to make it more difficult for you.

"The first thing that happens is that I'm firing the acting squad leaders. They should've been front and center, making sure this brawl never happened.

"Second, it's time to single out the people of note in this fight. Let's start with Recruit Baker. Front and center, Recruit."

Claudio stepped forward and stood at attention in front of Page. If he was frightened, Andrea couldn't tell.

"I want you to explain yourself, Recruit. Tell me exactly how this fight started and what the cause was. Save your justifications and just give me the facts."

"I was arguing with one of the other recruits about Recruit Tolliver, Drill Instructor. We shared a negative opinion of her, but he thought it was his place to pit himself against her. I disagreed. He swung at me, and I kicked him back into his friends. That's when the fight started."

Andrea blinked in surprise. That might *technically* have been when the fight started, but he hadn't mentioned anything about her instigating the general brawl. Not that she had, but that was what *everyone* else thought, since Diana had basically shoved her into it.

Should she correct the record? Just how much about the fight did Page know?

The drill instructor put his hands on his hips and shook his head disapprovingly. "So you couldn't be bothered defending your platoon mate? Why do you continue to feel the need to fight with Recruit Tolliver?"

"I've stated my reasons, Drill Instructor. She's not fit to be an Imperial Marine."

"What makes you worthier than her? You certainly haven't covered yourself in glory today. Did she start a brawl?"

Claudio opened his mouth to say something but then closed it. When he did speak, it was in a measured, clipped tone.

"No, Drill Instructor."

"Uh-huh. Get back in line, Recruit."

Page turned to look at Andrea. "Front and center, Tolliver."

She marched up in front of him and stood at attention, staring at the center of his chest.

He stared at her for a long moment and then shook his head. "You're coming into this training with a lot of things stacked against you, Tolliver. Why in the world would you order this entire platoon to attack?"

So he *had* known about the events that occurred during the

fighting, at least to a degree. Honesty was always the best policy, she supposed. Now he knew that Claudio had omitted some critical information.

Should she correct the record? Would it even matter? Since Diana had said that she'd said it, the effect had been the same. Her intent was almost irrelevant at this point.

"Once a group of recruits from the other platoon looked like they were going to attack Recruit Baker, it wouldn't have been right to just let them do so. We had to defend him. He's a prick, Drill Instructor, but he's *our* prick."

"While I laud the loyalty behind your actions, I cannot endorse the actions themselves," he said grimly. "What I will say is that you wouldn't have been in this position if Recruit Baker had shown any restraint whatsoever. Still, you displayed a serious lapse in judgment by starting a general fight."

The right thing to do would be to keep her mouth shut, but she'd never been any good at that. She was already in hot water, and this was only going to make it worse.

"What should I have done, Drill Instructor? I tried to talk the two of them out of fighting before it came to blows and failed. What was the correct course of action? We've never covered anything like this."

He stared into her eyes for several seconds without speaking before slowly nodding. "There is something to what you're saying. You haven't been trained in leadership techniques. We weren't expecting to need anything more than acting squad leaders, but it's clear that this platoon needs someone to direct it as a whole when the drill instructors are not present.

"That doesn't excuse you from the repercussions of ordering this platoon to attack, yet I think this can be turned into a teachable moment. If one wants to know what one does in a leadership position, the very best way to get that education is to be forced into the role.

"So, until relieved, I'm making you acting platoon leader, Recruit Tolliver. It's now *your* job to learn how to lead these savages. The drill instructors will educate you on this in addition to your other duties. Resume your place in line."

Andrea blinked in shock before she remembered to turn on her heel and march back to her place in line. What the hell was going on?

Page pointed at Claudio, Diana, and JR. "The three of you are now acting squad leaders. That makes you responsible for your squads, just as Recruit Tolliver is responsible for the platoon as a whole.

"I suggest the four of you examine the files that I'm about to send you and learn what you need to learn. You'd best make this work because their failures are yours. Is that clear?"

"Clear, Drill Instructor!" Andrea shouted.

What the hell had just happened? She wasn't cut out to be a leader. She was barely qualified to be here at all.

Yet what could she do? Page hadn't given her the option of declining, so she was stuck trying to make this work. Somehow.

She quickly checked the size of the file that he'd just sent her and almost groaned. There was a *lot* to learn and virtually no time to do it. She hadn't slept for more than an hour in the last full day, and it didn't look like she'd be getting any rest tonight.

32

As Fei walked inside the casino, she was struck by its opulence. The building and its contents seemed designed to exude an image of extreme wealth. She supposed she shouldn't be surprised. They wanted the patrons to feel as if they could win all of this for themselves.

That would be quite the trick. As any marine worth their salt knew, the odds always favored the house. If it seemed like you might just get ahead, there would be a hidden way for them to get your money.

"How do you want me to handle this?" she asked Still Water as she walked past a fountain shooting water high into the air while colored lights and lasers played over its surface, creating strange holographic effects.

"That's entirely up to you, but I'd recommend finding someone that looks like they work here and asking to speak with someone higher up. You're going to get some resistance, but if you say the right things, you'll get their attention, and someone will come looking for us."

Fei scanned the crowd without slowing down and spotted someone who looked like they were involved in security. At least the person was armed and dressed in a suit that didn't seem all that tailored for his form.

She changed course and walked right up to the man. "Pardon me, but you're security here, right?" she asked with a smile.

"Yes, ma'am. Can I help you?"

"My name is Lieutenant Na Fei of the Imperial Marines. I need to speak with someone about a matter regarding your operation and my marines."

He frowned, but it was only just enough for her to see a couple of wrinkles between his eyebrows. Whoever had trained him had done very well at showing him what needed to be done to minimize his responses. Frankly, she imagined he heard and saw any number of crazy things, so that was probably useful.

"You should probably call the corporate office and make an appointment," he said smoothly. "Management here is very busy."

She shook her head. "Let me be blunt. There was an incident on the base earlier today that resulted in a death. Evidence has come to light connecting that individual to the Mackie family and this casino. I'm hoping to figure out exactly what's going on before the higher-ups decide to blacklist this casino and the other Mackie family properties. I'd rather take care of this quietly and quickly."

The man considered her for a few long seconds. "May I see some identification?"

Since she was sure he'd have implants, she sent him her ID via implant com, which was exactly the same sort of thing as holding up a physical ID. She had a real ID if needed.

The man's eyes unfocused briefly, and he nodded. "Your identification appears to be in order, Lieutenant. If you'd wait over at the bar, I'll contact my direct superior and see if he wants to come to speak with you himself or contact someone higher up. I can't guarantee that anyone from management will speak with you, you understand."

"We can only do what we can do. Thank you."

Fei detoured to the bar the man had indicated with the earl on her heels. The two of them sat at a small table, and she ordered something nonalcoholic and fruity. He wasn't so restrained and ordered a pricey whiskey, paying for both their drinks.

"Do you think they're actually going to kick it up to someone inside the family itself?" she asked as she sipped the tart liquid.

"I do. The way you approached them was direct enough that they'll feel the need to let someone with actual authority make a decision. That doesn't mean they'll actually speak with us, of course, but I think they will."

"Any guide on how I should approach them about the attack?"

"Be direct, just like you're already doing. That's your strong suit, you know. If you try to be subtle, they'll wonder what's really going on because marines aren't typically indirect."

She chuckled. "You might be surprised. When it comes to fighting, marines can be shockingly subtle. Of course, they can also punch you in the face."

"A time for all seasons."

They sat there for about ten minutes before the man she'd spoken to walked up to their table with a short older woman at his side. She was dressed in business attire.

"Lieutenant Na," the woman said in a mellow tone. "My name is Leanna Mackie. Andrew tells me that you have a problem that you need to speak with someone in management about. Tonight, that's me. Would you care to come to my office, or is this something that can be discussed here?"

"I think it would be better if we went to your office," Fei said as she rose to her feet, finishing the last of her drink. "I'm afraid the details aren't exactly pleasant."

The woman turned and looked at Still Water. "Will you be accompanying us?"

The earl smiled slightly. "I believe it's probably best that I do. My name is J. Russell Macumber, Earl Still Water. I'm present in an official capacity."

The woman raised an eyebrow. "Even more curious. An Imperial noble of your standing and a marine lieutenant make an odd pair. Andrew, be a dear and call ahead to let them know that we're coming."

With that, the woman led them across the foyer and deeper into the casino. She veered away from the center of the large room and through a doorway mostly concealed behind a façade.

Once away from the glittering opulence, everything became very subdued. It was still well-built but no longer reeked of money.

The woman led them to a lift, which took them underneath the casino itself. It opened into a room with four more security officers who were openly armed.

"My associates will scan you for weapons," the woman said.

"I'm with the Imperial Department of Justice and must remain armed at all times," the earl said genially.

Fei wasn't armed, but she probably should've been. Something to bring up next time they confronted a crime family.

The woman pursed her lips. "I'll need to see your authorization and ID."

"Of course."

A few seconds later, the woman nodded. "Everything seems to be in order, so I'm not going to dispute your right to be armed. However, I will have my people scan you to determine what you're armed with."

Without waiting for a response, the four men closed in around them, and two of them produced scanner wands that they ran across Fei and the earl. Since his stunner was designed to be undetectable, she wondered what other weapons he had on his person.

In any case, moments later, the search was done, and the information likely relayed quietly to Leanna Mackie. She gestured for them to continue and led them into an area of what were obviously executive offices.

Seemingly at random, the woman walked through a door and nodded to an assistant seated at a desk. "We're not to be disturbed, Jimmy. Not unless the casino is burning down. Even then, I expect you to do your best to put out the fire before you call me."

The young man smiled and nodded without saying anything.

As soon as they were inside the office, the woman shut the door behind them and gestured toward a seating area off to the side of a rather large desk. "If you'll take a seat, I'll fix us something to drink while we speak.

"I believe you were having one of our top-line whiskeys, Earl Still Water, while you were having something nonalcoholic, Lieutenant. I'm afraid that I don't have anything nonalcoholic here other than ginger ale. Will that do?"

"I don't need anything," Fei said. "Thank you."

Unlike her, Earl Still Water ordered another drink. When the woman had poured for him, she sat in the chair nearby, crossed her legs, and raised one elegantly sculpted eyebrow.

"I understand that there was some kind of trouble on the base involving a marine or marines and my family. Perhaps you could explain the situation in more detail."

She was looking at Still Water, but he gestured to Fei. The woman tilted her head slightly and looked over at her.

"Unfortunately, some of the details are classified, but a marine on the base attacked me earlier today. I caught him trying to break into an area that he shouldn't have been in, and he tried to kill me."

If the news disturbed the woman, her expression didn't show it. "That's terrible, of course, but I don't see what that has to do with my family or this casino."

"The gentleman in question—Sergeant Evan Quint—didn't survive the encounter, but we've searched all of his communication and data equipment. We found some notes and messages. Those indicated that he had a substantial gambling debt here at this casino and that it was forgiven in exchange for him breaking into the area where the attack occurred."

That news made the woman frown more deeply, then her eyes unfocused briefly. "I just checked our records. The gentleman paid off his debt to us more than a week ago. He hasn't been into the casino since then."

"That would match up with the instructions he received which noted that his debt would be forgiven in exchange for the work that was done, but was banned from your properties," Fei said, crossing her legs. "He seemingly broke into a recruit's wall locker and planted drugs with the intent of having her banned from the Imperial Marines.

"If that information proves out, that's not only a crime that Earl

Still Water would be interested in but one that would cause the base to list all Mackie family properties as off-limits. As you might imagine, that would have a rather substantial effect on your bottom line."

The woman made an offhand gesture. "It would have an impact, yes, but it's not something that would critically injure our business. I'm not sure how I'm supposed to prove a negative, but we were not involved in this crime in any way.

"My family has been in the casino business for generations, and that's what we do. We have no reason to wish anyone inside the Imperial Marines harm. Far from it."

"Then someone is using your family as patsies. I'd imagine that you carry quite a lot of pull here on New Dallas. The list of people that would be willing to risk your wrath should be relatively small, I'd think. Whoever did it is willing to kill, after all.

"I suspect the drugs were their first foray, but it won't be the last. Now that their machinations are in the open, they're going to do whatever they have to to see that the recruit in question is eliminated. Permanently.

"So, while you can't prove a negative, you can find me someone that's more interesting to look at than your family."

The woman pursed her lips for a moment and then slowly nodded. "If someone attempted to use the Mackie family name like this, we'd be happy to assist the authorities in determining who they are. I'll need what information you can share to get some of my people on it.

"As it happens, we do have some knowledge of the various criminal organizations present on New Dallas. When one runs a casino, one has to do business with all sorts, you understand. Even upstanding people like the Mackie family."

Still Water smiled genially. "Of course. I'll be happy to give you everything we have on the attacker's identity and the communications and notes we've recovered. We don't really have much beyond that, but I'm confident that your contacts will be better than mine at figuring out who might have been interested in killing someone on the base.

"I'd ask that you expedite your inquiry because if another attack takes place before we have a better suspect, I'll have to send people to look through your systems myself. That would be *tremendously* disruptive for both your business and your clients. Personally, I'd prefer to avoid that."

The woman's gaze hardened. "As would we. Unfortunately for you, the information you have is insufficient for an Imperial warrant. You'd need significantly more than hearsay to get access to our systems and personnel."

The earl's smile turned cool. "You're not the only one that has contacts in interesting places. If it makes you feel better to think that I can't get a warrant, then, by all means, drag your feet. Otherwise, I suggest you treat this as an extremely time-sensitive matter."

The three of them sat in silence for longer than was comfortable, but the woman finally rose to her feet, smoothing her skirt with her hands. "I'll need your contact information, and I'll see what I can find. Cooperation in this matter is likely better than taking chances or making threats. Personally, I'd much rather take my ire out on the perpetrators than bicker with you."

"I'll let you interface with Lieutenant Na," Still Water said urbanely. "Since the attack happened on the base, she's a better point of contact."

Moments later, Fei's implants pinged with an incoming communication bearing the woman's contact information. She filed it away and returned her own.

"I believe that concludes our business," the woman said. "You're welcome to remain at the casino, but I'm afraid that I need to begin making calls and asking questions."

Fei extended her hand to the woman. "I look forward to working with you."

The barest hint of a smile flitted across the woman's lips, and she returned the handshake firmly. "As do I. I've always liked marines. So direct and forceful. If someone tried to kill you and they ended up dead, you're someone worth keeping an eye on. Until we meet again, Lieutenant Na."

The woman escorted them back out to where the security man

waited. Minutes later, they were back in front of the casino, and their car was pulling up.

Fei started to say something as soon as they climbed in, but Still Water held up a hand. He then brought out a compact scanner and began running it over himself and then her.

She was intrigued. She hadn't seen an opportunity for the woman to have planted bugs or tracking devices on either of them.

The device beeped when he brought it over Fei's right sleeve. He ran across the area until he found something that he retrieved with a pair of tweezers—a tiny device.

He put that into a small container and put it into his pocket. Then he scanned the rest of the car and found two more devices.

Only when he'd gone back over everything did he pull out a jammer and activate it. That done, he smiled at her and settled back in his seat.

"It seems that we've garnered their interest," he said with a smile.

"They're welcome to look at me all they want, so long as they figure out who's trying to kill Andrea. I'll work with the devil to keep her safe. Do you really think they'll be able to find out who's behind this?"

"I wouldn't bet against them. They've got a lot to lose if things go badly. Now, I suggest that we get you back to the base. You were injured earlier, and you need your rest. Besides, there's no telling what trouble Andrea is up to now."

That was only too true.

33

Peter was growing concerned. It had been five days since Jomos had slipped onto the orbital, and he hadn't sent back a single word.

It was mildly vexing because now that he'd committed to doing the murder, Peter wanted it to be finished.

It was unlike Jomos to be so quiet. Yes, the man was thorough and knew that communications would be problematic, yet he could've gotten *some* word back. Something was wrong.

Once he couldn't take it anymore, Peter summoned Lucinda to his office to brainstorm what they did next. He was lucky she was in the city, since she'd spent the last few days working on her plan near the marine base.

She came in with a scowl and closed the door with just a little extra force.

"Is something wrong?" he asked, an eyebrow raised.

"Yeah, something's wrong," she said belligerently. "I got word that the damned woman is asking around about hiring some side muscle. So far, I've been able to warn anybody that's been inclined to accept her offer, but it's only a matter of time before she makes a connection that I'm not aware of with someone too stupid to know better.

"This has gone on long enough. We need to end her. She and this job have both become liabilities."

He sighed. "More than you realize. I haven't heard from Jomos in almost a week, and I'm getting anxious. Even if he isn't able to act, he should've sent word by now. His silence makes me wonder what's going on."

"You think they caught him?" she asked as she took a seat on the other side of his desk. "If the marines got their hands on him, he's not going to tell them anything, but he might lead them back to us once they identify him."

He shook his head. "I don't think they have him. It wouldn't take them this long to link him to our organization. Still, I'm not sure what's going on, and it's got me concerned.

"I understand that he probably wants to do things carefully, and that is his nature, but it's been five days. Even if he couldn't directly act at this point, there's no reason he shouldn't be able to get word back to us. Whoever smuggled him onto the station has to have the ability to send a message to us."

"Do we know who that is?"

"No. Jomos has always been very protective of his contacts, and I can't blame him. In our line of work, everyone has their secrets, and his contacts have always been reliable in the past. I'm not certain what's going on, but his plans have gone off the rails. We have to come up with something new, or we're going to miss this opportunity."

Lucinda considered his words with a frown. "I've been working on direct action once the girl is back on the planet, but I don't have the necessary resources to get onto that station. It might be best to wait until she comes back down on her own. If Jomos wasn't able to act, my shooter could take her out down here."

That was the plan that his junior lieutenant had come up with. Part of marine training was working in the wilds of the base to learn how to operate without advanced support.

While they were out there, the girl was vulnerable because it was easy to slip someone into an area like that as long as one took the proper safeguards. There wouldn't be any security checks preventing someone from crossing the base perimeter as long as one made certain that the monitoring and alarm systems weren't triggered.

"I don't think it's a good idea for you to try to attack her on the station," he agreed. "Proceed with your plan. How certain are you that they won't detect your sniper?

"They will have advanced military gear that can find a person using infrared in environments like that. Setting up sentries to look for intruders is likely one of the tasks that they're going to be training in, and we don't want to accidentally stumble right into them."

"I've already taken that into account. There are certain fabrics backed by technology that can block infrared and other scanners. Our sniper will use all of that to get into place and take the shot. Once that's done, he'll use the ensuing chaos to slip away."

He considered that and slowly nodded. There would be risks, of course, but if their man was cool, calm, and collected, there was no reason why he shouldn't be able to avoid detection.

"I'll still be worried until this is over," he continued. "Have your contacts heard any specific timeframe for their return?"

She shook her head. "They're just getting into the meat and potatoes of vacuum training, so it's going to be slightly more than a week, based on what I've heard. We won't know for certain until they actually move the platoon, so we're going to have to be flexible.

"But what about the woman?" she demanded. "We need to take care of her. Wouldn't it be better just to eliminate her now and not deal with trying to take out the girl?"

"Don't I wish," he grumbled. "I agreed to this contract, and we'll carry it out, but don't sweat it. I've already contacted someone to make sure that she has an accident on the way back to wherever she calls home.

"He'll shadow her on whatever liner or ship she takes. As long as it isn't a private ship, he'll be able to get on board.

"Hell, he might even be able to get on board a private ship. He's that good. In any case, she won't make it home, and her death won't be linked to us."

Lucinda nodded. "Good. I still wish we could take her out first, but knowing that she will be gone when we're done will have to be good enough. Who did you pick to take her out? That guy you have at the port?"

Peter shook his head. "No. I decided that we needed somebody with a bit more skill, so I contracted it to Adrian Bolívar. He'll make the magic happen and get paid well for his trouble."

Adrian was an independent contractor, and that kind of deniability would be worthwhile if things went badly. The man wouldn't rat out his employer even if he got caught, but Peter didn't expect him to get caught. He really was that good.

"He's a good choice," Lucinda said with an approving nod. "He'll get it done."

"Yes, he will. Now, get back to work so that we can get this damned job done."

Once she'd left, he turned in his chair and gazed out the window, brooding. Something was going on up there, and he didn't like being in the dark. What the hell was Jomos doing?

* * *

Andrea wanted to facepalm, but she couldn't because she was in a vacuum suit. She settled for shaking her head sadly as Claudio and JR fumbled trying to maneuver around the depressurized small craft bay aboard the station.

Unlike the docking tubes, the bay was meant to service pinnaces and cutters in an open environment that could be accessed from the outside via a large hatch that would slide aside after the bay had been depressurized.

The gravity could also be turned off, which had led to the current hilarity. She'd taken her eyes off of them for *two seconds*, and now they were both floating free of the deck, tangled in their own safety lines.

Unlike the rest of the recruits who had no experience in zero gravity, she could handle herself in the environment. She could also use a thruster pack, which meant that she didn't have to be tied down to anything in particular, so she used it to float into the general area around her wayward squad leaders, making sure to steer clear of their flailing limbs and the twisting lines. She had absolutely no desire to end up tangled in their mess.

"Stop moving," she ordered. "Seriously. Just stick your arms directly out and stop moving so that I can stop your rotation and try to untangle you. What the hell happened?"

"Genius over here decided that he could jump to the cutter," Claudio said, his tone accusatory. "Only he didn't figure out that his line was going to hit my legs, and that yanked me off the deck too."

"Well, you're both lucky that we're in the bay and not floating around on the outside. Something like this could've gotten you yanked off a ship and out into open space, even with safety lines. Those connectors are made to be tough, but you shouldn't risk jumping because the odds are good that you're going to miss. Save that for the experts."

"You mean like you?" he sneered.

"No, I mean like fully trained combat marines. Somebody who's gone through doing that kind of thing over and over for months at a time. I know just enough to make sure that I know when I'm about to screw up. Nothing that I've learned makes me an expert on anything. That will come when I've been a marine for a while."

She had to unclip their lines to get them clear but used a temporary line to secure them to one another. That would keep them from floating off separately, at least.

All of that took time, which meant that they'd floated up to the overhead by the time she'd finished getting them in order. There was still plenty of time to gently reorient them so that they all landed on their feet rather than their heads.

"Try to take the impact on your feet and collapse into the overhead," she ordered. "That way you're not kicking us back off. Once we've stopped moving, I'll get us headed back toward the deck."

To her surprise, they managed to land without bouncing. Looking down on all the secured small craft below and the rest of the platoon, who were slowly making their way out to the craft they were supposed to be working on, gave her just a hint of vertigo.

Luckily, she had enough training that it was only just a hint. Up and down were just suggestions in zero gravity, after all.

"You know, you're not nearly as much of a jerk as I thought you'd be," Claudio said.

Andrea had to stop what she was doing to make sure that she hadn't suffered some kind of stroke. "What? Who are you, and what have you done with Claudio?"

He laughed. "Don't get me wrong, I still don't like you, and I don't think that you're marine material, but I expected you to come into this with a real chip on your shoulder, being superhuman and all. I was wrong."

She bit her tongue to avoid snapping back at him. After all, if anyone had come into basic training with a chip on their shoulder, it had been Claudio.

Still, this was a little bit of a thaw in their relationship, and she didn't want to screw it up. She was going to have to work with people like him for years to come, and the fewer of them that thought she was an enemy to the Empire, the better.

"My tattoos don't define me," she said with a sigh. "I hate what they represent even more than you. If I could be sure that having my skin peeled off would get rid of them, I'd do it."

He didn't answer, but maybe that was a positive thing. Claudio wasn't exactly known for holding back on negative comments, after all.

"I think there's a hydraulic leak," JR said in an offhand tone.

Andrea turned to look at him and saw that he was looking at the maintenance access panel just off to their left. Some kind of reddish fluid slowly leaked out from under the panel's edge where one of the fasteners wasn't fully latched down.

"Good eye," she said. "Float here while I check it out. Once I identify exactly what's going on, I can let Fleet maintenance know."

She used her thruster pack to slowly edge to the affected panel. While she wasn't familiar with all of the markings, she thought that the barcode printed on the panel indicated it was used for the exterior hatch's mechanical parts.

Andrea hadn't realized that Fleet used hydraulics for something like that, though. That seemed awfully old-school.

Because the recruits were supposed to be doing maintenance work on the cutters—or at least popping open some hatches to check the gross appearance of some of the mechanical items—she had a tool that would open the panel.

It only took a few moments to loosen the panel enough to open it on its hinges so that she could look inside to see how bad the leak was.

The panel popped open, but instead of seeing a leaking hose, she was confronted with a far grimmer sight: the mottled face of a dead man. The maintenance compartment's interior was coated in blood. The "leak" was blood boiling from his slit throat in the vacuum.

The shocking sight caused her to violently flinch, and she spun away from the ceiling before she righted herself with her thrusters.

That elicited a derisive laugh from Claudio. "What's the matter, pumpkin? Fingers slip on the controls?"

She almost snapped at him but clamped her mouth shut. This wasn't the time for them to be sniping at one another.

Should she tell him what she'd found? Probably not.

"That's exactly what happened," she said in the calmest tone she could manage. She closed the access panel but only secured one of the latches.

"The damage in there is a lot worse than I thought it was going to be. Let's get back down to the rest while I report it. Frankly, I think it might be bad enough that they cancel our little outing today."

Even as she got them started slowly back down toward the floor, she changed her com to the command channel on which the drill instructors communicated. As the acting platoon leader, she had access, though they knew when she was patched in.

"Drill Instructor Page," she said in a flat tone, "we have a situation."

34

P age floated just beneath the maintenance panel in the boat bay and stared at the dead man. At first he hadn't believed Tolliver when she'd said she'd found a murder victim, but the evidence was irrefutable. Someone had killed him and then stashed his body here.

Recently, based on the amount of still-liquid blood where the body had been discovered. The vacuum conditions—which no longer applied since they'd pressurized the bay—had acted to draw much of it out from the body through the wound, and it had foamed over *everything*.

Gunnarsdotter floated next to him. "Do you think the cover story is going to hold?"

"I don't see why it shouldn't, at least in the short run," he said. "Other than Tolliver, nobody saw anything. If she keeps her mouth shut—which I see no reason that she wouldn't—then no one else will realize that something happened here.

"This guy doesn't look like Fleet or a marine. I can sense that he's got implants, but that's about it. They're shut down now that he's dead, but maybe the investigator they're sending up can dig more information out of him. At this point, I think it has to be something related to Tolliver."

The other marine rotated gracefully in place with the touch of a single finger to the ceiling. She stopped herself as soon as she was facing him and hovered there in the open space.

"That girl really has someone hot and bothered."

He didn't disagree.

The man was wearing what looked like a plain jumpsuit under all the blood. Maybe he was some kind of contractor.

"How long until the specialist gets here?" she asked.

"They said they were sending him express, but I'll check and see exactly what that means. No matter how long it takes, we're going to have to wait until he gets here to do anything else. Fleet was told to stand down and let him do the investigating, which has *them* hot and bothered."

Page brought up his internal com and sent a message to the Fleet control center, asking the investigator's ETA. A few seconds later, the response came back that a cutter was going to dock in less than ten minutes.

Whoever it was, they'd been in a damned hurry to get here.

Once they docked, he expected it would take the specialist at least twenty minutes to find their way to the bay.

He was wrong.

After just fourteen minutes, a young man in a marine utility uniform came through the airlock with a bag over his shoulder. He crossed the zero-gravity line smoothly and launched himself toward them without bothering to hook a line.

Page immediately recognized him as Sophia's brother, the one that worked for Imperial Intelligence. He supposed that meant he'd definitely have the necessary experience to do what needed to be done.

The young man floated through the air with a grace that only came from long experience operating without gravity. He came to a stop about half a meter from them with a gentle touch of his hand against the ceiling.

"My name is—" he started.

"Riggio Gomez," Page said. "We've never met, but I work with your sister."

The young man raised an eyebrow. "You must know her pretty well if you know me. Do you know what I do for a living?"

"I do, but my associate does not. This is Senior Sergeant Ingrid Gunnarsdotter, the lead drill instructor for the other marine platoon here on the station. Even though you're dressed in that uniform, I think we need to start off with the fact that you're *not* a marine these days."

Riggio grinned. "I happen to disagree. Once a marine, always a marine. I'm a retired senior sergeant, but don't let appearances fool you. I might work for Imperial Intelligence these days, but I'm not one of their lapdogs.

"I came from a combat platoon, and I'm a tech expert that's seen his share of dead bodies. I also happen to be assigned to help keep watch over Andrea Tolliver."

Gunnarsdotter shook her head. "How many people do they have watching that kid?"

"More than you'd guess, Senior Sergeant. And considering the number of dead people turning up, I can't exactly say they're wrong."

"Your sister is pissed that you're working on this and didn't tell her," Page said. "She saw you in the barracks feed, and I think she's going to want some words with you about not being up-front with her."

"Sophia is always looking for something she can yell at me about. I'll deal with her when this is settled. Right now, we need to focus on this guy."

Page gestured for the young man to continue. "I think this is probably a stupid question, but do you think the two incidents are connected?"

"Undoubtedly. I don't know who this guy is, but people don't just get killed and stuffed into a maintenance area by happenstance. I have no idea how he's connected to Andrea, but he is."

The young man brought out a small device and held it next to the man's head. "His implants are still active, but they aren't Fleet or marine versions. They're some kind of hopped-up civilian gear that's illegally encrypted. I might be able to get in, but I'm not going to be able to do it quickly. I might have better luck getting his identity through DNA, fingerprints, retinal patterns, or facial recognition."

While Riggio started doing his work gathering the data that they needed, Gunnarsdotter scowled at him. "You're calling Tolliver by her first name. Why?"

"When you fight shoulder to shoulder with somebody, you get familiar that way," the young man said without looking over. "I can't give you any information about how we met, but the kid's got guts, and she's smart. It's my job to make sure that nobody keeps her from succeeding if she's got what it takes to be a marine—which she does."

"He can't tell you who he is, but I can," Page said. "He's the former tech specialist in a combat platoon that went on a raid into the Singularity. The same one that recovered Tolliver. Apparently, they had to fight to get out, and most of them didn't make it. Tolliver said that she's killed people. I'll assume it was on that mission."

Riggio spared him a small smile. "It was one hell of a trip. We almost didn't make it back at all. We had about a squad's worth of survivors.

"I'm going to assume that she never told you the details because she swore that she wouldn't. That means that if you got any serious intelligence, it came from Lieutenant Na. She was our platoon sergeant back then.

"The kid held up under fire. She killed experienced Singularity boarding troops with a damn sniper rifle from the backside of engineering on the ship we were fighting on. You can think whatever you like about her, but don't mistake her for someone who won't do whatever it takes to win.

"Help me get this guy out of here so I can see if he's got anything in his pockets."

"Is there a reason that we don't have Fleet security here giving us a hand?" Gunnarsdotter asked as she grabbed the dead man by the sleeve.

"The person behind this is an Imperial noble, and we're trying to keep this quiet. We've already got the marine MPs involved, and they're going to be taking lead on this as soon as they get up here. They're probably an hour behind me. I just didn't want to wait."

Page used one hand to brace himself against the ceiling and helped the others tug the body out of its hiding place. Whoever had put the man in there had wedged him in pretty good, but he finally popped out.

The two drill instructors held the corpse while Riggio searched its pockets. He found nothing.

"Well, I suppose that shouldn't be a shock," Riggio said. "If somebody is going to go to the trouble of killing someone, they're probably going to make sure that they don't leave any evidence behind. I'll take samples now and see if I can identify him."

The young man pulled more equipment out of his bag and began scanning the man's prints and retinal patterns and took DNA samples. After only a few seconds, he nodded.

"Got a hit on his prints. Meet Jomos Carfio. He worked for some type of criminal syndicate down on New Dallas. I'll wager that's the same group that was responsible for the attack on the LT."

"So, if this is one of the bad guys, he was obviously up here to cause mischief," Gunnarsdotter said slowly. "Who killed him and why? Do we have more than one set of bad guys? Or was this one of the so-called good guys?"

Riggio floated a little bit away from the body and stopped himself with a touch to the ceiling. "If you're wondering if this was Imperial Intelligence, it wasn't. I have the lead on this mission, and we didn't have anyone up here.

"I'm not sure exactly what's going on, but it has to be on the other end. We want to capture people and question them, not kill them."

The young man opened his mouth to say something else but froze. Then his eyes narrowed.

"You didn't lock down the feed to the bay. Fleet security is monitoring us, as are a number of drill instructors, but there's an extra pair of electronic eyes on us: Andrea's.

"There's no audio to the feed, so I'm going to be able to keep talking about this without worrying she'll overhear us. We're too far away from the vid camera for her to read lips.

"That said, she's on to me now for sure. How do I handle this?"

It might be against regulations for a recruit to tap into the feed that way, but it might not be. In any case, it wasn't something that Page was going to hold against the girl, though it was going to make his life more difficult.

"You'd better figure out what you're going to tell her," Page said tiredly. "I think she's going to figure out at least part of what's going on at this point. It might be time to lay some of your cards on the table."

35

Fei had to firmly restrain herself from going up to the orbital. That would ruin everything. It would also be useless, since Page and Riggio had this new situation under control. They'd figure out who the dead man was and how he'd been killed.

Her job was wrangling answers about who was behind it. Not that all her digging had done much good over the last week. The Mackie family had come up just as dry as Still Water.

Riggio had only been up on the orbital for ten or fifteen minutes. There wasn't any chance that he had any answers yet, so calling him would do her no good.

But she wanted to. Oh, how she wanted to.

How could officers sit back and wait for other people to do the work? This was driving her crazy. She needed to *do* something.

Her implant com pinged with an incoming call, and she answered it without even bothering to see who it was. "Na."

"Riggio. I've got an ID on the body and a problem."

"Give me the problem first."

"Andrea knows that I'm up here."

Fei cursed under her breath. "What have you told her? How did she find out?"

"She tapped into the vid feed to the bay, probably to watch the extraction of the body. Since that's where I'm at, she's no doubt seen me. I need to know how you want me to handle this."

Fei rubbed her face tiredly. "This whole damned thing is unraveling. I still think it's better if she doesn't know that I'm here, but that's beginning to look a lot less realistic at this point. You're going to have to lie pretty damn believably to fool her."

"Believe it or not, they've given me training in that. If you want me to cover for you, then that's what I'll do. I work for Imperial Intelligence, so there's no reason she has to know that you're here. I can give her the basic story without revealing your presence."

Fei hated lying to Andrea, but she wasn't going to lessen her ward's success. Yes, Riggio revealing himself was going to prove that *someone* was watching over her, but he wasn't interfering with her.

If Andrea discovered that one of her guardians was hovering over her shoulder to make sure that she made it, that would be damaging.

"Do it," she ordered. "Tell me about the dead guy."

"His name is Jomos Carfio, and he's associated with a crime syndicate down on New Dallas. You'll have to interface with Earl Still Water to get more details about them, but Peter Bryant is the overall boss. That should give you enough information to move your investigation forward.

"The dead guy has implants, but they're encrypted. It's going to take me a while to get into them if I can.

"The military police will be here in about half an hour to pick up the body and do an official investigation. I'm not going to be able to crack the encryption in that time."

She'd stopped pacing around her office as she'd listened, but now she started again. "If he works for the bad guys, who killed him? This doesn't make any sense."

"There has to be another player. I'm not sure whether the unknown party is on Andrea's side or simply acting against the first organization. We don't know enough about what's going on to even guess. We need more data."

"Is Andrea in any danger?"

"Undoubtedly," he said without hesitation. "They've failed at eliminating her through stealthy means. That means they're going to have to do something physical at this point.

"This guy's presence in the boat bay tells us something too. That's where their vacuum suits are stored, so he could've been there to mess with hers. I'll give it a good look as soon as I finish with the body.

"What I can't be sure of is how far this third party will be willing to go to accomplish their ends, whatever they are. If this is another group that wants to eliminate Andrea, they might be willing to take more chances.

"Planting the body behind a maintenance panel here risked having it discovered, even though that wasn't likely in the short term. It was pure chance that one of the recruits spotted the blood leaking through the seal."

"And now that plan is shot," Fei said grimly. "It's only going to be a matter of hours before *everyone* knows that there was a body up there. Too many people already know about it, so the word will get out, and you can bet your ass that these people are plugged into the right information networks, and they'll hear about it.

"I'm going to have to go talk with this Bryant. Maybe a direct threat can make him back down. I don't know how much Dayton is paying him, but there has to be a point of diminishing returns.

"With Still Water backing me, that's a real threat to any criminal organization. This isn't the local police. His organization will have to either pay attention or pay the price."

There was a brief knock at the door, and it opened before she could give her permission to enter. Earl Still Water slipped in and closed the door behind him.

She held up a finger to delay whatever it was he was about to say so she could finish the call.

"Do the best you can, Riggio. Talk with Andrea and make up a good cover. Use as much of the truth as you can, but keep me out of it. That's the bottom line."

"You got it. Riggio out."

She turned to face the earl. "I take it you heard."

He nodded. "Are you ready to go meet another crime syndicate?"

"Damned right. Let's go."

* * *

PETER'S worst fears were confirmed when his contact in the military police on the base sent him a brief message that a dead body had been found on the orbital. She couldn't provide an image, but her description left no doubt that Jomos was dead.

For the life of him, he couldn't imagine how this had happened. His lieutenant was a cautious man, and he wouldn't have allowed someone that he didn't know into a position where he could harm him. Frankly, it was astounding because people in their line of work trusted so very few people.

Yet what was done was done. Someone had decided to eliminate his lieutenant, and there had to be consequences for that. Worse, he knew that that meant that the authorities would come around asking questions. They wouldn't find any evidence, but their attention would be most unwelcome at a time like this.

The first thing he needed to do was brief Lucinda. Now she wasn't his junior lieutenant; she was his only lieutenant. She'd have to pick up the slack and help him figure out who had betrayed Jomos.

A quick check determined that she was still out in the field, working on getting her ambush finalized before the recruits returned to the surface. She acknowledged his instruction to return but said that it would take at least an hour.

He spent that time going through every bit of information that he could find to figure out who Jomos had been working with. He'd narrowed it down to half a dozen civilian organizations and perhaps two dozen people by the time Charlie told him that Lucinda had arrived.

"Send her in."

He hadn't been seated at his desk while he'd worked because he'd had too much anger coursing through him. It was hard to think straight when he was so pissed off.

He'd spent most of the last hour staring out his window. Watching the air cars flit around usually eased his thoughts and made it simpler for him to come up with new ideas.

That hadn't worked today, but it hadn't been for lack of trying.

He turned to face the door with his hands behind his back as Lucinda let herself in. Her expression showed mild concern.

"What's wrong?" she asked.

"Jomos is dead."

She'd been walking toward the chair on that side of the desk but stopped dead in her tracks. Then she took a deep breath and walked slowly forward, putting her hands on the back of the chair.

"What happened? Was he caught and fought back?"

Peter shook his head. "No. Someone slit his throat and then stashed his body."

"That... doesn't sound like something Fleet or the marines would do. Was it his contact up there?"

"I have no idea. It seems as though we've got another player in the game, and I'm wondering if this was something arranged for by the woman who hired us. It pissed her off that we weren't moving at her speed, and she might've managed to hire someone to make a go of it."

Lucinda pursed her lips and frowned deeply. "That makes no sense. Jomos was up there to kill the girl. What would killing him before he did the deed gain her?

"Since they've found his body, there's virtually no chance that we're going to be able to do anything up there. That makes the job harder. If it was the woman, she's an idiot."

"You're not wrong, but who else could it be? The circumstances are just too bizarre. There has to be something going on that we don't know about. Whoever this third party is, they've got their own endgame, and we need to figure out who they are.

"I'm going to put some people on figuring out who Jomos's contacts were. One of them is the killer or helped get the killer onto the station. Honestly, that's the only lead that we can chase."

"I'll take care of it," she said. "Nobody gets to attack one of our people and get away with it. I'll also increase the watch we have on the woman. If she's managed to hire somebody, I want to know who they are so that they can get their own share of payback."

Peter shook his head. "You got too much on your plate already. We need to finish taking out the girl, and that means we're basically going to have one chance when she gets back on planet. We can't afford to have another miss. Focus on your job, and I'll find out who killed Jomos."

"I think you're too close to this, Peter. Let me handle it."

"Somebody betrayed our organization, and it's my business to find out who it was. I'm never going to let this go, so I might as well be the one to figure out who they are. Once I do, I've got a special little room downstairs where I can keep them alive for weeks while I make sure they regret ever having been born."

Lucinda shrugged and took a step back from the chair. "You're the boss. I really am sorry that you made that call, though."

He'd only started to ask her what she meant when she reached into her jacket and pulled out a flechette pistol. At that moment, he knew who the traitor was, even though he had no idea why she'd done it.

He went for his own pistol, but he knew he was too late. He'd trusted her too much, and she'd gotten inside his defenses just like she'd gotten inside Jomos's. And that lapse in judgment was going to kill him just as dead.

He hadn't even gotten his hand onto his pistol when she opened fire.

36

Andrea felt as if she were being tortured. Having grown up in the crèche, that wasn't just some saying either. No, while this wasn't physical, psychological torture was just as real.

Everyone else was wondering what was going on. It was all they could talk about. They'd been in the bunkroom—a bunkroom suspiciously empty of other recruits—for over an hour now, and even the drill instructors weren't giving them a decent cover story.

The hydraulic leak had been good for a while, but even Claudio knew something was wrong at this point. He didn't know what, but it was apparent something was going on.

She knew what had to be happening but could say nothing. Not only wasn't it her place, she really didn't understand the implications of finding the murdered man. Or the fact that Riggio Gomez was here.

Of the two, the latter concerned her significantly more. It was terrible that a man had been killed, but why was somebody from the platoon that had rescued her helping investigate it?

The man was a tech genius, so if something needed his expertise, he'd undoubtedly be the one to call, but she knew that he'd retired.

Now he was back in marine coveralls, but she wasn't sure how he could even be here, considering how large the Empire was.

She wasn't a big fan of coincidence, and this just reeked of manipulation. Considering that she knew Riggio, that implied that she was the one being manipulated. She just didn't know why.

Oh, she could guess that it had something to do with her being here for training, but how could a retired marine possibly expect to help her?

The very idea that someone thought that she needed help pissed her off. She could do this on her own without any of the people who thought she was still a child trying to manipulate circumstances in her favor. She was an adult and could make her own way in the universe.

And yet, that brought her back to the troubling fact that there was a dead body on the orbital. Who had killed the man, and did it have some kind of connection to her?

She couldn't imagine how the two events could be connected, but now she was beginning to suspect there was more going on behind the scenes than she'd been aware of.

The suddenness of their relocation to the orbital before they'd finished their hand-to-hand combat training now seemed suspect. Had something happened down on New Dallas?

What was really going on? If she asked, would she get a straight answer?

While she was thinking about that, she was fielding questions and comments from various recruits in the platoon. Even though Claudio hadn't figured out exactly what was going on, Diana *definitely* had.

The normally bubbly and talkative girl was sitting nearby, silently watching Andrea. Anytime she looked over, her friend just raised an eyebrow meaningfully. She might not know the details, but she knew Andrea was mixed up in it somehow.

Maybe Andrea should ask her opinion on what she should do. Her friend could keep her mouth shut, she was sure.

She was still considering doing that when Senior Sergeant Page stepped into the compartment, locked eyes with her, and made a gesture for her to come over.

Andrea strode over to him. "Yes, Drill Instructor?"

"Maintenance has fixed the hydraulic leak, and we're clear to use the bay again. Get the platoon back in there and turn them over to the squad leaders to continue their training."

Since she knew damned well that there hadn't been a maintenance issue, that meant that they'd gotten the body out. She hadn't been able to see that for herself because someone had locked her out at the video monitoring system. Probably Riggio.

"Yes, Drill Instructor."

Without waiting for further instructions, she yelled for the platoon to form up and ordered the squad leaders to move their people back to the bay and get them back into vacuum suits to continue their training.

Getting them in place only took about ten minutes. She started getting her vacuum suit out of its locker to put it on, but Page stopped her.

"Bring that with you and come with me."

She wondered why but decided that she'd find out soon enough. Asking inane questions when a drill instructor told you to do something was an excellent way to get yelled at on the best of days, which this definitely wasn't.

He escorted her out of the bay and into a side compartment used for manufacturing parts for the cutters and pinnaces. At one of the tables stood Riggio and Senior Sergeant Gunnarsdotter.

Now that she could see him more clearly, she could see that it wasn't just marine coveralls he was wearing. They had rank tabs and everything. Had he gone back into the service?

"Recruit Tolliver, it's good to see you again," he said cheerfully. "You find the damnedest things. Put your vacuum suit on the table so I can take a look at it."

She did so and shot a sidelong look at Page. He gestured for her to proceed, and she took that as permission to start asking questions.

"What's going on?" she asked. "Finding that dead guy makes me wonder if we got moved up here because something happened down on the ground. Does it have something to do with me?"

He grinned at the two drill instructors. "I told you she was smart."

Even as he spoke, he was busy taking her vacuum suit apart. Not just in the ways that routine maintenance would require, but actually disassembling every part that could be taken apart and laying it out. What was he doing?

"You're not stupid, so you know it has something to do with you," he continued as he worked. "Somebody tried to mess with your locker down on the planet. Tried to plant some drugs that would've gotten you kicked out of training. He got caught in the act and resisted arrest. Shot the barracks up and got killed for his trouble.

"Senior Sergeant Page decided that it would be prudent to relocate the platoon up here without explaining the circumstances, and I don't disagree with him.

"Even though I'm in uniform, I'm not serving as an active-duty marine at this time. I took a job with Imperial Intelligence, and they tasked me with overseeing your stay here to make sure that nobody tried to put their thumbs on the scales."

"Someone killed that man so they could get to my vacuum suit?" she asked slowly.

"Not exactly. We think *he* was up here to mess with your suit. We've identified him as working for a criminal cartel on New Dallas. Someone paid them to make sure that you don't graduate.

"What I don't know is who killed him and whether that person wants you dead too. I figure it won't hurt to double-check your vacuum suit to be sure.

"Have you seen anything up here that seems odd to you? Is anyone asking questions that they shouldn't be? Looking at you strangely or with more hostility than you'd expect?"

She laughed. "I'm not exactly Miss Popular, if you know what I mean. Still, I can't say that I've gotten any strange looks that I didn't expect. We don't have a lot of interaction with people that aren't trainees or drill instructors."

Her brain was racing even as she spoke. Who would be willing to pay the kind of money it would take to have her killed or barred from serving? That couldn't be cheap.

"Just who have I made an enemy of?"

Riggio was plugging a device into the vacuum suit but stopped to shake his head. "You personally haven't made an enemy. They don't even know you. They *think* they know you based on where you're from and are willing to do anything to make sure that none of the genetically engineered people from the Singularity are legally recognized as human in the Empire. That's what they want to stop.

"I'm not going to mention any names, even though I have my suspicions. Someone higher placed than me is busy investigating all the angles to catch the person ultimately responsible for all this. What you need to do is focus on graduating."

The device he had plugged into the vacuum suit beeped, and he grunted. "Or maybe you had better keep an eye out for more trouble. Someone sabotaged this suit so that once it was actually in a vacuum, it would vent your atmosphere after an hour and twenty minutes. By that time, you'd have been so far away from any kind of help that it would've killed you."

A chill washed over her. She'd been in vacuum in the bay, but it hadn't been more than half an hour. Finding the body had disrupted their schedule. If it hadn't, she might be dead now.

Someone had tried to kill her.

"That tears it," Page said. "We need to wrap up the vacuum training as quickly as possible and get you back down to the surface, Tolliver."

"Is that going to make a difference, Drill Instructor? If they're willing to kill me here, they're going to have something in mind down on the surface as well."

Even though the man's expression didn't change, he clenched his fists. "I suppose we're just going to have to double-check everything while waiting for the investigators on the surface to unwind this conspiracy.

"Have you told anyone in the platoon what's going on?"

She shook her head. "No. It didn't seem prudent."

"Then we'll roll with that. Let them think that this was just a mechanical issue and that we're continuing the training and nothing is wrong. We've got about another week up here, and that should give the investigators time to pin down what's going on.

"Since you're now a target, we're going to have to keep a closer watch on you, Tolliver. I don't want you to be anywhere out into vacuum alone. We're instituting something a little bit more stringent than the buddy system.

"Normally, you'd have one of the other trainees close by at all times, but now we're going to stick Gomez with you. Until you're done with training one way or the other, he's going to be there to make sure that nothing else happens to you. Is that clear?"

"Clear, Drill Instructor."

She wasn't sure how that was going to go over with everyone else. How could they hide the presence of a marine just hanging around her without some type of excuse for it? No story would hold up for very long. Hell, Diana would be questioning it in seconds.

"What exactly am I going to tell everyone about this, Drill Instructor?"

He smiled coolly. "I'm told that you're smart, Tolliver. Come up with something believable and make it stick."

Perfect. Not only did she have to lie, but she also had to figure out something that wasn't going to come undone in ten minutes flat.

She sighed to herself. She'd figure something out. She had to.

37

Fei and Still Water arrived near the address they'd been given and landed the air car just up the street. Unlike the trip to the casino, this was more akin to confronting a lion in its den. If they made a wrong move, it could set off a chain of events that was completely out of their control.

While her initial impulse might be to march right in and find somebody to slap around, that wasn't the prudent thing to do, which Still Water had made perfectly clear on the ride over. They'd be going in but only once the place was secure.

Imperial Intelligence agents and some affiliated security assets were gathering a couple of blocks away. They'd raid the place much like the police would have, and their warrants were just as valid. Considering that this was a criminal organization, she expected there would be resistance.

The idea did not displease her.

Even though they didn't plan on directly confronting anyone personally, Still Water produced a flechette pistol and magazines for it, and handed them to her.

She immediately noticed that it had been crafted by the same person that had made her stunner. It was small, sleek, and deadly looking. If it was as undetectable as her stunner, it was a very, very serious crime to possess it.

"I think I need to order one of these," she said, more than a little jealous.

"If we can shepherd Andrea through this crisis, you can keep that one. Consider it a reward for a job well done if we succeed. I'll even get you a license."

"So, what's the plan?" she asked with a smile.

"My agents will rush the building in ten minutes or so. They'll stun anyone who shows even a hint of resistance. If they give up, they'll simply be taken into custody.

"The local authorities will be notified after the operation is underway. I expect that the organization we're dealing with has contacts within law enforcement, and I don't want to tip them off that we're coming.

"While that happens, we'll stay here and wait until the scene is secure. Then we'll go in and find the most interesting people to ask questions of."

She checked to make sure that the weapon was loaded and its safety engaged before slipping it into one of her pockets and putting the magazines in another. Under these circumstances, she didn't believe she'd need to be drawing it rapidly. In fact, if things went as planned, she wouldn't need it at all.

Pity.

The raid started off with a bang. Literally.

A couple of what looked like average citizens walking down the street in front of the building turned to go inside as one told the other some kind of story, complete with handwaving. Or at least that was what it looked like until they had the doors open and threw a couple of flashbangs inside the lobby.

Flashbangs were nonlethal munitions that created lots of noise and light, as well as a pressure wave. That had the effect of disorienting anyone in the area who wasn't protected.

Even as that was happening, a ground van pulled up outside the building, its back doors abruptly opened, and a large group of armed and armored men and women rushed into the building.

Other vehicles pulled up at various places along the block and disgorged people who began setting up a perimeter. She was confident the same was happening along the back of the building as well. They'd draw the net tight to make sure that no one escaped.

It was interesting to watch the operatives make their moves because she could see some parallels with how marines would carry out a similar exercise, though there were probably things to be learned here. She made mental notes just in case she needed to reference them later.

She was so focused on the operation taking place just up the block that she almost missed the door opening in the building beside the air car. A man and woman came out, and they wouldn't have caught her attention except for their behavior.

With all of the ruckus going on up the street, they never once turned their heads to look in that direction. Even when another flashbang went off inside the target building, it didn't make them flinch. They just kept walking.

"Heads up," she said as she put one hand on the door handle and the other on her pistol. "Looks like we got a couple of leakers. If we want to take them out before they escape, it's going to have to be us."

Without saying another word, the two of them opened their doors and stepped out, turning to follow after the man and woman.

That got the pair's attention. Either they had much better hearing than the average person, or they'd been keeping an eye on them somehow. The man whirled in place, his hand darting under his jacket for what she assumed was a weapon, while the woman sprinted forward and ducked into an alley just ahead of them.

With all of her training, Fei still only barely outdrew the man. Her flechettes took him in the gut just as his pistol was coming to bear on them. He still got a burst off as he went down, but it was unaimed and missed both of them, peppering the back of their vehicle instead.

Without waiting to see what Still Water did, Fei rushed forward to the alleyway, ducked low, and extended her head and weapon out to fire at the woman if need be.

Only she wasn't there. There was just a hint of rapid footsteps farther down the alley that indicated the woman had broken into a sprint and was attempting to escape.

Fei took a chance and raced after the woman, but by the time she got to the street on the other side, there was no sign of her. Whichever direction she'd gone, she'd managed to escape.

Somewhat disgusted with herself, Fei made her way back to where Still Water was examining the dead man. He looked up at her and raised an eyebrow questioningly.

"She got away," Fei grumbled. "Hopefully, she's not the one in charge."

Still Water shook his head and stood. "The man in charge of this organization is believed to be Peter Bryant. She didn't look like a Peter to me.

"According to my agents, they've about secured the entire building at this point. A fair number of people resisted and ended up being stunned. There are some injuries on our side but nothing too serious.

"I should've given you a stunner to replace the one that Riggio is holding for you. This fellow might have had some interesting things to say if we'd captured him. I won't complain about your reflexes, though. Thank you."

They could hear sirens in the distance. She supposed that meant that the local authorities were now involved. She wondered how much of an explanation they were going to need because of the dead man.

Even as the security vehicles were pulling up in front of the building, Still Water sighed and shook his head. "Well, things just got much more complicated."

"What's wrong?"

"My agents have found Peter Bryant in his office. It seems he was shot to death, probably within the last few minutes. This mystery just keeps getting more bizarre."

Fei turned back to face the alley down which the woman had escaped. "Do you think she was responsible?"

"I'm not ruling anything out at this point. We'll have to identify her, figure out how she fits into the organization, and see if anybody that we've captured can shed light on why someone murdered their boss."

Fei wasn't holding out much hope that they'd get a straight answer with the way their luck had been going. "Let's go find out."

They walked through the building and up to the office holding the boss's dead body. Now there were regular security forces intermixed with the Imperial Intelligence assault team. Nobody was unescorted, and no one on the local side looked happy.

Her sympathy for them was limited. Yes, it was rough when someone went around you to do something, but if they were as penetrated as Still Water had indicated, it had to be done, and they probably knew it.

That likely only made them more resentful.

She wasn't sure what she'd expected a mob boss's lair to look like, but this was a fairly spartan affair. The view out the window was nice, but the furnishings were plain and utilitarian.

The one thing that stood out about the office was the blood spattered against the wall and the dead body behind the desk. Several people were already standing around the dead man, taking images and speaking into recorders.

They wore shoe coverings and gloves. She imagined that there were others on the way who would be searching the scene in more depth. Even though the man was a criminal, they'd do their best to figure out who had killed him.

Fei didn't need to guess; she was already sure that she knew the answer. The woman who'd escaped had been identified as one of the lieutenants in the organization: Lucinda Drake.

Considering that the dead man on the station had also occupied a leadership position in the criminal organization, that really only left a couple of options. Either somebody was trying to kill the leadership, or it was a coup.

Personally, she was betting on the latter. The fact that the woman had fled before she'd even known that the building was being raided spoke volumes. The investigators could piece together all the facts in whatever order they wanted, but so far as she was concerned, the guilty fled even when no one pursued.

The more interesting question was why the woman had felt the need to kill her compatriot and then her boss. Was this an attempt to take over the organization? If so, striking at the man on the Fleet orbital was a huge risk. Why not wait until he was in a place that she was able to control more effectively?

Or was this somehow connected to Andrea? At the moment, it was hard to see how, but she couldn't rule it out.

It annoyed the hell out of her that they still hadn't managed to locate Dayton. How could she be hiding so effectively? She had to be *somewhere*. Maybe information in this building could point them to where the spider was lurking.

"He had a weapon, but didn't draw it," Still Water said from where he stood at the side of the desk. "I'll assume that means that he had little warning of the attack. Judging from the body's condition and the blood's relative freshness, this attack had to have happened very shortly before we arrived."

"There is an outer office, so the man had somebody vetting his visitors. He let someone in that he trusted, and they killed him. Why didn't the guard outside deal with the attacker after the fact?"

"Because the guard was in on the operation," Fei said without hesitation. "If I'm right, the big man I killed outside was sitting at that desk half an hour ago. Drake came in and spoke with Bryant. I have no idea what was said, but I'd call it a terminal conversation.

"Based on the angle of the blood spatter and the flechette damage to the wall, she was probably standing behind the chair here. He was behind his desk and didn't see the attack coming until too late."

Fei stepped around the edge of the desk and coolly examined the dead man. He hadn't been wearing any body armor, so the flechettes had ripped his torso apart. The expression on his face was one of both surprise and anger.

Yes. It had to have been Drake.

She looked at the desk and saw that there was a built-in computer. "It looks like he did work on this system. I wish we had Riggio to break into it, but I'd expect that you've got someone else who's qualified to get the information we need out of it. Is getting a warrant going to be a problem?"

He smiled indulgently at her. "No problem at all. My position comes with the authority to issue warrants, so I'll have a couple of specialists brought in to make sure that we can extract the equipment and data without tripping any security safeguards. What are you hoping to find?"

"Dayton. I want her *bad*. Once we take her out of play, the attacks on Andrea stop."

"Then let's hope the encryption isn't too difficult to break," Still Water said. "I'd like to get this taken care of before Andrea comes back down to the surface."

Fei resumed examining the dead man. He'd given the orders to frame Andrea and later to kill her, so she didn't regret his death.

All she regretted was not putting him to the question before he died. Now she'd have to do the hard work herself.

She could almost taste ultimate victory. Dayton was somewhere close, and she *was* going to find her. The only question was whether or not it would be in time to help Andrea.

38

Page was paranoid that the bad guys would make their next move quickly, particularly after Lieutenant Na and the noble with Imperial Intelligence found the suspected leader of the criminal organization dead, but things had been ominously quiet in the week since then.

They'd managed to identify the woman who'd gotten away. She'd been a senior member of the crime organization, just like the dead man up here had been.

To Page, it seemed as if this was some kind of power play inside the organization itself. How that connected to Tolliver, he wasn't quite sure. Nevertheless, he and his people kept a close watch on the recruits and everyone who came near them.

All the vacuum suits were regularly tested, and Tolliver ended up getting a different one each time, each requisitioned by Riggio Gomez and rigorously tested. He'd picked up a dozen of the appropriate size and had them under lock and key, but he still treated each one as if it had been tampered with.

Page approved of the man's paranoia. Having seen Riggio work, he was now fully willing to believe that the man had been a tech specialist with a combat platoon good enough to go on a raid into the Singularity.

He'd spent much of the past week making sure that the wilderness training area would be completely secure. There would be hidden marines surrounding the platoon even as they trained.

Sophia Gomez was his point person because he didn't need the distraction of her tearing her brother apart for the deception right now.

He hoped it would be enough.

The day for the final exercise rolled around, and he found himself more than ready to be done. Gunnarsdotter's people were making their run first, and his people were getting set up for their turn.

The exercise was simple. There was a powered-down ship that Fleet used for training. Today there was no one aboard other than the marine drill instructors and the recruits. The recruits would perform search and rescue tasks, some in a vacuum, while under remote observation.

There was some risk to this type of operation because it took time for the drill instructors to get to anyone who somehow managed to tear their suit.

The recruits were supposedly trained enough to handle that sort of thing themselves. Still, that didn't mean that recruits hadn't been injured or even killed on this type of operation before.

Yet the marines trained like they worked. Marines needed to perform these tasks, and the recruits required the confidence to believe that they could do so too.

Since Gunnarsdotter's recruits would be going first, it had made sense to let her instructors oversee his platoon when they made their run. The other lead drill instructor was more than competent enough to handle any problems, but he was still worried.

With Fleet on the lookout for anyone who wasn't supposed to be in this area, it was unlikely that any unauthorized small craft could get to the ship, so it should be safe enough.

It had been thoroughly searched before the operation had commenced. It wouldn't do to have someone hiding there and waiting for them.

After all, were you really paranoid if they *were* out to get you?

He had tapped into the feeds from his recruits and watched as they boarded the pinnace that would take them over. A second pinnace would typically take the drill instructors across, but it wasn't necessary in this case.

The only marines aboard the pinnace were the pilots and the crew chiefs keeping an eye on everything. And, of course, Riggio.

Tolliver was leading the search and rescue mission in her role as acting platoon leader. Once the pinnace had landed on the ship's hull, she and her people would begin the operation under her direction.

The landing went perfectly, and the recruits quickly exited the pinnace, using their magnetic boots to stay on the hull of the ship. Page focused his attention on the various feeds coming from their vacuum suits. Each recruit would be graded on how well they performed the tasks they'd learned and docked for any mistakes they made.

There were dummies aboard the ship that would be treated as casualties so they wouldn't have to deal with any living wounded. Coping with a ship full of screaming and panicked people wasn't something trainees should have to deal with. That would come later.

He was just pouring himself a cup of coffee and making some notes when there was a knock at the hatch. "Come in."

The hatch opened, and Ingrid Gunnarsdotter stepped through. "How's your run going?"

He blinked in surprise. "Shouldn't you be telling me that? You and your people are keeping watch on them."

It was her turn to blink. "You said your people would handle that."

Before he could say anything, she forwarded a message to his implants. It certainly looked like his codes, but it was a forgery.

"It wasn't me," he said, lurching to his feet. "They're walking into a trap."

And at that moment, all the feeds from the recruits cut out.

* * *

ANDREA FOCUSED on getting the platoon out of the pinnace and onto the hull of the ship. It wasn't her first time in space, but the sights still distracted her. Over her head, New Dallas hung, a blue and green globe coated in wisps of white.

All around them, the stars glowed, their colors solid, and the swath of the galaxy clear to the eye. The system's star wasn't visible because it was on the other side of the ship, but the globe above their heads was mostly lit, with the terminator creeping across its surface as the sun rose for the people living there.

It was beautiful, but she didn't have time to waste. She had to get her people inside the ship and begin searching for the dummies that represented injured or dead crewmen. This was a timed exercise, and they had certain milestones that had to be met, all while maintaining the protocols for their safety. Riggio was with them and would be on hand to act immediately if someone made an error that put them in danger.

As she'd expected, Diana hadn't bought her story that Riggio was following them around to audit the training process. Still, her friend hadn't challenged her on it, and the story seemed to have been good enough for everyone else, so she'd count it as a win.

The drill instructors would be watching from somewhere on board the ship, grading them but ready to act if need be. The pilots on the pinnace and the two crew chiefs would remain out here to take them back to the orbital when everything was done.

She was about to order Claudio to take his squad inside when a high-pitched squeal stabbed her ears. What the hell was that?

Andrea messed with the com unit in her suit and decided that someone was screwing with their channel. It had to be part of the test to see how they reacted to a communications failure.

That wasn't something she'd have expected to be thrown at them on this exercise. Well, they'd just have to improvise.

She tapped Claudio on the shoulder and gestured for him to lower his helmet until she could touch hers to his. The contact between them made for poor conductivity of sound, but if one spoke loudly enough, the other could make out what was said.

"Communications failure," she shouted. "Pass the word, have your people get the airlock open, and begin the initial assessment of conditions inside the ship. Send someone back out with a report as quickly as you can."

"Copy that," he said before breaking contact with her helmet and using his hands to convey his intent to his people.

Even as he was getting his people to access the emergency controls for the airlock, she saw Riggio walk toward her and could see the frown on his face even as he was leaning in to touch his helmet to hers.

"Was a communications failure part of the expected test?" he asked.

"No, but with the way things have been rolling, I suppose I should've expected something like this. It's going to make things more complicated, but we'll manage."

"It's been a long time since I went through basic training, but this isn't something that I'd call normal. Is your drill instructor the kind of guy that would do that?"

She laughed. "I've had so many roadblocks thrown at me over the last month that I'm not surprised by anything. Why?"

"I don't like it. Keep your eyes open."

That made both of her eyebrows rise. "Do you think this is enemy action? That's a little bold. We're in the middle of a Fleet-controlled area, and there are drill instructors on board this ship. The other platoon just finished their training, so we know that the ship is clear. What could possibly happen here?"

"I don't know, but after a while in a combat platoon, you get a sense for when things are going wrong. The little hairs on the back of my neck are standing up, telling me that this situation is hinky. I'm more than halfway inclined to just get everyone back onto the pinnace and wave off this exercise entirely."

The outer airlock door gave way for Claudio's people, and they entered to do the initial assessment before she could figure out how to respond to what Riggio was suggesting.

They were being watched over by their instructors. If something untoward happened, it would have to be via a ship or something coming in to attack them.

That seemed unlikely. Fleet had ships all around this area.

"I hear what you're saying," she said slowly, "but I can't go through life expecting everything to be a trap. You're watching out for me, and so are the drill instructors.

"They wouldn't be playing games. If the jamming wasn't their doing, you can be sure that they'll be talking to the trainees that just went through that airlock even as we speak.

"We'll proceed with the exercise as ordered. I'll keep my eyes open for anything that looks unusual, but this is a test that we all have to pass if we're going to become marines. I can't just run away every time something seems off. That kind of paranoia would destroy me."

From his expression, he wasn't convinced. "I suppose we'll play it your way because I can't be sure either. Keep your eyes open, though. If there really is something going on, we're not going to have much time to respond."

She felt him tap her stomach with his hand and pulled her head away to look down. In between their bodies, shielded from the view of everyone around them, he was holding a stunner. A sleek civilian model that was a lot smaller than the military-grade ones she'd trained with. It didn't take a genius to figure out why he was handing it to her.

Taking it would probably violate every kind of rule under the sun, but he was with Imperial Intelligence. Her drill instructors knew that he was responsible for her safety. If someone wanted to complain about her having a weapon, they'd blame him, wouldn't they?

And in any case, he'd have much more than a stunner on him. Even though he wasn't a combat marine anymore, he was still well-trained in the use of deadly weapons, and he wouldn't be under-armed for any fight.

She really hoped that there wasn't a fight. Who were these people who were trying to kill her? Just what kind of reach did they have? Was she going to have to watch out for this sort of thing for the rest of her life?

The airlock opened again, and Claudio came back out and made his way over to her. She stashed the stunner before he got close.

"All clear. We can go in. There's low pressure, but we have gravity."

That didn't sound like an ambush, so she hoped this was all much ado about nothing.

Using hand signals, she ordered the platoon to advance and enter the ship. It was time to get this exercise fully underway.

* * *

THE LAST WEEK had been pure torture for Fei. Not only had Imperial Intelligence failed to get into Peter Bryant's computer, no one had found any clues that led to where Dayton was hiding. All she'd heard was that every effort was being put into the task and every avenue of investigation explored.

It was utter bullshit.

They hadn't had any luck finding out who'd killed the man on the orbital, but at least there hadn't been any further sabotage. Every law enforcement agency on the planet was looking for Lucinda Drake, but she hadn't been seen either.

All in all, it didn't sound like they were going to catch a break. It felt to her as if she had no control over events, and that made her angry.

Andrea was conducting her final exercise in vacuum today, and that meant that the training platoon would be returning to the surface shortly. That opened up a vast swath of opportunity for their enemies to strike again.

Fei felt like a voyeur because all she could do was watch vid feeds of her girl doing her work and read reports about how she was performing.

She got reports about how *all* the recruits were doing and still had to do the work of a platoon leader, which was mind-numbing. She couldn't wait for this to be over so that she could go back to civilian life and her family.

Most of her family, anyway. Andrea was a grown woman now and would be living her own life from now on. Fei's job was to make sure that she wasn't under Imperial Intelligence's thumb while she did it.

Her desk link chimed, indicating that she had an incoming call. She answered it with more than a hint of trepidation. What else had gone wrong?

Still Water appeared on her screen, smiling. No, he was grinning.

"We've broken the encryption on Mister Bryant's computer, and I have a likely location for Countess Dayton. Could you free up the time that it would take to go pick her up and perhaps ask her a few pointed questions?"

"Oh, hell yes! Where are you?"

"I'll be landing outside the barracks in just a couple of minutes. Wear something that you can strap a stunner to because I want to take her alive."

"I'll be right down."

She killed the channel and raced for the stairs. She was in uniform, so she wouldn't have to worry about being able to wear a stunner. She'd strap it to her waist and be done with the nonsense.

Honestly, she hoped that she had a chance to use it too.

By the time she reached the ground floor and went out the back—the ground floor was still locked down—she could hear the air car approaching. She ran around the side of the building just as it came to the ground at the edge of the parade field.

She opened its passenger door and threw herself into the seat, slamming the door and securing herself all in one motion.

"Where is she?" Fei demanded.

"She's staying at one of the hotels that we checked, but not in the room where she's registered. It seems that she checked in under an assumed name to one of the regular rooms and had someone else rent the penthouse suite. At some point, she switched places with them, and that's why we were never able to tie her to the location.

"Someone with her apparently replaced the image of her that they captured during check-in. It was all very convoluted but effective enough, except that Peter Bryant had located her and had someone keeping tabs on her."

He brought the air car off the ground and took them toward the front gate at an irritatingly slow pace. Once they were outside the base, they'd head toward the city. It would take roughly an hour to get to the location that he'd sent her through her implants, but that was good. They'd have time to prepare a team to take her alive.

She was about to say something to that effect when an alert went out across the marine network. She knew it wasn't targeted solely at her based on the header. It was going out to all marines on the planet.

Fei quickly scanned the report and blanched.

"Something is going on in orbit," she said. "Someone activated a powerful jammer, and no one can communicate. Do you think it has something to do with Andrea?"

He shot her a worried look. "I'd be a fool not to. I know that you want to go up right now, but whatever is taking place would be over by the time you got there. I think we need to focus on capturing Dayton while we can. Are you going to give me any trouble?"

She wanted to rush up and protect Andrea, but she knew that he was right, damn his eyes. Riggio was there, and so were the drill instructors. They'd keep Andrea safe if anyone could. Fei needed to focus on catching that bitch.

"Can this thing go any faster?" she demanded. "I want her in my sights, and I want it now."

He grinned wolfishly. "Let's see just how fast this thing can go, shall we?"

39

Page raced out of his office with Gunnarsdotter hot on his heels. He ignored the lifts and ran straight up the stairs toward the Fleet control center. He didn't have time to waste standing around.

The marine guards at the control room hatch stopped him. He wanted to rage at them, but he knew that that was their duty. He controlled himself as much as he could and *urgently requested* that the officer of the watch see him.

It dismayed the hell out of him when the officer refused, and a harried-looking lieutenant stepped out of the control area instead, frowning at him.

"Whatever your problem is, Senior Sergeant, we don't have time to deal with it right now. We've got a crisis on our hands."

He started to snap at the man, but then he realized that he might be missing something. Besides, screaming at an officer wasn't a good way to get things done, no matter how much he wanted to. Officers made the strategic decisions, and if he tried to force this, the man could send him away. What the hell would he do then?

"We have trainees out aboard the training ship, sir," he said as calmly as he could. "We've lost communication with them, and I'm afraid that something has gone terribly wrong. We need a rescue team on its way there *right now*. An entire platoon full of recruits is at risk."

"*Everyone* has lost communication, Senior Sergeant," the man said distractedly. "We're not sure exactly what's going on, but there's some kind of jamming source in orbit, and Fleet is going to alert status in case we're under attack. I wish I could send someone to check on your recruits, but I'm sure they're okay.

"Right now, all of our ships are deploying into defensive positions, and we don't have anything to spare. You're just going to have to wait until we restore communications or take care of the problem yourself."

Without saying another word, the officer turned on his heel and went back into the control center.

"Well, that went well," Gunnarsdotter said grimly. "You heard the man. He said we could take care of the problem ourselves, and I'm sure this is a situation where it's going to be much easier to beg forgiveness than ask permission."

"Damn right," he said as he headed back toward marine country. "We're going to take one of the pinnaces, but we need to be armed. Let's get everyone to the armory and take care of that. We can also draw armored vacuum suits to make sure that we're covered once we get there.

"I hate spending the time, but it won't help them for us to rush into a hail of flechettes and die gloriously. The ship is empty right now, but you can bet somebody is bringing troops to bear. We've got to beat them to the punch."

A pinnace could hold seventy people, so long as they weren't in powered armor. With the drill instructors and half a dozen support staff, they weren't going to be close to that.

There was already a pinnace on-site with two pilots and two crew chiefs aboard. If he could figure out a way to get a message to them, they might be able to get inside the ship and retrieve Tolliver and the rest before things went straight to hell.

He wasn't going to count on that, though. With communications jammed, the only way to tell the pilots what was going on was face-to-face. Unless, of course, Fleet figured out where the jamming was coming from and stopped it.

It would be a point source of some kind, but it had to be powerful if it stopped all communications around the planet. Fleet was going on defense because that was what the book said to do. The odds of there actually being an attack here were so low that they were ludicrous.

This had to be something to distract Fleet to the point that they wouldn't react to someone coming in to kill Tolliver and the rest of the recruits. How those people planned to escape once the deed was done, he had no idea.

He supposed if they got back to New Dallas, they could scatter. Even identifying them might be impossible.

Right now, though, he had to focus on doing what he could. That meant drawing weapons and armor and getting his ass to that ship as fast as possible. He was responsible for those recruits, and he'd do everything in his power to keep them safe.

The armorer gave him shit, but he put a stop to that fast. With Gunnarsdotter at his side, they browbeat him into releasing the weapons and armored vacuum suits. By then, the remaining drill instructors and support staff were there.

Everyone armored up and drew weapons, including the armorer. Every single marine on this orbital was going on this mission.

That took ten long minutes that felt like four times the length. Yet it was time they had no choice but to spend.

As soon as everyone was ready, he and the rest raced to the boat bay. It was home to several cutters and the now-absent pinnace and its twin that had brought Gunnarsdotter and her people back. It would provide them their ride.

Only when they got into the bay, it was empty. There wasn't a single small craft in sight.

"Those Fleet bastards!" Gunnarsdotter raged. "They commandeered all our small craft. How the hell are we going to get out there now?"

Page turned toward the wall where the vacuum suits were stored and sighed. "We're going to have to do this the hard way. Grab thruster packs, everyone. I understand that we're going to be short on fuel for something like this, so we'll have to get it right the first time.

"I'll take a light and try to signal the pinnace pilots if the angle is good. No guarantees there, but it's worth a try."

Even as the marines were rushing to put the thruster packs on, Gunnarsdotter faced him. "The chances of us beating the bad guys there are pretty damn low."

"What else can we do?" he asked grimly. "Our only hope is that the bad guys are slower than we are. Come on. Let's get geared up and get on our way. The enemy waits for no one."

* * *

ANDREA CYCLED through the airlock and examined the area just inside the ship. The lighting was dim, but there was more illumination than just the emergency lights. Gravity was on, but something was wrong with the atmosphere. The pressure was low, and it wouldn't be safe to remove their helmets.

That was fine, since she didn't intend to put anybody at risk anyway. Thankfully, the pressure was high enough to use the external speakers on her suit to get her orders out to everyone simultaneously. That was necessary because the jamming still had their com systems locked up.

As each squad came through the airlock, she made sure they understood where they'd be searching. They'd gone over this already, but it never hurt to reinforce the plan.

Diana and her squad would head for engineering, Claudio and his people would head for the bridge, and JR was responsible for the crew quarters. As the platoon leader, she'd be coordinating the overall rescue effort, and, sadly for her, that meant the best place to go was the bridge.

The last thing she wanted to do was have to deal with Claudio, but those were the breaks. He knew what he had to do, and if he screwed around, then it was going to reflect poorly on him too.

Diana raced off with hardly a glance back. Her friend was utterly focused on the task at hand, like she had a mental checklist of things that she needed to accomplish. That probably wasn't far off the mark.

JR was a lot looser in his command style—if "style" was even the appropriate word. He gestured toward the corridor he intended to use, and his squad and he raced away in more of a mob than an orderly procession.

She stood against the bulkhead with Riggio as Claudio ordered his people to proceed toward the bridge, checking every hatch they came across for pressure on the other side as well as for injured or dead.

They began encountering those almost immediately, starting with a pair of dummies in the corridor with red bands around their necks. They represented dead crewmen, so Claudio had one of his people note where they'd found the bodies, and they all continued on. Things would get more complicated when they started encountering survivors.

If there were any survivors.

At the moment, the pressure was too low to support life, and anyone trapped in this particular section who wasn't in a vacuum suit was already dead.

To her surprise, they didn't encounter any wounded at all on the way to the bridge. In fact, all they found were dummies representing the dead. That included the bridge itself because every station had a dummy strapped in to represent a deceased crewmember.

The bridge was rather cramped compared to some of the ones she'd seen when she was younger. Of course, the bridge of a heavy cruiser was much larger than that of a civilian freighter. So was the one on the Singularity freighter that had been used as the raiding ship.

"Let's see if we can figure out why we have no power," she said as she moved over to one of the control panels. It was powered, and she was able to configure it to use the ship's internal communications array.

She started out with engineering and opened a channel to the central console back there. "What's the situation back there, Diana? Everyone on the bridge is gone. Why are we without power?"

A few seconds later, the channel came fully to life as Diana answered. Her friend's face appeared on the screen, still framed inside of her helmet.

"Engineering is in vacuum, but I spotted the flashing light on the console. I'm close enough to it that my suit com is connecting. Barely.

"It looks like the aft airlock is open, both doors. I suppose that's meant to represent some type of puncture. There aren't any dummies back here at all. I guess we're meant to assume that they were sucked out with the air.

"As for power, I'm not certain. My experience with that kind of equipment is almost zero. Do you want me to dig in and try to find an answer?"

Andrea shook her head. "Don't bother. Start bringing your people forward. Search every compartment, looking for survivors, and make note of any dead. If you happen across the drill instructors, pretend that they aren't there."

Her friend smiled. "Where do you think they're hiding?"

She answered with a shrug. "There's no telling. Probably the last place we'd look. Use one of the com consoles to call the bridge if you run into anything unexpected. Bridge out."

Her next call was more generalized because she wasn't sure exactly where JR and his people were. Instead of trying to speak to them, she made each of the com consoles in the crew area chime, hoping to draw one of his people over so that they could answer the call.

That worked because the screen cleared a couple of seconds later and showed JR grinning at her. "That's pretty smart, platoon leader. Good job."

She ignored the compliment and got right down to business. "What's going on in the crew quarters? Have you found any survivors?"

He shook his head. "All of the dummies we found so far indicate that they're dead, but I think we're about to find some survivors. Real ones. I see a couple of lights coming around the far end of the corridor. Maybe the drill instructors came looking for us."

Andrea frowned. Why would the drill instructors be interfering with the exercise? That didn't make any sense.

Well, she supposed she'd find out soon enough. If JR could see them, it would only be a few seconds before they'd be at the com console too.

JR turned his head and raised an arm, waving at someone. "Hey! It's not the drill instructors. It's the crew chiefs from the pinnace. Can we help you guys?"

The answer to his question turned out to be a hail of flechettes, which tore his torso apart in a bloody explosion.

40

F ei would've preferred to go straight to the penthouse suite and kick the doors open, but they had to have a special key to get the lift to take them all the way up. So, they made their way to the front desk at the head of a group of Imperial Intelligence agents.

Still Water displayed his identification to the young man smiling at him from behind the counter. "I am J. Russell Macumber, a roving director with the Imperial Department of Justice. I have a warrant to search the penthouse suite and another one of your rooms. I require a key to get into the rooms and use the lift to get to them.

"Here is the warrant. I require you not to tell anyone other than your direct supervisor, whom you can summon here before you tell only him or her, under penalty of immediate arrest for tampering with evidence and assisting a fugitive. Do you understand?"

The young man examined the identification closely and then took the old-fashioned paper warrant in his hand, frowning as he read it. "I'll call my supervisor, but there's not going to be any problem with this. Both those suites are empty. The occupants checked out perhaps half an hour ago."

Fei wanted to scream. They'd finally located that damned woman, and she'd flown the coop before they could pick her up.

"Do you have any idea where they went?" Still Water asked.

"Let me summon the bellhop and see if she can give you any information while I talk to my supervisor."

A young woman in a hotel uniform appeared moments later and listened to Still Water ask his questions and then nodded. "Even though they were in two separate rooms, the occupants left together. I called them a large air car and heard the woman in charge order the driver to head for the port.

"Apparently, they have a small craft there that's going to take them to a ship in orbit. From the way she was talking, the woman in charge expected them to be leaving the system in a few hours."

The young woman cast a glance over at the man behind the counter, who was explaining the situation to his supervisor, and lowered her voice. "I really shouldn't be saying, but they used a car from the Jackson Group. I recognized the driver. I can provide you with their number, but please don't tell my boss. He'd fire me for sure."

"Then why tell us?" Still Water asked.

"She was arrogant and a terrible tipper. She wanted every service possible but never left a tip. If she's a criminal, I really hope that you catch her because she was a bitch."

"We'll do everything we can to catch her," Still Water assured the girl. "You've been a terrific help, and if we can get our hands on her, you'll be eligible for part of the reward. The Empire is in your debt."

He turned toward Fei, his expression grim. "Whatever is going on in orbit, it looks like her doing. They're making their play now, and she expects everything to be finished in time for her to leave. I think we need to get to the port and find a ride of our own if we can't stop her."

Fei nodded. "Let's get moving. We're out of time."

The car company told them the area they'd dropped Dayton off, but that was where all the chartered craft left from, so it wasn't much help.

They sped to the port with Still Water talking to someone over the com, trying to identify which craft they needed to stop, but getting through to the right person proved particularly difficult. Perhaps they'd been paid to make sure that no one interrupted Dayton's escape. The woman certainly had enough money to spread it around for things like that.

The earl cursed as they pulled into the parking area. Once their vehicle was grounded, he turned to her and grimaced.

"I finally tracked down the cutter that she's using, and it lifted off fifteen minutes ago. She's already in orbit, and with all of this nonsense going on up there, we're not going to be able to isolate her transponder."

"Then we're just going to have to chase her," Fei said grimly. "There's only so many outgoing ships, and I'll assume that you can commandeer some of those Fleet vessels that are running around with their hair on fire.

"Better yet, we know that she's going to be involved in attacking Andrea in some way, so doesn't that narrow the range of potential locations?"

"Not if her contractors are the ones conducting the attack, which seems likely. If she were kidnapping her, yes. Honestly, I'm not certain that we'll be able to get our hands on her before she escapes. We might be best served going directly to the orbital."

"No. We won't let Dayton escape. Page and Riggio will keep Andrea safe."

"Then I'd best find us something to get us up into orbit."

Fei wished they had another choice, but they were out of time. She just had to hope that Andrea could save herself from what was coming so that they could swoop in and pick up the pieces once it was all over.

* * *

PAGE and the marines had to keep a tight formation because the jamming kept them from using anything but hand signals. Fortunately, all marines trained in them simply because there were times when it was too dangerous to use even short-range coms.

The problem with the suits was that they were limited to what they could see because they didn't have long-range scanners.

Normally for space operations, there would be a larger vehicle providing telemetry, or they'd have practiced going in blind to a specific location.

They couldn't even home in on the pinnace's transponder with all this jamming. They were just going to have to wing it.

The ship that the recruits were on was fully operational, but engineering had been shut down. The ship was operating on battery power and was more than capable of doing so for days.

When it was time to charge the batteries back up, a skeleton crew would come aboard, bring everything back to life and give it a good look before powering it back down.

Luckily, its location was well known, and the batteries were more than capable of maintaining running lights to be absolutely sure that no other vessels came close, in addition to the transponder signals that couldn't be heard over the jamming. Those lights were the only thing the marines could use to home in on it.

Gunnarsdotter was right about how slowly things were going. At this rate, it would take them another half an hour to get to the training ship. Whatever was going on might be over by then. Hopefully, the pinnace's crew would be of some use.

Motion off to his left made him turn his head to see what was going on. It was Gunnarsdotter waving to get his attention. Once she was sure she had it, she began using hand signs to direct his attention farther to the left of their course.

He immediately saw what had captured her attention. There were lights from another ship closing in on the training ship. It would pass relatively close to them. Most interestingly, the pattern of the lights indicated that it wasn't a Fleet vessel or small craft. It was some type of civilian ship.

That meant that it shouldn't be here. Could this be the ship that was bringing the attackers to the training vessel?

Well, at the very least, the ship could provide them a ride. He made the command decision to board the ship. Since they were being jammed, he couldn't challenge them, so he was going to have to do that in person.

If it was a ship full of civilians that was just off course, no harm, no foul. If it was a force on its way to attack his recruits, he was well armed, and they'd regret it.

Because they were in a restricted Fleet area, that relieved him of worrying about boarding the ship itself. If he'd had communications, he could've ordered them to heave to. Since he didn't, those extenuating circumstances would cover his unannounced boarding of the vessel.

Because it was traveling faster than they were, they'd have one chance to meet up with the ship, and it was going to be a very bumpy landing. The programs in his implants were more than capable of calculating the incoming vessel's distance and speed and matching it against their own. All it took was allowing his implants to direct the thruster pack to get them on an intercept course.

Once he'd double-checked the calculations and they were moving on the new course, he winced. They were basically going to slam into that ship as it closed with them, and he just hoped that no one was bounced back off or had their suits damaged to the point that they lost pressure.

Most approaches in vacuum were slow. This one was so fast that they barely had a chance to intercept before the ship ran them down.

When the ship was at its closest approach, Page maxed out his thrust and cut as much of the velocity difference as he could even as he slammed into the hull of the ship, scrabbling for purchase and turning on his magnetic boots.

He *almost* bounced off the damned thing before sliding to a halt against some antennas that absorbed his momentum at the cost of their integrity. That would probably set off an alarm, but they wouldn't know why they'd lost the antennas. Or, because of the jamming, they might not realize the problem was mechanical right away. In any case, the marines had to hurry.

Of the fourteen marines he'd brought with him, he was astonished to see that twelve of them were on the ship and in good condition. The other two had bounced off to be left rapidly behind.

He hoped that they were okay. The trajectory that they were on kept them out of direct danger, and they could call for help as soon as the jamming field went down.

Locating an exterior airlock wasn't difficult. Opening it also wasn't a problem, since it was designed to provide rescue personnel access if there was some kind of accident. That would *definitely* set off an alarm on the bridge, though, so if this ship was here to cause trouble, this would alert them.

Once he was sure that everyone had their weapons ready, he activated the airlock's emergency release. The exterior airlock hatch slid open, and half of them piled in, weapons at the ready.

Cycling the lock took thirty seconds, and that felt like an eternity. As soon the atmospheric pressure matched, the interior door cycled open, and the lead two marines entered the ship, already calling for surrender through their exterior speakers.

The craft's nature was answered moments later when someone up the corridor opened fire with a flechette rifle, and one of the marines went down, injured but still returning fire. His people joined in and began advancing.

This *had* to be the attacking force that was coming for his trainees. He'd caught them before they'd gotten there, and now he was going to end them. They held their location until the rest of the marines were inside, and then he gave his orders.

"Advance and secure the ship," he ordered via his speakers. "Take prisoners where you can. I want this ship secured in the next fifteen minutes."

* * *

ANDREA FLINCHED VIOLENTLY as she watched JR die. The shocking suddenness of it made her want to vomit, but she didn't have time for that. She had to save the rest of the platoon.

"We have hostiles aboard the ship," she said over the ship's all-hands channel so that her voice rang throughout every compartment of the vessel. Then she opened a channel to engineering and prayed that someone saw the flashing light on the console.

Moments later, Diana answered, and Andrea launched into giving her orders.

"Secure engineering and avoid contact with anyone not in the platoon, particularly the crew from the pinnace. They're trying to kill us. This is not a drill. JR is dead, and we need to avoid any more casualties."

Before the horrified Diana could answer, she killed the channel, drew the hidden stunner that Riggio had given her, and headed for the hatch. The ex-marine reached out to grab her, but Claudio beat him to it.

"You can't go out there," he said. "I don't know where you got that thing, but they're using real flechettes, and you'll die."

She shook his hand off her arm. "Sometimes the only thing you can do as a marine is to save someone else. Someone did that for me when I was a kid, and today might be my turn to do the same for all of you. That's what it means to be a marine."

"He's right, you know," Riggio said, stepping between her and the hatch. "They don't know where we are yet, so they're going to have to search for you.

"Now that they've killed someone, they're going to have to kill *everyone*. If anyone survives to tell the story of what really happened here, you can be sure that the Empire will never stop hunting them.

"I've got a flechette pistol, and it's my duty to see that you're safe. Seal the hatch. If you have to make a heroic last stand, make it here."

He didn't wait for her to respond, turning on his heel and racing out of the bridge.

"Those were pretty words, but screw that," she snarled. "Those bastards killed JR, and I'm going to make them bleed. Let's go."

She raced out of the bridge with Claudio and his squad at her heels.

Even though they only had two confirmed hostiles at this point, she knew that there had to be at least four. There was no way that the pilots on the pinnace were unaware of what the crew chiefs were doing. They'd have had to open the arms locker for them.

There had to be some other kind of plan in motion that would likely result in the destruction of this vessel. Fleet and the marines were probably supposed to think that everyone was killed in some type of engineering incident. An overloaded fusion plant would certainly do that.

Oh, hell. That was where the pilots were going.

She stopped at the first wall communicator and opened a channel to engineering. For long seconds, she was afraid that no one would answer, but Diana finally came on.

"Engineering."

"You've got hostiles incoming, and they'll probably want to overload the fusion plant. You've got to keep them out."

"I guessed that. We're locked down, but I'm not sure if they can get around it somehow. What do we do?"

"Jam it if you can. Use the airlock to get clear."

"Copy that. If the pilots are coming here, maybe I should secure the pinnace. They won't have sent a single person to take engineering, you know."

That wasn't a bad idea. Her friend was fast on the uptake.

"Do it. We'll be out there as soon as we can."

Without waiting for a response, Andrea killed the channel, raced down the corridor, and ran into the stairwell leading to the level where JR had encountered the hostiles. She could hear Riggio below her opening the hatch into the corridor at the appropriate level.

If she was going to make any difference in this at all, she had to catch up right now.

She pocketed the stunner, glanced over the railing, and vaulted over it. This was risky as hell, but if there was one time where she could use her physical enhancements to make a difference, this was it.

Andrea fell three flights and grabbed onto the railing when she got to Riggio's level, slamming against the rails hard as she came to an abrupt halt. It felt as if her arms were going to be ripped out of their sockets, but she was able to maintain her grip and grin at the gaping Riggio as he turned in surprise.

"Dammit!" he said as he reached back and helped her over the railing. "Do you *ever* listen?"

"Only when it suits me. Stop bitching and tell me what the plan is."

At that moment, someone down the corridor fired at them, and flechettes ricocheted off the upper part of the hatch he'd been about to go through.

Riggio and she both ducked, but he edged over to the hatch with his pistol at the ready. "I'll do my best to take them down, but you're going to have to follow me up and use that stunner to make sure. Good luck, marine."

"Wait! That's crazy. They know exactly where we are. You're going to die."

"Like you said, sometimes a good death is the best a marine can hope for. Make me proud."

And with that, Riggio raced into the corridor, firing his flechette pistol at enemies she couldn't yet see.

Without even thinking about it, she drew her stunner and followed.

41

Fei was pleased that Still Water quickly managed to find them a customs pinnace, complete with a trained crew, to pursue Dayton. Its regular duty was to inspect cargo in orbit. Occasionally someone tried to run, so the pinnace had to deal with any resistance when boarding.

She felt relatively confident that there was going to be resistance today.

While they now had the target cutter's transponder information, that wouldn't be useful with the jamming still active. Dayton's crew had filed a flight plan, so it was the only thing they had to go on. It claimed that a small yacht named *Exigent Circumstances* was waiting for the cutter in orbit.

Still Water thought the ship's name was hilarious, so Fei searched the data net and had found a reference to the term attributed to one of the premier universities of the Empire: the venerable Cornell University and its law school.

Its definition of exigent circumstances was "circumstances that would cause a reasonable person to believe that entry (or other relevant prompt action) was necessary to prevent physical harm to the officers or other persons, the destruction of relevant evidence, the escape of the suspect, or some other consequence improperly frustrating legitimate law enforcement efforts."

Basically, *they* were using exigent circumstances to board *Exigent Circumstances* without having a warrant or announcing themselves. Irony, indeed.

Their attacking force was made up of Imperial Intelligence agents and customs enforcement officers. Each of those two groups had different skill sets that might prove helpful. If they could pin Dayton down, they might be able to collect a lot of damaging information.

Still Water wanted to see that the target ship lost power as soon as possible. It was impossible to move and fight a vessel with no power. Also, if any computers on board had incriminating evidence, it would be hard to erase that data if the machine was powered down.

Since all vessels had emergency power, the only way to make sure that no power was available was to completely take out engineering. It didn't have to be destroyed, but if both the emergency power system and the standard fusion plant were taken offline together, the ship would be in utter darkness, and the crew and passengers would be trapped.

If, of course, everything went according to plan.

Luckily, the jamming didn't block regular scanners. They were able to see that the ship that they were supposedly chasing was still in orbit. It even had the cutter that had brought the passengers up from the surface still docked. That was easy enough to tell with scanners able to read the names and ID numbers right off the hulls.

The section of space where *Exigent Circumstances* was orbiting was fairly crowded. Their cutter passing by wasn't going to raise any eyebrows. That would happen when they changed course and latched on to the target ship's hull.

Because this was a customs vessel, it was outfitted with armored vacuum suits and weapons. The customs people were mostly limited to stunners with just a few flechette pistols for the officers, but that would do. The Imperial Intelligence agents had enough flechette rifles to provide necessary backup if it devolved into that kind of fight.

Right before they were set to dock, the chartered cutter

disengaged and began heading back down to the surface. After a brief conversation, Still Water decided to let them go.

Odds were that nobody they were looking for was on that boat. Dayton was making her escape, and they'd only brought her to orbit for pay. If need be, they could track them down later.

Their departure opened up a place to dock. As a small civilian vessel, *Exigent Circumstances* had a cutter of her own and one spare dock. With the spare docking port available, they wouldn't have to latch onto the hull and make their way to engineering in a vacuum.

The real question was going to be whether or not they'd take fire as soon as they entered.

Personally, Fei thought that if they acted quickly enough, they wouldn't run into any substantial resistance. After all, Dayton wasn't expecting anyone to know where she was.

That didn't mean there wouldn't be any fighting. A countess like Dayton would have a security force, and they would do their best to defend their mistress. It was Fei's job to make sure that they failed.

The chartered cutter had just entered the atmosphere when the customs cutter changed course and quickly latched on to the open port. Since the ship was often forced to board unwilling vessels, they had overrides built into the locks that either bypassed the electronics or mechanically forced the airlock to open.

In this case, the electronic version was sufficient to take out the security system, even though it was probably a high-end one. The customs people had all the manufacturer overrides, after all.

Fei noted that there was no one in the corridor outside the docking ring once they came through. It looked as if they'd surprised everyone on the ship. That wouldn't last.

Still Water led his people and some customs agents toward the bridge. That was where he expected to find Dayton. Three of his agents took station in the docking ring to make sure no one used the other cutter to escape.

It was Fei's job to make sure that power went out as soon as possible. They were almost to engineering when an alert began sounding over the speakers, and a warning was broadcast about hijackers. The enemy knew they were there.

The main hatch to engineering was already in sight when it started to close, so Fei raced forward and skidded through right before it sealed. If she'd been a few seconds late, that might have meant a grisly death, but she'd done this before.

The man who'd closed it gaped at her and then fumbled for a weapon on his belt. She stunned him, hit the control to reopen the hatch, and began methodically picking off everyone else who was scrambling around the engineering area.

Since she'd stopped the man from locking the hatch, it opened right back up, and Imperial Intelligence agents and customs officers flooded engineering. In less than fifteen seconds, the fight was over.

One of the customs agents was a trained engineer and quickly gained access to the fusion controls and shut the plant down. The emergency lighting immediately sprang to life, but he went to a different set of controls and extinguished them in just another few seconds.

"All power is off," she said. "So long as we hold engineering, we can keep it that way."

"Set up a team to repel any attempt to retake engineering," Fei ordered. "I'll lead a team to sweep the ship and make sure that we've got every single person aboard. I don't want any surprises, and we need to make absolutely certain that no one escapes."

She broke off from engineering with four Imperial Intelligence agents and started making her way forward. They stunned everyone they saw. They could sort them out later.

They were almost back to the docking ring when the hatch at the other end of the corridor opened, and half a dozen people raced out. In the lead was Dayton, clutching a heavy bag of some kind.

Fei brought her stunner up and shot the woman, smirking in satisfaction as she went down hard, the bag skidding up the corridor.

The agents also opened fire. In moments, the woman's guards were down as well, having not had an opportunity to return fire.

She walked over to the unconscious woman and resisted the powerful urge to kick her.

Instead, she settled for making sure there were no weapons on her and borrowing a pair of handcuffs to bind her. There was no way that she was allowing this bitch to somehow get away now.

Ten minutes later, the ship was secure. Still Water had them do another pass through, looking into every hiding place they could find to make sure that they hadn't missed a single person.

That proved a wise call, since they found two crewmen hiding. That spawned a third search just to be *absolutely* certain they had complete control. That one came back clean.

With that accomplished, they brought the power back online and headed toward the orbital where Andrea was. It was time to bring this sorry mess to a close.

She just hoped that they got there in time to make a difference.

* * *

PAGE LEAPFROGGED in front of the downed marine and put a burst of flechettes into the woman who had shot him. While she was well armed, she wasn't armored, and the burst tore her apart.

They couldn't count on being protected by their armored vacuum suits against every attack, but in this case, it had saved someone's life. They needed to end this fight as quickly as possible and on the most crushing terms possible.

He directed Gunnarsdotter and her team to head for engineering while he led his people toward the bridge. If they could gain control of the ship, that would make the fight significantly easier.

Right now, they had the advantage of surprise. The enemy knew they were there, but they hadn't had a chance to get armored up, and they were probably not all armed either.

They ran into a small group of fighters just short of the bridge. They also weren't armored, so the fight was brutally one-sided and quick.

"When we take the bridge, use your stunners," he said over the external speakers. "They'll probably be using flechettes, but we need someone to answer questions. We'll just have to take the risk."

The bridge hatch was locked, but the armorer was able to take care of that with an explosive charge that wrecked the mechanism and sent the hatch itself spinning into the bridge.

That sparked some flechette fire but far less than he'd expected. The defenders were disorganized, and that was perfect for the flashbangs he threw in. Smoke followed that, and his people raced in once the opaque cloud had filled the bridge.

Their optics was more than capable of seeing the enemy through the smoke, but the same wasn't true of the crew. The coughing and wheezing defenders tried to see through teary eyes and hear through deafened ears but failed.

He and the marines quickly stunned anyone who was still moving, and then they stunned the ones who weren't just on general principles.

With the bridge secure, he put a pair of marines on station to guard them against attacks from the rear while he got the life-support system working, drawing the smoke out and seeing what they'd captured. The fact that these people had been firing at him with flechette pistols meant that they weren't innocent bystanders. So far as he was concerned, they'd gotten what they'd deserved.

It took less than twenty minutes to fully secure the ship and account for everyone. Because he was thorough, they went through the ship a second time but found no holdouts.

The final tally on his side was five marines injured, one seriously. Two other marines had bounced off the hull, and their conditions were still unknown at this time.

They'd killed nine of the crew in the attack and severely injured seven. Half a dozen had been stunned in engineering or the bridge, and several others had been wounded in the breaching of both of those locations.

The most interesting thing about this was the course that the ship was on. It had definitely been moving to match speed with the training ship. They'd overshot it because no one was managing the ship during the fight, so it would take a while to get back into the general area in one of the small craft.

He gathered up his most combat-effective people, and they boarded the ship's cutter, detaching quickly and racing toward the distant training vessel. He only prayed that they weren't too late.

42

With Riggio going through the hatch first, he drew the initial fire. He went down, but he took down at least one of the attackers with him. It all happened so fast that Andrea barely got her stunner up and onto the second attacker before he fired on her.

Only the attacker's attention initially being focused on Riggio saved her from a fatal burst of flechettes before she took him down. Once she was sure that both of the attackers were down, she knelt beside Riggio.

He'd taken flechettes to his chest and had already succumbed to his wounds. The man who'd helped save her from the Singularity had saved her life once more, but now he was dead.

The rage that shot through her threatened to overwhelm her. She bent down, retrieved his flechette pistol and spare ammunition, and stalked over to the stunned attacker. She raised the pistol and aimed it at his head.

"Whoa!" Claudio said, pushing her hand to the side. "We don't shoot prisoners, no matter how much they deserve it."

Andrea hadn't even heard him and the rest of the squad arrive.

She considered what he'd said. She could kill this guy, but it wasn't going to bring Riggio back. It wasn't going to bring JR back.

"I don't think I agree with you right now, so it's probably better you take this," Andrea said as she handed him the flechette pistol. "Scavenge all the weapons you can. We've got to go find JR's squad ASAP. This guy will be stunned for the next several hours, but I still want him tied up. Make it fast."

They were still doing that when she heard someone racing up the corridor. She raised her stunner and found cover. If their attackers were coming this way, they'd deal with them.

Instead, the rest of JR's squad came racing around the corner ahead of them. Two of them were carrying the dead recruit.

Andrea pointed at Claudio. "Grab Riggio's body, the dead attacker, and the prisoner. We're going back out onto the hull and hope that Diana has gotten the pinnace open. We should be able to get far enough out that any explosion—if they're stupid enough to actually arm it before they have the ship secure—won't take us down."

She didn't want to look at JR or Riggio as they picked them up, but she forced herself to. They were *her* responsibility.

Once they had the bodies and the unconscious prisoner ready, they raced to the airlock they'd used to board the ship and cycled out as quickly as they could. The jamming was still in effect, so communication was impossible.

The ramp was down, but she had no idea whether Diana had done it or if the pilots had left the small craft open. In the end, it hardly mattered.

She used hand signals to indicate that she would try to bring the pinnace's controls to life. They'd be locked down, but the man who'd trained her to fly had been a smuggler. Getting around those types of lockouts was one of the *unofficial* lessons that he'd taught her when Grace and Fei were looking the other way.

Andrea raced into the control area and found Diana in the copilot's seat, trying unsuccessfully to get the controls to come to life.

She strapped herself into the pilot's seat, reached under the controls, and opened one of the access panels. Inside were a number of wires and control modules. She plucked out two control modules and ripped one specific wire free to wedge into a new location. Once she'd done so, the controls sprang to life.

"Who's your mama?" she asked in a purring tone as she started bringing the pinnace's systems online.

"You can hotwire a pinnace?" Diana asked, a hint of awe in her voice.

"I'm multitalented. Strap in. This might get rough."

She brought up the vid cameras scattered around the exterior hull and watched as the last of the recruits came out of the airlock, bearing the bodies. The vacuum had immediately begun to vaporize the leaking blood. The poor bastards were going to be covered with what was left of their comrades.

At the ramp's base, Claudio was urging them to move faster. She was astonished that no one accidentally broke their magnetic connection to the hull with everything that was going on.

As soon as the last of the recruits was inside, Claudio hit the com by the ramp as it was rising and opened a channel to the bridge. "Everyone is in. Let's get the hell out of Dodge."

Andrea didn't know where Dodge was or why it was important that people left it in a hurry, but she was all in favor of getting away from their attackers, particularly since they'd probably set the fusion plant to blow, and they were almost certainly racing back to the pinnace themselves.

Her training in flying a pinnace was not as thorough as she would've liked, but she could handle basic maneuvers. She'd even brought a pinnace down from orbit while under supervision a couple of times.

Technically, she could do it all. Realistically, she'd always had someone with far more experience standing by to give her pointers. Now she was doing it on her own, and one mistake could kill them all.

Andrea killed the magnetic lock that held the pinnace to the training ship and goosed the thrusters to lift them away. Then the caution and warning system lit up with indicators that they were taking fire from somewhere.

A glance back at the vid cameras showed that the pilots had come out onto the hull and were firing flechette pistols at them.

The odds of the flechettes causing damage to the armored pinnace were minimal but not zero. She needed to get away from them even faster than she had been, particularly if that ship's fusion plant was rigged to blow.

She activated the main engines and increased the thrust to maximum. A couple of minutes of this, and they'd be clear of any possible explosive radius around the training ship.

Andrea was starting to relax just a little when the proximity and collision alarms went off. She yanked her attention back to the scanners and saw a ship almost directly in front of them. She couldn't tell what course it was on, but it was *far* too close to them.

She pushed the control yoke down so that the pinnace dove beneath the other vessel. Scanners had tagged it as a civilian vessel: *Exigent Circumstances.*

That brought them closer to New Dallas. In fact, that brought them down to the edges of the atmosphere, and she felt a little drag on the pinnace's hull.

That other ship might not have been part of the attack, but there shouldn't have been any civilian ships inside the Fleet-controlled area. She needed to get her people entirely outside the reach of these bastards.

She tried bringing the communication system online to call someone—anyone—but there was still no connection. It had to be some kind of jamming to be this widespread. If they were being jammed, there had to be ships out there taking advantage of this, and she needed to act decisively.

Taking a deep breath, she put the pinnace into a deorbit flight pattern and tried to dredge up every single thing she could remember about what had to be done to safely get into the atmosphere. At this point, they were committed, and she needed to make sure they reached the ground alive.

"What are we doing?" Diana asked, staring at the planet growing larger beneath them.

"We're heading down to the surface. I don't suppose you know how to fly a pinnace."

Her friend shook her head, her eyes growing even wider. "Don't you?"

"Sort of. I really wish this jamming would go away so I could call somebody."

"Jamming? You mean this wasn't just some way they could cut off our communications on the ship?"

"I still can't connect with anybody," Andrea said. "It's got to be more widespread than we'd imagined. Find out how Claudio is doing back there."

"Claudio is fine," the boy said from the hatch behind them. "Everybody is strapped down. What's this I hear about landing? I didn't know you could fly a pinnace, particularly coming down from orbit."

She turned to smile at him cheerily. "I've done it a couple of times. Under supervision."

The young man pulled out one of the emergency seats that the flight engineers used when necessary and strapped himself in. "That doesn't sound very reassuring. How confident are you that you can get us down in one piece?"

"Mostly? I spotted another ship that looked like it might be part of the attack. If we'd stayed up there, we'd have gotten shot at or gotten more visitors. Someone is jamming the entire area. We've got to get out of here."

"If you can get us down in one piece, I'll withdraw all my objections to you being a marine. You'd have earned it."

"I've *already* earned it, jackass," she answered with a snort. "Still, I'll hold you to that."

Thankfully, she still had the recordings of the last couple of flights practicing atmospheric entry in her implant storage, and she was able to skim through them and get the data that she needed for the appropriate angle and speed references.

One of the keys to flexibility in flying that Kayden had taught her was not to lock up. There had to be some fluidity to your reactions and what the vehicle was doing, or you'd make the wrong call. Supposedly, the entry path was more forgiving than one might expect.

By the time the pinnace had fully penetrated the upper atmosphere and began slowing to something remotely normal, she was drenched in sweat. That didn't stop her from bringing up the map of the planet and locating the marine base. They were a couple of thousand kilometers away from it but could close the distance with just an extra ten or fifteen minutes at this speed.

In for a penny, in for a pound.

She was just beginning to see the base ahead of them when the jamming finally dropped, and someone on the base contacted them.

"Unknown pinnace, this is Control. Abort your approach."

"Negative, Control," Andrea said, forcing her voice to remain calm. "This is a flight full of recruits, and we are declaring an emergency. Clear the landing area and have crash rescue standing by."

With that, she killed the com. "I'm probably going to get into trouble for that, but I'd much rather be on the ground now than wonder who's going to shoot at us next."

The landing area came up much, *much* faster than she'd expected, so she applied even more deceleration. There was a relatively clear area off to the right-hand side as they were coming in, and she immediately selected it as their landing area. It was open ground rather than plascrete, so perhaps it would be a bit more forgiving if she blew the landing.

She overcorrected, and the nose of the pinnace rose into the air, causing her to juggle the flight controls at the last second, but she managed to get the landing struts down and locked into place just a couple of seconds before the pinnace stalled and dropped the last meter to the ground.

The impact was heavy and set off some alerts, but pinnaces were tough. That landing wouldn't have been the roughest it had ever seen.

She powered the major systems down and then hit the com controls to open a channel to the entire pinnace.

"This is your captain speaking. I'd like to thank you for flying Marine Recruit Spaceways and welcome you to your destination. We hope you'll consider us for your future spaceflight needs. Now, somebody drop the ramp so that the rescue personnel can get in."

She killed the com and almost collapsed in her seat. She'd made the landing, even if it had been sloppy. Now it was time for the consequences. There was going to be hell to pay no matter how this turned out, and she only hoped that her explanations would be good enough to see them through.

A hand clapped roughly on her shoulder.

"Good landing, marine," Claudio said as he rose. "I'll head back and get things moving. I think you should join us as soon as you can because they're going to want to get everybody off this pinnace ASAP. Diana, get her squared away. She can't afford to look shaken at a time like this."

With that, the tall boy headed back to the rear of the pinnace.

Outside, rescue vehicles were racing in from every direction, and armed marines were beginning to spread out around the grounded pinnace as well.

She'd better get back there and make sure that nobody got shot. And that they took possession of the prisoner. Probably arrested her too.

Diana put her hand on Andrea's shoulder far more gently than Claudio had. "You did it. You got us out of there. We didn't escape unscathed, and I know that you're already thinking about consequences, but you did everything you could."

Andrea sighed and started unbuckling herself. "I sure hope they think so."

"Stop. Look at me."

She blinked up at the girl. "What?"

"Breathe. You look panicked. Don't let the platoon or the rescuers see you like this. Get it together, marine."

Andrea took a deep breath and then another. The tension was still there, but she felt less like hyperventilating. It would have to do.

"Thanks. Let's do this."

With that, she rose to her feet, squared her shoulders, and marched back into the chaos already engulfing the rear compartment of the pinnace. It was time to face the music.

43

Fei stared at the vid feeds showing two separate rooms holding their prisoners at the Imperial Intelligence headquarters. One of them showed Dayton, who was handcuffed to a chair at an empty table. The other showed Lucinda Drake, who was in a medical bed, recovering from the abrupt amputation of her legs when the marine drill instructors had breached the hatch leading to the bridge.

Honestly, she wasn't certain who she wanted to speak to first. With Dayton, she could rub her failure in and trumpet the fact that Andrea would live and almost certainly become a marine.

With Drake, she could get into the details of what had been planned. She still didn't understand why the attack had taken place in orbit rather than somewhere on the planet. That just didn't make sense.

Still Water was on the marine base, interfacing with Major Martelle about Andrea. At this point, her girl knew far too much about what was going on, and there had to be some kind of explanation for her and the other recruits. Since Fei still didn't want to reveal her presence, he was the perfect choice and had graciously agreed to do so.

Technically, none of the questioning was official, but she'd promised to record everything with Dayton so that any interesting tidbits could be passed along to Imperial Intelligence, legally admissible or not.

She doubted that Dayton would tell her anything of note, so she might as well start with her. She was the one that Still Water was most interested in, after all. He'd keep her and turn Drake over to the local authorities to deal with.

With a sigh, Fei activated her implant recorders and went into the room holding Dayton. The woman smiled smugly at her, even though she had to be suffering from a massive headache from the stunner bolt.

"You failed, you know," Fei started off, sitting in the chair on the other side of the table. "Andrea is still alive, and she's going to stay that way."

"I don't know what you're talking about, Lady Na. I was simply here on vacation. I'm uncertain why you and those other thugs attacked me, but rest assured that there are going to be consequences."

It took an effort of will to stop her jaw from dropping. "So that's the line you're going to take? Bold, I'll give you that.

"Sadly for you, the criminal mastermind that you were working with made recordings of your meetings, and Imperial Intelligence has taken an interest in your case. I also don't think that the emperor is going to be very happy when he finds out how you tried to subvert his will."

In a flash, the woman's expression became almost feral. "He betrayed his oath to the Empire. We can't allow those *things* to get a foothold among us ever again. You might have captured me, though it's still far from certain that I'll face any punishment for my patriotic actions, but someone else will step in to take my place and keep the Empire safe."

"I suppose we'll see," Fei said. "For you, this little play is over. As soon as Imperial Intelligence wraps up questioning a few other people, they're going to take your ship and you back to Terra. I'd imagine they'll put you in a hole so deep that you'll never see the sun again. I say good riddance."

With that, Fei stood up and walked out of the compartment, terminating the recording as she closed the hatch firmly behind her.

She took a deep breath and bent her head, forcing the rage to dissipate. That woman was done. Her wealth, position, and friends might be able to save her from the worst of the consequences, but they wouldn't be able to shield her completely. She was going to pay a price, even if it wasn't to the fullest extent that Fei wished it could be.

That left the other woman. The criminal had been caught in the act with illegal weapons and resisted boarding by Imperial Marines. Even the jamming system that had been turned on to disrupt everything had finally been traced back to her, though Fei was confident that Dayton's money and connections had played a role.

Fei wished she could question the woman, but she'd already clammed up until she spoke with her lawyer. Well, Fei supposed that didn't stop her from trying.

She went into the makeshift hospital room and sat beside the bed. The woman turned her head somewhat lethargically and looked at her without real concern.

"I have nothing to say until I speak with my lawyer," the woman said, her voice listless.

"That's fine," Fei said. "I acknowledge that nothing you say is in any way binding or capable of being held against you. This is a private conversation without the legal representation you are entitled to. I just want to know something from a personal standpoint."

The woman blinked a couple of times, likely fighting the drugs in her system, and focused her attention more firmly on Fei. "I'm not entirely certain that the authorities would agree with your assertion, but I'll at least hear what you have to say."

"My name is Na Fei, and Andrea Tolliver is my ward. I understand that you were paid by Countess Dayton to kill her. That's someone else's problem, so you don't have to confess any crimes to me.

"I'm just confused about your process. Everything that happened in orbit could've been done so much more easily on the ground. And then you killed your boss and your associate. It just feels like I'm missing something, and I want to know what it is."

The woman stared at her for long seconds. "Nothing that I say in this conversation is being recorded? You swear that nothing I say will be used against me?"

Fei nodded. "That's correct. I'm not in law enforcement and am acting as a private citizen. I'm more interested in answers than revenge. You were the tool in this, not the cause, and you're done no matter what you tell me."

That actually earned her a chuckle from the woman. "I suppose I am. I didn't know the woman's name, but I'll assume that Countess Dayton is the woman who forced my organization to go after Tolliver."

At Fei's nod, the woman continued. "She wasn't satisfied with the speed things were being done and offered me a *lot* of money to take control of the organization and finish it—more money than I ever expected to see working as a junior lieutenant in the organization.

"I had nothing against Peter or Jomos, but if I could take control of our organization, then I'd basically be paid twice. The temptation was too much, so I did it.

"It was more than worth the price of bribing the marines to help me make it happen, though it took the woman's influence to get them transferred to the orbital to do the job.

"As for why the attack took place in orbit, that's simple. I ordered my people to capture Tolliver or at least recover her body. I'm pretty sure that the Singularity would've paid quite handsomely to get her back, dead or alive. That would've been a third payday, and I could've lived my life without ever having to work again.

"Their job was to allow the recruits into the ship and kill them all so that no one escaped into space. If they'd succeeded, no bodies would have been recovered, including the marines. They'd have left the system with me, though they'd never have been seen again."

Fei's blood ran cold. The Singularity getting word of Andrea's survival had always been a possibility, but this was the closest it had ever come to reality. Sadly, the Singularity would eventually learn that Andrea was alive and take action. They'd dodged a flechette today, but it was only a matter of time.

She was about to rise when Drake said something else.

"At least the woman won't live to gloat. It may take a while, since she's in custody, but she's a dead woman."

Fei sat back down, crossed one leg over the other, and raised an eyebrow, saying nothing.

Drake smiled coldly. "Peter paid someone to make certain that she never makes it home. I won't mention any names, but they're *very* good at what they do.

"Somewhere along the way, unless she's under a lot more protection than is likely, the woman is going to suffer a tragic accident or some kind of equipment malfunction. Who knows? All I care about is that she dies."

"Imperial Intelligence is pretty good. What kind of chance does your assassin have against them, particularly if they use her ship?"

"I suppose that'll make the job more challenging, but I'll still put my money on the assassin."

"I'd wish you good luck, but I have no sympathy for you," Fei said, rising and walking out of the room.

She stopped in the corridor and eyed the Imperial Intelligence agents watching over the prisoners. Would they be able to stop a trained assassin?

Maybe. Knowing about the situation would make it much more challenging to kill Dayton. Pity. If anyone deserved to die, it was that woman.

She almost said something to them, but then thought about all the times that Imperial Intelligence had withheld information that was critical to the missions that she and other marines had carried out. Of how many people they'd lost because of that.

She put the assassin out of her mind and headed for the exit. The potential assassin was Imperial Intelligence's problem. Let them deal with the unpleasant surprises for once.

* * *

PAGE SAT in Major Martelle's office, slumped into a chair with a drink that he really wanted to down in one gulp. Today had been a disaster. A complete and almost unmitigated disaster.

He'd come very close to losing the entire platoon. If not for Tolliver's actions, that outcome was almost a certainty, and it was all because he'd failed to take the danger seriously enough.

The major had mobilized an entire company to array around the temporary barracks where the recruits were staying. No one was getting in or out without being triple checked. Not even other marines.

The guards patrolled in groups that were always changing their makeup to make absolutely certain that no one made a deal to betray their oaths like the four marines that had taken the platoon out to the training ship.

One of them had been killed in the fighting, but the other three had been taken alive. One of them had been stunned by Tolliver, and he admired the girl's restraint in not killing the man. The two officers had tried to concoct a story to cover what happened, but no one was buying it. They'd sold out the Corps.

Riggio Gomez was dead, killed protecting the recruits. Sophia was devastated, of course, and she blamed Tolliver.

In a way, she was right. If Tolliver hadn't been here, her brother wouldn't have been put in the position that had killed him.

He rethought his situation and downed the drink he held in one gulp.

"I understand something of what you're going through," Martelle said from the seat next to his. "You're wondering what you did wrong and how you could've stopped this from happening.

"You couldn't have seen it coming. The situation was just so far outside what anyone could've expected, and we didn't account for all the potential mayhem.

"Don't think that I haven't noticed that you submitted your resignation. It won't be accepted. There's going to be an inquiry, but I already know that there was nothing you could've done differently with the knowledge that you had. It's going to take you a long time to accept that, but it's the truth."

Page sighed. "I let them down. Handley and Gomez are dead because I wasn't there. I don't think any amount of time is going to make that better."

"Better? No. Yet time heals all wounds like water washing away bits of stone and grinding a mountain down. In other words, slowly."

Page wasn't sure that he agreed, but it didn't seem the right time to argue.

"So, what do we do now?" he asked. "I think the danger is past, but I don't know that I can take that as a given."

Martelle shook his head. "No, we won't take that as a given. The recruits are going to finish their training under heavy guard. We're not even going to try to hide it anymore. That cat is well and truly out of the bag.

"They'll finish going through everything that they need to learn about being marines, but as far as I'm concerned, they've already made it.

"That isn't to say that some of them won't quit after having been through this, but they've seen the elephant now. They did what needed to be done, and they've proved themselves. Isn't that what basic training is for? To separate those who think they can from those who actually can?"

Page supposed that was true. There was still a lot of training to do, and it was always possible that a recruit would somehow fail to make the grade.

Still, they'd already been under more pressure than he'd ever have laid on them during training. So long as they stuck it out, each and every one of those recruits was going to graduate.

After that, who knew?

Once this was done, he was going to take some of that leave he'd never used. He needed to get away from this and figure out what he was going to do now.

That line of thought was apparently also prominent in the major's thinking because the next words out of his mouth mirrored Page's thoughts.

"As sooner this training cycle is finished, I want you to take a minimum of three months' leave. Frankly, I'd prefer six. You need to leave this entire thing behind you for a while and regain your perspective. Otherwise, I'm afraid we'll lose you."

"I've already decided to do something like that, sir. I think I'll do some of that wilderness camping that Gomez keeps encouraging me to do. Maybe I can convince her to come with me, and we can both help one another heal. When I get back, we can figure out what's going to happen next."

"You can figure it out with whoever my replacement is," Martelle said, raising his glass in salute. "I've decided that I've been in a rut as well, and I need to change my life. Training is rewarding, but I've been thinking about the Imperial Guard."

Page blinked in surprise. The Imperial Guard drew its forces from the Imperial Marines but was a much smaller and more focused organization. As one might imagine, they protected the Imperial family.

"Doesn't that come with a big cut in rank?"

Martelle nodded. "If accepted, I'd be the new guy. They'd bump me all the way down to sergeant, and I'd have to work my way back up if I wanted to become an officer again. You can bet your ass it would be a long, long time before I made it back to being a field grade officer like I am now.

"But I think it would still be worthwhile. I've been wanting a change, and they've sent me a couple of inquiries over the years, encouraging me to try out in one of the competitions.

"I think I'll see Tolliver and the rest of the recruits graduate and then give it a shot. I've got a lot more to give the Empire, and that might be how I can make it happen."

The two sat quietly and drank far more of the major's excellent whiskey than they should have. When they were finally done, they had a final toast to those who hadn't made it and he headed off to get a little bit of sleep before he got back to training the recruits who'd survived.

44

On the final day of basic training, Andrea stood at the platoon's head in the center of the graduation field and stared straight ahead. The drill instructors—minus Sophia Gomez, who'd taken bereavement leave—were arrayed in front of them. In front of those worthies was a platform that held Major Martelle and a number of other officers.

All around them, bleachers held family and friends of the graduating recruits, including her own. It was hard to keep herself from looking at them, but she forced herself to keep her attention focused on the moment.

She supposed she shouldn't be surprised that the main stage also held another man she knew: Earl Still Water. He'd been one of the people who'd delivered the offer for her to attend training in exchange for Imperial recognition as a human being.

He was seated just to the right of Major Martelle and looked for all the world like he was supposed to be there. She wondered where the woman who had been with him was.

While she couldn't see the recruits arrayed behind her with her eyes, she could tap into the feeds scattered around the graduation field that were meant to be used by their civilian visitors as well as those who couldn't attend. In those feeds, she could see Diana staring at Still Water.

Granted, her friend was masking her feelings quite well, but Andrea knew the signs after several months of close proximity.

She was pissed.

Now that the rest of the recruits had received their marine-grade implants, she was able to communicate with them directly. She took advantage of that and opened a private channel with her friend.

What's wrong? Why are you staring at that man?

I'm trying to figure out why he's on the stage. He should be sitting with the other parents, so that means he's up to something, and I don't like it.

Andrea blinked in surprise. *With the other parents? Why?*

Because he's my father.

Like a set of dominoes falling, everything suddenly dropped into place. *That* was why Diana was here and how she'd ended up as Andrea's bunkmate.

Diana's father had been pulling strings behind the scenes, including getting Riggio Gomez assigned to keep an eye on her. Diana was just one more arrow in his quiver.

Not that she was complaining. Diana was a close friend now, and she wasn't going to hold the manipulation against the man.

She suspected his daughter wasn't going to be as forgiving when she figured it all out.

Andrea considered not saying anything but knew that the truth would come out soon enough. It was far better to be honest with her friend than to conceal the truth and make her even angrier.

He's the one who delivered the emperor's offer for me to attend training in exchange for legal recognition. I suspect he pulled some strings and got you assigned to the platoon. He's also the one who made sure that Riggio Gomez was watching over me, I'm sure.

That sonofabitch, her friend silently snarled. *He arranged all of this. He's in Imperial Intelligence, you know.*

I'm not surprised.

And she wasn't. That really fit in with the manipulation that she suspected the man of engaging in. That thought prompted a thought about something her friend had said about her father when they'd first met.

So that's what you meant when you said that your father was a big fan of spy thrillers. I can also see why you wouldn't want to talk about him.

Diana, I've been manipulated more than you, and I'm not going to hold that against him. I ask that you at least consider that he was doing this for me. He thought that we'd make good friends, and we are. Let's let that be enough.

Her friend was silent for a moment before she spoke. *I suppose you're right. Ending up with you is one of the best things that's ever happened to me, and I'm not going to hold* that *against him, but I* am *going to make him pay for manipulating me. He's my father, and he deserves it.*

Before Andrea could respond, Major Martelle stepped up to the lectern. "Allow me to welcome all parents and visitors to this graduation ceremony for First Platoon, Bravo Company, of the 225th Training Battalion. The people you're here to support have worked long and hard to become Imperial Marines, and that dream is about to be realized.

"Though the details aren't something any of us can talk about, this has been a challenging training cycle. Each recruit standing here has gone above and beyond what was expected of them and should be congratulated on their achievements.

"The staff has done everything in their power to see that these fine young men and women have all the basic tools that they will require to serve the Empire, and that each and every one of them is ready for that signal honor. Recruits, raise your right hands and repeat after me."

Andrea did so and repeated the words that bound her to the Empire and the Imperial Marines.

"I do solemnly swear that I will support and defend the Empire against all enemies, foreign and domestic; that I will bear true faith and allegiance to the same; and that I will obey the orders of the emperor and the orders of the officers appointed over me, according to regulations and the Imperial Code of Military Justice. So help me God."

The last sentence was optional, but she said it anyway. She hadn't made up her mind about a higher being, but she wasn't declining any help at this point.

When the recruits finished taking the oath, the major stepped back from the lectern and gestured toward Earl Still Water.

The rotund man rose and stepped over to the lectern to gaze out at the recruits. Then his eyes settled on Andrea and stayed there.

"One of the young marines present today is a refugee from the Singularity. Unlike many who have come before her, she desired to serve the Empire as an Imperial Marine. The problem with that is that Imperial law dictates that genetically engineered beings aren't human in a legal sense.

"Emperor Marcus made an agreement that if she could complete her training as an Imperial Marine, he would grant her a permanent exemption from that law by Imperial Edict. She has done so with distinction, and it is now my privilege to be the voice of my liege in this matter.

"Andrea Tolliver, step forward and be recognized."

She swallowed, her throat suddenly dry, stepped forward three steps, and came to full attention. In front of her, the drill instructors turned on their heels and marched to the sides before wheeling to face her.

Earl Still Water looked down on her, his gaze profoundly heavier than it had been a moment before. It was as if the emperor himself was looking at her through his vassal's eyes. With implant recordings, that would undoubtedly be true at some point.

"In the name of Emperor Marcus and with the concurrence of the Imperial Senate, I hereby declare that an Imperial exemption is hereby granted to Andrea Tolliver. From this day forward, in all matters public and private, she is recognized as fully human by the Terran Empire.

"It is my signal honor and privilege to welcome you to the Terran Empire as its newest citizen. Let all who consider crossing you over your genetic heritage be wary of the enemies they make, because the emperor has spoken."

As one, all the marines on the field sounded off. "Oorah!"

With a nod, the earl stepped back, and the crowd in the stands went wild with applause.

Andrea almost fainted with relief. Her long fight for recognition was over, and now she could begin living the life that she'd dreamed of for so long.

Major Martelle stepped back up to the lectern. "Drill instructors, release the marines under your care for the final time. I believe many of them have family waiting to congratulate them."

Senior Sergeant Page marched back in front of the platoon and faced them. "Marines, you have your unit assignments and will attend further training before you get there, but on behalf of myself and my staff, I want to congratulate you on your accomplishments. Your achievements make me *proud*. Your success is a tribute to *our* beloved Corps.

"You are hereby dismissed. For those of you with family, I know that they're waiting for you. For those who have no one here, we've set up a small celebration at the mess hall, and we'd be honored if you'd attend. Dismissed."

Andrea expected to see Diana head for her father, but instead, she stepped over next to her and raised an eyebrow. "Did any of your family come to see you graduate? I want to meet them."

"Shouldn't you be going to chew out your father?"

"I'm making a point. Besides, I think that I like your parents better than I like him right now."

Andrea chuckled. "Sure. Let's go see them."

As they began walking toward her guardians, Andrea glanced at her friend. "Do you think it's weird that Claudio, you, and I are all assigned to the same unit? That seems kind of blatant, doesn't it?"

Diana shrugged. "Blatant or not, I'm happy with it. Not for being assigned with Claudio, though he's been less of an ass since the attack. He's sort of growing on me. As JR would've said, like a fungus."

That made Andrea hug her friend tightly against her and speed up. "Come on. I can't wait for you to meet my family. You'll love them."

* * *

FEI STOOD between Grace and Kayden and watched her girl graduate. Somehow, she'd managed to keep Andrea ignorant of her presence while still keeping her alive. It was a damned miracle.

Grace and Kayden had arrived a couple of days ago, and their reunion had been epic. She'd missed them so badly. She couldn't wait to get home again and resume her life with them. She'd loved the marines, but that part of her life was done.

Really done, once and for all. Finished. Over. She would never regret leaving the service again.

The four of them would spend the next couple of weeks celebrating Andrea's success. Then she'd see her girl off for her advanced training and permanent assignment. Unlike the last time, this time she really was sending her girl off to begin life on her own.

She'd miss her, but she was so proud of her.

Grace ran forward and grabbed Andrea into a hug, lifting her off the ground and spinning her in a circle. Her feet barely missed Private Randall, who jumped back with a grin.

"You did it!" Grace crowed. "We're so proud of you!"

Normally, Fei was too reserved for such public displays of affection but not this time. She pulled Kayden up with her, and they wrapped the other two in their arms.

That made her juggle the box she held to make sure that it didn't fall. It contained Andrea's graduation presents: the stunner that had saved her life and the matching flechette pistol that Still Water had given Fei. Together they would help keep her girl safe going forward.

Though both weapons were *highly* illegal thanks to their undetectable nature, Still Water had produced Imperial licenses for each and an Imperial dispensation allowing Andrea to retain and carry them, even on active duty.

That wouldn't make her new superiors very happy, but there was nothing they could do when the emperor was doing the talking through his vassal.

She'd give them to Andrea later in private, but she didn't trust leaving them just lying around while they were out. That was just begging for trouble.

Those were technically from Still Water, and there would be other gifts that came from Grace, Kayden, and Fei. Those could happen later.

Once all the hugging was done, Andrea introduced them to her friend, and at Grace's invitation, they all headed off to get dinner in the city. It was time to celebrate and put the troubles of the past behind them.

Tomorrow's troubles would just have to wait for another day.

* * *

ANDREA SEVEN SEVENTY-SIX stood in the largest room of the crèche. The sixty-five young women who stood in front of her were the ones that had survived her strict training regimen and would today be released to the Andrea Line. Her time as Keeper was done.

A few of the graduates deserved special note, including Andrea Thirty-One, who had proven to be one of the most ruthless and dedicated graduates that it had ever been her honor to train. That girl would go far, and she looked forward to advancing her education and position even further in the years to come.

After all, a woman had to look toward her own retirement, didn't she?

When the ceremony was complete, and other members of the Andrea Line had escorted their new sisters off to introduce them to life outside the crèche, she found a younger sister of the Line waiting for her just outside her office.

"What is it?" she asked, her tone irritated. She had other work to do.

"Forgive me, Keeper, but a message has just arrived from Line leadership. They wish you to see something from an intelligence briefing at once."

"What is it?"

"I don't know, Keeper. It's locked for your eyes only."

"Give it to me."

The girl proffered a tablet toward her.

Annoyed, she took the tablet and authenticated herself, unlocking the message. A video was already cued up and began playing. It showed a disgustingly diverse array of base caste men and women dressed in Imperial uniforms that she recognized as belonging to one of their branches of service. The Imperial Marines, she believed.

She started to wonder what this had to do with her, but then her eyes locked on one of the figures, and she froze. The girl had the genetics and tattoos of the Andrea Line.

That was impossible.

Andrea Seven Seventy-Six stared at the video without speaking or moving as her brain raced. It had to be One Twenty-Four. She'd assumed that the girl had died when the station they'd been on was destroyed, but that had obviously been an error on her part.

It seemed that her time managing the crèche wasn't quite done yet. There was still one problem left to be corrected. It wouldn't be easy, but issues that required personal attention from the Andrea Line rarely were.

Her time as Keeper wasn't over until she corrected this lapse.

"Prepare my ship," she ordered grimly. "I leave at once."

* * *

WANT to get updates from Terry about new books and other general nonsense going on in his life? He promises there will be cats. Go to TerryMixon.com/Mailing-List and sign up.

DID YOU ENJOY THIS BOOK? Please leave a review on Amazon. It only takes a minute to dash off a few words and that kind of thing helps Terry make a living as a writer and gets you new books faster.

WANT MORE BOOKS BY TERRY? Flip to the next page and grab one.

VISIT TERRY's Patreon page to find out how to get cool rewards and an early look at what he's working on at Patreon.com/TerryMixon.

ALSO BY TERRY MIXON

You can always find the most up to date listing of Terry's titles on his Amazon Author Page.

Note: the links below (ebook only, obviously) redirect you to my website where you can click a button to go to Amazon. This allows me to participate in Amazon's associates program and earn a little more. Sorry for any inconvenience.

The Last Hunter

The Last Hunter

Bonds of Blood

Alpha Strike

The Enemy Revealed

Command Authority

The Grand Conspiracy

Shield of Humanity

Fog of War

Ships of the Line

Operation Liberty

The Empire of Bones Saga

Empire of Bones

Veil of Shadows

Command Decisions

Ghosts of Empire

Paying the Price

Recon in Force

Behind Enemy Lines

The Terra Gambit

Hidden Enemies

Race to Terra

Ruined Terra

Victory on Terra

When Luck Runs Out

Gunboat Diplomacy

The Imperial Marines Saga

Spoils of War

Imperial Recruit

Enemy Action

The Humanity Unlimited Saga

Liberty Station

Freedom Express

Tree of Liberty

Blood of Patriots

Single Novels

Scorched Earth

Storm Divers

The Vigilante Series with Glynn Stewart

Heart of Vengeance

Oath of Vengeance

Bound By Law

Bound By Honor

Bound By Blood

Box Sets

The Empire of Bones Saga Volume 1

The Empire of Bones Saga Volume 2

The Empire of Bones Saga Volume 3

The Empire of Bones Saga Volume 4

Humanity Unlimited Publisher's Pack 1

Humanity Unlimited Publisher's Pack 2

ABOUT TERRY

#1 Bestselling Military Science Fiction author Terry Mixon served as a non-commissioned officer in the United States Army 101st Airborne Division. He later worked alongside the flight controllers in the Mission Control Center at the NASA Johnson Space Center supporting the Space Shuttle, the International Space Station, and other human spaceflight projects.

He now writes full time while living in Texas with his lovely wife and a pounce of cats.

TerryMixon.com

- [a] amazon.com/author/terrymixon
- [f] facebook.com/TerryLMixon
- [p] patreon.com/TerryMixon
- [BB] bookbub.com/authors/terry-mixon
- [g] goodreads.com/TerryMixon

www.ingramcontent.com/pod-product-compliance
Lightning Source LLC
Chambersburg PA
CBHW072307020726
47501CB00002B/431